Randall Lane

# The Reaping

# The Reaping

## By

# Randall Lane

"Oh my goodness!!! I just finished Devil's Den. What a roller coaster of a ride!!! I LOVED this book!! I can't wait to read your other stories, thanks again!!" — **Sherrie W Review for Devil's Den**

"This is not a book that I would have normally read, but I went to a reading by the author and was mesmerized by his incredible skill at drawing you in with sensational detail. I was right there in the story and was spellbound by this affecting and powerful book! The writing is excellent, the story is compelling, and the book has a message that touches your soul, one you will not forget! Looking forward to more from Randall Lane! I give the Devil's Den five big stars!" — **Janet B Review for Devil's Den**

"I loved Devil's Den. It was scary and quite intense as I read through it. I could not figure out, "who dun it." I really enjoy a book that has me guessing until the very end. I can't wait until your next novel is published! Thanks for such an enjoyable read." — **Sandra N Review for Devil's Den**

"I recommend this book highly. Devils Den. Can't put it down!"—**Marybeth L Review for Devil's Den**

"Awesome read! Once you start it's hard to put down! The way he tells the story keeps you captivated throughout the entire book." —**Tammy P Review for Devil's Den**

"I really enjoyed this book. The plot grew with an intense "who dun it" while surprising me with a twist I didn't anticipate. It's a great read in good vs. evil. You will find yourself questioning the validity of each character." — **Happy Amazon Customer's Review for Devil's Den**

"Mr. Lane writes with the eloquence of a storyteller. Deep, profound and superbly imaginative." — **Mark M Review for Devil's Den**

"This author's imagination will leave you spellbound! These stories will excite your senses, give you pause to think and excite your very soul! Can't wait for more!!!!" — **Happy Amazon Customer's Review for When Darkness Hides**

WELCOME TO
MAINE
The way life should be

# *Foreword*

The Reaping is a story I developed after visiting New England during the summer of 2017. I loved the area and particularly enjoyed seeing the many lighthouses and trying the different foods. It was when I visited Portland Headlight in Maine that my creative wheels began to turn. Now mind you at this point in time I would not have considered myself a writer. Other than countless college papers, the only thing I'd ever written were a handful of poems and a short story titled The Legend of Omah. Which as you may know would later become my novel, Omah.

So, The Reaping was my first real attempt at writing a novel. I came home after our trip to Maine and immediately began jotting down characters, scenes, and different plot ideas. I started crafting the storyline and characters around July of 2017. A few months later and I had the first draft complete. Now it was a very *rough* first draft to say the least, but it was complete. I had absolutely zero clue as to what I was doing. All I knew was that there was a story with a collection of characters bubbling within me that had to be let out.

It wasn't until two years later I picked The Reaping back up and refreshed myself with the plot and cast of characters. I kept most of the characters but did change and enhance the storyline. One of the characters in the original story was Paul Sealey who happened to be a real person and dear friend of my family and I. He was so happy and excited to learn that I'd placed him in the original book. From then on, I would give him a copy of every book and story I wrote.

Going back to last year (7/19/19) when I began rewriting The Reaping, I actually started exactly two weeks after Paul's passing. I decided that I would not only keep him in the book, but I would give him a larger role as well. Something I know would have brought him great joy. With that said, the timing of this book's release could not have come at a better time as it actually falls on what would have been Paul's 83rd birthday (7/26/20). I can already see him smiling with that big grin of his.

Aside from that, you'll also find that the cicada bug plays a large role in the story as well. It is important to note that this year (2020) actually marks the Magicicada's emergence after having spent the past 17 years underground. So, if you find yourself hearing them buzz about a little more this summer after reading the book, know that you're not going crazy. This is actually the year that one of their broods reemerge. Look it up on google or YouTube. It's actually a cool phenomenon that has baffled scientists for many years now.

You may ask why I choose to write the kind of stories I write. I think the biggest reason is I have always found it intriguing as to how and why criminals do the things they do. I'm not as interested in the what, but more so the how and why. I've always been interested in criminal psychology, and I love the battle between good and evil. I enjoy seeing good triumph over evil, and light conquer darkness. I guess that's why I'm drawn to write creepy mysteries and detective type thrillers. I enjoy the hunt for justice.

That said, as you read through this story and enter the journey alongside Detective Laurie Daniels, as scary and dark as it sometimes is, may you come to know that the Light shines in the darkness.

So, find a comfy reading nook to escape for a while, let the cicadas sing, and dive in. I hope you have as much fun reading this book as I did creating it. Enjoy!

–Randall Lane

July 16, 2020


*Dedicated in Loving Memory of Paul Sealey*

"Be not deceived; God is not mocked: for whatsoever a man soweth, that shall he also reap."

Galatians 6:7

"I have never met any really wicked person before. I feel rather frightened. I am so afraid he will look just like everyone else."

Oscar Wilde

**MICHAEL THE ARCHANGEL SLAYING THE DEVIL
BY GUIDO RENI (1636)**

# 2019

# DAY 1

---

# THE REEMERGENCE

# 1

**BLACKNESS FILLS** Amanda McCrae's vision. She's lightheaded and her mind swims with confusing thoughts. The acrid odor of soured trash churns her gut. A clock ticks away the seconds. Cicadas scream and crickets chirp in the shadows. A classical song plays through a static filled speaker. Yet, in an eerie kind of way, it's quiet and still. No movement. No talking. It's like the empty, dry stillness before a lightning strike.

She winces as the left side of her head pounds with each pulse. What happened? Is she dreaming? She must be, right? Her drumming headache says otherwise.

She remembers standing in the kitchen with her car keys in hand and being ready to leave. She called for their daughter to "hurry up," but Sarah never answered. Something stirred behind her and pulled her attention just before everything turned to black. Her memory after that is vague and full of drowsiness. She does not remember eating or drinking much but does remember the masked man inserting an IV into her arm. She tried asking him questions, but he chose to remain silent. She took notice though of how his demeanor changed when she questioned him about her husband and daughter. It was as if he were clutching a secret.

She tries to swallow a pool of saliva which has formed around her gums and teeth. Her eyes flash wide at the realization of a gag pulled tight between her lips. It's a wad of cotton material. Either a shirt or sock.

Dim light rushes her vision as it pierces the black hood encasing her head. She can see through the thin material enough to decipher her surroundings.

Above her hangs a light bulb with a beaded pull chain. Straight ahead is a wooden counter made of plywood and two by fours. A round, white clock hangs at eye level from a nail.

With a good squint she can see that the hands read 1:40. Whether a.m. or p.m., she doesn't know. An array of tools lies scattered across the counter. A rusty pair of pliers, spade shovel, a large handsaw, hammer, a vise, and . . . a STIHL chainsaw.

She jerks her shoulders in desperate attempts for freedom. She almost loses her balance as the metal chair tilts too far to one side. Warm tears trickle down her cheeks. Beneath her is a dirt floor. The chains are cold against her flesh and like a snake squeezing the life from its prey, they cinch tighter with each move she makes. She stops before her wrists and ankles begin to throb. She wants to scream, but all she can manage is a useless, muffled cry.

Exasperated and spent, she stops to collect her breath. She watches as it passes from her nostrils and pierces through the hood with small white clouds. A chill scatters across her body. She can feel her adrenaline begin to wane. With her breath now gathered, she sits and listens.

The bulb above flickers and hums.

The insects are quiet, but the classical tune continues to play. A cold draft meanders about the room and caresses her cheeks with ghostly fingers. It seeps through her hood the way spirits often blend through doors.

She feels her pulse quicken. The aching knot along her skull pounds once more. A heaviness weighs upon her chest and suffocates her breath. She blinks hard.

Something stirs behind her.

It could be a rat or may be the man's boots shifting across the ground.

More movement. He's here.

Has he been here the whole time? Watching her from the shadows?

The sound is out of her range of sight, but she tries anyhow. First, she twists her neck and looks over her shoulders. That doesn't work, so she tries angling her head backwards to her spine like a possessed soul would. That doesn't work either. Only blackness and thin patches of dismal light fill her vision. The chains have tightened. She returns her head to a normal position.

The horrible stench of soiled trash turns her gut once more. A wave of nausea begins to travel up her esophagus. She can't vomit. She'll choke. She fights hard to control the sickening feeling. She takes deep, calming breaths to keep the vomit down.

As her heart races at a violent pace, she hears him stir. He's edging closer.

A plastic wrapper twist open and is followed by the sound of teeth crushing a piece of hard candy. The crunching stops. Hot breath spreads across the back of her neck followed by a vicious aroma of peppermint. As if his breath carries a contagious virus, a deep, dark fear unlike anything she's ever known penetrates her soul. His warm, minty breath continues to crawl about her flesh.

She squeezes her eyes and tightens her jaw, biting hard onto the gag. The nightmare has to end. Any moment she'll awaken. She has to. This can't be happening.

She feels him step away.

A creaky metal hinge pierces the air and causes her to flinch. She hears his hands sort through metal nails or screws. He finishes and shuts the door which squeaks with a tight, rusty growl.

She tries hard to calm her quick breaths escaping through her nostrils. Her lips are becoming chilled and chapped. She wants to lick them to ease the discomfort but can't because of the gag.

A large, calloused hand plops upon the base of her neck.

Her heart starts, and her shoulders tense at the sudden touch.

She whimpers through the gag, but the owner of the hand is silent and still.

"Pwweeezzzee," her muffled voice says with tears.

Being gentle, the hand works its way up her neck. It's goes beneath the hood, one finger at a time, to the back of her head where the gag is secured. Another hand appears, and together the hands work the gag loose. It drops to the floor.

Neither of them says a word. The music continues to play.

She hears him step away and retreat into the darkness. She can feel him standing out of sight, only inches from her back. Watching.

"Do you know who I am?" his deep, contorted voice cuts the air.

He doesn't sound right. It's like he's purposely speaking in a different voice.

She shakes her head.

"I removed the gag for a reason. Speak."

She gulps, "No. No."

"Good. That's good."

She hears him move and watches as he crosses in front of her. He angles for the counter where the tools are. He's dressed in a red long sleeve t-shirt with blue jean pants, and he wears a navy-blue ball cap. With his wide and well sculpted back to her, he asks, "Do you smell that?"

The aroma of peppermint has faded and left only the odor of trash, so she answers, "Yes."

"Please, elaborate. Yes, what? What is it you smell? Be honest."

She thinks for a moment, "I-I-I smell trash. Soiled, soured trash."

He clanks a metal tool and wags his head, "It's more than trash. It's symbolic."

"Symbolic?"

He combs through more tools, "You do know the meaning? Surely, you are not that dense."

"It has a double meaning. The trash symbolizes something else."

He stops his searching, straightens his spine, and cracks his neck before pulling in a deep breath. "Excellent. Very good, Mrs. McCrae. You're not as ignorant as you almost lead me to fear. You should know . . ." He pauses as he holds up the pliers and gives them a good look, "I despise stupidity."

The man angles to the left and disappears within the corner shadow.

"The odor is symbolic to your sin. It's symbolic to the stench within your heart. It is the aroma, which day after day, your sinful soul offers to the almighty. A sickening, wicked, abomination," he drew out the last sentence with a sharp emphasis.

She watches his silhouette as he flanks her left side and moves back behind her.

"Please, you don't have to do this. We won't tell. I swear."

"Quiet. DO. NOT. BEG ME." he says with enough force to emit spittle. He takes a breath and adds, "Sarah is better off without you and Jeremy. She's going to love her new home."

She notices the quick shift in his mood and says, "No. No. Leave Sarah out of this. Do whatever you want with me and Jeremy, but . . ." she almost said please again, so she transitions with, "Don't hurt Sarah. She's only a girl."

Her words go unanswered for a long moment. She began to wonder if he was still behind her. Had he left through a back door without her knowing?

She waits to see if the crickets will return to their chatter, but they never do. She knows he's still here.

The clearing of phlegm startles her.

"Why has thy countenance fallen? If thou doest well, shalt thou not be accepted? If thou doest not well, sin crouches at the door and its desire is to have you. First book of the Bible. Genesis four verse six."

Another pause.

"You are bound in your sin, Mrs. McCrae, and as these chains confine your body, so do the chains of sin confine your heart. You're helpless. Hopeless."

Her shoulders jolt as the sobs return.

The man continues, "The wages of sin is death. Your payment is due Mrs. McCrae. However, I will be generous enough to give you two choices. A dilemma if you will. An ultimatum. Though, I shall warn you . . . you need choose wisely if you wish to save your daughter's life."

A warm sensation spreads across her groin followed by the foul odor of urine. She sniffles and attempts to quiet her sobs.

"You can offer me your life this very moment. Your life for your daughter's. That's the first choice. Life is all about choices you know. With every choice comes a consequence. If you do well, you'll reap a good harvest. If you do bad . . ." she hears him click his tongue against his teeth. "That's where I come in. Remember, sin crouches at your door, and is waiting to pounce. Now that we have your first choice on the table, are you ready for the second?"

She doesn't answer. Her mind is too scattered to gather a clear thought.

"Mrs. McCrae?"

She swallows hard and says, "Yes."

"Option two. I took you two days ago in case you were not sure. Judging by the reports coming through the scanner, authorities are aware of what happened. It'll soon be on every news outlet across the Country. Everyone will know your name. They'll see the family photos, and their hearts will be gripped by your daughter's blue eyes as Nancy Grace waxes poetic about all of the children disappearing in New England.

"Now, my second choice which I present to you is this: Wait and see if the authorities can find you within a hundred minutes. I'll give you until . . . say, three thirty. If they haven't found you by then, you'll die and possibly your daughter too. High risk. High reward. It's your choice. Either I can kill you now, or you can wait to see if the idiots can find you within a hundred minutes."

"What about Jeremy?"

"My dear . . ." he says with a scoff, "He's already paid his dues. He's not a part of the choice. This only involves you and Sarah."

His words were like a ram's head to the gut. Fear courses through her veins as reality begins to settle. All the talk and gossip on Facebook, the news stories, the detective shows, the missing children flyers posted around town . . . this is the man who's responsible for so many murders and disappearances over the years. This is the man they call Morty. The New England Killer. The Death Angel.

Taking inventory of her situation, she combs through his words. Would she offer her life for her daughter's? The slight hesitation in her answer floods her soul with a heavy dose of guilt, pulling her heart to the grave. What if he's lying? What if it's just his way of getting permission to kill her and ease his guilt in some twisted way? She can't allow him to kill her now. No. No way. She has to go with the option that buys her the most time. She must stay alive as long as possible and she has to find her daughter. She has to escape or survive long enough for the police to find her.

Tick. Tick. Tick. The clock holds her attention hostage for three precious seconds.

"I'm waiting, Amanda McCrae."

"I'll go with the second choice and take our chances with the
police."

He doesn't respond.

After a beat, she adds, "That was the other choice, right?'

"Yes, oh yes. High risk. High reward. That was a choice. If that's what you choose, then I'll give you until half past three o'clock. That's a little less than two hours from now. Considering my placement of the clue, it'll depend—"

"Depend on what?"

He gives a thin chuckle and says, "How quick miss Laurie Daniels finds the clue."

"Who's that?"

"She's the detective who'll be investigating your husband's murder, you and your daughter's disappearance, and quite possibly. . . your violent deaths. Remember, with every choice comes a consequence. A reaping of the seed that was sown."

Her lips tremble at his words.

Tears slip across her lips. She licks them away.

"But first, before we waste any more precious time, I'm going to need your hair."

"My hair? Why?"

"I like my victims bald, plus, I may use it later. I need all the disguise I can get. Oh, and I'll need a tooth from you as well to add to my collection."

Amanda McCrae begins to cry and tremble.

The classical music grows in volume, spitting out chords through the staticky speaker.

A sharp click followed by a loud buzzing sound emits behind her. The sound grows closer. A large hand spreads atop her head and takes hold of the hood. The hood slides off. Amanda McCrae keeps her eyes clinched tight. The buzzing of hair clippers penetrates her ears. Classical music continues to play behind the buzz.

As the hair clippers scratch and dig across her scalp, she squints open an eyelid and peeks at the clock.

1:50.

She has to make it to three thirty. Whatever it takes.

Did she make the right choice? Can this detective named Laurie Daniels find whatever it is the man has left for her?

Her and her daughter's lives now depend on a woman she's never met.

She pulls in a deep breath as the clippers eat away clumps of hair. The man brushes the trimmings to the ground.

One hundred minutes.

Tick. Tick. Tick.

# 2

**Tuesday**
**October 1st, 2019**
**24.5 miles NW of Portland, Maine**
**2:07 p.m.**

"GLENN SAYS IT'S BAD. They discovered the husband out back, and the wife and daughter are missing. Blood spatter was found inside, and there's no sign of forced entry." I sit my cell phone into the cup holder next to my thigh. I lean up on the wheel and peer through my rain battered windshield. I feel my partner's eyes on me from the passenger seat, so I continue. "He says it's the same MO and signature as the other cases." I turn to Detective Patrick Collins and add with a low, dreaded tone, the words neither of us want to hear. "Patrick . . . it's him. Morty's back."

Lightning strikes and thunder crackles as rain continues to pelt the hood of my black suburban. We both flinch while God's obvious disdain of me mentioning such a vile creature rumbles among us.

I watch as my speedometer needle continues a steady push to the right. Out of the corner of my eye I catch a glimpse of Collins gripping the safety handle next to the window. The stereo takes on a static hiss as he turns with his face drained of blood and says, "I know you're right but for heaven's sake, Laurie, I hope you're wrong."

We ride in silence for the next few moments while I traverse traffic and rummage the information passing through my brain. I only know as much as the Medical Examiner Glenn Giles has shared with me; however, it's enough to paint an eerie picture of what I am getting into. I knew by the tone in his voice that whatever he had was worthy of my immediate attention. Enough so to pull me off the drug related homicide we were on in South Portland. I turned things over to Detective Andrew Meyer and told Collins to ride with me to a possible "Morty case." Judging by his expression, you'd have thought I told him to leap from a plane with no parachute. I know the feeling.

I bump my turn signal and ease on the brakes as I exit I-95 en route for Gray. My heartbeat thumps strong in my carotid artery. My chest constricts, and I feel my gut begin to churn. A slight tremble has taken over my hands. If this turns out to be another crime by the UNSUB we've all come to know as Morty, then I have some long days and nights ahead of me.

It's been four years since the McNamara and Shelton murders. This next case could give Morty more than a dozen murders and kidnappings—that we know of—over the past seventeen years. His first murders occurred in 2002 during my rookie year as Homicide Detective. That was when he chose to end the lives of the Anthony's and Canton's. As for their children . . . nothing. They're still missing. It often leaves me wanting to turn in my badge to avoid the pain and torment of dealing with these types of cases. While another part of me could never do such a thing. That would be the ultimate let down. I'd be giving up on the children and their families. I can't do that. I can't give up on them now. Their little voices call out to me in my dreams every night, begging me to find them. I have to press on. I have to catch this guy, and I have to find the children.

"Did he say who found the husband?" Collins's question pulls me back.

I blink and swallow hard. "Yeah, the neighbor found him."

"Have they contacted the family yet?"

"No, not yet."

"Geeze."

I make a sharp right onto a tree-covered side street and continue to follow where the GPS leads.

"The next forty-eight hours will be crucial. If this is Morty, then let's hope and pray he's left something behind for us. If we're lucky, the wife may still be alive. We have to look at every detail. Everything matters. Nothing is pointless with this guy. There's a reason for everything he does. It's like a ritual.

The sooner we can piece things together, the better the odds of
. . ."

"Laurie."

"The better the odds of finding her alive."

My tone is not too convincing.

"Laurie. If this *is* Morty," he tightens his lips and shakes his
head, "It'll be a recovery and not a rescue. You know how he is.
He's been planning this for months. The odds are not good.
And the missing daughter is a whole other case within itself."

"I know, Patrick. We're playing catch up. But I'm hoping
he's slipped somewhere along the way. We have to remain
vigilant and we can't let our guards down."

We reach the McCrae's street, and I can see police lights
strobing in the distance. I fight to control the tremble in my
hands. The same sensation stirs within my chest.

"Are you okay?"

I wet my lips, bite my inner jaw, and nod.

The one thing I know for certain, is that in all my years of
investigating, Morty is the first criminal that scares me. I'm not
talking about a surface fear which you get from a jump scare in
a horror film. No, I'm talking about a deep-rooted kind that
sticks to your soul like the blackest tar known to man. A kind
of fear that haunts you while you sleep and chases you in your
dreams. The kind that watches your every move. A tormenting
type of fear. The kind of fear that knows you inside and out. It
knows your weaknesses, your strengths, and your very
breaking point.

This guy fits the profile of the perfect predator. He's
observant. Too observant. It's as if he knows me. And he's
different. Different in such a way that the textbooks failed to
mention. It's almost like that at each of the crime scenes, he
knows I will come. He knows where I will look and what I will
look for. Every time I get a case like this a fresh wave of dread
washes over me, and I can't help but wonder . . . is he the one
who took my sister thirty-five years ago?

# 3

I SNAKE OUR WAY through the myriad of flashing police cruisers, news vehicles, unmarked cars, and Sheriff vans all parked on the edge of the street. A slew of people line the perimeter of the crime scene tape which borders the front yard. A leaning mailbox has *McCrae* written along the side and it's wrapped twice with the yellow ribbon. The tape wrinkles in the breeze. The on-looker's gawk at the haggard home as they're pushed back by the officers standing next to a lady news reporter.

"Boy is this going to cause a stir," Collins says as he shakes out a toothpick from his wooden container which has *San Diego* swirled with palm trees on both sides of the words. He places the toothpick in his mouth and returns the pinky size container back to his pocket. A strong wintergreen aroma fills the air.

"Looks like it already has."

I pull the suburban into the driveway, and my tires crunch over pebbles as I do. I park next to the van belonging to Cumberland County's Chief Medical Examiner, Glenn Giles.

I can hear a news chopper or two overhead.

I retrieve a pair of black latex gloves from my coat pocket and stretch them on. I notice moving bodies next to numerous CSI vans parked around the side of the house.

"I've been worried this day would come. I knew sooner or later he'd reemerge," I say as I gaze toward the commotion of workers.

Collins curses beneath his breath and pinches his nose with two fingers between the eyes.

"Let's start with the body."

He nods and the toothpick bobs up and down between his teeth.

I take a deep breath and open my door.

A horrific odor, which I'm all too familiar with, confronts us.

Death.

A plethora of voices fill the air as reporters call my name. Begging me with their questions from the border of yellow tape. Chaos. Curiosity.

Yes, this is the scene of a homicide. A murder has been committed and everyone wants to know who, what, and why. So do I.

If it wasn't for the connections to Morty, Glenn would have already taken the body to the morgue. It's only in violent homicide cases such as this or in other suspicious circumstances that the Medical Examiner will leave the deceased behind for the detectives to see. So, anytime I get a call from an officer or Glenn, who is requesting I see a body on site, I immediately know why.

Standing outside my car door, I begin to take in the home and yard. A home can tell a lot about a person. My job is not only to find who did this, but to get to know the victims as well. The more I know about the victims, the more I'll learn about their killer. The house is two stories with white siding and black shutters. The front door is the color of blood, and two small white columns support an aging overhang. The yard wears high grass with scattered Miller Lite cans, brown Burger King bags, blonde headed barbie dolls, and a small trampoline with the safety net around it.

Was the husband an alcoholic? Was he abusive? Were drugs involved? Might explain why the home and yard are so unkept. If so, this wouldn't make for a good environment for a child to develop in. Which would make the McCrae's a prime target for Morty. I've yet to investigate a scene of Morty's where the parents were of good standing with their children or spouses. Every home so far has been unfit for a child and every family has been dysfunctional. His victims all match a similar profile. Bad parents. Abusive. Irresponsible. I have the feeling that the McCrae's will be no different than the rest. I'm not saying that every family with a trashy yard and beer cans scattered across it fit into this category, but knowing Morty, he wouldn't have picked the McCrae's if they didn't fit the profile. It just wouldn't match his taste.

He considers himself the "Angel of Death," or "God's Reaper." He's often left notes claiming to be called by God to render justice. I like to think maybe I have been too, though not in the same way. Now, I'm no theologian, but I think it's safe to say Morty's theology may be a bit twisted. If there is a god up there, I choose to believe he's a lot more gracious than some people give him credit for. I'm not saying everyone gets a free pass, because I do believe in a heaven and hell, and after seeing the things I have . . . I certainly hope there's a hell waiting for the monster's I've encountered over the years. I try to love people the best I can, give justice to those who've been wronged, and I leave the rest up to God. Afterall, who would want to live for a god who is always looking for a reason to deal out a lashing? If that's the way God is, then I guess you could consider me an unbeliever. Isn't he supposed to be like our father? A good father? Anyhow, enough with the theology, I have a case to solve.

A rumble of thunder sounds overhead. The rain has now slowed to a steady drizzle. I shut my car door, slip on my black rain jacket, and pull the hood over my head.

Officer Chris Williams stands next to the front door where a line of crime tape blocks the entrance. He nods when we lock eyes.

A brown dog with black streaks, who looks to be mixed with a Pit Bull, strides from behind the home. Another dog, who looks more Chow than Pit and years older, follows close behind with a bad limp. They make their way towards us with wagging tails. The sight gives a welcomed warmth in my heart. A nice primer before I'd be introduced to the dead.

I turn to Collins and ask, "They don't look mean, do they?"

He takes a moment to answer as he gives the dogs one last scan. "Doesn't appear so. Though they're likely hungry with it being two days since anyone heard from the family."

"Yeah, if it wasn't for the lady up the road there's no telling when he would've been found."

"Don't worry, they won't bother you," says Officer Williams.

"Good," I answer with a grin.

The dogs reach us, and the younger one is quick to lick and whine, while the older one does the same. I give them both some attention and raise my vision to the red front door.

Officer Williams catches my glare and holds out a closed fist by his side to signal the home is void of any dead bodies.

I nod at his gesture.

A bright light flashes against the windowpane of the door. It's followed by a loud hum. It's Glenn Giles hard at work, and being the old soul that he is, he denies the use of modern technology unless it's necessary. Rather, he chooses to use his camera from the good ole days instead. The kind that goes shutter, flash, hum. Yeah, that kind.

"Thanks, Chris. We'll give Glenn some time and start around back."

"Take your time. He's just taking pics of the blood spatter so he'll have it in his records."

"Okay, well be sure he doesn't leave without seeing me."

Williams gives a salute and says, "Will do."

If Morty did this, he would have spent a lot of time watching and observing them. And just with a quick glance, I can see that there would have been plenty of places for him to hide out here. The woods. The cornfield. He likely observed them long enough to learn their habits and routines. He also likely chose to strike at night, so the shadows could conceal him. He may have parked down the road for a quick getaway and chose to walk through the woods. There's no forced entry, which means the victims either knew their killer or he was silent enough to enter their home without them knowing. Another reason I believe he would have struck late in the night. Anything to make things easier for himself. His *modus operandi.* The pattern that aids in his success. The MO if you will.

Some may find it shocking to know that despite all the movies, shows, and books about serial killers, they're quite rare to tell you the truth. And thank God they are. I've served as the lead Homicide Detective of Portland for almost two decades now and Morty is only the third serial killer I've been cursed to deal with. To my knowledge he's only the fourth to reside along the New England Coast since the 70's.

Doesn't mean they don't exist, just means they're a lot less common than some people may tend to believe. The worst part though is they're all different. There's no cookie cutter formula for how to track these deranged individuals down. Each case brings about a unique set of circumstances. Which requires myself, my team at Portland Homicide, and our friends at Quantico to see each case with fresh eyes, void of any assumptions from those previous.

Having a Ph.D. in Psychology, the one thing I learned from my study and the thing that remains the same case after case, is this . . . pride. It's every killer's kryptonite. Sooner or later, their pride will demand they get the attention they desire, and they'll underestimate our task force. They'll leave behind a clue that gives just enough information to lead us into the devil's lair.

At least that's the common end, but with Morty it's been a bit different. Does he leave behind clues? Of course. But their vagueness eats at my psyche each time I discover them. They scratch upon the doors in the deep chambers of my mind, begging me to find their meaning. Lingering late into the night, repeating his blood scribbled words, over and over again.

When I'm thrust into these types of cases, no matter how hard I try to suppress it, my sister's voice always finds a way to flood my mind. I do my best to push away the memories from the night of her disappearance. It happens each time I stand before this type of crime scene. The sights and sounds from that night will slowly begin to appear in ghostly images and whispers. It's here I must feel my feet planted in the soil and be one with the breath entering my lungs. Otherwise, my mind will be too fogged to see past my scars and into the enigma lurking within the shadows of the scene.

A crime scene is never silent. It always speaks. The blood of the victims always cries out and begs for justice. You must be wise enough to listen and learn how to decipher the language.

I sigh out a breath and look to Collins, "Well . . . c'mon, let's head around back and see what we have."

Collins removes his toothpick and spits to the ground. "So, he left the body like the others, huh?"

"That's what I've been told."

"Oh boy."

# 4

I TAKE A STEP FORWARD, and the two dogs tag along just behind my heels. As we round the corner of the home, the backyard comes into view, and the horrid stench grows stronger. The dogs leave us and disperse among the officers and crime scene workers. People dressed in white Tyvek suits or khakis and black polos with cameras, video recorders, tweezers, and baggies, are scattered about like working ants. This is Sherrie Maynard's Crime Scene Investigation Unit. Or CSIU for short.

I feel my pulse quicken, and my veins constrict when my eyes land on the naked body of Jeremy McCrae. He hangs by his feet from a tall oak. A thick rope is tied about his ankles with the other end lapped over a branch and secured around the base of the tree. He appears to have been drained of blood as dark veins snake across his pale body like lightning strikes. His arms dangle to the earth as his stiff fingers brush the grass with each gentle sway.

I feel my feet grip the earth, freezing me in place. I grasp at my chest and wince at the sudden ache near my heart. I still haven't figured out what that pain is all about. Probably need to see the doctor before much longer. I take a deep breath, close my eyes, and swallow long and hard.

"You sure you're okay?" Collins asks as he gives my elbow a soft squeeze.

I dip my chin and march onward to the dangling body.

Two Cardinals, a male and female, sit together at the end of a branch. Together, they sing into the wind. A few branches over, sitting on the same branch supporting Jeremy McCrae, is a crow with his chest puffed out. He caws from the top of the oak and glares down at us with a tilted head.

I see Sherrie Maynard standing with Sheriff Steve Johnston by his truck. She has her clipboard propped atop her belly and is busy scribbling notes in between giving directions to two men in white suits. The men return to the body as we approach.

"So, this is Mr. McCrae?"

Sherrie and Sheriff Johnston turn.

"Oh, hey Laurie. Yeah, this is him," Sherrie says as she pauses from her writing and raises her eyeglasses to rest them atop her forehead

"And for heaven's sake, why the hell are you out here anyways? You could pop any minute. Sherrie, you should be at home getting your rest."

Sheriff Johnston turns to her and says, "See, I told you you shouldn't be here. The last thing we need right now is for you go into labor at a crime scene."

"I know, but you know me. I'd go crazy sitting at home thinking you guys were working a possible Morty case."

Sheriff Johnston takes a swig from his Coca Cola can and adjusts his gray wool beanie which matches the color of his beard. "Well don't look to me if your water breaks because I've never had kids let alone delivered any."

"Be careful, Sherrie. Don't push yourself too much," says Collins.

She rubs her eye and says, "I won't."

"So, it looks like he's been here for a while, huh? What, two or three days, maybe?"

She looks to me and I see a light flicker in her eye. "At least. He's in full rigor mortis and lividity has reached its maximum point. You can tell by how the blood tried to pull close to his face and hands. We know right off it's been more than fifteen hours. His core body temp is fifty-seven point two, so he's had plenty of time to cool down. Our current environment temp is fifty-four which puts him almost at equilibrium. Blowflies and maggots are present, but there's no pupae. That tells me he's been dead at least forty-eight hours, but I'm thinking more around . . . sixty to seventy-two, give or take. Meaning, this happened sometime between two p.m. Saturday and two p.m. Sunday. Likely closer to midnight though. Glenn agrees. We'll know for sure within the next few hours once our lab analysis is complete."

"Hmm," I say as I rub the nape of my neck.

"Oh, and come take a look at this," she says as she paces toward the body, "I'd wear a mask if you have one."

I was already reaching for mine as she turned and said it.

We slide our masks into place and come within three feet of Jeremy McCrae.

The first things I notice are his disfigured face, the stab wound near the heart region, and the absence of blood. A wound to the heart would have left a puddle. Especially with him hanging upside down. Another sure indicator that it's Morty. For whatever reason, he always takes the men's blood and the women's hair.

"The facial injuries are postmortem I'd guess."

"Yeah, the two dogs you see running around," Sherrie says while glancing about the yard, "I'd say they were hungry."

A knot of nausea grows in my chest.

"There's no blood. Judging by the injuries, I would have thought there'd been a puddle," says Collins.

I nod and say, "I was thinking the same thing."

I lean around and peak at the back of McCrae's shoulders. The deep, bloody imprint of molars and canines are present on his right shoulder blade. I count the number of visible teeth marks. The back rows are missing a total of eight teeth. I pull back and look to McCrae's mouth. I use a cotton swab and a flashlight to peer inside.

"The bite mark to the shoulder is missing eight teeth. Two less than last time. And Mr. McCrae is missing his second premolar. The tooth has recently been removed. This is definitely Morty."

"I'm afraid so. Looks like our biter is back," says Sheriff Johnston with a grim, raspy tone to his voice as he rubs at the hook shaped scar across his cheek and upper lip. It's the result of his face connecting with the blade of a drug dealer some twenty years ago when he was still on patrol.

Collins curses, "So, we were right last time then. He's making dentures from those he kills and is biting them with the teeth of prior victims."

I place my hands to my hips and shake my head as I step back in front of the body. My eyes land on the victim's arm where I notice what looks like a carving. I squat atop my calves and lean close. With one hand keeping pressure on my mask, I use my other to gently lift and rotate the man's arm. "What is this?"

"I was hoping you may know," says Sherrie.

"Looks to be a winged insect. A beetle or moth maybe. I'm guessing you didn't find the murder weapon?"

"No, but it does appear to be done with a sharp, double-sided blade. A dagger perhaps. Same as the others."

I nod and rise to my feet. I take my time observing the lay of the land, house, the body and rope supporting it, and lastly, the two dogs meandering among us.

I rub my forehead and return my eyes to the tree from which the body hangs. I allow my mind to wander for a moment. I begin to piece together a visual of Morty tugging on the rope while hoisting Jeremy McCrae into the air. I picture him biting Jeremy's shoulder, prying out his tooth, carving the insect into his arm, all before stabbing him in the heart and collecting his blood. He never kills first. According to Glenn and Sherrie's analysis of Morty's prior victims, he goes through his ritual before killing them. It appears he likes to make them suffer. He humiliates them by taking off their clothes. He's never been sexually motivated in any of the crimes. It's more like he's getting revenge. It's deeply personal. He wants to dominate, humiliate, and offer as much pain as he can before ultimately ending their life. With this place being so isolated, he would have had plenty of time to carry out his ritual without being seen. Morty always chooses the right location.

A cold wave washes over me and forces me to shiver away the gooseflesh. I look to one of the CSI tech's using a video camera and turn to Sherrie, "Be sure to send me copies of the film and pictures, will you?"

She dips her chin.

We spend another fifteen minutes combing the scene. Satisfied, I give the go ahead for them to remove the body and bag the evidence before they succumb to the elements.

"I think I've seen enough here. Patrick, you want to head inside and speak with Glenn?"

"Sure thing."

I look to Sherrie and Johnston, "We'll be inside should you need us."

As Collins and I cross for the front door, I notice the McCrae's dogs trailing us once again. I must admit that having learned of their actions, their cuteness has ebbed.

"Why does he do this?" Collins asks.

"That's the missing link to the equation. What plus why equals who, right? We know what's been done, but I am hoping that if we can learn why it's been done, then we can learn who has done it," I say while removing my mask.

We reach the front yard where Officer Williams still stands guard by the door.

"Anything?" I ask.

"No, not much."

I duck under the crime scene tape and open the screen door. It gives off a soft creak and whine. When my thumb touches the cold metal of the main door latch, I hear Glenn's old camera steal a snap. As I push the door open, we're greeted by a bright flash. My eyes wince but are quick to land on blood spatter at the end of the foyer going into the kitchen. Glenn is squatted like an old catcher with the camera to his eye. I hear Deputy Dean Ferrell ask a question, but it's never answered.

Collins shuts the door behind me.

The rest of the kitchen comes into view. More blood spatter. No doubt, this is the primary crime scene. The place where an assault or murder has occurred.

"Hey Laurie," Glenn says as he rises on unstable knees and looks to me and Collins.

I nod back, but my eyes are busy scanning the surroundings. The kitchen is quite a site. The dishes in the sink are dirty and scattered. The cabinet doors are left open. The fridge is stained a grungy yellow, and it's covered with Crayon drawings from the couple's nine-year-old daughter.

"What do we have so far?" I ask.

Glenn snaps another shot, so Deputy Ferrell goes first. "Well, Miss Carver," he says with a nod of his chin, "The neighbor up the road. Said she'd been trying to reach them for two days. Something about she was supposed to watch the daughter today while the wife went to the doctor. She said the girl had her tonsils removed last week and wasn't supposed to return to school until Thursday. The mom didn't want her to left at home alone. After not being able to get in touch with them, Miss Carver became concerned. Then once she noticed the odor from the driveway, she called us. I did a quick check outside, and that's when I found Mr. McCrae. I called for backup. We made our way in and found this, but no sign of the wife or daughter."

"Did you find anything unusual as you cleared the house?"

He nods, "I noticed something in the bathroom that you'll want to check out."

"Yeah . . . like what?" asks Collins.

"Writing," Ferrell says after a good swallow.

"On the mirror?" I ask.

His face turns to a frown, "Yeah."

My eyes linger to the living room. "Anything else?"

Ferrell rests his thumbs on each side of his gun belt and shakes his head.

I hear Glenn mumble something to himself as he squats back down. I notice he's quiet, and just as I turn to see what gave him pause, he begins to call out in a slow, unsettling tone, "Hey . . . hey Laurie . . . you need to see this."

Collins and Deputy Ferrell lean down to see.

I squint my eyes and move closer. Glenn holds a small flashlight to the bottom side of the kitchen island. I notice his hand has a slight tremble, but not from his old age.

Carved in the wood with a hairline slice is the following:

*PS 78:49*

It's not the first time I've seen this reference. It's the one about evil angels.

I stand to my feet, wag my head, and try to shake the feeling of being watched by invisible eyes. He knows I'm here. I have to see what's in the bathroom. I have to see what he's left me.

Collins follows me and calls for me to wait. I search the hall and check the first door I come to. The sight glues my feet to the floor.

It's a bedroom filled with pink and purple, and an array of Disney characters. No doubt the room of nine-year-old Sarah McCrae. I shut my eyes and hold onto the doorknob to steady myself. My palm is sweaty and has a slight tremor. All at once, my sister's voice floods my mind. It sweeps me to my childhood and inevitably to the night of her disappearance.

I feel Collins's hand on my shoulder. "Are you okay, Laurie?" he asks in a soothing tone.

I wipe away a small tear that tries to streak down my cheek. I bite the inside of my lip and nod. I swallow the knot of emotion climbing the ladder of my throat, open my eyes, and pull the door until it latches shut. I'll be spending lot of time in this room, but not now.

I pace down the hall and try another door. This one must be it. I'm right.

The moment I open the door, I'm greeted by his artistry. A skull beside a large scythe drawn with what looks like a bloody finger. Below it rests another scripture reference.

### REV 14:16

I've seen this one before too. The one about the scythe swinging from heaven to harvest the earth.

My eye catches something in the reflection. Collins notices it the same time as I. On the wall in front of the toilet is a drawing of bloody angel wings, followed by the word . . . *Mortis*. The name he always leaves behind. And below that . . .

*Laurie*

"Looks like you were right boss," says Collins. "It's our guy."

I try to control the tremble in my hands as I shake my head, "I wish I wasn't."

We'd combed the bathroom for a few moments, when I opened the sink cabinet and began to sort through it.

I looked in between the towels and that's when my eyes caught something. I lean close.

"What is this? Hey Pat, check this out."

Collins has his back to me as he's busy searching the bathtub with his light.

"Huh?"

"Looks like confetti, could be something the daughter did, but I think it's more than that," I say as I carefully lift the towel and try to cradle all the cuttings. Some float off onto the floor with the draft.

"Give me a hand here."

He steps from the tub and begins to pick up the dropped pieces of white paper confetti about the size of a dime.

"This could be something, Laurie," he says with wide eyes.

I take the towel of letters into the hall and place it on the hardwood floor where I try to sort through the jumbled mess. My heart pounds at the possibility of what might lie before me.

There are letters, some numbers, an apostrophe, and two odd shaped circles.

"Coordinates!" I blurt and begin shifting through the mess in a frantic pace. I hush Collins a time or two as his voice is too distracting for the moment. I hear Glenn and Deputy Ferrell thud towards us from the kitchen.

"What is it? What do you have?" Glenn asks.

"Sshh. Give her a minute," Collins says.

I arrange, rearrange, move a letter here, no that's not right, move it here, and . . .

W . . . E . . . ' . . . R . . . E . . . W . . . A . . . I . . . T . . . I . . . N . . . G.

I make a row of the two words.

Collins mumbles to himself and hovers over me.

The numbers and letters each have an exponent in their top right corner. One through twelve. I begin by laying them out in the order of their exponents. The odd shaped circles are the degrees. There's a capital N, and a capital W. North and West.

After giving it all a good shuffling, this is what I have:

$$38.6301° \text{ N}, 81.6462° \text{ W}$$

I stand and retrieve my cell.

"What are you doing?" Collins asks.

"Calling Agent Swanson. We're going to need the Bureau's help with this one. We need a Cessna citation flight ASAP."

"Shouldn't you talk to Chief Cunningham first?"

"I don't have time for his antics. I'll deal with the Chief later. The Bureau needs to know, and we need a flight out. Agent Swanson is our guy."

"You don't even know if these are real coordinates."

"Then Google it while I'm waiting for Swanson to answer."

Collins leans close to the numbers and thumbs them into his phone.

By the third ring for Agent Swanson I noticed Collins's eyes narrowed. Glenn and Deputy Ferrell huddle around him to peer at his phone.

"Where is it?"

He looks up and says, "It's in the middle of nowhere in West Virginia, near Devil's Den Hollow. It's a half an hour drive north from the capital of Charleston."

On the fourth ring he picks up. "Special Agent Frank Swanson. FBI."

"Frank, this is Laurie. How soon can you get me a citation flight to West Virginia?"

# 5

THE CESSNA CITATION FLIGHT into Charleston ate away five precious hours. It is now ten till eight, and I have been on the phone with field agents, the state police, and local detectives ever since Collins and I left the McCrae crime scene.

I spoke with Chief Cunningham prior to boarding. He was more than agitated, but after I offered some soothing words to entice his ego, he relented and said we would talk when I make it back to Portland. Now, not only do I dread my arrival to Devil's Den Hollow, but I dread the flight back to Cumberland County as well. Issues with the chain of command come with the territory, and my department is no different.

I received a call from Agent Frank Swanson about an hour into our flight, and he informed me of the news.

Amanda McCrae is dead.

She was discovered by a sheriff's deputy and two field agents at approximately 4:03 p.m. The coordinates left at the McCrae's were accurate to within three hundred feet. It's a deserted piece of property which belonged to an elderly deceased man whose estate has been tied up with probate since the 90's. Amanda McCrae's body was left in a trash can inside a wooden building full of the old man's tools. McCrae's head was sheared, and she had a puncture wound to her heart from a twelve-inch, double-sided blade. She also had a bite mark on the back of her right shoulder. Same type of wounds as those found on her husband.

I advised Swanson to be sure the scene remains untouched until I arrive, and not to move the body, nor contact the family.

That will be my job.

Although I am out of my jurisdiction, with my experience and knowledge of the Morty case files, Agent Swanson spoke on my behalf. He convinced the Jackson County authorities of West Virginia to follow my commands and allow me to lead the investigation. Experience and networks can take you a long way. Especially in my field.

So, Jackson County Detectives and their CSIU await my arrival, and the pounding thought in the back of my mind is . . . what has Morty done with Sarah McCrae?

† † † † † † † † † †

**AFTER THE PLANE LANDED,** we climbed into our state issued vehicle and made the half-hour drive to the secluded residence near Devil's Den Hollow. I could not help to notice how poverty stricken the area is. The scenery is mostly dilapidated single-wide trailers, fifth wheel campers, cars on blocks, dirt roads, open corn fields, and tree covered driveways for most of the way once you exit I-77.

We turned down an old gravel road and meandered along for a few minutes before seeing any houses again. Slowly, they began to reappear. These homes are even worse than the others. Young children, with stained clothes and dirty faces, played at the edge of one of the yards which was lit by a dim flood light. Their little hands waved from the darkness as we passed. I waved back and wondered how many times Morty has traveled this same route? How many times has he waved at these same children? Could they be next?

"Just a little further. It should be there on the left . . . just around that bend," Collins says as he glances at his phone and points a finger to the windshield.

"It's a minimum of a fourteen-hour drive. Why did he choose this place? Why go through such logistic trouble to bring her here?" I ask aloud as we travel down the dusty road.

With the sun sinking lower and lower, darkness encompasses us more and more the further we go. My headlamps cut through the blackness as dust particles float heavenward in gentle sways. The tires crawl onward as small rocks and debris ping against the under carriage. A crescent moon peaks around a passing cloud as cicadas sing among the trees. Like Morty, they hide within the shadows, announcing their presence from afar.

"Maybe it's to make our job more of a headache. Like a distraction or something," Collins says while scratching his chin.

Hmm . . . a distraction. It could be.

Collins continues, "For all we know he could be a third of the way back to Portland by now. If he's driving that is. If he has the money, he could've taken a flight. Who knows? He could be landing at Portland Jetport now."

"But where is Sarah?"

Collins tilts his head, "She could be here, or she could be locked away back in Portland."

I scratch my forehead with a thumbnail.

We reach the bend and dodge a large mud hole. The road straightens, and I can see an array of vehicles sitting just ahead. Police cruisers with Jackson County swirled along the sides, blacked out Tahoes, CSI and Sheriff vans, and one coroner van. They sit in the dark. Quiet. No lights or sirens. That is never a good sign.

I see the outcroppings of people moving about the yard, passing in and out between the vehicles. My headlights illuminate the scene as I turn left into the driveway. A ramshackle of a single-wide trailer, with a sagging porch and ripped patio screen, sits to the left-hand side. The torn screen flaps in the breeze like a villain's cape. A car port, with tattered blue and gray tarps covering the front opening, stands in the front yard. Next to it, surrounded by tall grass, is a vintage motorhome stained with rust and mold streaking from top to bottom. In the backyard, I notice bright crime scene lights and a gathering crowd. As we crawl closer, I can make out the building where Amanda McCrae was discovered. The doors face the west. A dozen or more FBI agents and officers stand next to the lights. I can see numerous CSI personnel and detectives entering in and out of the building's doors. Next to the building and tight against the wood line, is what looks like a pet cemetery which is full of wooden crosses. The thought of there being more than just pets beneath them rake across my mind like an axe being dragged across concrete. Though it would go against Morty's MO and signature, this place certainly matches the criteria of the perfect dumping grounds. For heaven's sake, how many people could he have buried here?

But why did he lead us here? Is he here somewhere, watching among the trees and soaking in a euphoric rush as we comb over his domain? Will there be another clue hidden within the fine details? Kind of like the box within a box within a box gag. That is what these cases always feel like.

Will we find Sarah McCrae? Will there be bodies beneath those crosses? Is there any tangible evidence waiting for me other than the dead body of Amanda McCrae?

God, please tell me this scumbag has slipped along the way and that we have the wits to catch him.

I shift to park. "The devil is in the details." I turn and face Collins, "Remember that."

He nods.

I kill the engine. The lights wink out, and I open the door.

Instead of going straight to the building where the body awaits, I take my time examining the exterior of the motorhome and glance inside to the forensics team.

"Hasn't seen any asphalt in quite a while," I say as I sweep my light over the rusted rims, dry rotted tires, and dead grass underneath.

"Yeah," Collins says as he shines a light inside the passenger window of the cab.

I hear what sounds like two, maybe three crime workers, speaking behind masks near the back bedroom of the RV.

I scan my light over the locks of the door which are old, rusted, and likely frozen shut. I notice what looks like pry bar marks along the metal door trim.

"Excuse me?" I call to the back bedroom.

No answer.

"Excuse me. Hello?"

I hear light feet thudding across the squeaky floor.

A middle-aged lady, no bigger than five foot and dressed in a white Tyvek suit with a mask, steps into view and stands in the doorway.

"Yes?" she asks with squinted eyes. "Who are you?"

I lift my badge from my neck and say, "Homicide Detective, Laurie Daniels."

I didn't add that I'm from Portland, Maine. Don't want to give her any reason not to talk. My southern accent is not quite as thick as it used to be, but it's there enough that I'll likely mingle in without her questioning me too much.

She nods with suspicious eyes.

"This door here. Did you do this, or was it already like this?"

"We did it when we arrived. This thing don't appear to be messed with for quite a while."

Her language and accent remind me that I'm not in Portland anymore.

"Thank you, ma'am. So, no signs of activity inside?"

She tightens her lips and shakes her head.

"Okay. Let me know if anything changes."

"I sure will."

I turn to Collins, who has stepped from the window and is crouched near the front of the RV. He sweeps his light across the ground directly beneath the motor.

"Anything?" I ask.

"No, doesn't appear to have any fresh oil or transmission leaks. You'd think something this old and with the shape it's in, would have some leaks if it's being driven."

He stands to his feet.

I turn my attention to the single-wide trailer.

"C'mon," I nudge with my chin as I stride over to it.

The only thing I noticed about the trailer was the addition of new locks. Though forensics have yet to find any meaningful evidence inside, the presence of new locks tells me Morty has been coming here for some time. Likely used the place as lodging while he plotted his crime. It'd be a quiet place for him to rake over the details, the logistics, the timing, and everything else.

"We'll need someone to canvas the neighborhood. Ask the neighbors if they've noticed any strange cars or activity. Be sure someone speaks with those kids we saw on the way in, and I want someone to reach out to this man's family to see when they were last around." I say to Collins as we cross toward the wooden building.

He nods, "I'll get right to it."

"Thanks. You can look around in here first if you want."

"That's okay. I'll go ahead and get started with the canvas."

"Okay. I'll be over here."

"Sounds good, boss."

As Collins walks off in search of a sergeant or detective, I make my way to the entrance of the building. The soft sound of classical music begins to fill the air. Morty has good taste. Like me, he favors Beethoven, Bach, and the other classics.

I pass by an old Chevrolet pick-up truck which is covered in debris, much the way the motorhome is.

Next to the red, paint chipping building, there are lidless Friskies cat food cans. The labels are peeled and some of the cans have teeth marks through the metal. They lie scattered across the leave and pine needle covered ground. Along the wood line rest those makeshift crosses. The pet cemetery. Nevertheless, I'll have someone dig up the graves to be sure it's not where all the missing children are buried.

Crickets chirp from the brush, and cicadas sing in the trees. The night sky is overcast with moving clouds. A gentle breeze rustles the leaves. I deepen my hands into my coat pockets and pull my arms tighter to my body. I lower my vision and set it to the open doorway into the building. Crime scene lights are stationed to the right and left, allowing an open pass through in between.

I notice a lady coroner looking over and into a trash can. The kind you see at the end of driveways in a nice neighborhood. Not typical in an area like this.

A well-built detective stands next to the coroner and busies himself with jotting notes.

Three CSI members dust the place for prints. A sheriff and his deputy stand with their hands in their pockets near a wooden counter where numerous tools are disbursed. A clock hangs to the right of them. It ticks in real time. 8:21 p.m.

Following my ears, I find the source of the music, and it's at this moment I realize it's neither Beethoven nor Bach. I've heard this tune before but can't immediately name it.

Odd that it's not the usual.

A yellow evidence marker with a black number thirteen sits on the ground next to a candy wrapper. I lower for a better view. Looks like a peppermint wrapper. Morty's favorite.

The detective notices me and stops his writing.

"You must be the one we've been waiting for?"

I nod and continue to scan the building. My eyes land on the trashcan. A piece of white 8.5 by 11 paper is taped to it with gray duct tape. Scribbled with what looks like a black Sharpie is the following:

*Job 1:21. "Naked came I out of my mother's womb, and naked shall I return thither: the LORD gave, and the LORD hath taken away; blessed be the name of the LORD."*

Everyone's eyes are on me. I step forward and lean over to see inside the trash can.

I'm met with the glazed eyes of Amanda McCrae. They're flashed wide in horror as she lays folded into a ball. Her head is free of hair, slick, and shiny. She's naked just like the others. And I can see the bite mark on the back of her shoulder.

After a few seconds of staring into her gripping eyes, I pull back from the trash can, place one hand on my hip, and the other to my forehead. Thank God I haven't discovered the kids like this. That'll be the day I retire.

I had to lean back in though because there were two things that grabbed my attention.

# 6

**WHAT STOLE MY** attention was the note he'd tied around Amanda McCrae's toe with a piece of twine. It looked like a morgue tag. I unraveled it and read:

*You're late . . . again.*

Fire spread across my body, and my cheeks burned while my eyes took in his written words. A harsh wave of guilt wasn't far behind as it crashed over me to distinguish the anger. My muscles released a knot of tension and my heart weighed heavy. I loathed myself for not getting someone here sooner. As much as I try not to blame myself for what happens in these cases . . . sometimes I can't help it.

Notes like that can take a toll on your psyche. I've almost learned to expect them though when I'm on a Morty case.

The other thing that grabbed my attention was the address on the inside of the trashcan lid: 3113 Brookford Lane, SW Portland.

Why is that significant? It's my home address.

Not only does the creep know my name, but apparently he now knows where I live.

He must've taken my trash can either Saturday night or Sunday morning right after he'd visited the McCrae's. I'd last took my trash out Friday night. They pick it up on Wednesday and Saturday mornings, so I always take out the trash on Tuesday and Friday nights. All of this tells me he's been watching closely enough to learn my habits and routines. I've suspected he's watched me before, but now I know for certain.

I'll be sure my trash can gets sent over to Sherrie and her team so they can dust for prints. I'll also have the note sent to Blake and Natalie with the handwriting analysis team. They can look it over to be sure it matches the writing discovered at the McCrae's and the other cases.

After finding the note and learning the trash can was mine, Collins and I stayed a few more hours at the scene. I thoroughly searched the building, motorhome, the truck, and did an intensive walk-through of the single-wide trailer. I had CSIU comb every square inch of the place in hopes of finding trace elements. I even directed them to go as far as vacuuming the carpet in both the trailer and motorhome to see if there were any unusual fibers from hair or clothing. They sprayed everything with luminol and used their lights to look for blood stains in case our UNSUB had injured himself during the murder. They dusted everything all for prints as well. If there are any unknown traces of DNA or other evidence such as secretions, blood, fibers, prints, boot tracks, tire impressions, anything at all, we'll know.

We finished a little after eleven o'clock. Instead of staying in a hotel for the night, which would delay our arrival back to Portland, Collins and I decided to take the Cessna to Portland International Jetport. It was twenty minutes after four in the morning when we reached the police station and a quarter to five when I made it home. I ordered two officers to use my spare key beneath the fake rock and check the place before I arrived. The last thing I wanted was to come home half asleep and have Morty waiting in my closet or beneath my bed.

I also cleared it myself once I made it in. You can never be too careful.

With my body and soul engulfed by a rapid, tugging need for sleep, it consumed me the instant my head hit the pillow. The last thing I remember seeing before drifting into the sea of unconsciousness was Amanda McCrae's lifeless glare staring at me from the bottom of my trash can. It was followed by the image of Jeremy McCrae swinging by his feet from that tall oak tree. Lucky for me, these images didn't follow me into my dreams. Only blackness did that.

✝ ✝ ✝ ✝ ✝ ✝ ✝ ✝ ✝ ✝

**AT SEVEN O'CLOCK MY** alarm began to wail. A two-hour nap would have to suffice. Although, I may have to detour from my usual cup of decaf and go with something a bit stronger. By eight, I was in my office and sifting through case files. It's now five after the hour and Collins has joined me. I've since shifted from the files and over to my desktop to comb through

Facebook profiles of the McCrae's and their connected friends. There doesn't appear to be much family between the two of them. Having scrolled through countless wallpapers and stupid selfies of people, I log out of Facebook and blink hard to rid the sting in my eye from too much screen time. I rub my eyes and ask, "Has any of this changed your thoughts on the profile?"

Collins takes a sip of coffee, then says, "No, not much. I still think it's someone you'd least expect. For there to not be any forced entry in the cases makes me think it's someone they knew or was acquainted with. I know we investigated the Postal Service and UPS payroll during the last case, but I think we should give it another glance. Regardless, he must have a harmless look and demeanor about him for these people to allow him into their home. Or perhaps, he has a way with locks and enters during the shadows of night." He sits his coffee cup on my desk and adds, "You know who this reminds me of, right?"

"Yeah. The GTK?"

He bobs his head and pulls out his toothpick container.

"I know, I 've already thought about it. Remember the GTK called his bunker 'Devil's Den.' I don't think it was any coincidence that Morty took us to Devil's Den Hallow."

"Me either. But what does it mean?"

"I think maybe he's trying to say he wants to outdo the GTK."

"I hope not. If that's the case, then I guess he's about halfway there, right?"

"Yeah. The GTK killed just over fifty I believe it was, and so far Morty is tied to around twenty that we know of. It doesn't feel copy catish' though. I think like I said, he just wants to outdo him."

Collins scratches his chin before biting down on the toothpick and says, "Yeah, I think you're right, But I still say we check out the cable man while we're at it. Whoever he is, he knows what he wants and is patient enough to be sure he gets it at the right time. He's a planner, so none of this is by chance. That's the difference between our guy and the GTK.

The GTK chose at random, this guy's not like that. Not at all. He spends a lot of time plotting. He could possibly be OCD. I'd say thirty to forty, white male, and well groomed. He will have average looks and stature, nothing that makes him stand out too much. He'll probably drive a well maintenance, dark colored car like a Honda or Toyota. With all the religious clues left behind, we know he has strong ties to the church. He's either a former member . . ." Collins pauses for a moment as he processes his thoughts, ". . . or current."

"And he's strong too."

"Yeah, and quick. You don't do all this without strength and speed. And with the kidnappings . . . there could be foreign ties. This could be a trafficking issue. Slave trade, you know?" he says as he pulls the toothpick away to talk with his hand. He looks at it and says, "I may need to change the flavor. I think I'm getting used to the Wintergreen. I need something with a little more thrust. You know any good flavors that might help?"

"Have you tried Cinnamon yet? I've heard it can help curb your nicotine craving."

"No. I don't think I have. I tried Peppermint before the Wintergreen. It's just hard to find something to get my mind off it, you know? I should have never picked up the habit in the Navy. I was young and naïve I guess."

"We all are at one point or another." I say as I take a moment to scan over the white board with pins and strings connecting the crimes. I take a sip from my second cup of self-ground, Columbian light roast coffee. It's the only caffeinated coffee I'll drink. All the others race my heart too much and give me the jitters, which I hate. It'll have to be my dose of caffeine for the day.

"You sure you want to help me with this?" I ask one last time before I plead my case to Chief Cunningham. I knew I'd have to do this when I placed the call to Agent Swanson yesterday. I can only hope the Chief will agree to speak to Director Ramsey about me and Collins remaining on the case despite the FBI's involvement.

Collins clears his throat and crosses one leg over the other. He tilts his cup and finishes the last sip. He chews on the toothpick as he looks to my picture hanging on the wall of

Michael the Archangel slaying the devil by Guido Reni. He turns to look me in the eye. Those blue eyes grip me for a moment. His black stubble and well-kept obsidian colored hair makes for a handsome man. If only we'd met before our time with the homicide team—oh who am I fooling. I'm not fit for any man. Not after all I've been through. Collins's lips move, but my mind doesn't listen. I catch his words near the end.

"... no matter what happens, we're in this together. I'm ready to bring this guy down. He's going to screw up sooner or later. It's just a matter of time."

I give a gentle smile and rise from my desk chair.

"Okay. Let me get the paperwork together, and I'll talk to Cunningham. If all goes well, we can spend the day here going over the Morty files, and plan to be at the McCrae's first thing in the morning. You can get a head start while I'm in there with the Chief."

"Sounds good."

I cross the room and pat Collins's shoulder. "Thanks."

He gives me a tight-lipped nod, and I step into the hallway.

I hear Cunningham say a few choice words from his office. His door is shut but with a slight crack. So much for meeting at eight-thirty. He'd started early and without me. Not that it surprises me though.

"I've got reporters crawling out of the woodpiles, and people coming from every angle wanting answers. I can't allow this psycho to continue feeding his sick appetite. We have one of the best forensic and investigative teams along the northern coast and it's time we start acting like it."

Then came the expletive rant which Cunningham is quite known for. I wait until he finishes before I ease my way in and take a seat at the cherry oak table next to Sheriff Johnston and Agent Frank Swanson. Johnston chews on a Zero candy bar as he clutches the blue and silver wrapper between his fingers. The FBI has arrived quicker than I thought. Agent Kim Weatherby sits two spaces down from me and is seated next to Detective John White. I give them a soft smile and settle into the chair. My gesture is returned from all but Chief

Cunningham and Kim. She just gives that fake grin of hers below those icy and deceiving eyes.

A jar of colored jellybeans sits next to the Chief's computer screen along with framed photos of his wife and kids. A set of Libra scales is mingled among them. On the wall behind his desk are multiple plaques with the name Leon James Cunningham swirled in bold script across them to honor his time in the Army. There are also a few photos of him on deployment in Vietnam.

"What do you think Lieutenant Daniels?" the Chief's loud and gravelly voice rips through the air. I raise my vision and hold his gaze until he looks away to his pudgy hands which cradle a Styrofoam cup of coffee. Probably the cheap stuff from the breakroom. I don't see how anyone can drink that black sludge. I'd puke.

He sits upon the table with crossed arms as the sleeves to his white pressed shirt are rolled halfway up. Thick black hairs rest along his forearms and wrists. His black-tie dangles atop his growing belly. He sips at the coffee as steam rises past his white mustache toward his balding head.

My initial words tumble from a dry throat, so I clear my airway and try again, "I know it's him. There's no doubt. I honestly believe he may be closer to me than I'd like to imagine."

I feel the air grow thin as all the eyes of the room lock onto mine. Cunningham cocks a brow and lowers his gaze.

"I think he knows me, and I think I may know him." I pause a moment to let my words settle.

"I just have a gut feeling that I've crossed paths with him before. I don't know how to explain it other than it's like at each crime scene I can almost hear him whispering in my ear. I can't make out the words, but it's a familiar voice. His character and tastes . . . the way he does things . . . it's all so familiar. I'm also believing more strongly in Collins's profile. I think he may be on to something."

Cunningham gives me a few slow nods before taking a long, deep breath. He pulls his black rimmed glasses down from his forehead and places them near the tip of his nose. He picks up a file and thumbs through the crime scene photos.

"Um Kim, would you mind?" he asks as he extends the pictures and gestures to the white board. She gives her faint little giggle and rises to accept the calling. She clears her throat as she passes behind me.

After a half hour of watching Agent Kim Weatherby pin the graphic photos to the board and draw lines and dots with a marker, I'd seen enough.

When a lull came in Cunningham's words I spoke up.

"Chief Cunningham . . ." had to say it in such a way that he'd at least find it inviting, ". . . I'd like it if Collins and I remained on the case. At least for the time being. I believe with the new evidence and profile that if given enough time, we will without a doubt catch our man. I feel we're closer now than we've ever been. I'm confident we're going to get him this time. I'm asking you to trust me on this one."

He pulls one corner of his mouth tight as if it were tugged with a string. He takes his time tasting my words. He passes another photo to Agent Weatherby and for the moment seems to ignore my request. I bite the inside of my lip and narrow my gaze.

He coughs into the crevice of his elbow and says, "I'll speak with Director Ramsey and fight for three weeks. I'll see to it that Detective White and Meyer handle the other cases till then. At the end of three weeks we'll access your progress and go from there. I expect a clearer vision of this by then." He raises his vision and takes off his glasses. He looks me in the eye, "For now, you're on the case until Ramsey says otherwise. He can be a real stickler sometimes, so don't hold your breath."

"You're telling me," Agent Swanson scoffs.

Kim sighs and pins a photo to the board with a round magnet, "With all due respect Chief Cunningham, I think the Bureau can handle this one. Besides Ramsey has had too many run-ins with detectives muddying the waters. I don't think he'd risk that again."

I give her a long look and say, "Well, we'll just have to see then, won't we? My partner and I know as much about Morty as anyone here, and I believe we'd be an asset to the case."

"We'll see."

I crane my head and rise from my seat. While crossing for the door I pass behind Agent Swanson. He gives me a subtle wink. Sheriff Johnston gives a friendly nod, and I thank the Chief as I angle for the door.

I can't resist the urge, so I pick up a marker and tap the cap end against the board. "Here's you another one Kim. Looks like that one's about to run dry."

Agent Weatherby hardly acknowledges me. It wasn't the first time and won't be the last.

I head for the record and database room with my mind on more files. I will collect what I need, sign everything out, and make copies for Collins.

I have a long day and night ahead of me.

I'll start by reacquainting myself with the files before searching the McCrae's house tomorrow. That's the way I work best. Long days. Long nights. I have to go with the flow. Whenever I have a lead, I have no choice but to continue pulling on the thread until it unravels the case one inch at a time.

A crack of thunder rattles the walls of the station. Heavy rain descends upon the roof as if dropped from a bucket. I hope this storm rolls out soon. It seems like ever since I received the call from Glenn about the McCrae's, the clouds have darkened. It's sort of eerie.

It's as if when Morty reemerges all of nature takes notice. He must watch the weather and plan things accordingly. It would not surprise me.

Who is he? How does he know me? Do I know him? Did I go to school with him? Did I cross paths with him in the police academy or something? These thoughts burn their way through my mind, nagging me and begging to be answered. To think there's a serial killer and kidnapper lurking beyond the shadows who knows my name and knows where I live . . . is quite unnerving to say the least.

# Missing Child

## Sarah McCrae

AGE: 9

SEX: FEMALE

HEIGHT: 4'1

WEIGHT: 60

HAIR: BLONDE

EYES: BLUE

LAST SEEN: 09/28/2019 WEARING KHAKI PANTS, A NAVY BLUE BOSTON RED SOX HOODIE, AND BLACK SNEAKERS.

### PLEASE HELP BRING ME HOME!!

#### IF SEEN, CALL 911!!

# 7

WE WORKED A twelve-hour shift at the station, and we know as much now as we did this morning. We're waiting on the official report from Glenn and Sherrie. They've completed the autopsies but are exchanging notes as they work to form a conclusion. We should know something by noon tomorrow.

The storm has taken on an eerie lull as I reach my street along the outskirts of Portland. Paul's porchlight still burned as I passed. I'll need to take him some food tomorrow. He's going to have a fit when I tell him about this case, but he needs to know.

I drive my Suburban onward and crawl beneath the tunnel of oaks leading to the edge of my driveway. It's within walking distance to Paul's place . . . if you're up to it. My headlamps shine upon my mailbox as I turn in.

The sun has retired for the night and like any fall day, the darkness came early. The clock from my stereo reads 9:12 pm. I turn off the ignition then grab my briefcase and purse. I open my door and step onto the pavement. The critters of the forest screech from the cloak of darkness. Frogs, cicadas, you name it.

Oddly enough, the moment my door latches shut they fall silent. As I lock the Suburban and tumble my fingers through my set of keys, an icy breeze washes over me. I stop halfway to the front door and scan my surroundings. The night is suddenly quiet. No bug or frog dares to make a sound, and a million eyes are on me at once. I can feel the sting of a monster's glare as it hides within the shadows. The grove of pines next to my home would be a nice spot for one to peer into my soul.

My Taurus Judge revolver still sits in its holster on my hip and packed with five .45 caliber rounds. I transition the keys to my crowded left hand and ease my right hand over the Judge. I feel my flesh tense as I decipher the eerie vibe penetrating my soul.

A cold gust dances through the trees as it howls at the waning moon, which climbs to its seat of honor tucked high in the starry sky. The storm clouds have rolled out, but more will be on their way. The air has a stillness to it that's more than unsettling.

As quick as the eerie vibe had filled the atmosphere . . . it vanished.

The frogs return to their wailing and the cicadas to their screeching into the dark night. My breath comes easier, and the tension in my muscles relax. The flight or fight instinct subsides.

I shake my head and chuckle at myself for being so on edge. With Morty's reemergence, I have a right to be, don't I?

I angle to the porch and reach with my right hand for the wooden bannister. A crunch tickles my palm and scrapes upon my senses. Gosh, I *hate* that sound. What the heck did I just grab? I pull my hand from the railing and can feel pieces of wings and legs sticking to my flesh. I open my hand, and it appears to be the remains of a cicada. Like the exoskeletons they leave behind after shedding their skin. Gross. Those little guys have always creeped me out. I shake my hand through the air as chills douse up and down my spine. I rid my palm of the remains by wiping them on the porch railing. I push out a huff of air and shiver the away the gooseflesh. I insert my house key and unlock the dead bolt. As I step in, I'm rushed and greeted by Sandy, my aging Border Collie. I rescued her from our local shelter six years ago when she was about three. I decided to name her Sandy because she is originally from Tampa Bay, Florida.

I lock the door behind me and kneel to give her some love. She trails me as I make my way into the kitchen. I sit my things on the counter and reach high into the top cabinet to retrieve a pink depression wine glass. I gently clanked it against another one on the way down.

Turning, I open the fridge and pull out the black bottle of Silver Oak. My last drink was four years ago, which was the last time I investigated a murder and kidnapping by Morty.

I pour a shallow offering and watch as the red liquid gracefully flows into the glass. It's just enough to settle me without all the buzz.

Within three sips the glass was empty. Sandy sits on her haunches by my feet, while she glares at me the way Boarder Collie's often do.

"I don't think you want any of this missy," I say in a half chuckle before lowering my glass to the counter.

One more serving, and I will be good for the night. I gather my briefcase and head for the bedroom. A nice steam shower calls my name, and the plate of leftover spaghetti never sounded so good.

After showering and enjoying my dinner, the time had come to enter the dark abyss where wickedness abides. In order for me to find the killer, I have to enter his mind and think the way he thinks.

Here I am, pacing the living room floor with one fist to my lips, and the other tucked beneath an elbow. I scan the crime scene photos scattered across the ottoman and couch. A few found their way to the rug as I had to make room.

The most recent cases are The Anthony's, Canton's, the McNamara's, Shelton's, and now . . . the McCrae's.

"Why? Why did you choose these people? What did they have that urged you to take their lives?" I mumble to myself as the eyes of the deceased glare back at me.

The pictures of their missing children are mostly school photos, or those from family outings. Of the missing children, two are boys and now with Sarah McCrae, three are girls.

The storm returns and the raindrops grow heavier by the minute. Within no time, my gutters begin to drain with their familiar gurgle. The tree frogs multiply as they add their singing to all the noise. Thunder rumbles in the distance.

Still the one question I just can't shake . . . why?

Why did Morty do this?

The one thing in common among the parents, is that they are in most people's eyes . . . unfit. From drug addicts to abusive alcoholics, to poverty stricken and careless living. None of the environments of the homes were ideal for a child to mature. Is it drug related? No. Sexually motivated? No. Does Morty believe he's heroic in some disturbed way by rescuing these kids from such dysfunction? Hmm. Does he find a sick nobility in his actions? Perhaps he suffers from delusion of grandeur? In his mind, is he doing the children a favor? On that thought, is Morty really such a monster? I mean what if we've got this all wrong? What if he has put on this evil persona with all the scripture references, bloody drawings, and violent methods to throw us off. For all we know, Morty may not be a man. What if it's a woman, and Collins's profile is all wrong? What if there are multiple people involved?

I shut my eyes and take a deep breath to let the moment pass as my mind wanders over the various possibilities. Though none offer much clarity to the situation.

When I do open my eyes, they're met again with those of the deceased. How many times have I seen their fished eyed glares in my dreams? I could never number. They linger deep into the night, begging me to bring them justice.

"What is it that you all have in common?" I say aloud as I scan over each of their photos.

That's the one thing I don't understand about these people. What is it that sparks such an interest for Morty? What is it that fuels his desire to kill? What scratches the urge he can't resist? The way that he humiliates, dominates, and inflicts pain leads me to believe it is deeply personal. An act of vengeance in some way. Did he know these people?

The Shelton's lived in a trailer park near Cumberland. The Canton's . . . a mansion outside of Portland. The Anthony's . . . a townhome in Naples. The McNamara's . . . a small neighborhood in Kennebunk, and now the McCrae's from the junky house in Gray. The races are mixed too, black and white, so what is it that attracts our killer? Despite the difference in living arrangements and monetary value, each of these people and those before had their issues. In a number of cases, the children had files with the DSS regarding abusive situations. So, apparently as I stated before, Morty targets abused children, rescues them, and then inflicts vile revenge upon the abusers. And he tends to favor families with only one child. It is rare for him to target a family with multiple children. Which all goes back to his MO. The pattern that aids in his success.

It'd certainly be more difficult to take two children rather than one.

I rub my hands down my face and take in the sounds around me: The pounding rain, draining gutters, the distant but growing thunder, frogs, and the singing cicadas. I also hear Sandy's toenails in the kitchen as she laps up some water from her bowl.

The buzzing in my pajama pocket gives me a start. I retrieve my phone and slide my thumb over the green button.

"Patrick?"

"Yeah, hey it's me. Sorry to bother you. You weren't asleep were you?"

"No. I'm still looking over the files and stuff."

"Good. Good. Hey, listen, I've been looking over the files too."

He pauses to grab a breath.

"Yeah?"

"I don't know if you know this or not, but Brett Stephenson—you know Amanda McCrae's brother?"

"Yeah."

"He goes to Freewill Holiness."

"*The* Freewill Holiness?"

"Yeah."

*The* Freewill Holiness. The church of snake handlers that were in so much trouble during the 80's. Their pastor kidnapped a boy to "protect him from the demons." That church has been the talk around town ever since. The one many believe may be involved in the murders and kidnappings.

Could be nothing. Could be everything.

"You there?"

"Sorry. Yeah, I'm here" I rub my forehead and add, "How about we bring him into the station tomorrow for questioning. I'll reach out to Miss Carver as well. Let's plan to spend the morning at the scene, and I'll arrange the meetings for the afternoon."

"Okay, sounds good."

A static hiss fills the line.

"How are you holding up with all this?"

I take a moment to answer as I have to suppress my sister's voice.

"Good. I'm handling it the best I can."

"Don't get yourself too deep into this, Laurie. I know it must be hard on you."

"Patrick, I appreciate you looking out for me, but I can take care of myself." I cringe as my words were sharper than I intended.

"Listen, I didn't mean it to come out that way. I really do appreciate your concern, and I value our friendship. It's just I'm growing a bit weary of people always thinking I'm struggling with my past."

"I'm sorry, I didn't mean to intrude. I just wanted to offer some comfort and remind you that you're not alone in all of this. There's a whole team of experts fighting alongside you. I'm always here for you. You know that."

Gosh, such a gentleman.

"I know, Patrick. Thank you. Well hey, let's get some sleep. We have some heavy days ahead of us. Plan to be at the station by seven. It'll be a long day, but it's necessary."

"Sounds good boss. Have a good night and call me if you need anything. See you in the morning."

"Thanks, see ya."

How I become so lucky to have a partner like Collins I'll never know. That man is as loyal and caring as they come, but he can be a ball of fire when need be.

I pocket my phone and take one last sip of wine before heading to bed. I gather the files and photos, tucking them away in the manila folder for another time. I look to the clock above my blank tv screen. Five minutes passed midnight. As my eyes fall over the shiny black glass on the television, my heart knocks so hard I feel the bones in my chest rattle.

A large hooded figure stands in the tv's reflection and glares back at me. I blink quick, but it's still there.

Sandy lets out a sharp bark as the hair on the back of my neck now stands erect. I yank around to face the man in the black hood. Without hesitation, I lurch for my Taurus Judge revolver sitting on the bookshelf. The instant I feel the rubber grip in my hand, I pull back the hammer and chamber a round.

My eyes reach where the figure stood, but they are left darting to and fro in frantic search of the intruder. There's nothing there.

Sandy stands at my feet with the hair on her back bristling. If it wasn't for her reaction, I would say it's just the wine not mixing too well with me, but for her to be acting this way I know something's up.

I clutch my Taurus Judge tight with sweaty palms and train it to eye level. When a dozen seconds pass without any movement from the shadows, I lower my weapon and slide my feet across the oak floor. My heart beats like a fist as I can feel my carotid artery thumping along my neck. I ease for the wall adjacent to the open doorway leading into the dining room.

Sandy creeps along beside me and keeps a low guttural growl. Her hair grows straighter with each step, and so does mine.

The rain beats harder upon the roof as the thunder grows more irate. The creatures of the night become drowned out by the rushing water that cascades through the gutters.

*Boom!*

The light in the living room flashes and winks out for a moment . . . then comes back to life. The thunder grumbles as it seems to crawl just on the opposite side of my ceiling. Judging by the flash and loud crack, the strike must've hit a tree in my front yard. I can still feel its vibration as it resonates deep within my chest.

Using the sound of the crack and the winking of light, I rush and press my back to the wall. I slide closer to the doorway of the dining room. I peer around and look towards the laundry room so I can see the door for my back deck.

The lights flicker again, but this time with a loud hum.

I peer around the wall just in time to get a glimpse of my door slamming shut. My heart sinks. It's really him. A mix of emotions flood my soul. Anger and fear gnaw at me from both sides in a violent tug of war. I'm fearful that this is Morty, and if so I may be the next victim to have my head sheered. While I'm also filled with anger that he had such audacity to enter my home.

A piercing screech claws at my mind. What the heck? Sandy barks in a viciousness tone I've never heard before. Her toenails rake against the wood floor as she scoots backward to the couch.

My dining room is full of blackness, but the light in the laundry room is bright. I can hear something scutter across the metal on my washing machine. The sound of little feet attempting to gain a footing while screeching for help. The sound is familiar. An insect.

Big feet pound down the steps of my deck. With my heart skipping beats, I force myself toward the noise and race for the back door. My breath comes in quick gasps.

I pass the source of the screeching. A black winged bug struggles on its back with its legs kicking at the air.

I yank my attention to the door. Fling it open. I aim my Judge down the steps. My eyes glimpse a tall figure. Who is that? They're dressed in black with a flowing cape. They land on the last step and bolt into the dense grove of pines.

I aim with trembling hands and squeeze the trigger. The crack of gun fire rings my ears as the muzzle flashes into the darkness. It sends orange hues spreading through the falling rain. The figure streaks into the woods and disappears.

I don't think I hit him, but at least my shots will show him I'm not afraid to kill.

I hear him tear through the thickets in quick thudding strides. His crashing footfalls ebb and are overtaken by the sound of rain.

*Boom!*

The sky flashes white as another lightning strike lands close. The rain falls heavy and fast, and I'm now soaked and chilled to the bone. I step inside, lock the door and retrieve my phone. With the Judge in hand and phone to my ear, I cross to the screaming critter still struggling on my washing machine.

I lean close . . . it's a cicada bug.

My heart thumps like a subwoofer as adrenaline speeds through my veins.

"Hello?"

"Patrick. Get over here now, and call Sheriff Johnston. I just had an intruder," I say in a quick breath, before adding, "I think it was Morty."

As Collins stutters and rambles, I back away and reach for the light switch. I don't want to give any advantage to Morty as he may be watching from the woods.

The room turns black, but the cicada continues to sing and squirm upon the metal.

**HE LATCHES THE DOOR** and sends the dead bolt home. The stale odor of molded earth fills the dismal basement. It greets his senses as he thuds lower into his dark abode. The train of his black robe caresses the steps behind him. He needs stillness. No lights, no noise, just himself and the black void.

It is here he will wait. It is here he will listen. He fights to control the tremor in his hands. His right hand has already taken to rolling the imaginary pill between his thumb and fingers.

He crosses for the center of the room. Water drips and splashes into a nearby pot. The kitchen above still needs to be fixed, but it'll have to wait. There are more important things that need attention than a broken pipe.

Possessed by the howling wind, a bush scrapes its bony branches against the cellar window. The effect causes it to look like curled claws grasping for another victim. The rain comes in at an angle against the cobweb covered glass. The darkness is only offset by the illumination of periodic lightning.

In all his years of watching, tonight marks only the third time he's entered Laurie's home. Physically at least.

This time was just as exhilarating as the last. Such a rush. He can still smell her floral perfume as it stings his senses. The sight of her ordered home rests fresh in his mind. After the third time, he now has the lay of her house stored perfectly within his memory chamber. Tucked away deep in the darkness and kept with a bolted latch. The key to get in is to do as he's doing now.

It requires stillness and meditation.

It's the way he allows his mind to comb over the senses and visualize his prey's domain.

He crosses to the center of the basement and folds to the earth, crossing his legs beneath him. He snarls his nose and pulls in a long breath. He allows his mind to settle. Sound begins to dissipate as he narrows his focus. He goes back in his mind and in a slow, apparition type manner, things begin to manifest. His body becomes numb as his mind transports him to Laurie's driveway. Classical music fills his ears as it emits in low registers from the home.

He steps softly upon her gravel. It crunches beneath his large black boots. Oh, how he wished he were truly here in body. The simple visual will have to suffice.

A tight grin stretches his lips as he angles for the porch. It's a single-story home which was likely built in the eighties but has been well kept. The cream-colored shake siding matches well with the brown shutters. Rose bushes, miniature crape myrtles, and small green shrubs sit atop the mulch. Not a weed in sight. Everything is in order, just the way the Laurie he's come to know would like it.

He sees the wide porch come into view. He notices it has a newly restored deck and fresh coat of cream paint. White wicker furniture line the wooden planks. A green and white swing set rest next to a window. A golden windchime dances in the air and sings with the breeze.

He reaches and twists the door handle and steps inside. The foyer is lined with paintings of the local lighthouses and pictures of childhood memories. At the end of the foyer is a familiar painting. One by Guido Reni that depicts Michael the Archangel as he slays the devil. He pauses here to give it the admiration it deserves.

Okay, time to move along. The kitchen is ornate with gray slate counter tops. A gorgeous sand and chocolate colored back splash leads to a deep farm style sink. The cabinets are dark cherry oak with large glass fronts to see into. Nice.

On the silver Maytag refrigerator are old photos of three children enjoying a day of creek tubing. Two girls and a boy. It's Laurie and her two siblings.

The soft and melodic tune from Beethoven's Moonlight Sonata plays elegantly upon a baby grand piano. Turning to the living room, his eyes ease upon Laurie's robed back. Her blonde hair flows along the black silk. Her fingers glide gracefully over the black and white keys. Sandy, her Border Collie, is asleep upon a pillow beneath the bookshelf.

As always, when Laurie hits the deep C with her left hand it pulls him back to reality. Laurie and her home evaporate like a spirit as his world spins into a rush of nausea.

His eyes flash wide. The cold dark basement fills his vision. The stale odor returns as does the sound of water dripping into the pot.

He shakes away the buzz and rises to his feet. He wipes his face with both palms and releases a deep breath.

The wind howls as it rushes along the windows like a mad Jinn begging to be let in. Sharp rain drops ping off the glass window.

The mind is such a beautiful gift which the Creator has bestowed to us. Some say we only use ten percent of our brains during this flash of a life, but Gary Wade Duncan uses more.

Much more.

Known by many names: The man in the black hood, man of shadows, the death angel, Morty, that creep, and so on. Gary Wade Duncan has managed to keep a glorious cover through the years. Which has allowed him to mingle among society without their ever knowing it. Of course, glasses, a wig, and a ball cap always helps when it's time to wander the streets. He's picked many a prey while simply shopping for groceries. Food Lion and Wally World have served as nice recruitment centers over the years. You wouldn't believe what you'd see and hear among the aisles. He enjoys his time in such places. He's always listening and watching. To fulfill his calling, a strong mind is required. Something he's grateful to have.

It's quite an advantage to be able to tap into the full essence of one's mushy, gooey, processor, we call a brain. Very few have ever done so. To think man has made all that he has while using only a fraction of his potential . . . one must shudder to wonder of the possibilities that exist if only mankind could become as Gary Wade Duncan.

It's a dying shame to think a mere insect could be wiser than most men and women. The cicada that is. It's such a beautiful gift bestowed upon us by the Creator.

Gary Wade Duncan reaches deep into his black coat pocket and retrieves a small pickle jar. He twirls it in the dark. It flashes before his eyes with each crack of lightning. A black bodied creature with bulging red eyes glares back at him as it cleanses its face with its little hands.

Some genus of cicadas only emerge every thirteen and seventeen years. The Magicicada, such as the one within his jar being one of them. They spend most of their lives tucked away deep within the cold dark earth, just before crawling out of the ground in abundance to over satiate their predators.

Majority of their predators only reproduce in even year cycles, two, four, six, and so forth. With the Magicicada choosing a prime number to develop their reproduction cycle, they enhance their chance of survival as most of their predators will be in a down year. Gary Wade Duncan has learned so much from their wisdom. They've been such a beautiful gift.

A twisted grin crosses his face as he watches in awe at such a creature. The cicada bug is so underappreciated. He twists off the lid and lowers a calloused hand into the opening. The critter scurries about but calms the moment he feels his master's touch.

Gary Wade Duncan grips the cicada in a tight palm and watches with glistening eyes as it struggles between his fingers. Finally, after persevering, it pokes its head out between the opening of his curled pointer finger and thumb. Duncan takes his free hand and rubs its head with gentle strokes. The creature begins to sing.

Indeed, such a wonderful gift. Such a beautiful creature.

# ·9

I SIT AT THE kitchen counter as Sheriff Steve Johnston and Detective John White question me. Collins sits upon a bar stool next to me.

"You locked the door behind you as you came in?" asks Steve.

I nod, "Yeah, like I always do, and I made sure of it tonight. I knew when I stepped out of my car something was off. It was like I was being watched." I curse beneath my breath and add, "He must've been watching me from the window. My *own* window."

I sigh and drop my face into my palm. I rub my temples with my middle finger and thumb. "I know I locked the door behind me, and I'd just got home so I know all of the other doors were still locked."

Detective White takes a breath and scratches the back of his bald head. "Laurie . . . either you left a door unlocked, or our guy has a key." That's Detective White for you, always honest whether I want to hear it or not. His words wash over me and cause my flesh to turn bumpy and cold.

Seeing my reaction, Collins offers a steadying grip upon my forearm and reassures me of his presence. I look to him and give a soft smile.

Sheriff Johnston places his hands to his hips and shakes his head. He curses as white flakes of spittle land on his salt and peppered beard. "He's taunting us. That sorry piece of scum. He's laughing in our faces," he then mumbles beneath his breath as he turns and faces my living room.

"Like I said, I knew something was off the moment I stepped out of the Suburban. I could just feel it, you know. I felt his eyes. He was already here. Waiting on—"

Johnston spins around and says, "I tell ya right now, if I get my hands on this sonofa . . ." Johnston gives a sarcastic chuckle and cranes his head, ". . . he'll be sorry."

Commotion trails down my foyer. I can distinguish that voice from a mile away. It belongs to Paul Sealey. He passes through the crowd of officers guarding my door. I'd called him right after I hung up with Collins. I told him to stay inside and lock the doors until an officer came to bring him to my place. His face is washed white with fear as he approaches me. His breath labors in and out with short gasps. Having smoked for more than half his life, the COPD can be nasty, especially when he gets worked up like this.

"Laurie, oh baby . . . what happen? Are ya alright?"

He hugs me tight like a father would. Afterall, he has basically been my dad for twenty plus years now. I met him shortly after I moved to Portland. With both of us having Southern ties and police backgrounds we were drawn like magnets.

"Yeah-yeah, I'm fine. Don't worry about me, everything's fine," I say against his white robe as he holds me close.

"I heard the shot, and it about near give me a heart attack. I jumped clean out of bed and grabbed my scatter gun. I knew something wasn't right. By the time I managed to get my light flicked on and reach the phone, you were already ringing."

I pulled back, "I figured you heard me fire. You can stay here for the night if you like. You can have the guest room. Collins said he would sleep on the couch."

He twists his head and clicks his tongue against his teeth. "Now I don't want to do that. I'll be alright," he tried to say in a convincing tone, but my look made him give it a second thought.

"Alright then. I reckon it wouldn't hurt to stay here for the night. You sure you don't mind?"

"Paul, you know I don't mind. Besides I wouldn't be able to sleep knowing you were up there by yourself after what just happened. It'd probably be a good idea for you to stay here for the next few nights until we get some things figured out."

He nods and pulls in a deep, raspy breath. His eyes drift off to Officer Williams and the others as they canvas my home, checking the doors and windows for any sign of forced entry.

"My. My. My. Mmhmm," Paul says with a dry cough at the end.

I turn to Detective White, who I swear is a clone of John Coffee from the Green Mile, and say, "Make sure we bag the cicada bug. I want that taken in with the evidence. I know they are really out right now so it might not be anything, but I don't want to leave any stone unturned. See if we can contact an entomologist to be sure it is a local species."

He nods, flips a page in his notepad, and makes some scribbles.

"I know, them jokers been keeping me up all night. I don't know which is worse, them or the frogs. They shouldn't be around much longer, though. Getting kind of cold for em, I think."

"Yeah, they've been bad this year," Collins says to Paul.

Officer Chris Williams strides back from the laundry room along with Deputy Dean Ferrell.

"Everything's tight and secure. It doesn't look like anything was tampered with. I mean you watched us check all the windows and doors. He must've had a key, or you left something unlocked."

I shake my head, "I know I didn't leave anything unlocked."

"That leaves us with only one possibility then," says Sheriff Johnston, "He has a key."

"Or he used your spare, Laurie," says Officer Williams.

I would be lying to you if I said the thought of it being Officer Williams or Deputy Ferrell didn't cross my mind. Afterall, they were the two that checked my home the night I was in West Virginia. I have known them both for over a decade now, and neither one could be capable of such a thing. They are both good men, but I take note of the sinister possibility and file it deep in the back corners of my mind. The more likely scenario is that Morty knew about the spare key beneath my fake rock.

"I guess it's time for me to change my locks then."

"Girl . . . I'm telling you, you need them cameras like I have."

I turn to Paul, "Yeah, I think that would be a good idea."

My eyes wander to the black glass of my tv screen, and a chill douses my spine as I recall its reflection of the dark figure that was standing behind me.

I had just been paid a visit by the man who calls himself the "Angel of Death," and a nagging question screams in the back of my mind . . . what if he really is?

My ears catch the ticking of the wall clock above my kitchen sink.

Tick. Tick. Tick.

Time rushes forward unabated, marching us closer to our coming ends.

*Geeze, will you listen to yourself? Knock it off.*

I blink hard and take a breath, but the clock continues to march us onward, eating away our time upon the earth. Tick. Tick. Tick.

# 10

**I CALLED FRED'S** Theft Protection as soon as he opened. After telling him my credentials and what happened last night, he arranged to have his guys at my place within the hour.

Deputy Ferrell arrived with a new set of door locks a little after 7:30 a.m. He dropped them off and went back on patrol. Fred's camera guys pulled in as Ferrell pulled out.

As the two men rummage about my home with wires, screws, and DeWalt drills, Collins busies himself with the locks. I supervise of course and sip on my cup of decaf coffee with chocolate almond milk. Paul is still asleep in the guest room.

I chose the cameras with the live footage option, and I can check into everything through an app on my phone. It will alert me should it pick up any movement or loud sound.

As Collins is twisting a screwdriver at my door, the cameramen are busy on their ladders around the corner of my house.

"You're going to be alright Laurie. We get the locks changed and the camera's installed, you won't have anything to worry about," he says as he glances at me with a faint grin. "Besides, I doubt he'll be back after getting shot at with that elephant gun of yours. He's probably still shaking like a leaf."

I chuckle and steal a sip of coffee while diverting my eyes to the men on the ladders.

No matter how hard I try, thoughts of the GTK will not go away. He is the serial killer from Georgetown, South Carolina who murdered over fifty people within a span of about two and a half decades. The acronym GTK is short for, "The Georgetown Killer." It's a long story, but to sum it up: Jessie Randolph was kidnapped around the age of five while he and his older brother James were walking through a wooded path to their local playground. George Thompson leapt from the brush and beat James into a comma before running away with little Jessie. George and his wife Lorraine would go on to spend the next six and a half years brainwashing him into their cult known as, "For the Greater Good." The cult progressively grew more and more sadistic and twisted as they often do. George claimed to be a prophet sent from God and would routinely declare that God had spoken to him about how someone within the group had sinned. Therefore, God would require a sacrifice and George would force young Jessie Randolph to participate in the ritualistic slayings. The cult broke up on the day an eleven-year-old Jessie came home from school and found Lorraine, who he called mother, crucified in the barn. George Thompson was knelt in the hay only feet away and lost in a trance as he rocked back and forth in earnest prayer. He slumped to the ground when Jessie shoved a pitchfork through his gut. Jessie buried their bodies beneath the house and then staged the barn with two bodies of those who had been recently sacrificed. He set the barn ablaze, scripted a tragic story, and was sent to live with his supposed aunt and uncle. It was later discovered that they were not blood relatives, only members of the cult. Randolph spent the next seven years with the couple. The cult known as "For the Greater Good," died that day, but an even more sinister thing was born . . . the GTK.

Upon turning eighteen during the spring of 1989, the GTK became an employee at the Georgetown International Papermill. It was around this time that he began his killing spree. Bodies began to surface, and after causing a horrendous accident at the papermill which almost cost a man his life, the GTK fled to Southern California. It was there he would go on to reign terror for the next twenty-five years. In total he murdered over forty people in San Bernardino County from 1989 to 2014. He worked as a local handyman and cable tv installer. Using his occupation wisely, he would store the layout of the customer's home within his mind and go back in the midnight hours. He would sneak in, hide within their home and attic, and wait patiently for his moment to strike. The term, "San Bernardino Phantom," was quickly coined by the locals as one murdered family after another was discovered.

The GTK eventually moved back East in 2014. Leaving behind a wife and teenage son who were oblivious to his crimes. He would kill almost a dozen people before finally being apprehended late one night in Holden Beach, North Carolina. As I understand it, he is currently on death row in North Carolina and awaiting his verdict. As strange as it may sound, he claims to of had a transformation experience. He is now in the process of helping FBI and authorities in tracking serial killers. I've been pleading with Chief Cunningham for three years now to let me go down and interview him. I'm hoping I can twist his arm enough to give me the green light.

Anyhow, now that you're up to speed on all of that, maybe you can understand why I keep having the thought that one of the men dressed in cable man clothes may have been the one inside my home last night.

I watch as one of them reach high with both arms extended to the corner of my roof. I burn the image of the rosary bead tattoos snaking down his arms, deep into my mind. His skin has an olive tint, and his hair is black. He's maybe six-foot-one, a hundred and eighty pounds, but he looks sneaky strong. Feeling my glare, his eyes shift to mine. I take a sip of coffee and use the cup as a cover. I return my eyes to Collins who is saying something about a memory of his time in the Navy.

Finding me suddenly quiet, Collins stops twisting the screwdriver and looks up at me. He glances to rosary bead tattoo man, then turns back to me and says in a low tone, "You're thinking too much, Laurie. Not everyone new is Morty."

I bite my inner lip and look over my shoulder to the inside of my home. My place of security which has now been infiltrated by the serial killer I'm supposed to be tracking. Who's doing the tracking now?

I hear a door creak open, followed by feet thudding across the oak floor. It's Paul, and he is still dressed in his robe from the night before. The one I'd bought him for his birthday this past July.

"Good morning sweetheart, how in the world are you doing?" he asks with a big grin below his thick white mustache.

"I'm doing good. How about you?" I ask as I give him a hug.

"I'm good, I'm good. Let me tell ya something . . . that bed in there must've fell straight out of heaven because I slept like a baby last night. Mmhmm. Like sleeping on a cloud."

The three of us share a laugh.

"Getting ya some new locks I see," he says before lifting his eyes to the guys installing the camera system, "And some cameras too. Boy, them there will sure ease your mind."

"Oh yeah. I got the live footage too, so I can watch it on my phone. It'll alert me if someone's fooling around."

"Oh, well that's good darling. That's good. I tell ya, I remember when those things first came out. They sure helped me catch a bunch of bad guys during my days in the swamp lands."

"Oh, I bet so. How long were you detective again?" asks Collins.

"Six years in North Carolina, and twenty in Nah-Leans as they say down there. Moved there to be closer to my wife's folks after her daddy passed. They owned a French plantation home back in the sticks and swamps of Southern Louisiana. Hotter than a rat in a wool sock during the summers, though. Whew wee."

Collins's shoulders jiggle as he says with a grin, "I bet so. Did you like the food?"

Paul scoffs, "Shoot, are you asking Paul Sealey if he liked the food?"

"I bet your wife could cook, couldn't she?" I ask.

"If you only knew," Paul says as his eyes turn distant with eighty-year's worth of memories. He glares out into my front yard and takes a hard swallow.

"Well, after we're done here, Collins and I are heading to the crime scene in Gray. I talked to Allen this morning, and he said he would come stay with you for the day as long as you don't mind."

"I don't care. That's fine with me."

"I have some food that you can take back with you too. I figured we could drop you off as we leave."

"Oh, got me something to chow on, huh?" he grins, "Is there a turkey burger in the mix?"

"You know it."

Paul belts out a deep belly laugh and gives Collins a good slap on the shoulder. The man sure loves his food.

I notice rosary bead tattoo man in my peripheral as he steps down the ladder. We lock eyes for a moment before he disappears around the corner of my house.

Whether my gut is trying to tell me something, or I am being too paranoid I can't tell. Either way, I had a full description of the man etched on the notepad of my mind before he left. I even stored his voice in there too. The name tag on his breast read, ***Vernon.*** Which seems kind of an odd name for a man who looks to be of Hispanic descent. Strange as it may seem, I'll take an odd name over no name any day of the week.

It was eight-fifty-two when the cameramen left and nine-o-four when we loaded into my Suburban. We dropped Paul off at his place and did a thorough search of it as we waited for Allen Poteat.

Allen's another neighbor who is like family. He lives through the woods behind me and Paul. If Paul is my dad, then I guess Allen is my uncle. He is a full decade younger than Paul, and he is a good friend and caretaker. They get alone like any two men in their seventies and eighties would. They can sit hours on end talking about the 'good ole days', until one of them becomes too grumpy to go another minute.

"Alright now, you two 'youngins' behave, you hear?" I tease with a southern twang as Collins and I head for the door.

"Oh foot. Don't you be worrying about us. We the sheriff and deputy of this here town. Y'all two the ones that need behaving," Paul says with a grin as he wags a finger at us.

"Yeah, except I'm no Barney Fife," Allen says with down cast brows.

"That's right. We're more like Wyatt and Doc."

Allen lifts a thumb in the air, "Amen, brother."

"Well, you two be good. Keep your eyes and ears open. Call me if you need anything."

They both nod.

"Be careful out there, Laurie. And Patrick, you better take good care of my girl now," Paul says with a down tilt of his head.

Collins glances to me, then looks to Paul, "Don't worry Mr. Sealey, I will."

"Take care, love you guys," I say as we pass through the door.

They return our love and start chatting in old man verbiage.

When I reach my car door, Paul calls out from the patio window, "Y'all be careful now, and call me when you start heading home."

"I will. Love you, Paul."

"Love you too, darling."

I settle into my seat and shut the door.

"He's a mess isn't he?" Collins says with a grin as he waves through the front window.

"Yeah, he's rotten."

I back out of the driveway and glance to Paul's patio. He sits in his rocker, waving a lamp shade up and down in front of the light as if he were a night watchman calling ships into port.

We chuckle and wave back.

I shut my eyes and sigh. That will likely be my last laugh for a while. The McCrae's place pulls me like a magnet. The images of Amanda folded up inside the trash can, Jeremy dangling from the oak, and the girly colors of little Sarah's room, all flash like strobe lights before my mind's eye.

Okay, it's time to focus. Time to zero in and find this guy. It's time to put an end to all of this and bring these kids home.

# 11

"TOXICOLOGY SHOWS THAT JEREMY doesn't have any trace of chloroform, but Amanda does," Glenn says over the phone as I pull into the McCrae's driveway.

"Anything else?"

"Yeah, she has a contusion and laceration on the right side of her head near the back juncture of her skull. There was no fracture or subdural bleeding, so this was not a severe injury but would have certainly been enough to render her unconscious. Which makes me wonder why he didn't just use the chloroform?"

"Well, if you know she had chloroform in her system, perhaps he didn't use it then because he didn't have any at that time. The chloroform must've been something he used over the past few days to keep her out. It sounds as if he were caught off guard and forced to act. Amanda could have caught him in the home." My mind flashes through what happened to me last night, and I shake away the images of the figure in the dark hood.

"That's certainly a plausible theory. Anyhow, I also discovered higher than usual amounts of saline and magnesium in her system. It appears he had her hooked to an IV while she may have been unconscious from the chloroform, which explains some of the needle marks on her arm. The others are where she likely used. Jeremy has more marks than Amanda, but there is no evidence of anything other than heroin or cocaine. They have both used within the last thirty days."

I scribble quick notes to keep up.

"I believe Jeremy was attacked in the kitchen after he discovered his wife's blood spatter. He was then dragged outside and hanged from the tree. With the high levels of blood alcohol content in Jeremy's system, it would not have been hard to do. As dark and isolated as it is out there, no one would have seen Morty do it either."

"So, you're saying it's true that Jeremy was alive when Morty did this to him?" I ask as I pull the Suburban behind Sherrie's black CSI van. The Tahoe of Agent Frank Swanson and Kim Weatherby is parked in front of Sherrie's van. A silver Chevy truck belonging to Barry Tyson is parked at the mailbox by the road.

"Yes. Because all of the blood had drained to his face and upper body. Morty did it this way, so he'd get the most blood. Had he killed McCrae before hanging—"

"Lividity would've occurred much sooner, and he wouldn't have been able to drain as much blood."

"Correct."

"He knows his human anatomy."

"He sure does."

"A doctor perhaps?"

I hear Glenn click his tongue before saying, "You know, I don't think so Laurie. I feel that a doctor would be more prone to slice than to stab."

"Yeah, you're probably right. Why would he want the blood though?" I ask more to myself than to Glenn.

"It could be a trophy or maybe we have a vampire on our hands."

I scoff and add, "What, like on Salem's Lot or something?"

"Never know. People are strange these days, Laurie."

"I'm with you on that one, Glenn. People are strange indeed."

Collins opens the car door and stands between its gap with a hand atop the roof and the other above the window of the door. He leans down below the door frame, aims a thumb, and mimes, "I'm going on inside."

I nod.

"Okay, so Jeremy comes home after a night out with some friends, learns that his wife and daughter are missing, notices blood on the kitchen floor, and gets attacked from behind. He's possibly choked out and is then transported out back to the oak tree where he's hung and bled like a hog."

"That's the way I see it."

I lean my right elbow onto the center console and rub my forehead. "I need to speak with the neighbor today, and I'll be bringing in Amanda's brother this evening. Detective White is working on speaking with Jeremy's boss and co-workers to see if anyone knows where he was the night it all happened. I have some people who'll be speaking with Sarah's teachers as well. I'll also get Meyer to swing by a few of the bars when he gets a chance to see if anyone knows a Jeremy McCrae."

"Good. Yeah, I would be sure to check out the bars. You never know, Jeremy may have even shared a beer with his murderer. Morty could have followed him home. Maybe someone noticed Jeremy speaking with a strange man or something. Despite their reputation, some of the best witnesses can come from bars."

"I know."

"I wonder why he would not have burned everything like last time? It's odd that he set flame to the McNamara's place but not any of the others. I thought maybe it would become a new pattern for him. It sure made my job hell to have them all burned up like that."

"I know. I remember Glenn. There's no need to remind me."

The smell of smoke and fire still gives me chills. The acrid stench of burnt hair and flesh is something one can never rid from the nostril's memory glands.

"Glenn, I appreciate you calling. If anything else comes up, be sure to give me a ring. How late are you planning to be at the morgue?"

"We'll do. Uh, I should be here until six or seven unless I get a call. I have a few autopsies to do and some paperwork for two unclaimed remains."

"Okay, I'll try to swing by before you leave. I want to speak with you in person and take a look at the McCrae's."

"Sounds good. Call me before you head this way in case I'm on the road."

"I will. Take care Glenn."

"You do the same Laurie."

I pocket my cell and climb out of the car. The two dogs from the day before greet me as I shut the door. They trail my heels with wagging tails.

I reach the blood colored door, shut my eyes, and take a breath.

*It'll all be over soon.*

I repeat to myself while hoping there is some truth to the words.

I can hear Swanson and Weatherby inside. I open the door, and a holy hush fills the home. Weatherby pokes her head from the kitchen and drills me with an icy glare.

I nod and retrieve my notepad.

*Just ignore her, she's not worth it.* I tell myself.

She gives a fake grin and goes back to her business.

"How are we doing Lieutenant?" comes Swanson's voice.

"Doing well, how about yourself?" I say as I scan over the family photos on the wall. Two of them are crooked a touch or two to the left. I fix them and make my way to the kitchen where Weatherby and Swanson stand looking like Mulder and Scully from the X-files.

Sherrie Maynard and two of her assistants, who are dressed in white Tyvek suits, busy themselves with blood spatter on the cabinets.

"Anything of significance, Sherrie?"

"Hey Laurie. I'm glad you're okay," she says with a sincere look before adding, "Nothing yet. The blood belongs only to Amanda's. It's standard spatter from blunt force trauma. Enough to knock her unconscious, nothing more."

"Yeah, I just spoke with Glenn."

"Oh okay, so I won't bother repeating what you already know then. It all makes sense though, right?"

"Yeah. After what happened last night at my place, I believe he was already in the house when he took Amanda and Sarah. That explains why there's no forced entry. Either he has a key, or he's good with locks. He may even work at an anti-theft store like Fred's Theft Protection."

Kim Weatherby scoffs at my words, "I don't buy it."

"You think?" asks Agent Frank Swanson with scrunched brows.

"At this point, everyone is a suspect," I say and allow my eyes to linger to Kim's.

"What are you looking at me for?"

"You trimmed your hair since the last case."

"Yeah. Why, does that bother you?"

"Don't ask me, ask Morty," I say with raised brows.

"Maybe you should have asked him yourself last night."

Fire spreads across every inch of my body.

"Whoa. Calm down now ladies. I don't feel like breaking up any cat fights," Swanson says with a slight chuckle as he steps between us.

I look her in the eyes and give my choice words some thought, but decide she isn't worth my time. I have more important things to focus my energy on, and I'd be a fool to waste any on her.

I rearrange my comeback with, "That was uncalled for, perhaps my comment was to, but rather than add fuel to the fire I think I'll be an adult and get to work," I say as I lick a thumb and flip to an empty page in my notepad.

She doesn't say a word but only gives me the same smirk I've received for the past seven years.

"Let me know if you need me, Sherrie."

"I will. I'm glad you're okay Laurie. I know that must've been scary."

"It's all good. I did change my locks and install some security cameras this morning."

"That's good. That makes me feel a little better."

"Well, maybe he'll think twice about showing up again," says Swanson.

I nod. "Anyone know where Collins went to?"

"I believe he's out back with Barry."

"Okay. I'll start in Sarah's room and go from there."

"Sounds good."

I slip on a pair of latex gloves and head for the hallway. I have to step over a plate of food scraps along the way. A black tv sits in the corner on a table. A chill rushes over me as I recall that dark reflection standing in my dining room last night. I shake off the image and angle past a beige recliner.

Sarah's room is the first door on the right. I come to it and close my eyes. I prepare myself to face the flood of memories that are sure to confront me the moment I open the door. The sound of my sister's voice is already a faint whisper in the back of my mind.

I breathe deep and press on.

The door opens and swings against the wall. My sight is once again filled with pink and purple. There is fairies and Disney characters galore. The ceiling fan, wallpaper, and bed are all dressed in the same theme. It's a typical bedroom of any nine-year-old American girl.

The covers are thrown back in a hurried fashion. Did she hear commotion from the kitchen and come running? Did she see her mom's assault? For the girl's sake, I hope not.

I notice the window beside the foot of her bed. I check it and find it locked. I unlock it and peer outside. A wooden swing set sits in the yard to my left, a chicken coop to my right, and in the center is Jeremy's McCrae's red Toyota Tacoma truck.

The AC unit kicks on with a rattled hiss. It sits about ten feet to the right of me and is tight against the house. Empty Mountain Dew bottles lie scattered with Bud Light cans and other trash among the high grass. A black pushing lawn mower, which looks two decades outdated, sits next to the AC unit. There's an empty bag of Kibbles-N-Bits, a pair of gray hand trucks, and two barbie dolls to my left against the house.

Lining the tall, but dying cornfield is a white tin building with orange rust blotches scattered across it like chicken pox. A piece of the tin roof flaps in the breeze.

My eyes scan the dying cornfield, and I imagine Morty being out there watching me this same instant.

"Finding anything?"

My heart starts, and I pull back inside.

"Just taking a peek to see what the view is like."

"The place is a mess isn't it?" Collins asks.

"You can say that again."

I lock the window back. My eyes turn to the nightstand beside Sarah's bed. Drawing me closer is a small, white piece of cloth sticking out from the drawer.

Collins opens the folding closet doors behind me as I kneel to pull the drawer open. The white cloth is spread over a small rectangle outline.

"Patrick . . . come here a second."

"Whatchagot?"

I don't answer as my attention is too focused on what lies beneath the white cloth. I pull it off as Collins approaches me.

A voice recorder rests upon a diary.

A piece of white paper is taped over it that reads:

*My Dearest Laurie...*

# 12

BEFORE I PRESSED PLAY, I retrieved my phone and turned on my voice recorder app. This way I'd have a copy for myself after I send the recorder to Nancy and Morgan with the voice analysis team.

"Lieutenant Daniels here with Detective Collins . . . nine-forty-two am, October third, twenty-nineteen. Listening to discovered voice recorder from Sarah McCrae's nightstand."

Collins stands next to me with his hands to his hips.

I press play.

A static hiss begins and continues for ten seconds. I begin to wonder if there's anything on here. That wonder is shoved to the side when the deep contorted voice of a demon begins. Sounds like a voice altering app of some sort.

"Why hello my little darling."

My skin crawls as if there are maggots beneath it.

"Glad you found my voice. If only you were this good at finding children. First your sister and now nine more. You'd make for a terrible mother, much like your own," the voice snickers as it relishes the insult it'd just given me.

I rub my brows and glance to Collins, whose eyes are drilling into the device clutched between my hand.

"I'm assuming you've found my gift by now. I left it upon the washing machine. I have to say Laurie, you have a lovely place. Perhaps we could enjoy dinner sometime. I'm a marvelous cook, and my specialty is homemade spaghetti just like the Italians make it. I'll be sure to bring some Silver Oak wine as well. It'll be my treat."

My heart now rests in my bowels. How long has he been watching me? I swallow hard.

"Would you be as kind to indulge me with a playing of Beethoven's Moonlight Sonata? Only if you play it in your silk gown that is."

I smash the pause button and utter a curse. I'm only seconds from slinging the stupid thing against the wall where it would surely shatter in a million different directions. I'd already pulled back to launch it when I felt a gentle touch upon my arm. Collins. I turn and see his wide blue eyes as he slowly wags his head.

I let out my breath and sit upon the bed. The springs squeak as I do so. Collins sits next to me.

"Go on, we need to hear the rest."

I nod ever slightly, maybe not at all. "I know."

I press play.

"I'm always watching Laurie. Always. And the cicadas will continue to sing. Watching you with their bulging red eyes as they hide within the shadows. They sing of your coming demise. '*Laurie will succumb to Morty. Laurie will succumb to Morty.*' Over and over they sing."

He pauses for a moment as his words eat the courage from my heart like a ravaged lion tearing into a fawn. In a slow fade, the sounds of night begin. First crickets, then tree frogs, and finally there comes a hoard of cicadas. Where was he while he recorded this? My back yard? My back porch? Paul's yard?

"Do you hear them? Can't you hear them sing, Laurie? They're beautiful, aren't they? *Laurie will succumb to Morty. Laurie will succumb to Morty.*

"Face it my dear, you're never going to find me. You will never find the children. Ever. All of your efforts are in vain. You'd do wise to use your energy on the others. There is plenty of other killers and criminals you could be catching. They're the ones who use only ten percent. Those you can catch, but not me. It's all in vain. Vanity. It's all vanity. Besides, I've already chosen the next field to reap. You'll know who within three days."

Static returns and is followed by the sound of night critters.

"Hear them sing Laurie! Hear them sing! Their eyes are upon you, their tongues speak of you, and their hearts despise you. This is the year Laurie. This is the year of their emergence. Out of the darkness and into the marvelous light. Shedding their skin to grow into what they've been chosen to become. You can't stop destiny. You must only watch and listen. Sleep tight and don't let the cicadas bite. Bye now."

He ends with an eerie chuckle, and the cicadas screech grows louder.

I draw a deep breath.

Collins doesn't say a word. What can he say?

I turn off the recording app on my phone and begin to ramble through my thoughts.

"Okay, so it's an older recorder. At least a decade old judging by the looks of it. It's not like it's something he picked up at Walmart last week. We can try searching the pawn shops and consignment stores. I honestly doubt he'd make such a mistake, but it's something we do need to look at."

I pause.

Collins is deep in thought.

I continue, "I knew the cicada wasn't a coincidence. I wonder if White has found an entomologist yet?"

I pick up the diary and leaf through it. Nothing out of the ordinary jumps out. It looks like it's mostly words and doodles until . . . what is this?

Right before my eyes is a child's drawing of the man in the black hood. The Angel of Death. He stands at the edge of the cornfield with his big red eyes glaring through the window I'd just looked out. The chicken coop, the building, and her dad's truck are all drawn in as well. She'd seen him before he came. He'd been watching her, just as he's been watching me.

# 13

**WE COMBED SARAH'S ROOM** and the rest of the home for another two hours. Our biggest find was the voice recorder and diary. I spoke with Detective White over the phone and learned we have an appointment at three with Zach Feltner. He's an entomologist at the museum in downtown Portland.

Brett Stephenson will be in at one, so that gives us about an hour to spend with Miss Carver. Deputy Ferrell said yesterday that she's a widow with a paraplegic son. The lady has enough stress as it is, so I hate she's having to deal with this too. The report says she was close to the family, especially Sarah.

Collins and I finish searching the living room and remove our latex gloves. We pass Sherrie and her crew in the hallway.

"Sherrie, we're going to speak with the neighbor. I'll be back tomorrow. If you find anything significant, let me know. And take care of yourself and your baby for me, will you?"

"We'll do."

I hear people talking on the back porch. It sounds like Barry and the duo from Quantico.

"C'mon, let's see what they're up to," I say to Collins.

I reach the back door and gently push it open. Barry Tyson stands pulling a drag on a cigarette while holding the leash to Rusty, his German Shepherd. Agent Swanson and Agent Weatherby stand across from him with crossed arms.

"Hey Barry, how's it going?"

He raises his eyes and flicks ash from his cigarette as he coughs out his reply. "Pretty good. How are you?"

"Not too bad, all things considered. Find anything out there?"

He shakes his head, lowers his eyes, and takes another drag on the cigarette.

"What do you have there?" asks Swanson.

I hold up the bags containing the voice recorder and diary.

"He left boss a message. He's been watching her for a while now. The girl too. She's got sketching's of him outside her window," says Collins.

Barry and Frank raise their brows, but Kim doesn't budge. Why she hates me so much I could never tell you. She's the type of person that no matter what I do, she'll always find something negative to say about me. I can never do anything right in her eyes. It reminds me of my mother. I think if it wasn't for my blonde hair and desire to take care of myself, perhaps she would be more friendly. Jealousy is a strong vice. One in which I don't think will ever let miss Weatherby out of its grip. It's a shame too, because she could be a cute girl if she took better care of herself and lost the attitude. There has to be something working under the surface that keeps her from doing so. Likely a sour relationship with her dad. Probably never complimented her. As much as I dislike her, a part of me feels sorry for her.

Anyhow, after letting them listen to the copy recording on my phone, we climbed in the suburban and headed up the road to Miss Carver's.

# 14

**MISS CARVER'S HOME** is a half mile up the windy road and is only one of the few I've seen around here. Large oak's and pines, with dying leaves and needles, stand on each side of the roadway. A black mailbox leans to the right upon a ragged post. I turn off the road and enter onto a gravel drive. The woods are thick like bristles on a hairbrush, but it thins out the further we continue along. The trees give way to dead corn fields and the driveway snakes its way a hundred yards or more between them, before finally ending at a wooden two-story home. A dust storm trails behind us.

The house has a large front porch with rocking chairs on each end. A few of the shutters are crooked and hang only by a nail. Most of the paint is chipping upon the cedar shakes. The shingles are ruffled, and a few have holes in them.

A brown 1980's Oldsmobile, with more rust patches than paint, sits on cinder blocks in the front yard. The passenger window is shattered, and the seats are ripped. Pieces of yellow foam lie spread across the floorboards.

I pull to a stop and shift to park. A chocolate Labrador, with gray whiskers, rises from a nap on the porch.

"So, this is the neighbor that called it in, huh?"

"Yeah, this is Miss Carver's place," I say as my eyes take it all in.

"Dang," is all Collins manages to say, but his point is clear.

The lab stands with a feeble wobble at the top of the steps and struggles to give a few raspy grunts to alert its owner.

I turn off the ignition and step out. A crow caws overhead before disappearing into the patch of woods behind the home.

The sky is gray but with a glimmer of hope as the sun attempts to peek through the curtain of clouds. I zip my jacket before we stride for the front door.

We pass the guard dog, who only sniffs us, and I pull on the screen door. It felt like it may come off the hinges as I did so. The main door has a black iron door knocker, so I put it to use. It may be the only thing that works around here.

No answer, so I knock again.

"Coming, hold on a sec," a gruff but feminine voice calls out.

I turn to Collins and see him with his wool beanie in hand and bent at the waist to pet the dog.

Footsteps thud across the floor and edge closer. I step back and watch as the door opens to a slight crack. An eyeball that looks like a pig's eye, peeks out and looks me up and down. "Yeah . . . who are ya?"

I clear my throat and hold up my badge which dangles around my neck.

"Miss Carver, I'm Lieutenant Daniels with Portland Homicide. This is my partner . . . Detective Collins. We would like to speak with you regarding the McCrae's. Would you have a moment to answer a few questions?"

The lady's mood shifts and she's quick to slide away the chain latch. The door pops open as the lady yanks it from its stubborn stick. A large elderly woman, dressed in a gown and robe, stands before me. A long coffee stain is spread between her breast. She looks to be in her mid-sixties and not in the greatest of health. A warm smile spreads across her face as she welcomes us with an inviting sweep of her arm.

"Of course-of course. I'm sorry. Wasn't sure who ya were. Come on in," then turning over her shoulder she calls out, "Phillip, we have some company."

We step in, and she shuts the door behind us. I watch as she angles for a corner lamp beside the sofa. It lights up the living room and exposes a million dust particles. Newspaper is scattered across a glass coffee table. A farm patterned, brown sofa with barns and tractors sits against the window. An end table separates it from the recliner. A box television set rests upon a wooden table in the corner. A fireplace and mantle line the wall next to it. Upon the mantle stands numerous pictures which look like family photos from days past.

The creaking of floorboards pulls my attention and causes me to spin around. My eyes land on Miss Carver as she stands

behind an old wheelchair which supports a young man still in
his pajamas. His hand is bent and tucked tight to his chest.

"Phillip, now these here are two police officers . . .
detectives actually. They're names are Laurie and Patrick. Can
you say hi to them?"

The man has curly red hair, a cleanshaven face void of any
acne, pale skin, and hazel eyes. He can't be any older than
twenty-five. He wears red and black pajama pants with a navy
Boston Red Sox shirt.

He raises his head, which resembles an infant struggling to
gain its strength, and looks to Miss Carver with wild eyes. He
smiles, then turns to me and Collins. In a raspy tone, he says,
"Hi . . . I'm Phil-phillll-*lip*."

Compassion washes over me. I swallow hard and say, "Why
hello there Phillip. It's nice to meet you."

He smiles and lowers his head, grinning at the floorboards.
He looks to Collins and says, "You-you-you're Pat-pat-atrick?"

"Yes sir, I am. I love your shirt there. I'm a big Red Sox fan
myself. I bet you like watching them on TV, don't you?"

Phillip nods with a toothy grin.

Miss Carver wheels him to the opposite side of the coffee
table and says with a half chuckle, "If you only knew. The boy
loves his Red Sox," she locks the wheels with her foot and
adds, "Please, have a seat. Can I get you some coffee or tea . . .
water?"

"No, thank you ma'am. We'll be okay," I answer as I lower
myself to the sofa. Collins sits next to me.

Miss Carver turns the recliner so to be at a better angle to
me and Collins. She falls into its embrace and searches the
pockets of her chair. After some thorough digging, she retrieves
the remote for the tv. She aims it and smashes buttons with her
thumb.

"Sorry, he'll get upset if I don't put something on for him."

She stops flipping channels when she finds ESPN.

Phillip begins to rock back and forth. His eyes grow wide to
match the grin stretching across his face.

The volume is faint as the Top Ten Plays of the Week
begins to count down.

"Hey where are you from anyway? Don't sound like a Northern accent." Miss Carver asks me.

"North Carolina."

"Is that right? I had some family that used to live in Georgia and South Carolina. What brought you up this way?"

"Other than the cozy atmosphere and scenery, school and job opportunities, I guess."

"I see. I see. New England's a fine place to be. So, what I can I do to help?"

We go on to spend the next half hour asking questions pertaining to the McCrae's while Phillip laughed, drooled, and clapped at the tv. Miss Carver sipped on her cup of coffee, cleaned her glasses, and fed Midnight. Midnight is her black cat with white socks and a white spot between its eyes.

"Them two never got alone much, you know. They were always fighting about something. Poor Sarah had it rough."

At the mention of the name, Phillip cranes his head around and grins.

"Yeah, I'm talking about your girl aren't I?"

She looks to me and Collins, "She was such a sweet little girl . . . wouldn't harm a fly. She spent a lot of the summers up here with me and Phillip. Watching movies and messing around outside," her eyes wander back to Phillip and his tv. She breathes deep.

"Well, I'm sorry for all of this Miss Carver. I really am," I say as I place a gentle hand upon her forearm. She tightens her lips, shuts her eyes, and nods.

As I form my next question, my phone begins to buzz.

"Excuse me just a moment. I need to take this," I hold up a finger and tell Collins to continue on without me while I step onto the front porch.

The air is warmer now as the sun has finally peeked through the low hanging clouds. The porch creaks as I angle for the bannister. I recognize the number as someone from the Bureau, but I'm not sure who.

"Lieutenant Daniels."

"Laurie . . . this is Director Scott Ramsey from the Bureau." He pauses a moment.

"Yes, I believe we've spoken before."

"Four years ago. The last Morty case."

"Sounds about right. What do you have for me? I'm assuming you received the info I sent in for ViCAP?"

"I did and it's been updated into the system. I've also received word about your incident last night."

I didn't answer but waited for him to continue.

"Well, I wanted to let you know, that I'd be more than happy to set up a surveillance if it helps you sleep any better."

"Thank you, Director Ramsey but that won't be necessary. I have it all under control."

"Okay. Remember the resources are available should you feel the need for them."

"Thank you, I'll keep that in mind."

"I also wanted to inform you that we've come up empty on the background of the camera man that you'd sent in this morning. He has a clean record. We also hit a wall with cable installers and handymen in the ViCAP system. And I spoke with Agent Vasquez and Agent Turner who spent some time on the GTK case a few years ago. They have your number, so expect a call from them shortly. They're busy with a sting operation at the moment, but they've both been informed to give you a call when they can. As soon as they can pull away from their current assignment, they'll be joining you in Portland. They'll both be a tremendous asset to your team. They're good."

Nice. Maybe that'll crowd the space for Miss Smarty Pants. I'm sure Weatherby could use a vacation anyhow.

"Okay, sounds good. Thank you, Director Ramsey. I appreciate you reaching out, and I look forward to meeting Agent Vasquez and Agent Turner. I've heard a lot of good things about them. I'll continue to send information to ViCAP and NCIC as I receive it, so keep an eye out."

"I sure will, and you're very welcome. Stay safe out there. We'll be in touch."

"Thank you, bye now."

I end the call and rest both my hands upon the wooden banister. Looking out past the long, gravel drive, my sight stretches and strains to reach the roadway. My thoughts wander and search for answers while looking for an opening as if stranded in a maze of corn.

I chew on the inside of my lip while I allow my mind to rake over the words Morty had left me on the voice recorder.

*The cicadas will continue to sing. Watching you with their bulging red eyes as they hide within the shadows. Singing of your coming demise. 'Laurie will succumb to Morty. Laurie will succumb to Morty.' Over and over they will sing."*

Somewhere in the dusty corner of the porch, tucked behind one of the rocking chairs, a cricket begins its magic. My heart would have left me if it had been a cicada's screech.

A crow caws as it lights upon the roof of my Suburban. It watches me with a twitch in its eye. It takes flight and heads for the road.

"Yeah, get out while you still can, pal."

# 15

THE MORNING HAS slipped away as I now find myself seated in my office and hunched at my computer screen, while typing away into every database we have. ViCAP, NCIC, and everything else Quantico and my department has to offer.

Frustration and anger eat away at what little hope I have. The harder I look, the less I find.

I pull away from the keyboard in a huff and glance to the clock above my desk. *12:48.* Brett Stephenson should be here any minute.

A knuckle rap to my open door pulls my attention. I spin around in my chair. Collins leans on my door frame with a manila folder in hand.

"Found some information on Jeremy. Like the things you'd asked for."

I raise my brows and hold out a hand, "Oh, yeah?"

"He has a history of assault and battery, which matches what Miss Carver said. He worked third shift at the Walmart here in Portland. He was a night stocker. I spoke with his boss, and he said Jeremy hadn't been in for the Sunday and Monday shifts. Apparently, it wasn't the first time he'd skipped work, but the boss said he'd planned for it to be the last. He also has numerous drug charges, and so does Amanda. They both have long rap sheets, so they definitely fit Morty's victim profile."

I bob my head and flip through the papers, glancing over the backgrounds and records of the McCrae's.

"What about Meyer? Has he had the chance to stop by the bars yet?"

"He said he spoke with the owner of Jimbo's by phone but didn't get anywhere. Said he has the numbers for three other bars and will stop by a few others this evening when he has the chance."

"Good. Thanks.

"Anything on the voice recording yet?" he asks.

"Nancy and Morgan are still working on it. They're trying to strip it down for any background sound or voices. They should be finished by the time we're done with Mr. Stephenson."

"What about Glenn and Sherrie?"

"Glenn's report is the same, but Sherrie did say they found a wine glass and glass plate that had been cleansed with Clorox."

"Interesting."

"It appears Morty may have had dinner and a glass of wine before he left. They're analyzing everything in the lab now."

"So, you think he subdued Sarah and Amanda, murdered Jeremy, and then sat down for a meal and glass of wine before he left?

"Appears so."

I could paint a perfect picture of the man in the black hood seated at the kitchen counter while a dead man swings by his feet out back. Did he offer a toast? Where was Sarah and Amanda while this happened? Are there more involved than just Morty?

My office phone jingles in its cradle. I shake away the thoughts and images. I pick up. "Okay, sounds good. Thanks, Deb."

I return the phone to its receiver and look to Collins.

"Alright, lets head over to the interrogation room. Mr. Stephenson's here."

# 16

**MY FIRST IMPRESSION** of Brett Stephenson was not that impressive. A thin framed man who could use a good home cooked meal. Sedate and reserved, yet wiser than his own good. He could quote scripture forward and backward from any testament, prophet, or apostle. He's dressed in jeans and a plaid blue shirt. He wears solid black shoes with frayed laces and white paint stains.

He cried when we tried to discuss his sister and her family. He dabbed his eyes with a Kleenex he had stuffed in his front shirt pocket. His concern and grief seem legit, but I don't like the way he covers his mouth when he speaks. His voice changes pitch when I ask tough questions. Too many red flags for lying. I didn't get my Ph. D in Psychology yesterday. I know a liar when I see one.

He fidgets when I ask about the last time he saw his sister. His eyes wandered about the room too much when Collins questioned his involvement with the snake handlers at Freewill Holiness. It's all signs of uttering false evidence.

"Do you participate in these events Mr. Stephenson?"

"Oh yes. It took a few years before I really got involved, but I've been practicing snake handling with them for about five years now I guess."

I scratch the back of my head and ask, "You're not afraid of being bitten? I mean I know you have faith and all, but that's pushing it a little, isn't it? Doesn't scripture say not to put God to the test?"

"When you've seen and felt what I have . . ." he leans forward and rest his elbows upon the table. He interlocks his hands and looks me deep in the eye as if to probe for something he has no right to search for. "Fear dissolves like the passing of time. It loses its grip the more I learn to trust the father."

I raise my brows and twist my head. I jot some notes on my pad and rub my tear ducts in effort to pinch away the migraine seeping in. I need some water to ward it off. I clear my throat and reach for the bottle in front of me.

Collins ask the next question as I take a swig.

"Now Mr. Stephenson, I'm sure you are aware of the talk that goes around about you guys? You know, with the whole deal that took place in the eighties?"

His eye lids disappear as his gaze wanders to the ceiling. He strokes his chin. It sounds like sandpaper. He swallows hard, lowers his eyes to Collins and says, "Yeah. Yeah, I'm aware. Archie's a good man. It's a shame what they've done with him."

"Not when you look at the facts. He was charged with kidnapping and child endangerment. I'd say he's lucky to be where he's at." I answered as I sat my bottle of alkaline water back to the table. I lean back, cross my arms, and cup my mouth while I await a response.

"Yeah, but Archie meant well. He thought he was doing it for Richie's good. You know, protecting him from the man in the black—"

I stopped him with a raised finger, "Save it. I've heard it before. Hiding a kid in the church basement for three days doesn't exactly sit well with many people. Including myself."

"Well, have you spoken with Archie?"

"Uh-huh, I visited him once in 2002. Can't say I enjoyed my time, and he didn't appear to either."

"You know he's been writing us about Morty, right? About the end times, all the weird sightings, and the crazy stuff that goes inside of that wacky asylum he's in?"

My ears must've perked like a doe when she hears a hunter twitch his aim.

Collins almost spit his coffee.

"He's been writing you about Morty?"

Brett Stephenson leans back and dips his head.

"Do you have copies of the letters?"

"I'm sure Pastor Wicker does somewhere. You could speak with him. Have you two met yet?"

"No, but I met his brother and sister-in-law four years ago. His brother conducted the Shelton's funeral."

"I see, well if I were you, I'd speak with Pastor Wicker and pay Archie a visit."

"Is he still at the same facility? I don't recall the name."

"Cumberland Behavioral Health Center for the Gifted."

"The old Ottawa house on Cushing Island, right?"

"Yup. You have to take a ferry to get to it."

"Yeah, that's the same one."

"Is that where the lady drowned all those years ago?" Collins asks.

"Mm-hmm. I led the investigation. It was my first year on the job. Everyone suspected that one of the nurses did it, because of the way the lady was wrapped in a sheet. Turns out that's just the way she wanted to go. She said in the note that 'It'd be like she went to sleep in the sea.' I'll never forget that one."

"You never told me you investigated that one."

"Guess I didn't did I?"

Not too many people know of the things I've had to witness. It's not that I'm keeping secrets, I just try not to remind myself of certain cases.

Collins questions me with his brows then turns back to Stephenson and says, "What does he have to say about Morty?"

"That he doesn't believe he's finished and that he thinks he may be tied to witchcraft or something."

I lean forward and ask, "Really? And when was the last letter sent out?"

"Uh, I 'dunno, must've been a couple weeks ago I guess."

"What kind of 'crazy stuff' does he say goes on within the asylum?"

Stephenson scoffs and looks to his right while bringing a thumbnail to his teeth. "Archie says he thinks they're experimenting on people in there."

"Oh, c'mon you can't be serious." Collins says.

Stephenson leans forward and with big eyes, says, "No. No. I'm serious. He says he'll wake up in the middle of the night to the awefullest sound of screaming. Like someone's being murdered. The next day there'll be a few patients with bandages wrapped around their heads and they'll be acting all drugged up and zombie like. And he says all the nurses and doctors are acting funny. Whispering to each other and such. Really starting to worry him. He says there's a rumor going around about them performing transorbital lobotomies."

Collins curses. "You're full of it man. No way."

"Go see for yourself then. I know Archie. He wouldn't lie to us. He's not like that."

I take a deep breath and add, "So, you're saying that place is sticking icepicks into people's eyes and digging around until they tickle the right spot in hopes of reversing the patient's illness?"

Collins restrains a laugh beneath a fake cough.

I look to him.

"What? My throat got tickled."

I look back to Stephenson. He tightens his lips and says with a hand tossed in the air, "Hey, I'm just the messenger. Like I said, go check the place out for yourself. Don't say I didn't warn you, though."

"Okay. Moving on. You said he mentioned something about the weird sightings. What do you mean by weird sightings?"

"Oh, umm, you see there's been a handful of children at our church who claim to have seen a shadow like figure in their rooms at night. Said he just stands there and looms over their beds. Really creeped the kids out. There's a good friend of mine and Pastor Wicker's who lives up around Augusta. Craig Foster is his name. He comes down to help with the sound systems in the church from time to time. Well, he said he was working on his car late one night out in the garage and started feeling like he was being watched, you know? Said he just had that creepy feeling that he couldn't shake. He ignored it at first, but said it just kept getting stronger. So, finally he takes a break and steps out of his garage to look around the place. It's when he walked around the side of the house where his son's window is at, that he saw it."

"Saw what?"

"The man in black. The one the kids at church are calling, 'The man of Shadows.' Said he was standing at the wood line and staring through his kid's window."

"I see. And then what happened?"

"Well, when Craig saw the man, he yelled at him, but he said the man just kept standing there. Craig yelled again and started walking towards him. He said that's when the man darted off and slipped into the woods. Craig chased after him, but he said it was like chasing a ghost. He ended up all by himself, in the dark, in the woods, and with that feeling of being watched again. He's been kind of creeped out ever since."

"Did he file a police report?"

"No, you see Craig doesn't have a good repour with the police. His lengthy background of course from his drug days don't help much."

"Okay. And you said Archie mentioned the end times."

"Oh yeah, you know just him giving his two cents of what he thinks is going on in the world. Talking about how things are lining up with what the Bible has to say about how it's all going to wrap up and such."

"So, he probably talks a lot about the book of Revelation, I bet?"

"Yeah, a little. I mean who doesn't when they're talking about the end times, right?"

Collins asks, "Going back to the 'man of shadows', as you called him."

"Uh-huh."

"Was your friend able to give a description of him?"

"Just said he was big and dressed in black."

"I see."

Mr. Stephenson glances at his watch and looks up, "I've been here an hour, do you thank you have enough from me? I've told you all I know."

I scratch the back of my head once again. "Yeah, if we think of anything else we'll be sure to give you a call. I expect you'll do the same."

"Of course."

With that, we thanked him for his cooperation, and Collins showed him to the door. I watched as he walked with a limp to a 90's model red Ford Ranger pick-up that may not get him home. By the looks of it, he'd be doing to good to leave the parking lot with the rear bumper still intact. Duct tape looked to be the only thing holding it in place.

I pull a finger from the blind in my office and turn to Collins as he passes through the door. "That was interesting, huh?"

"Looks like we may be paying a visit to Cushing Island."

"Perhaps tomorrow. I'll have to give Vicky a call. If she's still there that is. What time is it now?"

"Two-twenty-three."

"The Entomologist is expecting us at three. It'd be nice to catch Glenn before he leaves the morgue."

"How come you never told me you investigated the lady on the Island?"

I bought some time to answer by digging in my drawer for the key to the evidence room.

"Patrick—"

"I'm just curious you know?"

"My mother did the same thing after Amy disappeared. Except she went to sleep in our pond. I found her wrapped in a sheet after our last argument."

Collins eyes grow wide. He lowers his head and rubs the nape of his neck.

"Laurie . . . I'm sorry. I had no idea."

"It's okay. I should've told you."

I found the key, grabbed my Judge on the desk and holstered it.

"Let's get the cicada to this guy and see what he can tell us."

# MISSING

# CHILD

## RICHARD "RICHIE" JENKINS

AGE: 8

SEX: MALE

HEIGHT: 4'0

WEIGHT: 72

HAIR: BROWN

EYES: BLUE

LAST SEEN: 4/22/88 EXITING SCHOOL BUS IN HIS NEIGHBORHOOD OF GRAY, M.E.

LAST SEEN WEARING: BLUE JEANS, RED TEE-SHIRT, NEW ENGLAND PATRIOTS BALL CAP, AND WHITE SNEAKERS.

## PLEASE HELP!!

### IF SEEN, CONTACT YOUR LOCAL AUTHORITIES

### IMMEDIATELY!

# 17

**PORTLAND MUSEUM** of the Natural World is a red two-story brick building located at the edge of town. A block or two from Main Street, it rests in a corner along a cliff. As we proceed from the parking lot, of which I counted fourteen cars, a majestic view of the Atlantic is to our right. Gulls hover and squawk in the salty breeze. Cushing Island sits off in the distance. With this fog, it's only a lurking silhouette. To the far right of us, jutting out from the jagged coastline, is the Portland Headlight.

My place of solace.

The place I turn to when I'm faced with a tough case like the one I'm currently on. I need to make time to pay the light a visit. God knows I need it. Walking the trail along the rocky edge and leaning over the rail to gaze out into the endless sea, always helps to clear my head. A peaceful sensation wafts over me as I anticipate my next visit to the light. I watch as shrimp and lobster boats journey out into the deep in search of another bounty. The sights and sounds sweep me back to my youth.

You see, I grew up in a small coastal town in Brunswick County, North Carolina called Southport. My family and I would often take the ferry over to Bald Head Island. We'd catch crabs with homemade pods, cast nets for shrimp, and fish until the biting bugs drove us away. Mom would cook our catch of the day and we'd celebrate with a feast. I remember one time my brother Jared got stuck in the hand by a stingray. I caught it and he was trying to get the hook out, so he always blamed me for it. That was a bad day. Mom made him keep his hand in hot water for most of the day to ease the pain and swelling. If we weren't fishing or crabbing, we were swimming in the ocean or back water somewhere. I've been stung by jellyfish more times than I can remember. Though my family was by no means perfect, which no family is, we had fun together most of the days. Dad was always doing something with us, unless his pain was unbearable that day. He'd served in Vietnam and suffered a severe back injury during a deployment which led to chronic pain and pill popping. When he was pain free and sober, he was a fun and loving man to be around, but when he took to the pills, he became a irritable roaming zombie and a man neither of us knew.

My times in Southport are filled mostly with good memories. It wasn't until around my high school days that things begin to change. My dad was diagnosed with bladder cancer during my freshman year. He went downhill quicker than any of us expected. Mom began drinking, and by the time of Dad's funeral a year later, she'd become a sold out drunk. She'd often times take out her frustration on us kids by beating us for no apparent reason. Surprisingly, I actually began to excel in school. Mostly, because I knew it was my only way out of the hell my mother had created. With my success came numerous scholarship opportunities. The best being from NC State University. I accepted the offer and feeling a tug toward criminal justice, I made an early decision to study criminal law and minor in psychology. Something I knew would eventually help me deal with my mother. So, I moved to Raleigh and began working towards my degree. My brother Jared had just become a Freshman in high school and my baby sister Amy was about to turn four. I felt terrible for leaving them, but knew I had no other choice.

It was during my sophomore year that everything changed. After my mother's suicide and Amy's disappearance, Jared went to live with our aunt and uncle in Colorado. To this day he still blames me for what happened. If I'm lucky I may talk to him once every few years. Though I've tried desperately to amend things with him, he just won't forgive me. A part of me believes that maybe he shouldn't. Maybe I deserve his wrath. If I'd stayed at home, none of this would have likely happened. Maybe one day he can forgive me. I just hope it's before one of us ends up on our death bed.

Even after our family tragedy, I continued to have success in school. I found some good internships over the summer, worked part-time jobs and roomed with friends while I worked to complete my degree. What should have taken me four years to do, I did in about three and a half. Realizing my passion for learning how the mind works, after earning my undergrad degree, I immediately applied for a master's in Psychology. I secured a part-time job with the campus police department and helped the investigative team conduct interviews and follow ups on campus crime. Mostly which involved drugs, theft, or sexual assaults.

A good friend of mine and fellow co-worker at the campus PD, who happened to be a former Boston police officer, spoke on my behalf and was able to help secure an internship for me in Boston that summer. It was during my time there that I was able to explore New England for the first time. I knew after that summer that New England was where I wanted to be. And it certainly helped that it was a thousand miles away from my childhood home.

After returning that summer to complete my master's at NC State, I later secured a job at the Police Department in Bangor and enrolled at the University of Maine to begin working towards my Ph. D in Psychology. It took me four years to earn my degree. Soon afterwards I got an investigator assistant job at Portland PD and never looked back.

So, you see it's the little things that sometimes jar my memory. The smell of fresh fish. The taste of salty air caressing my lips. The sight of an overhead seagull. The sound of a crashing wave or seawater lapping against the bank. Or maybe the touch of sunshine spreading across the back of your neck, kissing the salt flecks, and building freckles. These are the things that give life to my good memories of childhood. These are the things I cherish.

I smile and breathe deep before angling onwards for the entrance of the museum.

"What's this guy's name again? Jack?"

Collins question disrupts my daze.

I clear my throat and continue toward the entrance of the museum.

"No, Zach. Zach Feltner."

Collins nods as he chews on a toothpick.

A double sliding glass door parts as we near. We pass through the front entrance. A T-rex skeleton, which almost scrapes the twenty-foot ceiling, greets us. Along with the theme song to Jurassic Park of course.

A group of young school kids streak past us and are yelled at by two teachers. Judging by the looks on their faces, they are not too enthused about having the unfortunate job of babysitting a dozen rug rats for the day. With faces drained of energy, they barely have enough thrust in their voice to reach the children.

To the right of the T-Rex is the information desk, which sits next to a long glass display counter full of fossils and petrified plants.

A middle-aged lady with kind eyes acknowledges us and smiles, "Hi, how are you?"

"Good, how are you?"

"Doing well, I'm assuming you're here for Dr. Feltner?" she asks while looking to my badge, then to the plastic bag containing the cicada.

"Yes ma'am. Lieutenant Daniels and Detective Collins. We have an appointment for three." I say with a glance to my watch. 2:54.

"Yup, follow me. I'm Stacy by the way. Zach's in the back doing some research. It's a cicada you have there, correct?"

"Yeah, that's right."

We follow the brown headed lady, dressed in a black skirt with a white button-down blouse, to a long hallway with tan walls and maroon colored carpet. Picture frames of local artwork decorate the corridor lined with large oak doors and brass handles.

She turns and says over her shoulder, "I've been following the case."

I move my eyes from the artwork and grant her my full attention.

She continues to glance at us when not watching where she's going. "Gosh, I hope you catch this guy soon. It has all of us locals really worried. I believe there's more gossip spreading now than ever before."

"I can only imagine," says Collins.

"Still talking about the man in the black hood?"

"Oh yes. The man in the black hood. Some disturbed parishioner from Freewill Holiness, a Native American legend, you name it. There's all sorts of things being said."

Stacy stops outside the half open door numbered *149*. A plaque is nailed to the wall, *Z. Feltner Ph. D.*

She raises her hand, "Here it is. Let me know if you need anything. I'll be at the front desk."

"Thank you, Stacy."

A classical arrangement from Johann Bach plays over a static speaker. It sounds like the beginning to *Adagio.* I give two knuckle raps upon the door before pushing it open.

If insects make it to Heaven, then this must be their port of entry. It's as if I've stepped into the breeding ground of every insect known to man. In the center of the room is a round glass display filled with countless species. Everything from spiders, beetles, bees, and moths. Their Latin names are printed on angled white cards next to them. Upon the walls are paintings and magnified photos of various insects in the wild.

Draping from the ceiling and tied with fishing line is a swarm of locust.

"Why hello there. I've been quite anxious to meet you." A thin, high pitch voice carries from the corner of the small room.

As I turn to find his voice, my eyes are drawn to a large model hanging from the ceiling. It's a cicada about the size of a child's piñata and with its bulging red eyes, it stares straight into my soul.

Below the model insect is a fragile, blond headed man.

I swallow and assume the man to be Zach Feltner.

He's dressed in a pair of black slacks with a brown turtleneck sweater. He lowers the black rimmed glasses to the edge of his abnormally large nose and tilts his head at me with a slight grin. He clutches a stack of paperwork close to his chest with tiny, skeleton like hands.

*Laurie, you're supposed to say 'Hi Dr. Feltner. It's a pleasure to meet you.'*

I thought it but could not force my mouth to form the words. I feel paralyzed. The classical music caresses my ears as I take in his knowledge and love for the cicadas. Is this Morty? Is his sedate and harmless demeanor only a cover up? A costume to hide the monster?

"Why hello Professor. Thank you for meeting with us. I appreciate your willingness to help," says Collins.

I clear my throat and watch as the two of them shake hands.

"I'm sorry Doctor, but you remind me of someone I used to know. There's such a striking resemblance, it caught me off guard for a second. I'm Lieutenant Daniels," I say with an extended hand. As he takes my hand, I can't help but notice how cold and soft his flesh is. He looks me deep into the eye, and something within me quivers with disgust. A creepy disgust. I swear his eyes even have a red tint to them. Maybe he's been studying the cicada for too long. My hand slides from his sweaty but cold grip. I fight the urge to wipe my palm free of his touch. A strong sense of bile fills my mouth.

"You have a different accent. Where are you from?"

"North Carolina."

"I figured it to be somewhere in the South. Have you lived here long?"

"Over twenty years now."

"Oh, so you're a local then."

"You could say that."

He smiles without showing his teeth, and his beady eyes examine my soul. "I was told you have a specimen for me?"

I hold up the bag and glance at it before handing it over to him. I'm careful not to let our hands touch again.

By the look on his face, you would've thought I'd just given candy to one of those field trip kids outside.

Dr. Feltner crosses the room and settles into a desk chair. Collins and I follow him and watch as he lowers his glasses. He takes a moment to thumb over the thick bag marked *Evidence*. He squints his eyes and bites his lip.

"Hmm?" he says before rising and angling to a counter full of microscopes and magnifying glasses.

"Looks like a Magi at first glance but let me get her under the lens to be sure."

We watch as he retrieves a large blue handled magnifying glass and pair of silver tweezers.

I glance to Collins. He has one hand cupped to his mouth and the other tucked beneath his elbow. His toothpick bobs in a vertical rhythm. He tilts his head and raises his brows. I give him a tight grin and scratch the back of my ear before sweeping a strand of hair behind it.

Dr. Feltner cranes his head, narrows his gaze and mumbles, before finally offering, "Yeah, she's a Magicicada. Which is odd though because they're not common here in Maine. This species usually stays to the south of us. They're more typical for the Southeast and lower Midwest states."

Using the tweezers, he extends a wing and scans over the stained glassed like design.

"Perhaps with it being the year of the brood, they've decided to travel a little farther north."

Detecting our questioning glare, he pulls away from the specimen and explains, "You see the Magi are what is known as a periodical cicada. The ones that only emerge every thirteen and seventeen years. It's the prime number enigma that have baffled scientist for centuries. They do so to over satiate their predators. Their natural predators: Birds, cats, reptiles, and the like, all produce in even numbered years, two, four, six, and so on. So, with the Magi's only emerging every thirteen and seventeen years, they show up when the population of predators is at their lowest. Survival of the fittest and Natural Selection at its finest."

His Bose speaker changed from a classical of Bach to Mozart's Piano Sonata 12. It's really blaring now. I turn and glance toward his phone lying screen up on his desk. He takes my hint and turns the volume down.

"Sorry, I'm not used to having visitors. Is classical not much for your taste?" he asks.

"Oh, no. I enjoy classical music, just not while I'm knee deep trying to learn about a gift an allusive serial killer left on my washing machine the night before."

"My goodness. He left this in your home?"

I only nod.

"My apologies. That must be awfully frightening. You don't think he'll be back do you?"

As hard as it is to do, I don't answer, but only stare into his beady dark eyes.

When I sense him grow uncomfortable, I answer his question with a question. "A fan of Beethoven I'd guess?"

"Why of course. The genius," he says in a half chuckle.

"Are you familiar with scripture?"

He wags his head with squinted eyes behind his thick black rimmed glasses.

I zero in on the diameter of his pupils and ask, "So the church or religion has never interest you?"

When his eyes don't change, I switch to his bony hands. No tremble, fidgeting, or knuckle popping. All the signs of fibbing. His feet are firmly planted to the carpet. If he's being dishonest, he's doing an honest of job of keeping his outer shell from showing it. Which makes me wonder, is he like the cicada? Is there a whole other separate being beneath the surface?

"No, can't say I've ever been too fond of organized religion. Not that I'm against it or anything, I guess it's just not my cup of tea."

I raise my eyes to meet his, "Mine either."

"Now pardon me Detective, but what does all this have to do with my expertise of the cicada? I'm an entomologist, not a priest, remember?"

"Of course, just sifting wheat that's all. Now, back to the cicada. You said it's more prone to the southern states and Midwest. Do you have any Magicicadas on hand? Live that is."

"No, not Magi's. I do have some annual cicadas in the hatchery below us. The one's more common here in Maine belong to the genus *Tibicen*, which are comprised of the 'annual' or 'dog-day' cicadas. They emerge in July and August and hang around until late October or November, depending on the weather. It's more common to discover a cicada's shed exoskeleton than it is to find a live one."

"It's possible then that the cicada left on my washing machine was someone's pet?"

"That's a safe bet."

We spend another fifteen minutes or so listening to him ramble on about the characteristics of different insects. More than once, I had to steer him back on course to be sure our time here was being spent most efficiently. The more he talked, the stronger my creep-o-meter became. I finally decided to just say it bluntly. "Dr. Feltner, I won't insult your intelligence. I know you're a wise man. You know since I'm a detective, it's my job to rule things out. Every case is a process of elimination. Would you be kind enough to do us all a favor and come to the station for an interview and DNA swab? Just so we can clear you from the investigation and make our job a bit easier."

Insulted anyway, he crosses his arms, pulls a hand tight against his mouth, and stares at me the way I imagined a cicada might. His eyes narrow, and he doesn't say a word for a moment. Finally, his eyes drift to the array of bugs hanging from the ceiling. His gaze stays there longer than it should, and with a toss of his hand, "Sure, what the hell. Go for it. When do you want me in?"

"Eight o'clock sharp. Tomorrow morning."

"I'll be there."

"Thank you, Dr. Feltner. I appreciate your time and insight. We'll let you get back to your research and music. We can show ourselves out."

"My pleasure. Glad I could be of service," he says with nods to me and Collins.

Out in the hall, halfway to Stacy's desk, Collins says, "We may have our first real suspect. He seems promising. I just hope he doesn't decide to fall off the face of the earth."

"If he's really Morty than he won't."

"What do you mean?"

"Morty is too proud to run. It would rub his ego the wrong way. He's a sociopath. He doesn't believe anyone is ever on to him. He believes he's smarter than everyone else and that no one will ever figure him out. If he runs, he'd be giving me credit for outsmarting him. He may hide, but he'll never run. He'll stay close, trust me."

"I hope you're right, because that guy was some type of weird back there. He gave me the creeps. I wish we had enough probable cause to search his office."

"Yeah me too, but as long as he comes in tomorrow I won't much care. I could use some food right about now. How about you?"

"Ted's would be nice. Whadayasay?"

"Sounds good, but first I need to get a copy of the payroll from Miss Stacy. I need to see who Feltner's colleagues are."

# 18

GARY WADE DUNCAN sits at a booth and points to the menu while calling out his order. The waitress, Christine as her name tag says, is a thin framed, black haired woman with curls barely touching her shoulders who is likely in her thirty's. Much to Gary Wade Duncan's preference. He's dressed in his "going out attire" and keeps a steady grin. He thanks Christine when he finishes, and hands her back the menu.

His skin is smooth and glistens from the recent oiling. He tugs his gray fedora an inch lower to sharpen the angle of his continence. He glances around the diner, and being sure no one is watching, he unbuttons another rung on his Ralph Lauren polo. Solid white with no blemishes, and perfectly steamed pressed. Business like, because after all, he is on business. Looking through his lightly oil tinted Ray Bans, which could pass for a type of reading glasses, he watches with his abnormally large eyes as people crowd and pack themselves among him. If only they knew what manner of man sat before them. A shame they couldn't perceive his glory.

He cranes his head and steals a sip through the straw to his iced tea. No sugar, only salt. Joe Cocker sings above about getting some help from his friends. Lovely voice. In the corner high upon the wall, there is a small television set showing a local reporter interviewing Sheriff Johnston about the recent murders and the disappearance of Sarah McCrae.

Though he couldn't show it, Gary Wade Duncan grinned inside as he watched. Shaded by his glasses, he scans his eyes about the customers at the diner. He never once moves his head, only the eyes. He drinks in the ecstasy of watching them stare and mumble at the Sheriff.

Fear.

It's such a marvelous gift when tamed and orchestrated for one's benefit. Striking fear in the locals' hearts is the fuel that powers Gary Wade Duncan. It increases his power over them. Inch by inch and taking by taking. Such a joy to do God's work. Carrying out the reaping of sins is so fulfilling. He sips on the straw again and drains the cup of tea. Much the way he drains the life out of the residents. One sip at a time. Such a genius.

He scratches an itch on the back of his head. Black strands of hair tickle his fingers. He'd never had such thick hair before, what a pleasure to enjoy. Finishing, he steals a quick glance about the diner, then sniffs his fingers. A tingling rush crawls across his body. He can still smell Amanda McCrae. So fresh. Nothing like the smell of the recently taken. Mrs. McCrae's hair is so soft. Wonder what kind of conditioner she used. Could be the same that Laurie uses. The Lavender and Jasmine one by head and shoulders. It does have that sweet aroma. Must be the same.

The news report goes to a commercial break. The customers return to their loud chatter. It's mostly gossip about the crimes. Though he does notice a few conversations involve local sports and how the Red Sox had such a disappointing year after taking home the gold from last season. Two lady friends go back and forth about narcissistic in-laws. Seated at the bar, a group of old men chat about their Lobster and Crab season over coffee and apple pie.

As he occupies his time by deciphering the language, cute little Christine comes scampering along with his favorite. Meatloaf with mashed potatoes and green beans.

He neatly stretches a napkin across his lap. He rubs his knife and fork against one another while watching with a tight grin as Christine lowers the platter in front of him.

"Here you go, sir. Anything I can get for you?"

"Why yes, some mayo, mustard, and how about some relish?"

She eyes him with a cocked brow for a moment.

"Oh, you're not discriminating my tastes, now are you?" he asks as he glances up at her.

"Of course not, it's just I've never seen anyo—"

"I know, I know. It's strange, but it wouldn't be if you knew me," he says with a tight-lipped grin.

"Okay, I'll be right back. And I'll bring another tea for you as well."

"Thank you, darling."

As he waits for his condiments, he stares out the window and into the parking lot. He watches and listens as dead leaves skitter across the pavement, being carried about by an unseen force. They're obedient to the invisible power acting upon them.

Doth nature not teach us?

Such a blessing to have been chosen by the creator to be the bringer of justice. To be the reaper and the hero. If people only knew why he did what he did, they wouldn't stop him from doing it. It's really a virtuous thing to defend the weak.

Lost in his thoughts, he doesn't hear Christine return.

"Sir. Sir, here are your condiments."

"My apologies. I was lost in the beauty of the day. Thank you, Christine. Lovely eyes by the way, and that hair of yours is just beautiful. I love your natural curl. Is your hair really that black, or is that color you've added?"

"Oh, well thank you sir. This is all-natural."

"Hmm. It's gorgeous. Don't ever change it."

She gives him an uncomfortable smile and says, "Thank you. Let me know if you need anything else."

With that, she quickly moves to another customer.

As his stomach growls from all the labor he'd exerted over recent days, he hurries to dress the meatloaf, beans, and mashed potatoes with thick lumps of mayo, mustard, and relish. He mixes it all together like a shepherd's pie. He savors each and every bite.

Ten minutes pass, and he takes one last sip of salt tea before tossing the napkin onto his plate. He retrieves his wallet to pull out a twenty and takes hold of the ink pen tucked in his breast pocket. He scribbles across Jackson's face and rises from the booth before crossing for the door. He pulls the fedora lower upon his head and adjusts his oil tinted glasses to be sure his eyes are concealed. A deep chuckle resonates within as he marvels at his wit.

# 19

**REACHING FOR THE DOOR** to Ted's Diner, Collins says, "Feltner's a little frail to be our guy though don't you think?"

"Yeah, but doesn't mean—"

I start to say as I go to enter but notice a tall, lanky older gentleman, in a white polo and gray fedora, coming out. I stop to exchange smiles, step aside and motion for him to go first.

"Why thank you ma'am," he says with a touch to the fedora's brim and dip of his head.

I told him he was welcomed and stepped on through.

"Doesn't mean Feltner's not connected. He might not be Morty, but he could be an accomplice," I say while pulling out a chair at the bar counter.

"Yeah, that's true. There's no telling how many people could be involved in all of this."

Stormy, an elderly lady with red but graying hair which she likes to keep in buns, steps from the kitchen with a bright smile.

"Hey there Detectives. How you two holding up?" she asks as she ties a white apron behind her back.

"Hey Stormy, we're doing good. Wow, we timed that just right. Are you coming from lunch or just starting your shift?

"I know, right? Yeah, I just came from lunch. It's nice to see you. How have you two been?"

I look to Collins, and he looks to me. I look back to Stormy.

"We've been better, but considering the circumstances, I'm not complaining. How about you and Ted?"

"Same. We've been better, but I guess it could always be worse. Ted's been struggling with his ulcers again. He's having a hard time with them. On a good note though, I got the results back from my testing. I'm free and clear. That makes it two years since the last bout of cancer."

"Oh, thank goodness. I'm glad to hear that, Stormy. I've been thinking about you two," I say as I reach out and touch her hand.

She touches it back with a soft pat and smile.

"Thank you, Laurie."

Collins says, "That's good news Stormy. I'm happy for you."

Stormy nods at Collins and pulls her hand from mine to wipe at a tear rolling down her cheek.

I smile softly and say, "And tell Ted I hope he gets to feeling better."

"Thank you, Laurie. I'll be sure to do that. So, enough with the small talk, you two look like you could use a good meal. You want the usual?"

"Yup, the Cesar salad with grilled chicken, and a water please."

"How about you Patrick? Usual?"

"Yes ma'am. Fish tacos with extra sauce and a Sprite."

"You got it. I'll turn it in and get your drinks and fried pickles."

"Thanks, Stormy."

"My pleasure."

I sigh out a long breath and rub my temples. I pull out my phone and check the live footage at my house. Everything looks to be in order. There's no tall black figure glairing back at me from the living room. Not yet at least.

I talked to Paul on the way to the museum, and everything was good with him and Allen. I'll call him again once we finish at the morgue.

"Hey, are you seeing this?" Collins asks as he taps my arm.

"What?" I blink away the slag in my eye, pocket my phone and follow his hand pointing to the corner television hanging to our right.

A news reporter stands outside a home in Bangor where the headline reads, *Enraged, nude man, shot by police.*

Reading the subtitles, the lady said a man who appeared to be in a drug-crazed delirium was spotted by a neighbor outside a home, fully nude and smashing his head against the front door. His mother was discovered lying in the yard with a fatal wound to the neck where he'd . . . bitten her. Inside was the sister who'd luckily locked the crazed man out. As police arrived on scene, the man crashed through the front window, causing the sister to run out the back door and around the house where the man chased her before being shot by police.

"My goodness, this world is going to hell in a hand basket isn't it?" Collins mumbles.

My mind was instantly taken to a time and place where a similar thing happened to me. I've never told Collins and I don't feel like telling him now. It'd be nice to enjoy a good meal first. My story will wait for another time.

"It's that synthetic mess they get hooked on. It possesses them and lets the devils out," I say while wagging my head.

"Man."

"Remember the guy in Miami a few years back? The one who ate that man's face off? Yeah, he was on the same type of drug. It warps their mind and turns them into a zombie. It's scary."

"Yeah. I remember that."

The news shifts to another story. A headline about business and the stock market. The Dow is up two percent and the S and P is up just a tad below that. I pay special attention when they mention the stocks I have nice positions in. Like Facebook, Dollar General, Home Depot, and AbbVie, just to name a few. There are a handful of others I'm in, but those have been my best performers so far.

Anyway, the news shifts to sports and I notice Stormy as she treads from the kitchen with our drinks and fried pickles. Mexican restaurants have salsa and chips and steak houses have their bread, but Ted's has fried pickles and no one complains.

A few pickles later, and I had the overwhelming feeling of being watched. In a subtle way, I twist as if my back is giving me a hard time. I take the opportunity to glance about the diner. A man and woman sit at a booth behind me and a group of old men dressed in overalls sit at another.

The old men don't pay me any attention. They're too caught up in a brew about fishing and crabbing. They seem to be getting on one another's nerves. Reminds me of two crab sparring.

The man and woman, though they're not looking at me, seem nervous. The man is dressed in a blue and gray plaid shirt which is tucked behind a pair of Levi jeans. The lady wears a long black skirt which touches the ground and a white blouse that reaches her hands. Her hair is tied tightly upon her head. Looks like they belong to an old-fashioned church. Perhaps freewill holiness.

Collins asks, "What's the matter?"

I turn around and shake my head, "Nothing, I'll tell you later."

He cocks his brow.

"Later," I say with emphasis.

He nods.

"The tacos remind you of San Diego, don't they?"

"Huh?"

"You get fish tacos to remind you of your days in the Navy."

"You're good, Laurie. You're good," he chuckles as he takes a sip of Sprite.

"Do you ever miss it?"

"Yeah those were some of the best years of my life, other than the three I spent with Kelsey."

"I'm sorry you had to go through that," I say as I reach out and touch his folded hands which sit upon the counter.

"Thank you. I'll never forget the day we received the news. We had everything going for us. We were set to close on a new house the next month. She'd just got promoted to CFO with the company. I was retiring from the Navy and had a promising job lined up with the CIA. Then . . . boom. Stage three breast cancer," he tightens his lips, takes a deep breath and glances up at the television set. "I still feel her in my heart, you know? It's like she never left me," he turns and says with strained and glassed eyes.

"I know Patrick. I know. That's proof of your love. Don't ever let that go. I still feel my sister even after all these years. It's a beautiful thing."

He dips his chin and lowers his eyes.

"Thank you, Laurie. Don't know what I'd do without you," he places his hand atop mine and smiles.

"Who are you kidding? I'd be lost with *you*."

We smile and turn to see Stormy coming with the food.

Moments later as I pull the fork close to take my second bite of Cesar salad, the song emitting over the speakers, stalls my heart. A soft play of piano keys, which I knew would lead into an arrangement by Beethoven, sends chills over my entire body.

I sit my fork down, dab my mouth, and listen.

Beethoven.

I jerk my head side to side and scan the entire diner. Is Morty here? Is he watching? Did he request a classical song? The customers take notice of my actions. Some stopped midways with a cup of coffee and stared with squinted eyes to learn what had me so worked up.

I feel Collins place a hand on my arm.

I turn to him.

"The music."

He nods with big eyes.

"Stormy. Stormy!" I yell into the back.

I watch as she hurries from the kitchen.

"What dear? What is it?"

"Who changed the music?"

Her face is puzzled.

"Who changed the music?"

"Uh." she stutters with raised hands and a blank face.

I shot off the stool and began to call out, "Who changed the music?"

A middle-aged lady with black curls, who was busy emptying a tray of food by a corner booth, looks up and says, "I did, ma'am. That man asked me too."

"What man?" I ask while marching to her.

The whole diner goes silent. Except for the classical music.

"The gentleman who left a few moments ago. He wrote a note on the twenty he left me on the table."

My mind races a thousand miles a minute, "What did it say?"

"Umm , uh, something about his soulmate liking classical music and he asked if I'd play her a song or two. I figured he was talking about his wife that must've passed or something. At first I thought he was weird, but then I read that and felt guilty for judging him, so I switched the station to something classical."

"Where's the twenty he gave you?"

"Right here," she says reaching into her apron.

"What did he look like?"

"Uh. He was an older man. Sixties maybe, I don't know. He was wearing a gray fedora with brown lensed Ray Bans and a white polo."

Collins curses, "We passed him coming in. I held the door for him."

I turn and look about the diner, "Anyone see what he left in?"

A room full of blank stares and wagging heads return my question.

"I saw him walk around the building, he may have parked over on the side," one of the old men in overalls says.

"Thank you, sir. Stormy, please tell me you have surveillance cameras for the parking lot."

"I do."

# 20

I MADE PHONE CALLS to let all of Cumberland and our neighboring counties know to be on the lookout for a middle-aged man dressed as Christine had described. We checked the cameras in the back of the diner with Stormy but didn't get anything. He must've known where they were and was vigilant enough to avoid their glare. My only guess was he must have parked somewhere else and walked through the woods to get to the diner.

The thing that bothers me though, is how did he know we were coming to Ted's Diner? Was it purely coincidence? I hate that word. Or did someone tip him off? Collins and I discussed Ted's as we were leaving the museum, so did someone hear us? Stacy? Was Dr. Feltner standing outside his door and overheard us?

Or is this all a false hope for a lead? Is the man in the gray fedora a lonely widower who'd requested the music for his lost lover as he claimed?

Either way, I went ahead and bagged the evidence. The silverware and drinking glass the man used, and of course, the twenty-dollar bill. Collins and I took witness reports and spoke at length with them and Christine.

There's too many questions and not enough answers.

Within an hour, we'd done all we could do. On the way to meet Glenn I had Collins run the evidence into the station.

My phone has blown up ever since we left with calls from Chief Cunningham, Director Ramsey, Agent Swanson, Detective White, and everyone in between.

After arriving at the morgue, as always, out of respect for the dead I turned my phone off. Everyone knew where I was and could expect to not reach me until I left.

So, now I find myself in a cold room looking at a white sheet upon a metal slab. Collins stands with crossed arms to my right and Glenn Giles, dressed in a white lab coat, stands to my left.

"You ready?" Glenn asks.

I nod with a fist tucked tight to my mouth as I stare at the sheet.

Glenn takes a step and eases the sheet back to reveal the remains of Amanda McCrae. Her body is a dark shade of purple with even darker veins snaking up and down it. Her bare chest wears a stitched Y incision.

"What are you thinking Glenn?" I ask as I lean over the body.

"Well, it's much the same as our last female victim. The hair has been sheered, a molar has been extracted, her shoulder has been bitten, and her heart has been stabbed." Glenn takes a breath and adds, "This is personal Laurie. It's a type of revenge somehow."

I pull back and rub my forehead.

"No latent prints, hair samples, or semen?" asks Collins.

"No. Nothing."

I pinch my bottom lip with my pointer and thumb before saying, "Morty's too good for that. He knows better."

"But Laurie, he has to make a mistake somewhere. No body's perfect."

I nod at Collins and then turn to Glenn, "What about Jeremy? Anything new since we spoke earlier?"

Glenn turns and looks at a clothed table about ten feet behind him and says, "No, I'm afraid not. I just finished examining his brain before you got here. I'll need to sew his scalp back into place before I leave tonight. I'm assuming the family will want an open casket."

I know the procedure well and an image of Jeremy McCrae's forehead flesh pulled down over his eyebrows flashes before my mind. I blink and rub at my tear ducts.

"I need to spend some time at the McCrae's tonight."

I feel glares from Collins and Glenn, and neither say a word for a long minute.

"I have to do it. It's the only way I'm going to connect with the case and see things through both the victim's and killer's eyes."

Glenn clears his throat and starts to say something, but Collins beats him to it, "Laurie, I know, but—"

"I have to do it," I say in a straight, no questions asked tone.

Glenn pulls the sheet back over Amanda McCrae.

"Laurie, listen to me." Collins face tilts down, his voice enters a different tone, "Please, think this through. Don't walk into a trap."

"Patrick, I know what I'm doing. Don't try to talk me out of this. Our briefing with Cunningham and Ramsey is at nine in the morning. I'll stay at the McCrae's until a little after midnight, come home, get a few hours of sleep and see you at the briefing."

Collins sighs and places his hands to his hips, spinning away from me.

"You're wasting your breath trying to talk her out of it son. Once she's made her mind up, its set. She knows what she's doing, you have to trust her on this one," says Glenn as he wheels the slab of metal back to the proper room.

I take Collins by the elbow, "I'll be okay. If it makes you feel any better, you can sit in the driveway until I'm finished."

He gives it some thought and turns to face me.

His eyes are glassy. "I can't deal with losing anyone else. You have to promise me you want let that happen. Promise me, Laurie."

A knot the size of a baseball swells in my throat. My lips, heart, and face turn hot and begin to quiver.

I swallow hard and place my hand atop his shoulder, almost having to stand to my tiptoes to do it. "I won't let that happen. I promise."

He wipes a tear and says through a cracked voice, "Thank you."

I dry my eyes and take a breath.

Seeing all I needed to see, we finished, thanked Glenn for his time and made our way to the station.

I have a lot of people I need to speak with. Hopefully, they'll have a lot to tell me. I also need to pick up Sarah McCrae's diary if Sherrie and her crew are finished with it.

# 21

WE MADE IT BACK to the station and spoke with Sherrie, Detective White, and Chief Cunningham. Sherrie had dusted the diary for prints and made copies of the interesting parts. There were no latent prints, not that I expected any, but there were a few entries which she said I needed to read. She had me a list of the page numbers. I will read it once I get to the McCrae's. As for the voice recording, Nancy and Morgan were able to pick up the voice of a young female child in the background. It's too distorted to make out the words, but it's clear there's a second voice. Which offers both hope and fear. Hope, being that Sarah McCrae may still be alive, but fear in that she's living with a monster such as Morty.

Detective White spent some time questioning the local pawn shops and electronic stores. He asked about recent purchases of a used voice recorder such as the one left in Sarah's drawer, but came up empty.

Agent Swanson and Agent Weatherby investigated the lead with the man at Ted's diner and was able to get a sketch based on witness testimonies. The sketch will be released to the public tomorrow morning. If it was just a crazy coincidence, then hopefully the gentleman will see his face connected to the murders and decide to come forth to clear the air. Otherwise, when enough time passes with no appearance from such a man, then I'll know for certain, the man in the gray fedora is either Morty or a close accomplice.

In my office, written on the white board with an assortment of colored markers is the list of suspects which are front and center in my mind.

Dr. Feltner
The tattooed camera installer
The man in the gray fedora
Brett Stephenson
Pastor Wicker

The part I don't understand though, is how do any of these people tie into me and my past? How can any of them be connected to my sister's disappearance? When and where did I cross paths with them? Or did I? Is Morty's taunts and clues just a way to throw another wrench into the enigma?

I'm not even considering all the suspects I've dealt with in the past while investigating the Morty murders. Sam Carter was convicted of 1st degree murder for slaying a man and woman in Augusta back in 2010. He was a promising suspect, but after a thorough investigation we were able to rule him out of the Morty files.

Then there was Gene Montgomery who was sentenced to death for conviction of 1st degree murder and kidnapping of Jessica Rozelle in 2006. I really thought he was our man, but after a deeper dive into the investigation, we were able to rule him out. A few others were considered, but those are the two that stick out the most.

Then the question of a possible connection to the GTK murders always makes its way to the surface as well. Could it be someone from that cult that the GTK was a part of when he was younger? Hopefully, one day soon I can convince the Chief to book me a flight to North Carolina and conduct an interview. If not, maybe I can try a skype session. Anything to help me get into the mind of a serial killer. And with the GTK's transformation, I think he would be a good place to start.

Anyhow, after gathering and signing out what I need for the stake out at the McCrae's, such as case files, Sarah's diary, crime photos, and of course my Taurus Judge revolver, I locked my office door and checked my watch. *8:49 p.m.*

I march down to Collins's office and find him reading through a stack of case files. He's reclined in a rolling chair with his feet propped upon his desk.

I give a few knocks on the open door and say, "You ready to do this?"

# 22

A GHOSTLY FOG CRAWLS for the ocean, being pushed by the cool night breeze. Miss Carver's place is dark in the distance and lit only by a flickering porch light. She must've turned in for the night. I checked the clock on the radio as we pulled into the McCrae's driveway.

9:27 p.m.

The yard is dark and void of any light. The house is even darker as it lurks like a spirit beyond the patch of fog.

Darkness.

I ease over the pebbles and sigh when I shift the gear stick. I rest my arm upon the ledge of the open window for a moment and stare at the McCrae's home. I rub my eyes and look to Collins.

"You sure you want to do this?" he asks.

"I have to."

He tightens his lips and looks out the window to the trampoline which hides within the blackness.

"I'll be okay. Keep an eye on things and if I need anything, you'll know."

He turns and faces me, "Be careful."

I nod, retrieve a black Maglite from the center console, and check the rounds in my Judge. I step out and open the back door to get my briefcase.

I shut the door and move to the front where the window is still down, "Give me some time and let me do my thing. Like I said, if I need you, you'll know."

"Be careful, Laurie."

I turn away and march to the blood colored door. My brief case is strapped over my shoulder. My revolver is on my hip and the flashlight is clinched within my left hand. I wasn't greeted by the dogs, only the darkness and fog. Barry had taken them to the K-9 kennel where they will be held until we find a good home.

I shine my light to the door. In the center is an official taped X from Glenn. In the corner of the door and its frame, just above the handle, is a white square sticker from Cumberland County Police Department. The seal.

I remove the key we had made from the McCrae's original. I slice through the seal and insert the key into the dead bolt. A gentle breeze wafts by and stirs a windchime hanging next to the door. It looks to be handmade with colorful glass fragments. Geeze, I feel like I'm on a horror movie or something. Is this a sign I shouldn't enter the domain of the dead?

The door creaks open as the halo of my light pierces the darkness. The home is eerily quiet. An uneasy vibe hangs in the air. The overwhelming feeling of being watched causes me to glance over my shoulder.

Collins is leaned low and looking through the driver's window to me. I take a breath and return my attention to the entrance of this sepulture like abode.

I step in and pull the door shut behind me.

The odor of old blood still lingers. The air is filled with the unmistakable sense of dread. You can just feel that something terrible occurred here only days before. There's a presence here. I can feel it. I often feel it at other murder scenes, but it's stronger here. Lives have been taken too soon, and in some odd way I can hear the McCrae's voices calling out from their graves. There's a verse in the Bible about the voice of murdered blood crying out. I never understood that until I became a homicide detective.

Even though the McCrae's were known drug addicts, it doesn't change my resolve to bring them justice. Every life matters to me, and no one deserves to be murdered in such a brutal manner. I don't care what your background is or what you've done, you don't deserve to be murdered and humiliated the way Morty does things. Life is sacred and it should be treated as such.

All of this causes me to wonder . . . if I see things this way, why doesn't God? I mean if he is who he says he is, then why am I here investigating the McCrae's murder? Couldn't he have prevented such an atrocity? Where were the angels that people talk about? I hate questions like this, but I can't help asking them when I'm faced with these kind of cases.

I hear people talk about hope and how God will make all things right one day. You want to know the truth? Deep down, I believe it's all non-sense. The fact of the matter is . . . there is no hope. This is all there is. I think we create gods to soothe our anxiety and dread of forever being alone. Deep down, I think we know we're all alone, and that's what scares us into believing in a higher power. There is no man upstairs watching out for us, only clouds and stars among a million other galaxies. It's up to us to fight for justice, because the sad reality is we're just a grain of sand sinking to the bottom of life's ever treacherous and unpredictable sea.

I hate having these ugly thoughts come to surface like this. Part of me wants to believe and have faith in a higher power, but another part says, "what's the point?" Perhaps I'm bitter, but I have a right to be, don't I? For crying out loud, my sister vanished before she even learned how to drive. Before she even felt the emotions of having a first love. She was stripped from this world and dragged into the ocean of unknows by an ever hungry rip current.

My mother who I came to despise for the way she treated me and my siblings, finally succumbed to the root of her problems. She didn't hate me, but she hated herself. That's the reason she slipped into the dark waters of our pond one crisp winter morning. Dressed in her nightgown and wrapped in a white sheet, she too, left me.

My older brother Jared left me shortly after he graduated high school. I always had it in my head that somehow Jared and Amy would never leave me, but they did. One by choice, the other snatched by one of the world's many monsters.

That's my story.

The reason I'm where I'm at. I realized long ago that justice is not for the man upstairs to decide, because quite frankly, he left too. Justice is up to us. That is the only reason I'm capable of doing what I do. It's my responsibility to do what everyone says God will do in time.

My past is like the dark, quiet, and odor filled home I stand in now. Standing here, I can see the deep, inner chambers of my own heart. Darkened by the cruel world we all live in.

For heaven's sake, what am I thinking? Where's your faith, Laurie? This is one of the reasons Morty scares me so much. His cases always bring these questions and doubts to surface. It's like he has a way of eroding what little faith I have. Like there's always a supernatural presence lurking at the murder scenes, feasting on my faith. I've always thought there's more going on than meets the eye. I never believed in supernatural stuff until I began investigating his crimes. Sure, I've seen enough Stephen King movies and read enough of his novels to at least consider the possibility of there being something behind the veil but I never really believed it. Now, I not only entertain the possibility, but I find myself believing there might really be something at work in the unseen realm.

Goodness gracious listen to me.

I didn't come here for no pity party or moment of truth on faith and the supernatural. I came here to solve a murder. Enough with the wandering thoughts, it's time to get to work.

† † † † † † † † † †

**AN HOUR HAD PASSED WHEN I CHECKED** my phone. So far, I'd spent my time walking the darkened floor with no light just as Morty must've done. I quietly crept through each room, placing myself in the dark world of a killer's mind. A daunting place to go, but it's vital to track down such a deranged individual. To catch a killer, you almost need to become one. You have to learn to think the way they think, and you have to view the world through their eyes.

Even with it being my third time in the McCrae's home I still find myself stumbling into things more often than I would have imagined. I thought I had a good idea of the layout of the home, but I realize now that it's dark just how much I was wrong. Which says to me, Morty had been here more than once. Likely even in the dark more than once. Like the way he was at my house last night.

How many times had the McCrae's come home and unbeknownst to them, a serial killer lurked beyond the shadows of their own nest? How many times had he hid in a closet or empty shower? Beneath their bed? The attic? As he waited for the late hours of the night to emerge from hiding. Like a hungry roach looking for a snack. Meandering among the home like a spirit as he watched, plotted, and anxiously anticipated the McCrae's coming demise. How many times has he done that in my home?

Wait . . . what if Morty never had to sneak in? What if they knew him and willingly invited him into their home? What if he'd stored the layout of the home each time they welcomed him over for a chat or dinner? Maybe even for one of Sarah's birthday parties. Could it be Amanda's brother, Brett Stephenson? If so, why? What would be the motive?

To do what Morty did, he had to be someone they knew or someone who could gain access to the home and learn its blueprints even in the dark.

I place one hand to my hip and shine the light about the living room with my other. I scan the tv and coffee table it sits upon. DVD cases and discs lie scattered across it. A glass half full of dark soda sits crooked on cork coaster. A small black box catches my attention. At first glance I thought it was a DVR or cable box, but one of those sit to the right of the tv. They wouldn't have two DVR's would they? Unless . . . it's a DVR box for security cameras.

I feel my pulse quicken as I step closer for a better look. With my gloved hands, I pick up the box and give it a quick glance over. Yeah, it's for surveillance cameras, but where are they?

Clinching the mag lite between my teeth, I follow the wires leading from the box. I'm directed to the corner of a sliding glass window. Tucked away and hidden within the coverage of blinds that pull away with a string, is a camera. It's on the inside looking out to the backyard. Its glare covers the building which I was told is full of Jeremy's tools.

That begs the question . . . who installed the cameras? The guy with the rosary bead tattoos which installed mine? Vernon Martinez? That's the name Detective White gave me. With the Maglite still clamped between my teeth, I take note in my pad

How did we miss this? The DVR box may hold the answers we've been searching for. It could have footage of Morty. The camera is on the inside, so if it's one with sound recording ability, it may even have recorded what took place. This could be our big break in the case.

The anxious hope that this little camera and DVR box may contain video and or sound which could help catch one of New England's most daunting serial killer's, is enough to get me off track. My heart pounds at the possibility. I take a deep breath and steady myself. I still have work to do.

As I make my way toward the master bedroom and pass by the kitchen, Glenn and Sherrie's words about Morty enjoying a meal at their kitchen counter fills my mind. I imagine him sitting there on a stool. I see his dark silhouette raise a toast to me. His face is hidden beneath the black hood like the grim reaper. The image sends a chill down my spine. I also wonder if he may have propped an unconscious Amanda McCrae up in a chair to watch him. Chill bumps ravage my arms and neck at the thought.

Why would he do that? Is it a way to feed his ego? To prove his power and control over them? All of this passes through my mind as I follow the halo of my light to the back of the house, where the McCrae's bedroom awaits.

The door is shut. I twist the knob and push it open. The room is black, and I can barely make out the silhouette of the bed and nightstands. Morty could easily be standing in a darkened corner right now, and I would never know. I swing my light about the room, sweeping away any questioning shadow. I shiver and rub the upper part of my right arm. The room is colder than the rest of the house.

I would turn the light on, but as is the case in most violent crimes, the power to the house has been turned off to ward away any squatter from disturbing evidence. Something that had become quite the problem a few years back. We corrected that by cutting the power. Not too many people willingly enter a darkened home where a murder has taken place. Unless you're getting paid to do it.

The covers on the bed are raked to the foot of the mattress and left in a tangled mess.

I cover the room with sweeps of my light. Besides the empty cups lying on the nightstands and clothes scattered about, the room is clean of any obvious evidence. If there is anything here, it'd take some digging and searching to find. I go on to spend another half hour searching every drawer, pile of clothes, and closet, but didn't find anything that stirred questions.

I need to read Sarah's diary, and I should do it in her bedroom so I can read it from her perspective and vantage point. The same way I needed to become Morty, now I need to become Sarah McCrae.

I leave Jeremy and Amanda's bedroom and head for Sarah's.

I check my phone, 11:38 p.m. I have 63% battery life left.

Diary clinched in my right hand and light shining from my left, I push her door open. I sit gently at the edge of her bed. The springs whine as they receive my weight. I lay the diary in my lap and rub my forehead.

The room is black other than a circle of light and a tree's shadow on her wall which is cast from the moonlight outside her window. It looks like bony fingers stretching forth to snatch me by the arm. The wind begins to howl as it streaks past her window.

I swallow and push away the eerie vibe.

I open the diary to the first page that Sherrie had marked for me. I shine my light to the scribbles and fractured sentences. Messy flowers and failed attempts to draw cats and dogs are scattered about the page.

This is the first entry I read:

*Thurs Sept 26th 2019*

*I saw him agan. The man in blak. He stood outsid my windoe. I told mommy and daddy but they dont listin. All they do is fite. They dont care. They dont love me. I wish he wuud take me. I thank I wuud be beter off.*

For heaven's sake. Did she willingly go with him? Did she know what was going to happen?

I flip the page.

*Sat Sept 28th 2019*

*I saw him in the feld at sunset. He promised it wuud be okay. He says they have lots of toys. Hes really nice. He says my new family will love me lots. He said I wuud have to rid on a big bird to go where they are. I cant wait.*

*He said he will come tomorow nite. But he says its a secret and will be like a dream. I cant wait.*

Emotion swims up from the pit of my gut and knots in my throat. She thought this was her way out. The only way for her to escape this hell hole. Her chance to get away from the drugs and fighting. A chance to be loved. To have a normal life. To have a family. What kind of monster can deceive a child like this? It's an unspeakable act of evil.

I click out my light and rise from the bed. The springs squeak again. I pace to the window and rest my palms along the seal. Looking out into the darkness and across the field, my mind tosses and turns with questions, theories, and pain. My head swims as a bout of nausea begins to swell. I take deep breaths to calm it.

Why I put myself through the torture of examining these cases, I guess in a way is like penitence for leaving my sister Amy with that monster we were forced to call mother. What would have happened if I'd stayed home and worked a local job, instead of running away to college. Would Amy still be here? Could I have prevented her disappearance? The questions that will haunt me until I enter the grave.

At that thought, my heart sinks and knocks hard at the sight outside Sarah's window. My pulse surges through my veins. A large figure, dressed in a black trench coat, stands in the field staring into my soul.

I gasp and blink hard. Nothing.

Sighing out a long breath, I lower my head and pinch my tear ducts. Get a grip on yourself Laurie. C'mon now.

My gut twist and crawls as nausea is hard at work. My head spins as I do my best to keep the vomit at bay. What in the world? I take a deep swallow to push down the knot growing in my throat. Breathing in and out of mouth, I steady myself with a hand on the window seal.

*Tap. Tap. Tap. Tap. Tap.*

The sudden tapping of glass gives my heart another stir. I jerk and spin to face the open door. It taps again. Sounds like it's coming from the front door. I snatch up my light from the bed and unsnap the button to my Judge's holster. I ease my right hand over it and make my way out.

It must be Collins, but why didn't he call me?

*Tap. Tap. Tap. Tap.*

Coming down the hall, I can see a small halo of light piercing the window and into the darkened home.

I pull back the hammer to my revolver, "Patrick . . . is that you?"

"Yeah, let me in. The Chief just called," he says in a tight tone.

I holster my weapon and open the door.

"What?"

"Dr. Feltner hung himself."

"What?"

"Janitor found him hanging in his office about an hour ago."

I take both palms and trace them over my face and scalp.

"White is there now. You want to go check it out?"

"Yeah, let's go."

# 23

"I TRIED TO CALL YOU. The chief said he and White have been blowing your phone up too."

"Really?" I ask as I sit in the driver seat and retrieve my phone. "It's dead. What in the world? I just checked it and it had 63%."

"That's strange."

"Yeah and I became nauseous in there too. Kind of weird."

"Really? Yeah, that is weird."

I turn over the ignition and back out of the driveway.

Collins begins to fill me in on things as we make our way down the road.

"White said Feltner left a note behind saying he knew the name of the killer."

I snap my head to him.

"Gary Wade Duncan."

"Gary Wade Duncan?"

"Yeah, said he met him over the summer. Said he was asking a bunch of questions about the cicada. Claimed to be a professor from UMass and was doing research on the emergence of the prime numbered cicadas."

"Has White sent the name to ViCAP?"

"Yeah, it's a blank slate though. And there's no record of a professor from UMass by that name. There were only three Gary Wade Duncan's that fit the profile. One in Oregon, Texas, and Georgia. Swanson and Weatherby have sent field agents to each state to question the individuals."

Coming around a curve a tad quicker than I should have, I catch glimpse of Collins gripping the handle above his shoulder.

"Slow it down will ya? I want to be alive when we get there."

"Sorry. My foot gets heavy when I have a lot to think about. Does there appear to be any sign of foul play?"

"White said it's a straightforward case. Suicide by hanging."

"Will you plug that in for me?" I ask as I pass him my phone. "I still don't understand how it died that fast."

"Yeah, that's strange. Are you feeling any better?"

"A little bit. I still have a hint of nausea working, but it's not as bad. Oh, we've got to check the DVR box from the McCrae's."

"Huh?"

"They had a camera in the corner of their sliding glass door. Might be another break. Especially if it had sound."

"Dang, we'll have to check that out."

"Why would Feltner kill himself?"

"He was guilty of something."

"Well obviously, but what?"

"Hopefully we can find out."

✝ ✝ ✝ ✝ ✝ ✝ ✝ ✝ ✝ ✝

**THE FRONT OF THE MUSEUM IS ROPED** off in yellow caution tape and accompanied by numerous police cruisers. Glenn's coroner van sits near the entrance.

The inside is bright but without any music. Chatter from the officers and CSI members fill the air. The janitor, a balding white male perhaps in his early seventies, is questioned by Deputy Ferrell next to the skeletal T-Rex that scrapes the ceiling.

We continue down the hall to a group of officers standing outside Feltner's door. One of Sherrie's helpers steps out as we approach. I think his name is Corey if I remember correctly. I've only met him once or twice, but I will always remember him for his bright orange hair and the way he wears his glasses at the tip of his nose. Even though he can't be a day over thirty.

"Hey Lieutenant. Sherrie's inside. It looks to be a pretty cut and dry case."

"Thank you."

We step through the door. Glenn and Sherrie stand by the feet of Dr. Feltner. His body hangs from a beam and sways between his collection of bugs which are suspended by fishing line. A white rope is tied above Feltner's brown turtleneck sweater, and a wooden stool is overturned below him. The rope creaks with his movement.

"Sorry you couldn't reach me. My phone died on me."

"Hey Laurie." Sherrie and Glenn say together.

"So, he left a note and name?"

"Yeah. Gary Wade Duncan," says Glenn.

"We just finished dusting the area. Nothing. There doesn't appear to be any foul play," says Sherrie.

"What did you do to fill you with such guilt?" I question as I stare up into Feltner's lifeless eyes. His glasses lie on the floor next to the chair.

Glenn clears his throat, "Maybe he was afraid to spill the beans and suffer the consequences. He'd rather take his own life than leave it in the hands of Mr. Duncan."

I bob my head. "He definitely knew something about our new named suspect. I just wish he would have told us before he did this."

"Where's Detective White?" Collins asks.

"Downstairs in the hatchery," says Sherrie. "He has the note bagged if you want to see it."

I nod, "Yeah, that'd be nice. You guys okay here?"

"Of course. We've got you covered," Glenn says.

"Okay. Collins, you want to give the place a good look over, see if anything catches your eye while I go talk with White?"

"Sure thing."

"Alright." I turn to Glenn and Sherrie, "How do I get to the hatchery?"

Glenn tosses a thumb over his shoulder, "Go through that door and take the elevator down to the basement. Get off and make a right, it'll be on your left-hand side."

"Thanks, let me know if you need me."

"We'll do."

With that I head for the elevator.

Along the way, I pass numerous pictures and paintings of every creepy crawly known to man.

I reach a hallway with white walls and salt and peppered colored tile. It reminds me of a hospital. It also reminds me of the hallway leading to the Cumberland County morgue where

Glenn examines the dead. The air is chill which causes my skin to turn to gooseflesh.

I press the button with a down facing arrow and wait for the silver doors to open.

A loud ding fills the air, the doors slide open, creaking and whining in protest.

I step in and press *B*, among only three other options. The doors lock me in and begin the descent. The light flickers and hisses on the way down.

The elevator jolts to a stop and does a shimmy like move as if emptying a crumb from a food container. I make the right and to my left is a wooden door next to a large rectangular glass window. The lights are on inside and I can see White, Agent Swanson and Agent Weatherby studying a wooden contraption wrapped in tiny mesh wire.

I push the door open and step in.

The three of them raise their vision.

"Oh, nice of you to join us," Kim says with a smirk.

"Agent Weatherby."

"Hey Laurie. I tried to call you but kept getting your voicemail."

"Yeah sorry John, my phone was dead."

"Where were you?" asks Agent Frank Swanson.

"I was at the McCrae's place."

He nods and turns back to the darkened cage. It's lit only with a small lamp, like the kind you'd expect a snake owner to have. Only this cage doesn't house snakes. It houses cicadas. Lots of them, and they all sing.

"So, you turned the name into ViCAP and NCIC?" I ask Agent Swanson.

He bobs his head and breathes out a sigh, "Yeah, it's a clean slate. We did find three men within the age range of the profile. Only problem is, they're all over a thousand miles away. We have field agents planning to stop by tomorrow morning to pay them each a visit. Ramsey is flying in Agent Turner and Agent Vasquez tomorrow too. We'll see what happens."

"Where's your partner?" Kim asks.

I turn to her after fighting the urge to ignore her, "Upstairs with Glenn and Sherrie."

"Mmm," she says with thin lips and a bob of her head. Her brunette hair is pulled into a tight bun.

I lean close to the cage, and gaze at all the crawling insects. One is up against the screen, taking its time ascending a tree branch in the corner. Squinting my eyes, I zero my focus.

Wait a second.

I began to mumble to myself.

"What?" asks Detective White as I can feel the three of them leaning in with me.

"Feltner said he didn't have any Magicicadas."

"And?" asks Kim.

"I swear this looks like the exact same kind that I brought in. The kind that was left on my washing machine. A Magicicada. The one's that stay underground and only emerge every thirteen and seventeen years. He lied. Why would Feltner lie about this?"

"Are you sure it's the same kind? I mean there's probably a hundred different species," Swanson says.

"No, it looks just like the one I showed him. We need to figure out what genus these all belong to. Was Feltner our man? Did he get nervous that we were on to him and couldn't handle the thought of being caught? What if the name he left in the letter is all just to throw us off?"

Detective White straightens his back and takes a step back. He rubs the nape of his neck.

Swanson crosses his arms and places a fist to his mouth, "Laurie, even if Feltner's our man, I still don't believe he worked alone. There is going to be more than one person involved in all of this."

"Oh, I know. I've already come to terms with that."

"I know you've had a long day, how about you go get you some rest. We can handle it from here. You're still going to Ottawa tomorrow, right?"

"Frank, I'm fine. Don't worry about me. Yeah, the ferry departs at 10:15 and Professor Langston is expecting us between 10:30 and 11."

"Enjoy your time with the creeps. I'm sure that'll be fun," Kim says out the corner of her mouth.

"Oh, that reminds me Kim. Can you contact the list of Feltner's colleagues? Clear some alibis and see if any of them can identify the cicadas down here."

In a short, icy tone, "Sure."

"Thank you, Agent Weatherby."

"Laurie, Frank's right. How about you call it a night. We can regroup in the morning, go over things at the office before you leave for Ottawa."

"Alright, if anything comes alive through the night, be sure to give me call."

"We will."

It was 1:07 when Collins and I left the museum. Unfortunately, I left with more questions than answers.

Hopefully, our trip to the mental asylum will answer a few. We'll see.

# 24

AFTER SOME CONVINCING, Collins reluctantly agreed for me to go home by myself. Like always, if I needed him, he'd know. I talked to Paul before we went to the McCrae's, so he knew it'd be late when I made it home. Allen's Toyota truck was still in the driveway when I went by. As long as I know Allen's with him, I don't worry too much.

I ease over the gravel and stop next to my cobblestone walkway. The air is brisk with a stiff breeze and chill enough for my breath to steam. An owl hoots in the distance. I shut my driver door and open the back to retrieve my briefcase. It contains the files and information on Archie Whitaker who is the former pastor of Freewill Holiness I'll be going to see tomorrow.

The door slams and the night goes silent. I glance around, sweeping my eyes side to side in search of the man in black. I spin around with my back pressed firm to my Suburban. I press my fingers between my eyes and look to my porch, checking the darkened corners for any sign of life.

Nothing.

I lock the Suburban and stride along the stones to the steps of my porch. Fighting to stay awake, I blink and expand my eyelids. The nausea has returned. It'd be a heck of time to catch the flu. I swallow and rub my eye. My hearts leaps when my last step lands on the deck board. My flood light surrounds me and my ears fill with the screeching of a disturbed cicada. I drop my belongings and pull my Judge. I pull the hammer and sweep my aim side to side. Sitting before me on my welcome mat is a glass mason jar with a folded piece of white paper tied to the lid. Inside there is a cicada with its bulging red eyes, who squirms and screams.

My heart pounds. My gut twists into a knot. My throat turns dry as if filled with sand, and my blood pulses through my veins like a light rail train.

A bead of sweat tickles my spine as a tiny bead trails along my flesh like rain descending a glass window on a cold winters dawn.

My breath is short and only travels through my open mouth to keep rhythm with the drumming beat of my heart.

He's here.

"Show yourself you coward." I scream while bracing myself in a trained police stance.

Sandy rushes to the front door, barking hysterically at the wild woman outside her home.

"C'mon. What, are you afraid? I'm right here!"

There is no answer. There's no crunch of a twig or dried leaf. The night is silent, but the cicada continues to sing. Taunting me with Morty's words, *Laurie will succumb to Morty. Laurie will succumb to Morty.* Over and over the words repeat in my head. Scraping along the walls of my mind like nails to a chalkboard.

I march to the jar, snatch it into my hand and in a moment of hot unquenchable anger, I slam the jar onto my stone walkway, shattering it in a million different pieces. The cicada lies on its back, stunned from the crash. I pound down the steps and in one rage filled motion, slam my foot as hard as I can upon Morty's pet. I did it so hard my foot screamed in protest, sending a fire of pain up my leg, begging me to wake from my manic episode.

Focus.

This is what he wants. He wants you to lose control. He wants you to act out of impulse.

With my breath in huffs, and my face hotter than fire, I dart my eyes about the darkened wood line in search of the foul beast. I know he's watching me. Gazing upon me like a lion in the Safari waiting for its moment to pounce. As I glare into the woods, I allow my breath to settle. I can feel my flesh release the flush of anger, and my head begins to clear. The contrary winds of furious thoughts subside. At least for the moment.

I squat atop my calves and pick up the note. I stick it into my pocket and turn to my front door. I use the mini flashlight on my key set and shine it along the crease of the door. Earlier in the day, I'd placed a small piece of paper into the top left corner, so I'd know if anyone had opened the door after I left. The paper is still there and untouched. If Morty or an acquaintance had entered my home, they didn't come through the front.

I insert the key and give the door a gentle push. Feeling like I could be attacked any moment, my palms grease as I tighten my grip around the black rubber grip of my Judge. I've yet to switch to my .410 shells, so I have five rounds of .45's.

I peep through the crack in my door and push Sandy back with my left hand. I steady my gun's aim with my right and ease through the door in a slight crouch. My tired eyes fight away the intruding sleep. I blink and dart my vision this way and that. The house is dark except for flashes of light coming from the TV. I left it on like I always do to give Sandy some company while I'm gone. It was still on the Animal Planet channel and at the same volume. Sounds like Northwoods Law is on. The screens light flashes along the floor and walls. It fills the kitchen and attempts to crawl its way down the hall. Before I shut the door behind me, I reach outside and grab my briefcase lying near the welcome mat. I place it upon my wooden table in the hallway beneath the oval mirror with a cherry oak frame.

With Sandy by my side, I ease down the hall and press my back tight to the wall. Facing the kitchen, I look into the reflection on the microwave and peer into my living room. I count to three.

I jolt around the corner and sweep my gun about the room. Nothing.

I ease myself into the kitchen to check the other side of my island. Clear. I make my way through the living room and into the dining area, sweeping, looking, clear. I reach my laundry room and door leading to my back deck. All good.

I head to the other end of the house to check the bedrooms and bathrooms. Clear.

All the doors and windows are still locked. No sign of forced entry, everything seems tight and secure.

I take some breaths and allow the tension to ease in my shoulders. I go on to pour myself a half glass of Silver Oak and relax in my recliner. My Judge lies across my lap and Sandy sits curled at my feet.

With my head in my left hand, and empty glass in my right, I slip off into another world.

† † † † † † † † † †

**THICK, SUFFOCATING BLACKNESS FILLS** my vision. A heavy weight sits upon my chest, pressing down, binding my every breath. I force my eyes open. I'm lying in a bed which is not my own. I throw the covers to the side and stand to my feet. I'm dressed in work clothes, and my badge dangles around my neck. I can feel myself being pulled out of this bedroom and into the hallway. A squeaking, swooshing sound fills the air. Followed by a loud scratching sound on what appears to be hard wood floor. I ease out of this bedroom and stand in the open doorway. To my right is a desk with a computer monitor. In front of the monitor is a computer chair which spins faster and faster as if a child is playing in it. Faster and faster it spins, demanding my eyes to watch its sickening spin. My head grows faint as I begin to totter. My feet instinctively spread in effort to support my swaying mind. Nausea returns with a vengeance.

Bang!

The chair comes to a sudden halt.

I follow the origin of the sound.

Bang!

It's coming from the front door.

Bang!

The door jolts and rattles upon the hinges.

I glide across the floor as you often seem to do in dreams. I don't remember taking any steps, it was all one fluid sweep. I reach the door.

Bang! The door rattles again. My heart jolts. I feel my breath leave me. Fear grips my soul with an iron fist. The sound of a soft breeze enters my ears. I can feel *something* curling around my ankles. I lower my eyes to see tendrils of fog swirling about my feet.

Bang!

I return my eyes to the door and though every part of me rebuked the thought of opening it, *something* made me want to. I had to. I just had to, didn't I?

With a trembling hand, I reach for the doorknob.

Before I could open it, an abundance of hissing sounds emit from the other side. I drop my eyes to the bottom of the door and catch glimpse of a hoard of snakes slithering their way under the door. How? I don't know.

Stumbling, I force myself backward as the snakes pour in, slithering across the floor, pulling themselves towards me. Their tongues reaching out to taste my scent.

Bam!

The door flies open, sending in a swarm of flying and screeching insects. Cicadas. Their big red eyes zeroing in on mine. Standing tall like a statue in the doorway, staring into my soul is the man in the black hood.

Morty.

I thought at this moment I would awake. It's as if someone has pressed paused. Sound disappears. Movement halts.

I stare into the shadows covering his face, trying desperately to make out his features. It's useless, he's nothing but a big, black shadow.

Pop!

Like the sound of a bone cracking.

Two red dots flash wide upon the being's face. A loud hiss follows as those red eyes glare deep into my soul. All of sound and movement return.

I let out a gasping scream and at that very moment, he breaks from his stillness and bolts for me. His heavy feet pound upon the floor.

I jerk around and attempt to enter into a sprint, but it's as if I'm running in quicksand. I can't go anywhere. The snakes slither closer and hiss, their forked tongues stretching forth. The cicadas scream, all singing . . . *Laurie will succumb to Morty! Laurie will succumb to Morty!*

Within seconds, I'm engulfed by a swarm of them. They flutter and screech about my face, before landing on me, crawling about my lips and eyes.

Morty's feet slam closer with each torturous second, but I still can't go anywhere. He will reach me any moment.

Finally, I break free from the ghost's grip. I bolt towards the back door. I pass the spinning desk chair. An array of children's voices string together in a harmonious, eerie laughter.

I come to a sliding glass door like the McCrae's. I try opening it, but it's locked.

Pulling. Tugging. Yanking.

I'm stuck. Nowhere to go. Nowhere to hide.

He's coming.

I hear the flutter of the cicada's wings and they continue to scream his words.

*Laurie will succumb to Morty! Laurie will succumb to Morty!*

He inches closer, taking his time.

As much as I want to flee, something keeps me in place. The unseen presence holds me tight within its grip. I can feel something curling around my arms and legs. I look to my arms and see the fog swirling about them like rope. I glance to my feet and see the oily, scaly skin of snakes as they coil around my legs

Morty's heavy feet continue to thud closer.

I begin to scream. Pleading. Begging.

I begin to cry and gasp for breath. The snakes and fog squeeze tighter and tighter.

A bright flash pierces the darkness outside of the sliding glass door. The yard lights up as if it were day.

The sounds within this darkened home cease. The snakes disappear, and the cicada's grow quiet. Morty has vanished.

I peer through this glass door and notice a home across the street. At the front door stands a man dressed from head to toe in black. He bangs his head upon the door in rapid fashion. I catch glimpse of a curtain pull back from a window next to the front door. I can see a young girl, close to the same age as Sarah McCrae and my sister Amy when she disappeared.

Her face twists in frantic horror, she pleads to me with innocent eyes, begging me to do something. Her hand spreads upon the windowpane. The crazed man hears her. He jerks his head to her and takes a step. I immediately begin to slam my fist upon the glass door, screaming, doing all I can to get his attention.

The girl moves from the window, allowing the white curtain to swing back into place. The man bolts away from the glass and enters into a crouch.

I continue to scream and pound upon the glass.

I watch as the man races to the window, takes a leap and crashes through it.

Horrified, I drop my head and begin to weep with an unexplainable heaviness. Knowing full well another innocent soul has fallen victim to Morty's evil desires.

Lost in my despair, my attention is pulled to the high pitch scream of the girl, followed by deep grotesque laughter. I look and catch glimpse of the girl racing from the back of the home, pounding towards me. Running just behind her heels is the man in black.

Everything grows dark. All light begins to fade as it's swallowed by this dark presence. As if someone turned off the light switch, everything goes black. I can still hear the girls screams and Morty's eerie laughter, but my sight is void of any light. A piercing hum enters the air, growing louder and louder, until it overtakes all other sound. I clinch my teeth, grab at my ears, and slam my eyes shut. I can feel my energy being sucked away as if someone or *something* is stealing my soul. I crumble to the floor.

The hum grows louder and higher in pitch.

A loud click rips through the air, and in that instant, I'm engulfed by a pure white light. The hum dissipates. Despite the sting and ache from the sudden light, I flash open my eyes. I see a magnificent white mountain, bigger and more beautiful than anything I've ever seen. Standing at the base of it, next to a crystal-clear river which rushes with soft sounding ripples, is the girl. She's clothed in radiant white. She has her back to me, but the moment my eyes find her, she begins to slowly turn. One moment, she looks like Sarah McCrae, but the next she looks like my sister Amy.

She smiles with pearly whites and mouths in a slow abbreviated gesture . . . *It's okay.*

Then she raises her hand and points skyward. I try to follow but am overtaken by the light.

The next thing I know, I'm swimming to the surface of this world. Gasping for breath, I jolt awake in my recliner. I drop my glass onto the floor. The TV is still airing reruns of Northwoods Law. Breathing faster than I can manage, my heart races with each pounding pulse. I blink and rub my eyes. I jerk my head about the room. Knowing I'm in distress, Sandy begins to paw at my leg.

Overtaken with a sudden wave of emotion, all I can do is cry.

I'd seen my sister. I'd seen Sarah McCrae, and I'd seen their abductor, but it was the light they were surrounded by that brought tears to my eyes. And her words . . . *It's okay.*

All I can do is weep.

I feel like this is the answer I've been searching for. They're gone, but they're *okay*. I'll never see my sister again. This is her way of showing me that. Sarah McCrae will never be found, but *it's okay.*

My heart rate continues to surge. What have I just experienced? The darkness, such evil in its truest form, yet the light was there, and it was brighter, purer, and more powerful than anything I'd ever experienced. It's real. It's tangible.

What is it?

# 25

**THE NEXT MORNING,** I awoke to the beeping and buzzing of my phone's alarm. Still seated in my recliner, I'm relieved to see the sunlight. My eyes have a slight bit of morning sting and are full of sand, but the sleep was good. I shut off the alarm on my phone. It's 6:50.

I managed to get about four hours of sleep, which when coupled with a few cups of caffeinated coffee rather than my usual decaf, should be enough to get me through the day. Collins and Detective White along with the FBI duo, expect me to conduct a briefing at eight-thirty. I expect them to brief me on a few things as well. Afterwards, Collins and I will be making the trip to Cushing Island where we will meet with Archie Whitaker and Dr. William Langston.

I rub my face with both palms, rise and head for the bedroom. A nice shower will be well received.

I freshen up, put on a change of clothes, black slacks with a white button down, and make my way into the kitchen. I put on a pot of coffee, and as I wait, I fix half of an almond butter sandwich on wheat bread with organic honey drizzled over it. I pick a banana from its cluster as well.

Moments later when the coffee finished, I poured a splash of chocolate almond milk into my cup, gave Sandy a treat, and sat at my table.

I sip at my coffee and retrieve the piece of paper which was tied to the mason jar last night. I had removed it from my pants last night and stuck in my fresh pair to read as I eat.

I take a bite of sandwich and unfold the paper. Almost not wanting to read it, I shut my eyes and draw a breath. I finish chewing the bread and almond butter with a hint of sweet honey before washing it down with coffee. I open my eyes and begin to read the Courier typed words.

Why hello there my little darling,
At the reading of this letter, you will
have likely searched my dear friend Dr.
Feltner's office and hatchery. I heard he
was found swinging among his friends. I
always enjoyed my time with Dr. Feltner.
Such a mysterious, yet wise little man. He
never ceased to amaze me with his
brilliance regarding the cicada. One of
God's greatest gifts. I must say, I am
pained to see him go. I shall miss our
enlightening conversations. We had a lot
in common you know, the two of us. Lovers
of insects, lovers of classical music, he
was a dear friend and oh how I wish he
would have kept his mind to himself. You
see towards the end, Dr. Feltner became
increasingly curious of my dealings with
the cicada. So much so, that he
investigated my credentials and claims of
study at UMass. He was more brazen than I
originally believed. Just last week, he
confronted me with my false giving's. I of
course told him that if he were to tell
anyone, I would be sure to flay him much
in the same manner of which he dissects
his specimens. After my work was finished,
I'd hang him from the beam which his dear
friends fly. I told him, if he ever felt
the need to turn me over, than it'd be
better if he hung himself rather than
force me to carry out my wrath upon his
vile transgression against God's servant.
And thanks to you Miss Daniels, I had no
need to carry out any more harm. With your
help, Dr. Feltner took matters into his
own hands, just as I had commanded. So,
for that, I thank you my dear Laurie. May
my little friend here serve as a reminder
that I'm always watching, and the cicada's

```
will continue to sing. Hear them wail
'Laurie will succumb to Morty.' Whether by
your own hands or mine, I have yet to
decide. To be quite honest, after all
these years, I've kind of taken a liking
to you Laurie. Although you never pay me
much mind, it's always a pleasure to see
you. Mostly from afar, but when I'm lucky
enough, in close proximity.
    Easy goings.
    Your friend,
    Morty
    GWD
```

The nausea returns and I can hardly continue to eat my breakfast. So, Dr. Feltner was not our man. Wait a second, what about my cameras? They would show him coming to my porch.

I sit my coffee cup down and leave the table with a plate half full of breakfast. I rush to the living room and grab the controller, pressing input until I reach the channel the camera screens are on. Once there I work my way through the previous recordings, fast forwarding at 16x from nine o'clock on. At *12:23*, my eye catches glimmer of a dark figure racing up to my porch. I slam the pause button, hit rewind, and mash play.

About ten seconds pass before the man of shadows appears. Angling around the side of my house and dressed in black with a dark hood. The first thing that stands out to me is his size. It was definitely not Dr. Feltner.

This is a big man. At least six-foot-two I'd say. I try zooming in on the face, but he appears to be wearing some sort of dark mask with big red eyes. Like the cicada.

I watch as he casually strides to my front door and lowers the mason jar onto the welcome mat. He straightens his spine and stands for a long moment, not moving an inch. His head is stiff as he glares at my front door as if he'd turned into a statue.

I check to be sure I hadn't pressed pause. In a quick snap that startles my heart, he jerks his head straight to the camera. In a slow, mechanical motion, he raises his hand and waves.

With my heart thumping, I cover my mouth and watch as he turns away before angling back the way he came. All in a slow, carefree gait.

A chill caresses my spine.

I need to set up a police surveillance.

I pocket the letter, unplug my DVR, and tote it into the kitchen. I take a bite of sandwich and sip the rest of my coffee. I fix a to-go thermos, pick up the banana, and head for the door. Passing my mirror in the hallway, I steal a glance and find the need to spruce up a few strands of hair. If I had a dollar for every time someone told I could pass for Buffy the Vampire Slayer, perhaps I could afford retirement. Not that I would of course, because money is not the reason I do what I do. It's the reward of bringing justice for the victims that keeps me going. If it wasn't for that I would have retired long ago.

Here I stand though with puffy eyes and dark circles beneath them that will need more coffee to liven up. I take a sip from my thermos and squat to pet Sandy.

Allen will be by later to pick her up. He and Paul offered to take her to the park for me. I know how rough it can be on her when I get on a case like this. I hardly ever have time for her as I barely have time for myself.

I give her a few last pats to the head and make my way out the door.

I pay special attention in securing the deadbolt.

† † † † † † † † † †

**I BEEPED THE HORN WHEN** I passed Paul's house. I got a good chuckle when I saw him flash his lamp light back at me. It wasn't a few seconds later my phone began to buzz.

Before I could even say hello, "I's sitting here watching my TV and saw you going out. I said boy she's up early," he said through the deep chuckle of his.

"Hey Paul, yeah I have a meeting at eight-thirty, so I'm heading in to get some things together."

"Yeah-yeah, well how are you doing? You okay?"

"I'm fine. You know how I get with a case like this. I go from seven hours of sleep down to four if I'm lucky."

"Well, be sure you taking care of yourself now. Don't overdo it."

"I won't. You and Allen will be heading to my house in a little bit."

"Yeah we sure will. Going take ole Sandy to the park."

"Thank you, I appreciate you two doing that for me. I feel bad being gone all day. I know she enjoys getting out for a change. Just be sure you both keep an eye out as you go down there. You know in case anyone is messing around."

"Oh, don't you worry about that now. I'll have Mr. Colt by my side. I was the finest shot in all of Jefferson Parish back in my day."

"I know. Just be careful. And if you want, you can keep Sandy at your place until I make it home. I shouldn't be gone quite as long today. If all goes as planned, I should be back around seven."

"Okay honey, y'alls be careful now. I'll talk to ya later."

"Alright we will, you be careful too. Love ya."

"Love you too honey. Bye bye."

"Bye."

† † † † † † † † † †

**"BLAKE AND NATALIE ARE WORKING** on the handwriting analysis for the twenty-dollar bill. They're also examining the letter left on my porch. Ronnie's looking over the film from my DVR, and Officer Williams and Deputy Ferrell are heading to the McCrae's now to pick up their DVR. Hopefully, there will be something there too. John, have we heard from Feltner's colleagues yet to see if the cicada's in the hatchery are Magi's?" I ask standing before he, Collins, Chief Cunningham and Agents Swanson and Weatherby.

"Yeah, Mr. Roestein said the majority of those in the hatchery are Magicicada's. He said he thought he remembered Feltner saying something about giving a few to a professor from UMass for research purposes."

"Keep talking with Mr. Roestein. I want to know everything there is to know about these bugs. If you could have me a file when I return from Ottawa, I'd be grateful. And Kim please let me know what your field agents find out once they approach our Gary Wade Duncan's."

"Yes ma'am," she said crossing her legs while writing on a note pad in her lap, never bothering to look at me.

"What time are Agent Turner and Agent Vasquez arriving?" I ask looking to Agent Swanson.

He removes his glasses and scratches the corner of his eye. His white hair seems whiter today for some reason.

"Said they'd be here by noon."

"Are they bringing anyone from Behavioral Analysis?"

"Yeah, Agent Shannon Carter is the best profiler we currently have. She's good. She was a part of the team that worked on the GTK case and she's worked on countless others. She's been with us for almost thirty years now. She's worked in the NCAVC most of her years, so she's seen some dark stuff and has helped shackle some evil men in her years."

"Good. That's nice to know. I'm sure Collins and her can work together to strengthen our profile," I say with a glance his way. He was busy chewing on a pen while looking at the files. His white sleeves are cuffed at hairy and tan forearms. He glances up and nods with a slight smile.

I look to my watch, 9:28.

"The ferry departs at 10:15. I expect we will be gone for most of the afternoon. I do have a meeting arranged with Pastor Wicker at four and I'd like for us to meet back here . . . say by five-thirty, so we can reconvene. Chief, is there anything you'd like to add?"

He clears his throat and stands from sitting on the desk with a crossed leg. He rubs his chin and begins to pace in front of the white board. Numerous pictures of the crime scenes and our victims are arrayed like post it notes. Scribbled handwriting with large question marks are scattered here and there on the board.

He begins with his deep gravelly voice, "Listen, I know we are growing anxious to catch this guy. Believe me, nobody wants this sick lowlife brought in more than me. But I don't want us to get too caught up in our emotions that we miss a piece of the puzzle that may very well lie right under our noses. I know we're all aware that today is the second day and according to the voice recording, he's going to take another victim tomorrow. We can't let that happen. We can't allow him to gain any more power than he already has. We have all the resources we need. We are smarter than this guy, and he's vastly outnumbered. We have everyone Washington has to offer working on these cases. It's only a matter of time before we find our man.

"However, we have to remain vigilant. We cannot let our guard down for one second. Everyone is a suspect until proven innocent. Remember that. Don't count anyone out until you know beyond a reasonable doubt. Because as you have already discovered, he likely walks among us. He eats at the same restaurants, and he travels our same roads. He's likely a local. He knows the territory. But so do we. Keep your heads screwed on tight and pay attention to everyone you come in contact with, because you very well may be speaking with a serial killer. Good luck to you, stay safe. See you this evening."

With that, Collins and I grab our things and head for the ferry.

# 26

AS WE DRIVE through downtown Portland, a light mist begins to fall. We continue and make our way to Long Wharf where the passenger ferry St. Croix awaits us. We park in a crowded lot next to the marina where numerous commercial fishing, crab, and lobster boats are ported. Tourist roam about like disturbed ants as seagulls squawk above, floating in the ocean breeze.

Seeing people's breath steam into the air, I retrieve my gray wool beanie and button up my black peacoat. Street venders and food trucks are scattered about the area, offering lobsta rolls, bisque, chowder, and anything else Maine has to offer. We have fifteen minutes before the ferry departs, so Collins and I grab some rolls for a quick brunch. Standing by the waterside, I squeeze a wedge of lemon over my toasted bread containing lobster and chive among other tasty ingredients.

We discuss the case and watch as two Asian kids toss bread into the water, feeding the birds and small fish. Laughing like the gulls, the kids enjoy their time and are oblivious of the monster lurking these very streets.

"You know Laurie, these past few days I've really been given the profile some thought."

"Yeah?"

"I feel the profile's right, it's just—"

"Just what?" I question as I wad and toss my trash into a nearby bin.

Following behind me, he hands me his napkin and wrapper, and says "What if it's someone close to us?"

I give him the look.

"What if it's someone within the department?"

"Patrick."

He raises a hand and tilts his head, "I know, I know. Hear me out for a second."

I sigh and walk to the water's edge, a few yards down from the two Asian kids who appear to be brother and sister. I turn back to the food truck to see their relatives seated at a picnic table, eyeing me like a hawk. Their glare gives my heart some relief. The last thing I want is to have to be sifting through case files filled with these children's photos.

"Laurie, I don't think the man at Ted's Diner is Morty. My gut's telling me the whole thing was just a strange coincidence. Think about it, the witness sketch and description doesn't even match the man in your footage."

"I know that, but we also know Morty isn't working alone either."

Collins rubs the back of his neck then reaches for his toothpick container and shakes one out.

"Who are you suggesting? What are you suggesting?"

He takes a breath and inserts a toothpick. I get a faint aroma of cinnamon as he says, "I don't know, but I keep getting this feeling that Morty is somebody we already know and possibly. . .work with."

"C'mon now Pat, you and me both know that's a road we don't want to venture."

"I know. I can't get the thought out of my head though. Maybe I'm getting paranoid." He sips on his coffee and looks out to the array of boats anchored in the harbor. A thick rolling fog hovers above their hulls. I follow his gaze and marinate on his words.

Hearing heavy heels thud along the boardwalk, I turn to my right to see a daunting figure striding my way. Glaring at me with a stern face, is a white bearded man with dark eyes and a white captain's hat. His skin is a ghostly pale. Our eyes lock as he passes us by. I offer a friendly grin, but my gesture is returned with a cold glare. I feel my heart knock hard against my chest before coming to a halt. If looks could kill, this man just committed murder. Satisfied after searing his eyes into my soul, he turns his attention to the ferry and proceeds to step on board. Collins mumbles something, but his voice is like elevator music to me. I hear him, but I'm not listening. Instead, I watch from a distance as the weathered old man pulls himself up a set of spiraled black iron stairs leading to the helm. Great, of all people, of course this'll be our captain.

A loud ding-ding-ding pierces the air.

The time to board has come and a crowd of people rush together to meet the ticket master. In total, there's not any more than thirty or forty passengers on board. Most are tourists, though a few may be locals of Cushing Island. Then of course there's the two brave detectives heading to the Cumberland Behavioral Health Center for the Gifted. The place was formerly known as the Ottawa House for the Criminally Insane.

We step aboard and make our way through the crowd. The ferry's cabin has large windows and booth type seating which is similar to that of a subway train. Up front at the bow is where most of the people naturally gather, so we decide to head for the stern instead. We lean over the rail facing Portland Headlight. She sits high upon the rocky cliff with her amber hue of light rotating and piercing through the fog for all to see. Salty air caresses our faces as blue water and white sea foam lap against the hull. In unison we begin to rise and fall, crashing over the swells. Gulls squawk above, waiting for a tossed crumb.

A moment passes when a deep, unnerving voice crackles over the microphone to set our attention to Cushing Island. We both turn and proceed over to the opposite railing for a better view. My heart begins to thump like a subwoofer at the sight of the silhouette hiding behind the fog. It's been over a decade since my last visit, and I told myself I'd never come back but look at me now.

The mountain of darkness grows with each passing second as it begins to loom over us, stripping away my courage inch by tantalizing inch. As memories of the place consume my resolve, I find myself questioning if it's all worth it. Is the trail of leads worth jeopardizing my life and sanity? Visons of last night's dream resurface. What kind of monster is waiting for me at the end of all this?

Gliding closer to the island, I watch as angry waves crash against the rocks. A buzzard stirs from a nest along the cliff and flaps its big black wings to send it away into the gray abyss above the white capped sea. A deep heaviness fills my body, weighing down my heart. It's as if the island is speaking to me, warning me not to awaken the beast. Dread leaks into my soul at an alarming rate as an eerie presence fills the air, snuffing away the oxygen and stealing my breath. My pulse soars as icy adrenaline trails down my spine. I shake away the fear seeping into my bones and tilt my cup of coffee for a sip. I soak in its warmth, hoping it'll soothe the chill flowing through my veins.

The piercing cry of a raven sends my flesh leaping from the bone. I raise my vision to find him strutting along the ferry's roof next to an array of antennas and flashing red lights. He watches me with twitchy eyes and begins to let out sharp, screechy caws. The feeling of being watched overtakes me, so my eyes shift to one of the glass windows looking into the helm. I catch glimpse of that ghostly captain turning his head from me as he steers the ship onward to Cushing Island.

Collins words pull my attention, "What are we getting ourselves into?"

I turn to him and can see the questions lurking in his dark blue eyes. His five o'clock shadow has thickened over the past few days. His large hands turn white as they clinch the railing. At least I won't be doing this alone like last time.

I look back to the island, "I don't know, but this place may just let the cat out of the bag."

"Yeah and let's hope it's a tame one," he scoffs.

The ferry cuts to the left as the engine picks up speed, causing it to growl and huff out a puff of black smoke.

If the new rumors are true about Cushing Island . . . what *are* we getting into?

Cushing
Island

# 27

A TAXI WAS AWAITING us when we made it onto the island. It took us further inland to reach the Ottawa Home which is now known as Cumberland Behavioral Health Center for the Gifted. The ride has been sedate but bumpy as we snake and spiral our way higher up the mountain. The angry white capped sea has vanished behind the veil of fog which slithers about like a serpent. The amber hue from Portland Headlight has waned.

Our driver, Don Graves, couldn't be any nicer. Although he seemed a bit timid when I first mentioned where we were heading. He's an older gentleman with white curly hair. He wears a black beret hat with a slight bill over his large wrinkled forehead. The few times he removed his cap to scratch an itch, I noticed the crown of his head was slick and shiny with red sunspots tossed here and there. His hands are decorated with black leather gloves. A gray peacoat is buttoned tight around his thin waist. He has the thickest Boston accent I've heard in years. I thought Collins's was bad, huh, he has nothing on Mr. Graves.

The whole way over, Don has been fixated on the death of Maria Santorum. The lady who wrapped herself in a sheet and leapt from the cliffs. I've yet to tell him I was the lead investigator of the case.

As we finish climbing the remaining hill, the topography flattens out and the Asylum comes into view along with my distant memories of the place. People screaming and banging pee pots against the wall. A few even barked and howled at the moon. Yeah, it was that bad. Those few were the worst of the worst and the worst appeared when the meds began to ebb.

The others either sat silently against the windows and glared out into the horizon or argued over a poker or chess match. Some others were busy drawing, painting, or playing dress-up. Then there were a few who I'd hardly ever see. They were less spaced out and more attune to their situation. They stayed in their rooms like hermits, reading, writing, or listening to small Victrola record players they'd been gifted for their good behavior.

When I did see this type of patient, they'd often watch me with tilted heads and mysterious eyes. They were the outcast of society. They'd been left to rot in a man-made hell, and they had no problem telling you that. They often slipped notes to the more extroverted among the home and would persuade them into passing the notes on to me. They would mention how they didn't belong in such a place, and they'd swear on their mother's grave they weren't insane or *gifted*.

But they were. They just didn't acknowledge it, and that small simple fact *was* their insanity.

Heck, we're all gifted in one way or another.

"Neva been in such a place. I can only imagine what it's like in there. I've heard some wicked stories about what goes on inside of this place. Heard a lot rumors. Some true, some not so true." Don places a hand on the back of the passenger head rest and looks to me and Collins in the back seat. "I'm anxious to hear the truth from a reliable source. Just don't get to close to some of em. I heard they don't like it too much when they space is invaded. That one nurse had to have her nose put back together. I imagine they can be a hand full when backed into a corner."

"Thank you for the heads-up, Don. We don't plan on backing anyone in a corner though, we're just trying to get some answers. We'll fill you in, in a bit. Can you be back here by two?"

"I'll do my best."

Collins opens the door and we step out.

I go to the passenger window and look through. "Thank you, sir. I enjoyed the ride over. Take care."

"My pleasure miss. See you folks in a jiff."

With that I patted the roof of the yellow Ford Taurus and turned to Collins, who was standing with his hands in his pockets, looking to the gray and black, three-story home beyond the black iron gates.

It has more windows than I can count, but each one is barricaded with thick iron bars and opened black hurricane shutters.

The entire lot is surrounded in a high black fence that curls inward at the top with barbwire. Something you'd expect to see at a prison yard. Must be left over from their time of being a home for the criminally insane.

We stride to the gate where a small box is stationed with a pad of numbers. On the corner of a brick column is a bubbled camera which looks like a cicada's eye. It's just black instead of red. It watches our every move.

"They know we're coming, right?"

"Yeah, I spoke with Dr. Langston yesterday," I say as I push the button.

A static hiss answers, "Yes, how can I help you?"

"Hi, Lieutenant Daniels here with my partner, Detective Collins . . . we're here to speak with a few of your patients on the approval of Dr. Langston. He's expecting us between 10:30 and 11."

"One moment please."

I step back and cup my hands to my face to blow some warmth into them. I look to my right and see the vast Atlantic peeking through the rolling fog. I can hear its waves crashing against the rocks beyond the cliff.

"Despite the eerie vibe, the place looks quite nice inside," Collins says as he peers between the gates with his hands coiled around the bars. "Carved statues and fountains, nice gardens . . . oh and look, some of the patients are even tending to them."

I cross to him with hands tucked deep into my coat pockets. I lean into the bars and look at all the patients wandering about mindlessly among the gardens and sculptures.

The place hasn't changed much. It's just as I remember it.

The keeper, Maryann Cusick, once told me that they designed this place based on the biblical account of Eden. It's quite metaphorical when you stop and think about it. It's a place for the outcast to retreat into heaven. A place to feel wanted and valued. A place where they can see the hidden beauties of this world. According to Cusick, once they begin to see that, it opens a whole other world in which they can then see themselves the way they were created. Without spot or blemish, and without the tarnish of man's contraptions. In Cusick's own words, "There is an Eden within us all. A gift. A place of paradise that only we can find."

This was their reminder of such a gift.

*Bam!*

"Get me out of here mista! I don't belong here! They're crazy! They're crazy!"

A wild-eyed woman, perhaps in her early sixties, grasps the bars and grips Collins forearm with such strength it takes all he has to yank away. She's dressed in a white gown that is spotted with fresh soil, likely from her time of tending to her garden. Her hair is brown with slightly curled strands that stretch to her belly. She's barefoot, her toenails are unkept, and her skin is a dead looking shade of pale. Though her voice is strained, there's no anger or ill will connected to it. If I'd stumbled upon her on the street, I would have thought she was a victim of some horrible crime. One in which I would spend the rest of my days attempting to solve.

Collins rubs his wrist and watches her with curious eyes.

She grips the iron bars with both hands and sticks her face between the gap. Tears fall from her big brown eyes, drenching the soil below her.

Her voice cracks and sounds like a child after a spanking, "Please. Please, jut get me outdahere. My babies need me. Please, they need tha mothder."

She clinches her teeth and bares them like a rapid dog. Spittle leaks through, popping out in small flakes as she speaks.

"Ma'am. You're okay. Everything's okay. I need you take a deep breath for me, okay? Is there a nurse nearby?"

A woman's voice returns over the speaker, "Okay, ma'am you're welcome to come in. I'll open the gate."

"No. Wait!"

I jolt for the box.

"Miss Wellington, now what have we told you about journeying near the gate?"

A younger feminine voice arises behind me just as I near the speaker box. I spin on my heals and see a dark skin lady who looks to be of Eastern Indian decent. She has kind eyes and a gentle smile. She's dressed in white with a white nurses cap.

I angle back.

"I'm sorry. I had my back to her just for a moment," she says as she tightens her grip around the lady's arm.

"You sure you got her there?" asks Collins.

"Yeah-yeah, we're fine," she says as she steps away from the gate with the lady. It begins to open on squeaky hinges, pushing inward. The whole scope of the place is now unobstructed as it comes into full view. It kind of feels the way the dark mountain of Cushing Island made me feel from the ferry. Like the place is looming over us with outstretched arms, stretching forth for its next victim.

I feel Collins's eyes.

I turn and find him looking at me with raised brows. He swallows hard.

"Don't worry . . . it's not as bad as it seems. I've seen worse."

He twists his head and rubs the nape of his neck.

"You must be the detectives?"

"Yes, we ar—"

"You have to save us! Please!"

"Sshh . . . easy now Margaret. You're okay," the nurse says as she gently combs the lady's long locks.

"You'll have to excuse her. It's time for her meds. Follow us, we can show you to Dr. Langston. I'm nurse Omora by the way."

We step inside the gate and watch as it shuts slowly behind us to lock us in.

A long-paved walkway leads to a wide set of brick steps angling up to the entrance of the home. White columns support an overhang which creates dark shadows from the crest of the steps to the humongous white double doors that could welcome a giant. The doors are tucked deep within the shadows of the overhang.

To the right and left of the walkway is luscious green grass, mixed with an array of water fountains, sculptures, and floral gardens. If I remember correctly from my past visit, each patient is given a garden in which they are tasked the responsibility of tending. It serves as a symbol to the chore of striving to keep their minds free of any weeds or unwanted thoughts. Which is the reason many are here. To learn the art of a keeping a garden. Their own inner garden. Their own Eden.

Despite the weather, the yard is full of patients in flowing white gowns. Some eye their gardens, others walk the perimeter of the walls. Some sit along on benches and gaze to the heavens while listening to the waves beyond the walls. You'll see them point to passing gulls, and sense the envy they have for the bird's freedom.

Collins and the nurse are speaking, but I'm too busy observing to pick up their conversation.

One such patient to my left demands my attention. It's a young lady, dressed in the standard issued white gown, with blonde hair parted down the center and strands resting along each shoulder. Her beauty is striking even from a distance. She'd be easy to mistake for an angel. She seems out of place here. How can someone with such exterior beauty belong in a place like this?

She stands there within a stone's cast, with her hands dangling along her sides and eyes locked on mine. A blank, empty, and soulless glare.

Then, in a slow, mechanical motion she raises her hand and waves. A slow grin stretches across her face.

I smile and wave back.

Heat rises to my eyes as my heart grows in weight. That was more than just a simple wave.

I put my head down, wipe a tear, sniffle, and look back over my left shoulder. She'd turned away with her head hung low, and I watch as she crosses toward a garden where three other patients are gathered.

I swallow the knot of emotion in my throat and interrupt Collins and the nurse's conversation. I did so out of impulse, void of manners, "Excuse me, ma'am. Who's that?" I point to the girl.

"Oh, that? Why that's Hope Jamison. She's special. One of the most gifted we have."

I watch as she mingles quietly among the others with her arms crossed at the chest. She steals glances toward us with cuts of her eyes.

"Is she a local?"

"No, she was transferred here from Virginia two years ago. Spent most of her life in and out of orphanages since she was about nine or ten. She lived a rough life."

"You said she was gifted. How so?"

"She possesses some psychic abilities that therapists and scientists have yet to explain."

"Such as?"

Omora adjusts her grip on Margaret once more, half dragging her to the steps.

"Well . . . you see, she has dreams that are not really dreams. They're more like visions. She will sometimes have a dream only to watch it unfold in real life days or weeks later."

"Déjà vu?" asks Collins.

"Sort of, but different."

"Paul's friend from New Orleans did the same thing," I mumble.

"Yeah, you're right."

"Remember the stories about all of that?"

Collins nods.

"So, you're familiar with the condition?" Omora asks.

"A little, yes."

"She's really a nice and interesting girl. It just takes some time for you to gain her trust. Which is understandable when considering her circumstances. I should also mention that she is schizophrenic."

"I see. Perhaps we could speak with her later if it's okay."

"You'll have to speak with Dr. Langston. I'm sure he wouldn't mind," Omora says as she and Margaret reach the first step.

As we conquer them and step into the overhang's shadow, I turn one last time to look out at the yard full of the gifted and watch as they continue to wander among the gardens in their flowing gowns.

This place is such an enigma.

I take a deep breath and turn at the unlatching of the big doors. They must be at least twenty feet in height. Omora steps in with Margaret who is significantly more docile now that she's in a controlled environment.

The interior is the same as I remember it.

It looks like a wealthy 1950's hotel lobby. Bronze and gold mixed with red velvet carpet decorates every inch of the place. Long black curtains with gold trim stretch to the floor. Old European style furniture is scattered about. Large pictures of local figures rest high on the walls. Some photos are more distinct. Like paintings of Michael Angelo and Picasso. Then, of course there's an old painting of a man with a white beard who looks strikingly similar to the captain of the ferry. He's dressed in suit and tie and wears a docile grin as his hands are interlocked across a lifted knee. The name *Dr. William J. Langston Sr.* is inscribed at the bottom, along with the dates: *1889-1969*. As I understand it, the Dr. Langston we will be meeting with today is of the third generation. Apparently, the man in this photo was his grandfather.

A long, drawn out gargle of a scream emits from somewhere deep within the walls. The loud ting of a pee pot follows close behind. Not much has changed from the last time.

We've entered the chambers of the gifted. For how long we stay . . . who's to say?

# 28

STANDING BEHIND Officer Chris Williams and Deputy Dean Ferrell inside the McCrae's living room, Assistant Special Agent in Charge Kim Weatherby watches with crossed arms as the men unplug the cords connecting the DVR and camera.

"Man, I really hope there's something on here," Williams says as he wags his head while glaring at the cords in his hands.

Deputy Ferrell nods and stands from a squat, "Yeah, what if this thing has audio? And where it's placed, our man probably never knew they had it."

"Hopefully, Ronnie can get into it and find what we need. Well . . . Agent Weatherby I guess we'll head back to the station. You going to seal it back up?"

Weatherby bobs her head, "Soon as you boys get out of here, I'll slap the seal back on it."

"Alright, we'll get going. You and Swanson talking with Feltner's co-workers today?"

"He's there at the museum now with Dr. Roestein. I'll be heading that way after I leave here."

"Okay, call if you need us. Take care ma'am," Williams says with a polite nod. Ferrell follows suit.

† † † † † † † † † †

**LYING ON HIS BELLY, DRESSED IN CAMO,** and tucked away in a thick patch of woods, Gary Wade Duncan watches as the two police officers tote the DVR box to their patrol car.

Luckily for him, the footage on the DVR box would only be a distraction. Something for the police and detectives to chew on while he commits another murder. Today he serves as pest control, but tomorrow he'll be back to serving as the reaper. The one chosen by God to carry out the punishment of sins.

*It's just like killing a deer, boy. There isn't any difference. These people are animals.*

Is what his father would tell him each time he found himself in the cellar beneath the barn. It was there they'd stare at the upside-down flailing body of the one God had chosen to punish. The person's eyes would bulge, and Gary Wade Duncan could see their pulse thumping along their neck where all the blood swam. Even their breathing would become animalistic as they panted out through their nostrils. Their mouths would of course be gagged to prevent screaming. Loud screaming that is. They all screamed, but the gag helped to keep it muffled so it sounded more like snorts and grunts. Animal like.

The classical music, which his father played, helped to drown out the sound as well.

His father would then hand him the knife and pliers—the same pair of pliers his father had used to pull one of his baby teeth a few years before that—and he'd go to work. He had to because if he didn't it'd be him hanging from the ceiling with his head almost touching the straw and earth covered floor.

Once he gained the courage to carry out his father's deeds, he managed to avoid the long nights in the woods of being bound to a tree in order to "become a man," as his father would tell him. From the age of seven to twelve his father would routinely take him deep into the woods, bind him to a tree, shave off his hair, strip him naked, and leave him for twenty-four hours. "God will be with you," he'd tell him, and it was during those long nights that he learned to cherish one of God's greatest gifts. The cicada. They'd be sent to watch over him. They'd come out late in the night and crawl across his body. Their little feet would tickle his flesh, and they would sing him songs of comfort. If he was lucky he may get a few hours of sleep before his father came to get him the next morning. As he grew older, his father began leaving him bound for longer periods of time. His father was finally satisfied that he'd become a man after he'd survived three days and nights during the fall of his twelfth year of life. When he asked his father about food and drink, he'd simply told him to fast. Which he did, though not without being on the verge of dehydration and malnutrition. That was the last time his father ever tied him to a tree in the woods. From then on, Gary Wade Duncan was the one doing most of the binding as he helped his father slay the "animals."

It was a noble thing that they did, and it is a noble thing he does now. He should be considered a form of savior. Something people should admirer. He does what no one else has the courage to do, but deep down wish they did. Tomorrow he'd take another child from a destructive home to give them the chance to fulfill their wildest dreams. That's quite admirable.

Lost in his thoughts, the sound of the engine cranking brings him back. He watches as the muffler of the police car puffs gray smoke into the air. It proceeds to back away and do a *180* as it heads for the roadway.

The ASAC is still inside, and about to be brought home in a sack. He snickers silently at his self. He always has had a sense of humor. His breath rises in a slow steam among the thicket.

A little Sparrow rummages about in a tree above him, singing its morning song and oblivious to the manner of man lurking below.

Gary Wade Duncan begins to tremble as he can hardly wait for the taking. His gut quakes, his pulse soars, and a bead of cold sweat snakes its way down his forehead. Leaving a white trail as it strips away the skin cream application he'd used earlier this morning.

He reaches deep into his pants pocket and retrieves a handmade strangling device. A piece of cheese wire between two hand grips. He twirls the grips in each hand, tightening the wire. The coast is clear. He shuts his eyes, says a quick prayer, grins and takes in a long, deep breath to steady his anxious soul. He quivers at the thought of what's to come.

He pushes himself off the ground, hunches his back, and emerges from the woods. It's time to make Laurie proud. It's time to kill another animal.

God will understand.

# 29

DR. WILLIAM LANGSTON is what you'd expect to see when meeting a Psychiatric doctor at a behavioral health center. A large man, with black glasses, white hair, a neatly trimmed white beard, broad shoulders, and a thick British accent.

A nice fellow, but blunt and straight to the point. No kidding or messing around. You either liked him or you didn't, and he couldn't care less either way.

After we met in his office, the three of us proceeded to the 2nd floor where Archie Whitaker resides.

Dr. Langston discusses the rules and requirements of the floor as he paces beside us with his hands interlocked behind his back.

"You will need to remove your badges, weapons, jewelry, keys, and things of that matter once we reach the front desk. We keep a three-foot rule. Meaning, that under no circumstances are we to get within three feet of our patients unless for medical or assistant reasons. Do not invade their space and do not allow them to invade yours. This is a rule that is ingrained in each patient, so you shouldn't have any issue."

"Why do you need our badges?" Collins asks.

"So there's no temptation for them to reach out and touch it. A few of them would see it as a way to pull you closer. You don't want them pulling you closer."

"Touché."

As we near the end of the long white hallway, we come to a set of double doors like you'd find in a hospital.

Dr. Langston stops before pushing through them and turns to me, "Detective, I trust you have good intentions, but remember . . . this is a home for the gifted and mentally insane so keep your expectations to a reasonable level. And be sure to remember the three-foot rule. Don't forget."

I nod.

He turns and pushes through the doors. They clank and reveal a small room where a nurse sits at a check-in desk with a phone cradled to her ear while sifting through files.

"Miss Ann will take care of you. I'll be in my office should you need me."

"Uh, Dr. Langston."

"Yes?"

"I would like to speak with Hope before I leave."

"Hope Jamison?"

"Yes. I believe so."

He gazes at the salt and peppered floor tiles and mulls over my words as he gently rubs his beard.

"I'll consider it. Your interactions here will serve as a prerequisite," he says with a nod behind me, "If everything goes well in there, then we'll see."

"Thank you, Doctor."

He dips his head and crosses for the doors to the long corridor. The doors automatically open once he flashes a card to the box on the wall. I watch as he strides down the hall with his white coat trailing in the draft by his feet. The doors shut and block my view of him.

The nurse was still speaking on the phone when I turned back around. She holds up a finger with a kind smile.

Collins nudges my arm, "The three-foot rule, huh?"

I grin, "Don't worry, I'll protect you."

He scoffs and crosses to a small window overlooking the front yard. With his hands in his black slacks, I watch as he lowers his gaze to the patients below.

I remove my necklace containing my badge and bunch it up in my palm before angling to Collins.

We watch at least a dozen or more patients enjoy their chance for fresh air as they wander and mingle among the sculptures and gardens.

"Can you imagine what it must be like to live in their world?" Collins says softly, almost as if to himself.

"I'd rather not."

He turns and looks me in the eye. Captivated by his striking blue eyes, I freeze as I wait a response.

"Laurie . . . it's for that reason these people are here."

I swallow a gulp and bat my eyes for a moment, waiting for his elaboration.

In a tone just above a whisper, "They're the outcast. The misunderstood. Where's their families? It's the families failed attempt to understand and walk in their shoes that placed them here. They all must be begging for someone to understand them. To step into their world and see things the way they do. It must be a longing they all have. If we want answers from this Archie Whitaker fellow, then we have to step into his shoes and connect with him on a deeper level."

I turn and look out the window, watching as the wandering souls roam about, searching for belonging. To be wanted. To be loved. To be home.

Was I not the same? Did I not have the same longings? We all do, right?

I have more in common with these people than I would like to believe.

I hear the phone land in its cradle, "I'm sorry about that, Detectives. I assume you're here to see Mr. Whitaker, correct?"

"Yes, hi. I'm Homicide Lieutenant Laurie Daniels and this is my partner, Detective Patrick Collins."

Ann dips her head, "Nice to meet you both. Please fill these bins with any items that may serve as a weapon. And I'll need your badges too," she says as she passes us two plastic bins.

She's a small middle-aged lady with olive skin and dark hair that rest just below her ears. She wears red lipstick and a black hand band keeping the hair from her hazel eyes.

"They have many visitors?" I ask.

She shakes her head and frowns, "I'm afraid not. When they reach this point, the family has likely given up hope. If the patient is lucky enough, they may get a visit on their birthday or holidays but that usually ends after the first couple years. Then they're left here all alone. We become the only family they have left. It's a sad deal, but it is what it is. We do our best to make the most of it."

Collins sighs and asks, "Is there any chance of them ever being rehabilitated and released?"

Ann shakes her head again, "No, not much. Once they arrive here, they rarely ever leave. There have been a few over the years who've been rehabilitated, but like I say, it's rare. Most of them are beyond a cure. They're to a point where they could never live on their own. They're like children in a sense."

Collins and I pass the bins of our belongings back to her.

"Thank you. Okay, right this way."

She uses a card like Langston did, and a loud beep emits. The double doors swing open. Sudden chatter, screams, and laughter rip the air as if everyone within knew the meaning of such a beep.

We step into another long hallway, but this one is lined with rooms on each side. Most of the doors are open, though a few are shut. Patients dressed in white gowns of all ages, genders, and races stand in the hall like statutes as they watch us with curious gazes.

Some snicker with angled eyes and mischievous grins, while others stare without expression or ever blinking. One older gentleman watches us with a twitchy head as he scratches nervously upon his stubbled face, drawing red marks and welts on his cheeks. He acts much the way a meth addict does when in need of a hit.

I breathe deep and force a smile as we begin our way down the hall.

"Ann, is he okay? He's scratching his face."

She turns, "Hurman stop that! Enough!"

His fingers stop and immediately drop to his sides. He still has a quick twitch to him as his eyes dart left and right, searching, scanning, and watching.

We continue down the hall and are startled when an elderly heavy-set lady leaps from her room into the hallway, screaming and lifting her gown to show the goods.

Collins and I immediately yank our heads away as Ann lashes out at such behavior.

"Stop that! Get back in your room! Now! You know better than that Barbra. You *know* better!"

Her scathing rebuke sends big Barbra sulking back to her room, where she slams the door like a grounded teenager.

"You have your hands full," I say.

"You could say that."

A small elderly man, with white hair and a hunched back, stands at the end of the hall looking out a large glass window protected by bars. As we near, he turns and faces us. He stares for a moment before hobbling into his room.

Ann nudges her chins and says, "That was Archie there."

Hearing footsteps, I turn to see we're being followed by three individuals. A man and two women. They look to be in their sixties or seventies. They stride close behind, almost breaking the three-foot rule.

"There's the gang you have to keep an eye on there," Ann says with a cut of her eyes and grin.

One of the women giggles like a preschooler.

Ann slows to a halt just outside Archie's door and turns to face us. "How about you three introduce yourselves to our fine guests?"

"Oh-oh-oh, hi-hi, I-I I'm Will-wi-illis Fr-Frank. Pleased to m-meet-meet you," the man says stretching forth his hand. I shoot a glance to Ann. She nods.

"Hi Willis, I'm Laurie Daniels. It's nice to meet you."

"And I'm Cynthia Harden. Actress and winner of eight golden globes for my outstanding performances in three star-studded films alongside the fabulous Miss Marylyn Monroe. Have you seen my films dear?" the lady says in an elegant and glamorous tone.

I take a moment to answer, while smiling and eying the lady with caution, "Why yes, yes I have. You're a lovely actor. I enjoy your work."

She blushes and covers her face with a bony, frail hand, while smiling with what little teeth she has. Her long red hair drapes over her left shoulder.

"See Dorothy, I told you I have fans," Cynthia says with a half squeal.

Dorothy bobs her head in a slow, uninterested manner. She raises her bright blue eyes to meet mine and says with a smack of her tongue against her teeth, "What can I say, she's the ambitious one among us. Dorothy Bledsoe, pleased to meet you."

I shake her hand and introduce Collins.

"My, my, my, how handsome. Whew-we. Darling you should play the lead role in my upcoming film. We'd have to fight the ladies off with a stick. You know who you remind me of?"

I watch as Collins's face turns a different shade of red. He swallows hard and paws at his cheek.

"Gregory Peck. You sure do. My, you are just gorgeous. I could eat you with a spoon."

"Cynthia! Mind your manners," Dorothy blurts with a gasp.

"Well it's true. Just look at him."

Collins clears his throat and starts to say something.

"We-well-well what abo-about the misses? Sh-she-she's quite the si-si-site to behold is-isn't she?" says Willis as he tosses his hands up in front of him while looking to Dorothy and Cynthia. He steals glances at me out the corner of his eye and grins.

"Yes, she sure is. She's strikingly beautiful with a natural beauty that can be hard to find. You would make a fine actress my dear," Cynthia smiles.

"Okay, well if you will excuse us, these fine people have business to tend to," says Ann.

"Business? What do you do?" asks Dorothy.

I look to Ann. She bites her lip and raises a brow.

"We're detectives. We're here to ask Archie a few questions about the church he used to pastor."

Cynthia bounds up and down on her toes, clutches her hands to her mouth, and squeals with excitement.

Willis grabs at his ears, squinting and wagging his head in rapid fashion.

Ann shushes Cynthia. Willis eases his wince.

Dorothy just stands there staring at us and eying us up and down as if sizing us up.

"Detectives, huh?" she asks.

I nod with tight lips as I turn from her and look to Ann who's assisting Willis.

"You'll never catch him."

I shot my head back to her.

"Catch who?"

She stares at me for the longest time. Her pupils change in size, and her eyes shift from hazel to green.

Her breath begins to quicken as she snaps her head side to side. Her eyes dart about at a frantic pace.

"Who are you? Who are you?" she begins to scream as she scratches and claws at her head.

It's amazing how fast her demeanor has changed. She's like a totally different person.

Ann looks to Dorothy and pats down a palm at her, "Shh sh . . . it's okay Delores. Go to your room now. I'll be right there. Everything's okay. Go on honey, I'll be right there. Omora! I need you."

Nurse Omora steps out from one of the rooms near the entrance and heads our way. Taking Dorothy by the arm she gently leads her to a room.

Still attending to Willis Frank, Ann looks at me and apologizes.

"Delores? I thought her name was Dorothy?" I ask.

Ann nods, "Yes, but Dorothy is only one of her many personalities. She currently has seven that we know of."

"Seven?" Collins says in a lowered tone.

"Seven."

I turn to the door frame leading to Archie Whitaker's room, wondering what I was about to witness.

"You can go on in. He's expecting you."

# 30

**WITH EVERYTHING GOING** as planned, Gary Wade Duncan accomplished his work in record time. It was in the rushing to beat the officers to Laurie's house that he received his biggest thrill. He used Weatherby's hair to make a wig like he has from all the other victims. The floral scent of lavender filled the cab of the car. Weatherby had good taste when it came to shampoo. Lavender is always a good choice. He spruced up a few strands along his forehead and put on a pair of glasses he found in Weatherby's glove compartment. He even scrunched lower in the seat to appear more feminine. His efforts aided his disguise in case he was to pass any of her colleagues along the roadway. They would have likely though it was Agent Weatherby and even tossed up a few fingers in a passing greeting.

Having arrived at his destination and just begun his work, he checks the GPS bug which he planted on the patrol car. He has ten minutes before the officers will arrive to set up surveillance. Which gives him enough time to do the deed and hit the road without being seen.

He continues to work as minute's tick by in rapid cessation, eating away his time to flee. He checks his phone. The officers are 3.4 miles away, which gives him approximately five minutes if they're travelling 45 miles an hour. He can be finished within the next two if he hurries.

C'mon-c'mon.

He finishes his work and scurries out of the dark like a cicada emerging from its nest beneath the soil. He makes it to the light and dusts himself free of the stale earth. He sneezes into the crevice of his elbow for the third time since having begun his work. With his knees damp and dirty, he stands and angles from the back side of the house. He runs in a crouch and steals glances over his shoulders. He rushes to the black Tahoe and climbs in. He turns the ignition. His black leather gloves are gritty with fresh soil. He pulls away a cobweb which had stretched over his forehead and lowers the window to toss it out. He shifts gears, backs away, and heads for the road. He takes a right to avoid passing the old man's house. He adjusts the long brown hair and puts on a wool beanie he found in the center console. He slouches in the seat again, being sure to mimic where he imagined the late Agent Weatherby would've sat.

Then the thought hits him like a ram's head to the gut.

His mask.

He'd left it. What an idiot. His mind was so busy on planting the body that he'd forgotten about the mask. He grimaces and bangs the heel of his palm upon the wheel. He grinds his teeth and utters curses. God forgive him.

He takes a deep breath and allows his nerves to settle. Besides, even if they did find the mask, it's not like they'd ever find him. They would never link him to the hair or skin cells found in it. He needn't worry. Let them find it. It'd just give them something to occupy their useless time with. Besides, no one can track the reaper.

He feels his carotid artery pump hard along his neck as his heart knocks against his ribs. Adrenaline and dopamine rifle through his body.

The rush. The thrill.

He breathes deep and takes it all in, basking in it. He's sure to enjoy every last moment before the guilt sets in.

Had he deviated from God's plan? Maybe.

Would God understand?

Of course.

He always does.

# 31

**I GIVE A SOFT KNUCKLE** rap to Archie's door which is cracked half-way. I wonder if he will remember me. He has his back to us as he stands with a slouch while gazing out his window. Six black iron bars stand erect within the frame, each about six inches apart.

I watch as he cranes his head over his left shoulder. It takes him a full three seconds to look at us with both eyes.

His face is decorated with thick white brows and day's old stubble. Harsh lines cut into his skin around the eyes and mouth as all his years of living are packed tightly within the wrinkles snaking across his sagging flesh. He's dressed in white pants and a baggy white shirt that looks a size or two too big. His head is tilted to one side like a crow, and his eyes are glassy with glaucoma. A tremble controls his whole body as if he has Parkinson's. Keeping his tilted head in place, he turns his body to face us. A slow grin stretches across his lips.

"Hello. Archie Whitaker?"

He dips his head amid the array of tremors.

"I'm Laurie Daniels . . . this is Patrick Collins."

I search his eyes to see if he has any recollection of my name.

"Hello. Pleasure to meet you." His voice is horse as if he has gravel stuck in his throat. He doesn't remember me.

Since he doesn't offer his hand, a simple nod and smile will have to suffice. The three-foot rule, remember?

I notice his eyes are fixed on the gap between me and Collins.

I turn to see what holds his attention, but the hall behind us is empty. Yet, he still stares as if someone is there. I feel gooseflesh begin to work its way down my neck and arms.

"And you are?" Archie's voice crackles.

I turn back to Archie.

He's still staring into the empty hallway. He nods his head and says, "Pleasure to meet you, Bill."

I look to Collins. His face is blank as he raises his brows and swallows.

Footsteps patter down the hall toward us.

"Everything okay, Archie?" Ann asks as she steps into the room with us.

Archie eases himself down upon the bed. The springs squeak as he lets himself drop onto it from a safe distance. Once settled he looks to Nurse Ann and dips his chin.

I nudge her and ask about this Bill fellow.

She lifts the corner of her lip and sighs.

"Archie . . . it's only us three in here. There's no Bill. Just Laurie, Patrick, and I. Okay?"

He lifts his head, looks out into the hall, squints his eyes, takes a long breath, and rubs his eye lids with a trembling hand.

I look to Ann for an explanation. In a low tone I offer, "Schizophrenia?"

She nods, "He suffers with psychosis and delusions as well."

"I see."

"Okay, I'll let you return to your visit. If you need anything, Omora and Pam will be in the hallway."

"Thank you, Ann."

She smiles and pulls the door shut behind her as she steps out.

To lessen the intimidation factor by standing while Archie sat, I lower myself onto a small sofa against the wall. I pat next to me and motion for Collins. He lowers himself next me and retrieves his notepad.

Archie has his hands atop his bony knees as he stares at the floor.

"Nice view," I offer.

Archie snickers and looks to the glass, "Yeah, it can be. At least I have one I guess," looking to us, "I'm sorry you had to see all that coming in. I know how unsettling it can be. I had nightmares for the first few months upon arrival. The human mind can become a scary thing when left up for grabs."

He breathes deep.

"The sad part is, today's a good day."

Collins shifts his weight and places his right ankle atop his left knee, "Today's a good day?"

"Yes sir, you wouldn't want to be here on any other," his eyes linger to the end of the couch next to Collins.

"You're treated well though, right?" I venture.

His eyes are still locked to the empty spot on the couch.

Collins follows Archie's eyes and rubs his hand across the cloth material of the vacant spot.

Archie notices and diverts his eyes to meet mine. He clears his throat, "Oh yes. Of course. Three meals a day, two hours of outside activity, a comfy bed," he gestures a trembling hand toward the window, "A nice view. Though I wish the circumstance were different . . ." shifting his gaze back to me, "I have no complaints. So far." He ends with a chuckle.

"So far. After what, thirty or so years?"

"Something like that."

A moment of awkward silence rises among us as I contemplate my next move.

"Listen . . ." he leans to the edge of his bed and interlocks his fingers between his knees, "I don't want to waste any more of your time. I know you're both detectives and I know you have cases to solve. So, what really brings you here? What do you want to know?"

His bluntness catches me off guard.

Collins shifts his weight again and readies himself with the pad and pen.

"Okay, well I'll be frank with you Mr. Whitaker. We're investigating another Morty case."

He straightens his spine and pulls a hand to his mouth. His brows furrow. He lowers his head and rubs his forehead.

"Yeah. He's back."

With a twisted face, he looks up at me, "I know. God have mercy. How long has it been since he went dark?"

"Four years. Thirteen before that."

He clinches his eyes and lowers his head again.

"He's become fearless, Archie. He's taunting me by leaving notes, and voice recordings like he has in the past, but these are more brazen. And there's something else."

Raising his vision, "What?"

"Cicadas. He's infatuated with them."

"You're positive it's cicadas?"

I nod.

He scratches the back of his head and looks out the window. His breath still ebbing and flowing through his mouth.

"Archie . . . I need to know what really happened. I need to know why you're here."

Sighing out a deep breath, "I did what I had to do to protect the kid. If I hadn't hid him at the church, the demons would have gotten him. It was the only way to protect him. I knew they wouldn't enter the church, so I hid him in the basement. I knew his parents weren't living right and figured they be the next to go. Richie was such a fine boy, I couldn't allow some demon possessed man to take him, like he had all the others. Then once I started seeing them . . . I had no choice."

"Seeing them?"

"Yeah, I'd see them emit from the clouds, swooping down with a large scythe, flapping their wings before disappearing into the woods. Then they started harassing me as I slept. I'd wake up in the middle of the night to the awful feeling of being watched. The whole room would be filled with the foul odor of urine and I'd have to start praying to make them leave. Frances noticed them too."

Collins scribbles on the notepad.

"I've always wondered if it was someone within the church. You see, I began having my doubts about the whole snake handling mess. But when a church has been practicing a certain doctrine for so long, it's hard to get them off the stuff. It's like a drug. They become addicted to it, and if you try and take it from them they'll damn you to hell and call you a heretic. I even wondered if a few of them were delving into some sort of witchcraft. It wasn't long after I started revoking my beliefs in snake handling that I began having strange sudden ailments, almost to the point of vomit. And the lights and power at my house began to flicker constantly. I wondered then, if some of the ones I'd upset weren't casting a spell or curse on me."

His words cause my spine to tingle as a douse of ice water trails up it. I did the same thing at the McCrae's last night. Then I had that crazy dream with the snakes and cicadas, and the man in black. Is someone doing the same to me? Has someone cursed me?

"Sam Wicker seems to be a good man. He's visited me a few times over the years, asking my advice about this and that. I know they still practice snake handling despite my warnings. I now believe that all it does is open a door to the other side which you'll wish you never opened. I believe that's why I have this sickness. I think something got a hold of me and ruined my mind."

He glances again to the empty spot on the couch, "You have any idea how terrible it is to question the reality of everyone you meet? I mean you two could just be a figment of my imagination and I'd never know. Heck, I could be living in some abandoned hospital for all I know and all this . . ." he sweeps his arms about the room, "Could just be a grand delusion. I could be sitting right here speaking to an empty couch and I'd never know the difference."

"I'm sorry, Archie, but I can assure you we're real. Us. The nurses. Cynthia. Dorothy. Willis. And all the others. We're real. Feel." I stretch forth my hand slowly.

He stares at it for a long moment, exchanging glances between it and my eyes.

I nod, "Go on, it's okay."

He swallows hard and reaches out with his sun spotted hand as it trembles and hangs within the air between us. He brushes his fingers across the top of my hand. His bottom lip begins to quiver as tears well in his eyes. "Thank you." He pulls back and wipes his eyes with the sleeve of his shirt. "I want to help. I want to do whatever I can to put a stop to all of this."

His voice is strained like his eyes.

"Thank you, Mr. Whitaker. That's why we're here. I need the details. Anything you can remember."

"Well . . . at first I thought it was the demons that were doing all this. I thought they were murdering the parents and taking the children. I know how much they hate God, I know how much God loves children, so I figured the demons best way to hurt God would be to hurt his children. But then I started thinking maybe it was a man or a group of people doing those things as they're directed by the demons. Governed by the devil, you know?"

"So, you believed it was someone within your church who may have been practicing in the occult while under the pretense of orthodox religion?" Collins asks.

"Exactly. They only used the church as a cover up."

"Do you believe Freewill Holiness is responsible for the killings?" I ask.

"Whether its current members or former, I think the roots of the matter is tied to the church. If I were you, I'd spend a lot of my time there. I'm not saying Wicker's a bad man. It might not be him. The whole congregation may be innocent, yet oblivious to a murderer within their church. I think Morty is connected to the church somehow. My gut just tells me that the truth lurks beyond those doors of Freewill Holiness."

"Why would they want the kids?" Collins asks.

Archie shrugs, "I couldn't say. That's the thing that always stumps me. Why anyone would do such a thing was beyond me. That's why I finally took matters into my own hands. You have any idea how many nasty letters I've gotten over the years? I don't even bother reading them anymore."

A crow scurries by the window and pulls our attention.

"Does the name Gary Wade Duncan sound familiar to you?" I ask with a curious brow.

He wags his head and turns to face me. "No."

"Other than *Mortis*, which is the name he leaves at the scenes, Gary Wade Duncan is the only name we have." I look to the door, thinking. "What's with all the scripture references? The evil angels, the scythe swinging from heaven to harvest the earth? He's claiming to be the Angel of Death. What do you make of that?"

Archie takes a swallow. "That's old testament stuff. The evil angels. They were sent by God to carry out His wrath. With the death of Jesus there is no more wrath. Jesus took care of that on Calvary. The scythe I believe you're referring to is from Revelation, in which it mentions the Son of Man seated in the clouds who is given the sickle to harvest the earth. The great sifting of wheat, separating the good from the bad, the tares from the wheat and so forth."

He gets my attention at the mention of sifting wheat.

"So, the reference in Revelation is speaking of the rapture?" I ask.

"I think so. I'm no expert, but I've read enough that I like to think I have a fair understanding of scripture. If you read the entire passage in context, it's not nearly as frightening or treacherous as one may first believe. It's actually speaking of the grace of God, in a sense that after all these years, He's still waiting for people to turn to Him before he finally has taken all He can and has no choice but to harvest the earth. That's when He'll come to restore peace and vanquish evil for all of eternity.

"It's a glimpse into how patient God really is. He's been waiting all these years, watching in heartache as us finite humans fight and devour one another. He has held out hope, giving us all an equal opportunity to turn from the wickedness we so often fall victims to, and turn to the very Creator of all that's good in the earth that we too often take for granted."

"That's one way to look at it," I say.

"It's the only way I know how."

I scratch my scalp as Collins jots something down.

Archie coughs and then asks, "Have you spoken with Frances or Hal?"

"No, we haven't. Should we?"

"I'd like it if you did. I'm sure she could use the company. Do you think you could give her something for me?"

"Sure, what is it?"

He stands from the squeaky bed and crouches to open the drawer to his nightstand.

Collins and I lean to the edge of our seat.

"She'll know the significance," Archie says as he hands me a paper origami of a white swan.

I hold it gently as if it could shatter with the wrong touch. His eyes sparkle as he watches it rest in my palms.

"Our first date was at Swan Lake. That's also the place I proposed . . ." his voice trails off.

"I'll be glad to pass it along to Mrs. Whitaker. It'd be my pleasure."

"Thank you."

He sighs and looks out the window into a free but distant world.

"Who's Hal?" Collins asks.

Archie snickers at the thought as he sniffles and dries his face.

"Hal Resnick. An old pal of mine. He was my assistant back in the day. He took over after everything happened. He held down the fort for twenty some years, before turning it over to Sam Wicker. I think it'd do you both some good to speak with him too. You'll just have to mind all of his cats. Always was an animal lover. He's a good soul though. Tell him old Archie said hello, will ya?"

"Does he go to Freewill Holiness?"

"No, he quit once Wicker took the church back into snake handling. He was on my side with all of that, so as soon as Wicker picked it back up, Hal hit the road. No hard feelings or nothing like that, they just agreed to disagree."

"I see. You know where he lives?"

"He should still be off Oak Street in Yarmouth. He's got a small place on a big plot of land that his daddy left him."

"What about your wife? Is she still at Morningside?" I question.

"The last letter I got was from this Valentine's and that's where she was at. I haven't got her to respond to any of my letters since and no one will tell me anything. So, she may have been moved I don't know."

"Did you have any children?"

I could sense my question picked at a scab. He grimaces and answers, "We had a daughter once. She passed a month before her nineteenth birthday. Her name was Cindy."

"I'm sorry."

He nods and takes a deep swallow before turning his eyes back to the window.

"I lost my mother during my sophomore year of college. She couldn't handle my sister's disappearance. She took her own life."

"Oh sweetie, that's a terrible thing to go through. I'm so sorry."

Collins pats my hand as I do my best to hold back the emotion growing in my gut, attempting to travel to my eyes.

"Well, looks like we have something in common after all," Archie says with a faint grin.

"Yeah, we all do," I say as I squeeze Collins's hand.

We go on to spend another hour with Archie as we alternate between talking about life, the cases, and his past at Freewill Holiness. I take the swan origami, cradle it gently in my palms, and promise Archie that I'll see it makes it to the rightful owner. We say our goodbyes and spend a few minutes speaking with Cynthia and Willis in the hallway. Once we finish, we make our way to Dr. Langston's office to see if we can speak with Hope Jamison before we leave.

# 32

Friday
October 4th, 2019
12:08 pm

AGENT FRANK SWANSON leaves Portland Museum of the Natural World after having gathered the info he needed from Dr. Roestein on the cicada bug. The professor enjoyed his time as he waxed poetic on the details of the life and habits of the creature. He even showed Swanson numerous videos on YouTube explaining the mystery of the creature's emergence and how it sheds its skin. Swanson felt his own skin crawl at the thought of the killer's fascination with the sophisticated insect. Swanson decided it would be best to explain to Laurie what he'd learned, in person. It's too much to go over on the phone. He'll wait until the briefing later this evening to fill her in.

He's tried reaching Agent Weatherby, but it keeps going to voicemail. She must still be busy at the McCrae's. Perhaps she's conducting a walk through before sealing the place up again.

He continued to try and reach her as he travele north along I-95, heading for the McCrae's.

† † † † † † † † † †

**TUCKED DEEP WITHIN A THICK CANOPY** of woods somewhere outside of Gray, Gary Wade Duncan empties out the remnants of a red gas container onto the black Tahoe. He grins at the anticipation of the coming blaze as his mind travels back to the horde of childhood memories of his first attempts at fire starting. Gas, fire, and Gary Wade Duncan have always been a dynamic trio, and he has no plans for any changes.

He tosses the empty gas container to the side and retrieves a box of matches from his pocket. He rakes one across the box and drinks in the electrifying sound of the black powder igniting to mix with the Carbon Dioxide, Oxygen, and Nitrogen. His eyes glisten as orange light dances at his fingertips. It's only a small flame, yet it's capable of mass destruction when fed the right ingredients and given the right environment. His eyes widen as the little flame licks skyward. He imagines what it must look like in the reflection of his glassy and dark retinas.

He closes his eyes and breathes deep, sucking in the glorious aroma of sulfur dioxide. His muscles tremble as the euphoric rush spreads across his body. The grin stretches his lips wide and in a slow, meticulous motion, he flicks the little stick of flame onto the hood of the Tahoe. It's engulfed by flames with a quick *whoosh* sound.

Gary Wade Duncan steps back while being pushed away by the hissing flame and scorching heat. He strides backwards with his eyes locked onto the destruction before him. Once at a safe distance, he squats to the ground and gazes at the sight, basking in the moment. He picks at small sticks and stones and tosses them into the flame. A few stones ping off the hood. When that no longer satisfies him, he begins to grab at dried leaves before crunching and spreading their particles into the wind.

The flames dance higher as they rake the branches of the trees above, darkening their leaves. The embers continue to rise to the heavens.

Gary Wade Duncan looks up. He knows God understands.

He always does. God is well pleased, and he'd be even more pleased when Sarah finds a home.

Then his work with the McCrae's will be complete.

Even still, there is work to be done.

# 33

ONCE INSIDE DR. LANGSTON'S office, he informed us from his black leather and gold studded chair as he drew on a Cuban cigar, that Hope Jamison would be available for us to interview. However, we'd have to speak outside, so she felt less enclosed and cornered. Which is understandable.

Langston disposes of his cigar and ushers us from his office. We stand in the hallway now. "I would advise you not to get your hopes up. Hope is a very shy girl who comes from a treacherous past. She's been broken more than you could imagine and is still enormously fragile. Be careful with your words and tone or else she'll withdraw and never speak to you again. She is strong and wiser beyond her years, yet she retains the emotional stability of a child. She's an enigma we've yet to solve. However, if you tread lightly, perhaps you'll have some success."

With that he turns and begins to walk away. As our footsteps thud and echo down the empty corridor, I say behind him, "Thank you, Dr. Langston. We have nothing but good intentions."

He turns and dips his head, "I know Detective. I admire you for what you do."

We reach the end of the hall, and a white door with a small square window stands before us. Dr. Langston swipes the card reader with his ID. It emits a loud buzz.

I look up and over my right shoulder to see another black bubbled camera watching our every move.

Langston pushes through the door, allowing light to flood in. The sound of chatter and laughter fills the air, followed by a few screams from the patients and scathing rebukes from the nurses.

Dr. Langston stands in the door frame and holds the door open for us with an outstretched arm.

"I wish you the best with the investigation. My door is always open. A nurse will see you out once you're finished with Miss Jamison. Be careful Detective. Tread lightly."

Collins gives a quick two finger salute as I say, "Thank you, Doctor. I'll be in touch."

He smiles and shuts the door, latching it back into place.

Here we stand before a sea of hovering fog and gifted patients tending to their gardens among the eerie glares of the life-like sculptures.

I scan the yard, looking for Hope Jamison. I look over at least a half dozen patients before finding her. She is squatted behind a large Davidian type stone statue which overlooks a flower garden full of yellow daisy's, purple Virginia spiderworts, and roses.

"C'mon. That's her over there by the statue," I turn to Collins and point my chin.

We angle over and pass a few gawking patients along the way. They either giggled and hid their mouth or eyed us like they could murder us with a toothpick. Either way, I smiled and nodded at each of them.

Reaching the garden, Hope busies herself with picking weeds as she's still squatted on her calves. She never once raises her head to acknowledge our presence as our shadows pour over her.

I attempt to break the ice by offering a compliment, "Hello. It's a beautiful garden you have here. Are those Virginia spiderworts? They're gorgeous."

Nothing. She continues to fiddle with the weeds.

"I love the array of colors you have here. Quite the collection. You know purple represents wisdom, peace, and creativity among other virtues, right?"

Finally Hope raises her head. I can see her eyes are leery of my prodding as she searches hard for any sign of deceit. I can't blame her.

I give her a gentle nod and smile.

"Everyone thinks yellow only stands for happiness, but did you know it is also symbolic for enlightenment, intellect, and remembrance?"

Her lips part for the first time and her voice comes out with an awkward pitch as if from the lack of use. "What about white and red?"

I smile and say, "White can represent a number of things. Purity, cleanliness, safety, innocence, and in most religions it is considered to be connected to the light."

"The light?"

"You know . . . a higher being I guess."

She bobs her head and shifts her eyes to a red rose. "And red?"

"Red is one of the most emotionally intense colors we have as it can mean a lot of things too. Mostly though, desire, love, energy, and determination."

I skip the part about it having its connection to war and danger.

"And who are you? Doctors? Let me guess you have a new kind of medicine you want to shove down my throat? Am I Right?"

I wrinkle my face with a grin. "Not quite. I do have a background in psychology, but I'm a detective. We both are." I say as I tilt my head to Collins standing next to me.

One cannot deny the beauty this girl has. Though she'd likely argue and dismiss my observation, she'd make for a refreshing sight to the eyes of any man.

My heart pounds the more I observe her. It's as if I'm gazing upon my sister. She even has the same curvature to her nose that me and her share. My grandpa used to say we got it from our great grandmother who was part Cherokee. This is exactly how I would imagine Amy to look as an adult. She also has a striking similarity to the girl in my vision last night, only much older.

Feeling my silent glare, Hope cranes her head. She clutches a lump of weeds in her right hand, "Why do you have interest in me? What could I possibly offer? I'm just a mental handicap. We all are." She scans the field of gown covered patients and shakes her head in gentle sways.

"No. That's not true. You're gifted."

She sighs, tightens her lips, and returns to plucking weeds.

"Did you ever know a girl by the name of Amy Daniels?" I zero my focus onto her reaction. Any shift in mannerism, fidgeting, swallowing, a pumping carotid artery, all the things which my Ph. D and training with the police academy has taught me to look for when digging for the truth.

Hope shifts her position, rotates her knees slightly to the left as she continues to pick weeds. Her skin tone slowly turns a faint shade of red, beginning at her neck and swimming to her face. She avoids eye contact and avoids saying another word. I'd crossed the line, just as Dr. Langston had warned me. I'd backed her into a corner, and she retreated into her shell.

I squat on my calves to reach eye level. In a soft, non-threatening tone I say, "You can tell me anything. I want you to know that. If there is something you need to say, I'll listen."

Collins squats next to me. "It's okay. If you're not comfortable telling us here, we can move somewhere else," he offers gently.

I watch as Hope stops her weeding, shuts her eyes, and pulls in two long, deep breaths. The muscles in her jaw go taut.

I lean back, anticipating her to lash out.

She opens her hazel, almond shaped eyes with the speed of a sunrise, and peers deep into my soul. Her vision has a distant look to it as her breath is held captive behind her cheeks.

She sighs out her breath and in a slow, mechanical like fashion begins to wag her head.

Feeling a knot growing in my throat, I mutter out, "Amy?"

With confusion and horror swimming about her eyes, tears slowly begin to well. She shakes her head in rapid successions. Her shoulders jerk side to side as she wraps herself in a tight hug and begins to rock to and fro.

My heart breaks as the dam holding an ocean of lifetime emotion begins to crack. With a trembling hand, I reach out to touch her. Just to pat the arm of my sister.

You would have thought I was trying to pet an injured cat. She jolts back, hisses and spits like a mad kitten. She lands on her haunches and scurries across the ground, kicking her feet and clawing with her hands to propel her backwards. Her eyes are wild as saliva bumbles between her lips and emits like popcorn.

My dam brakes. Tears sting my eyes. All these years have passed and here she was. No visitor. No family. All alone. Is this really my sister? It has to be, right?

Hearing the scuffle, two nurses spring into action as a herd of on looking patients begin to cheer and gawk at the excitement.

I stand and turn away with a hand to my mouth. My lips quiver, and so does my heart and soul.

The nurses rush to Hope's side and hook their hands under her arms to lift her to her feet. It's then that I see one retrieve a syringe filled to full capacity of a milky like fluid.

"No. Don't do that!"

As the words leave my lips, I watch in horror at the sight of the dagger like needle plunge into her neck.

Collins grabs me and holds me in his arms.

I watch as the beautiful young woman, who I now believe to be my sister, goes from a feral human to a drugged zombie. She slumps to the earth as gravity pulls her into its grip.

A harsh breeze sweeps in and brushes past us.

I watch as the nurses drag her off.

Dead leaves skitter across the paved walkway behind the nurses clacking heels.

I turn and bury my face into Collins's chest.

The chatter and gawking among the patients continue.

A firecracker of pain rips through my brain just behind my left eye. My head begins to sink hard into a migraine. The bitter taste of bile fills my mouth, snaking its way around my teeth and gums.

That's my sister. I know it is. It has to be.

# 34

**SEEING THE GIRL**, who I believed to be my sister, drugged and dragged away into what the nurses call the "holding room," my anguish was quickly overridden by a fire that began to work its way across my body. The muscles in my jaw tightened, and I felt the weight of my burning anger boiling in my chest.

I march back into the home and pound my way to Langston's office. My mind races, and my heart thumps hard as the blood grows hotter by the second. Collins is right on my heels as he tries to calm me, but his voice sounds so distant.

I force my way past a nurse at the check-in desk. I hear her clopping in her heels upon the tile floor as she rushes after me.

"Ma'am you can't go back there. Stop."

Reaching us, "Ma'am you can't go back there! Who are you?"

I shove my badge to her face and say through gritted teeth, "I'm Lieutenant Daniels with Portland Homicide. I need to speak to Dr. Langston. Now."

The blonde headed nurse swallows hard and with big eyes says, "Uh-um-uh-but—"

A door opens at the end of the hall. The sound of it echoes down the corridor through the thin air.

My teeth are clinched, and I feel my hot breath pouring in and out through my nostrils.

It's Dr. Langston.

I march onward with angled eyes and a tight jaw.

Collins says, "Laurie, be careful now. You need to think this throu—"

"I've got it. Stay out of this."

We meet in the center of the hall, stopping two paces away. Langston, obviously seeing my anger, "Why, what has stirred such a ruckus? I heard all of the commotion."

"I want a copy of every file you have on Hope Jamison, and I'm not leaving until I have them in hand. Understood?"

"Good heavens. What seems to be the problem?"

"If you are not willing to offer up the files, then I'll attain a search warrant in which case we will turn this place upside down to see what shakes out. You wouldn't want that to happen, now would you?"

"Miss Daniels. Please, slow down," Langston pleads with outstretched hands.

"It's Lieutenant Daniels to you. You either hand over the files, or I'll get them myself. Otherwise, an investigation will ensue."

His whole demeanor shifts. A blank, hardened look darkens his face, casting a long shadow across his smooth skin. Even his voice takes to a deeper octave, "What are you suggesting?"

"You know what I'm suggesting. Judging by what I've witness so far, I could likely have you strung in the courtyard by noon tomorrow. We can do this the easy way or the hard way. It's your choice."

Dr. Langston drops his head, removes his glasses, and drags for sand. His breath comes in thick huffs as his face begins to turn two shades of red.

I look to Collins, then check the nurse standing between us and back a few steps. I sidestep to create distance from any would be needle from her.

Collins notices and wrinkles a brow.

I shift my eye to the lady as she looks to Dr. Langston with her face twisted in a strange grimace.

He moves two steps to his left.

Every sense in my body is on full alert as I anticipate an attack or ambush. My eyes dart this way and that as I gently pull my right hand to my hip to close the distance for my Judge.

Heart knocking. Blood pulsing.

I want answers.

Dr. Langston cleans his glasses with the tail of his white coat, places them back on to the tip of his nose and says, "I'll need to speak with you in my office. There's a lot I should tell you."

I swallow. "Okay, now we're getting somewhere."

# 35

WE ENTER LANGSTON'S office. He stands by the door and waits for us to enter. I toss my chin toward his chair. He steps back and gives us a clear lane. I scan the room for any others. It's just us three. I sit in the chair across the desk from Dr. Langston. Collins sits next to me.

"If it's okay with you Doctor, I'd like to have this conversation recorded. Would you be opposed to that?"

He marinates my words and leans back with his hands interlocked at his navel.

"No, I suppose that'll be just fine."

"Good. In that case, I'll begin recording."

I pull my phone from my pocket, thumb to my voice recorder app and press the red button.

"Lieutenant Daniels present with Detective Collins and Dr. William Langston from the Cumberland Behavioral Health Center for the Gifted. Friday the fourth of October . . . *12:39* pm. You may begin Doctor."

He stares at me for the longest moment as if unsure whether he should proceed.

I tilt my head and bite my lip.

He huffs out a breath and leans to the edge of his seat, eying the phone in my lap before locking eyes with me.

"Lieutenant Daniels . . . what I am about to say must not under any circumstances be released to the public. I want this conversation to remain within this room and within whichever room the recorded audio is replayed. Understood?"

"That's a reasonable request, and I'll do my best to be sure that's the case."

He coats his dry lips with a smooth tongue, nods and says, "Thank you."

"Well then, what is it you need to tell me?"

"Hope Jamison is not your sister. I am well aware of the resemblance, but—"

"And how is that? How do you know what my sister looked like?"

"Lieutenant Daniels, everyone in Portland who has lived here for more than a decade, knows of your history or has at least heard of the rumors. With a quick search of the web, you are bound to come across numerous articles on your sister's disappearance."

I cross my legs and fold the back of my right hand beneath my elbow. My left hand is cradled to my chin.

"Hope Jamison arrived from an orphanage in Virginia shortly after her sixteenth birthday. Two months prior to her arrival we were dealing with the horrific death of Maria Santorum."

"The patient who escaped and leapt from the cliffs. Where were you at that time? Because I was the lead investigator, and I do not recall having met you prior to today."

"That's because I was in Liverpool undergoing my third round of chemo. I would spend ten months on sabbatical that year," he says with his eyes rising to the ceiling. His face twist as if he'd just bit into a molded batch of fish and chips. Bad memories I guess. Whether from the cancer or the death of Santorum, I can't say.

Langston sucks in a room full of air and lowers his gaze to the table where he adjusts a few of his knick knacks: A snow globe with Big Ben in the center, and an old feather ended ink pen that Shakespeare would've enjoyed. "Miss Jamison was deemed unfit for the orphanage due to her violent outburst and extreme delusions. Shortly after her arrival, our doctors quickly diagnosed her with severe forms of schizophrenia, bipolarism, and psychosis delusions. Hope Jamison was in a very ill and vulnerable state when she arrived. A year after her arrival the orphanage from which she came was convicted of several misconduct and sexual assault charges. The agency permanently closed within the following weeks." Langston raises his vision and scratches a spot above his right eyebrow which is so thick it looks like a bird could nest in it. "It was around this time that Miss Jamison began to not only speak of her time at the orphanage, but of her time before it."

"I'm listening."

"She told myself and Doctor Montgomery of how she'd been taken from her home at an early age, late in the night by a man dressed in black with a black hood."

My heart sinks at his words.

Langston continues in a slow, methodical tone. "Jamison claims the man held her with numerous other children in a dark basement. Over a few months span as she guessed, he would come and take the children one by one, until it was just her and another girl named . . . Amy."

I gasp.

My head spins and my entire body begins to tremble as I hang onto Langston's every word. I place my elbows to my knees and cover my mouth. Tears begin to form as the familiar sting pierces my eyes. I can feel my breath hitting my palms.

"Jamison says the two were held captive in the basement for a number of weeks. During which time they became as close as sisters. They relied on each other and genuinely cared for one another. Amy was eventually taken just as the others, leaving Hope all alone. Until one day the man came to her and told her he'd found her a home. He threatened her by saying that he'd kill her if she did anything stupid. She says it was later that day when a man and woman came and took her from the basement. Together they boarded a plane to the orphanage in Virginia."

I form a teepee with my hands. Collins places a gentle hand on my back.

"What orphanage is this? Please tell me you've checked into it?"

"Saint Ann's of Alexandria. We have. Yes." Langston shakes his head. "There's no record of any girl by the name of Amy or of the description given by Hope. Now, here is the reason I have withheld this information and the reason I intend for this to remain between us," he says with a gentle wave of his hand.

"Go on." Collins says while doing circular motions on my back.

"Not long after Hope was transported here, I began receiving phone calls from a restricted number. The voice was very odd and . . . quite disturbing. As if they were using some sort of voice contortion device or what have you. They knew we had Miss Jamison and threatened if anything she said were to escape our walls, they would wait until the patients were asleep, chain the doors shut, and set the home ablaze."

"My goodness," I say straightening in my chair.

"The individual threatened myself, my family, along with the nurses and their families as well. They claimed if the police were to learn of the call or of Hope's stories, it would be within a day that the home would be set to flame. This is the first time anyone besides myself and the remaining nurses from that day has learned of such threats. So, I beg you, please keep our conversation confidential. Lives may very well be at stake here."

I don't answer. I can't answer.

I turn to the side and give my face a good rubbing.

I rake over his words, think of what Archie Whitaker said, and relive my dream from the night before.

Where is the truth? What do I believe? Who do I believe?

A long, guttural howl full of anguish creeps through the room. I hear a nurse clack down the hallway in a rush.

Voices. Laughter. More screaming.

I look to my phone as it buzzes in my lap.

It's Agent Swanson.

I sniffle and gather myself enough to answer.

"This is Daniels."

"Laurie, have you seen Kim?" his voice is quick and tight.

"No. Why?"

"No one has spoken with her since she was at the McCrae's earlier. We've been trying to call but goes straight to voicemail. I'm getting worried."

"Have you tracked her vehicle?"

"Yeah, but there's no data. The bug was either disactivated or destroyed. I've spoken with everyone at the station and field office. No one has heard anything. Williams and Ferrell were the last to see her and said they passed her a few minutes from your place as they went over to set up surveillance."

"Gosh, not now."

"Do what?"

"Nothing. I'm kind of tied up here at the Ottawa House. I mean Cumberland Behavioral. I have some leads I'm working on. I will try to be at the station within an hour. Call me if anything changes."

"I will."

I hang up and turn to Collins.

"What is it?" he asks.

"Agent Weatherby is missing."

"What?"

I look to Dr. Langston. "The files, Doctor."

"My goodness. Of course."

# 36

**WITH THE FILES IN HAND,** Collins and I walked out of the asylum and took the taxi back to the port where we loaded onto the ferry. The ride to the mainland was a little less crowded as it was mostly locals mingled among a few tourists. The fog was still low and heavy as the gulls squawked overhead, begging for a crumb.

We eased into the marina, unloaded and headed for the parking lot. I was too distraught to drive, so Collins did the honor. My mind was too foggy. With the hope of having found my sister now crushed, along with the added pressure of tracking down a serial killer who knows my name, knows where I live, and has possibly taken a FBI agent, all combined to give me a drumming headache and gut churning case of nausea.

With my right hand cradled to my forehead and my elbow propped along the window's ledge, I drifted into a daze.

Collins notices my state and drives along in silence, allowing me to think.

I have a puzzle with a million different pieces, but no picture to go by. Everything is essentially guesswork by this point.

Where does Hope Jamison and this orphanage fit into all this? How does Cumberland Behavioral tie in? What about Archie Whitaker's theory? Are the Wickers involved? Is Collins right, is it someone within our department? How does all this tie back into my sister's disappearance? Is there witchcraft involved? Supernatural entities? God?

Yeah. God.

Where is he?

If he is real, why would anyone want to serve a god that allows these types of things to happen? How cruel and distant is that? God. Nothing but a gimmick for cruel minds to steal from the gullible.

But what about the vision last night? What about the light, the vision of paradise entering the darkness? Had I so soon forgotten?

What was that?

Is that hope? Real authentic hope? Or is it just my longing for something greater than myself?

My soul is torn between these thoughts and stuck in an inner turmoil. Longing for something more but knowing there isn't anything more than I can see in front of me.

It is what is.

At this point, I'd have to see God in the flesh to believe he's really out there. Even then, it wouldn't be a nice meeting because the words I've stored deep within my heart, can slice through the thickest bone and marrow.

We're nothing but a horde of wild animals. Beast carried about by our ever need for more. It's like a sickness. A disease that finds its way into our blood stream and works slowly but ever surely to our hearts and mind, until finally succeeding in turning some of us into the monsters we see walking among us. It creates an eating, consuming passion for more of whatever drives our dopamine. Never satisfied, always needing more . . . more . . . more.

We're all different with different desires.

For those who I have been given the task of bringing to justice, it's a sick and twisted game of gaining more power, more authority, more dominance, and ultimately . . . more control.

Whether it's a onetime murderer who killed out of passion while being driven by a sudden rush of anger that overtook their rationale, or you're dealing with a multiple offender. It's the need for more that drives them both.

This is what keeps a serial killer motivated and driven. It's a craving for more power and control. It becomes an all-consuming fire that only grows with each breath. Never satisfied, always wanting more.

And Morty fits into this mold as if it were custom designed just for him.

The reason for the notes and taunts, the sheering of his victims, it's all about dominance and control. Nothing makes a detective feel powerless, than a taunting killer who's outwitted you at every corner of your game. And he knows it. Everything he does is a slap in the face, proving he's smarter than me and my team.

Maybe he is.

Because maybe Morty is more than a man.

Maybe Morty really is the angel of death as he claims with his bloody drawings.

Maybe he's been sent by God.

When you really stop and think about it all, is that such a bad thing? Because the *modus operandi* of Morty . . . is killing bad parents and taking the children. Is it really such a horrible thing? As horrible as that is to even consider. I've never been one to dismiss a murder as "well they deserved it" or "they had it coming", that's just never been my mentality during an investigation. I don't care who the victim is, I have never once thought such a thing. Should I start now?

Is Morty using all of this creepy, evil, serial killer-like stuff to cover his real motive? Taking the children from abusive or worthless parents? Is he killing the parents, then shipping the children to orphanages in hopes of giving them a better life? Is that his ultimate motive? The eating, consuming fire that drives him? Is everything else just fluff to lead us down a darkened rabbit hole? The scriptures, the sheering, the cicadas, is it all just useless fluff? Puzzle pieces that don't fit?

Listen to me.

I don't know what to believe anymore. There're too many pieces to place together, and I honestly don't even know what the puzzle is supposed to look like. That's the thing that really scares me.

I need an anchor, something that'll plant my feet and steady my mind upon this troubled sea.

I need God, but a different version of the one I've seen.

I feel Collins apply the brakes and hear the pebbles ting underneath the Suburban. I know where we were.

The McCrae's.

One of the last places Agent Weatherby was seen.

Kim and I have always been at odds with one another, but I would never wish for her to fall into the hands of someone like Morty. I don't wish that upon my worst enemy.

A growing, troubled feeling rises in my gut as something tells me I may never see Agent Weatherby again.

The nausea and headache begin to ebb like a slow falling tide, still there but not as strong. I need coffee.

I climb out of the passenger seat, plant my feet onto the gravel, and look on at the swarm of police cars and blacked out SUV'S surrounding the McCrae's home.

I turn and say to Collins, "I have a bad feeling about this."

"You're not the only one."

# 37

**ONCE INSIDE,** we were met by Agent Swanson and Sheriff Johnston.

"Anything?"

Agent Swanson answers with a shake of his head and a strain in his voice, "No. We can't get anything with her phone or the GPS on the car. We have numerous officers and field agents patrolling the roads now. She said she was leaving here and coming straight to the museum."

"Williams and Ferrell said they saw her not too far from your place," Sheriff Johnston says as he bumps his chin toward me.

I rub my forehead.

Static voices chatter over radios as officers and agents scurry about.

"Why would she be out my way?"

Johnston shrugs his shoulders, "I asked the same thing."

"You've searched for any sign of struggle or disturbance I gather?"

Swanson breathes out a deep sigh, "Yeah. There's nothing. The door was even sealed back up. Whatever happened must've took place outside."

"Where's Detective White?"

Sheriff Johnston tosses a thumb to the right, "He's up there talking with the lady and her son."

"Miss Carver?"

"Yeah."

"I was just about to ask if anyone has spoken with her. We'll go up here and see what she's telling John. Let me know if you find anything."

"We will."

Collins and I leave the McCrae's and take the short ride over to Miss Carver's. We proceed down the long, dusty driveway sandwiched between the old cornfields.

Detective White's black Crown Victoria is parked next to a turquoise 1970's square bodied Ford pick-up that has more rust spots than I can count.

Miss Carver's old lab rises from the porch as soon as we pull behind White's car. He strides to the steps on sore joints and lets out a deep bark that steals all of his breath.

I pat his head and pull open the storm door to give a good knuckle rap.

I can hear White's deep voice asking a question, but I can't make out the words.

Heavy feet thuds toward us and the door opens to reveal Miss Carver.

"Why hi there, c'mon in," she says as she pushes open the storm door and holds it to welcome us in.

"How are you doing today, Miss Carver?"

"Doing well-doing well. Good to see you folks again."

We step in and sit next to Detective White on the sofa. Phillip is in his chair stationed in front of the television set watching a replay of a Red Sox game.

"Anything?"

White wags his head as he stuffs his note pad inside the inner pocket of his blazer.

Miss Carver shoves her weight into the door to get it to latch shut.

"Darn door has always given me trouble. The handyman said the house is so unlevel it's like it was built on top of a waterbed. I guess it's just something I have to live with, you know. Can I get you anything? Coffee? Tea? Pie?"

I nod and say, "Coffee would be nice if its not too much of a hassle."

"Course not. Got a fresh pot brewing right now. Boys, would you like some?"

"No thank you, ma'am," Collins replies.

"I'm good, thank you though," White says with a raised hand.

Miss Carver disappears into the kitchen.

White turns to me and Collins. "Any luck at the asylum?"

I crane my head and tighten my lips, "More than I expected."

He raises an eyebrow. "Really?"

I give him a quick rundown of Hope Jamison and the files I was able to pull from Langston's tight grip.

"Sounds promising."

"I'd like to believe so."

Phillip begins to clap and cheer. The Red Sox must've scored.

"What's the score Phillip?" Collins asks.

He cranes his head and speaks over his shoulder with words that tumble from a crooked tongue, "S-seven-seven to-to-to fo-fo-four." A line of saliva drips onto the floor.

"Oh wow. Are the Red Sox winning?" I ask.

"Yeahhhh!" he says in a slur.

"Awesome."

"I love you Laurie."

His words catch me off guard. A warm wave washes over me.

"Oh, you're a sweetheart. I love you too," I say as I rise from the couch. I walk over and squat next to his chair. I rub his arm. Despite him seemingly having the mind of a child, the bent hand tucked to his chest, and his inability to steady his head, he seems quite normal. Doesn't appear to have down syndrome, or any other mental illness.

"That was sweet of you Phillip. You're a fine boy, you know that?"

He grins and turns his head from me.

Miss Carver comes back to the room with my cup of coffee and one for herself.

I pat Phillip's hand and straighten my legs. I take my coffee and cross back to the sofa where I sit between Collins and White.

"Thank you, Miss Carver."

"You're welcome. Do you need any sugar or cream?"

"No thank you, this is fine."

She sits her cup on the table next to her and crashes into the recliner.

I lean up to the edge of my seat, "If you don't mind me asking Miss Carver, what condition does your son have?"

She takes a sip of coffee and breathes deep.

"He fell off the back of his father's truck when he was seven. Hit his head on the pavement, causing severe trauma which resulted in mental retardation. He was perfectly fine until the fall," she says with glazed eyes.

"Goodness. I'm sorry."

She gazes upon Phillip as he cheers on his Red Sox. "It was tough adjusting to everything. I lost one son but gained another. An angel took his place."

I swallow hard, "You're right about that."

Phillip claps and jolts in his chair as he laughs and giggles at the television.

"So, are you getting any closer to finding Sarah?"

"We have some good leads, but we're still in desperate need of more information." I sip my coffee.

"I see. I wish there was something I could do. I can't believe the FBI agent is missing. That's scary."

I nod.

"You didn't see any strange cars or people down by the McCrae's today? Other than the officers."

"No, I saw the police car and black SUV, but never saw anything else."

"Did you see them leave?"

"No."

Something small and black catches my attention. It comes from the hallway and paces toward us.

The cat.

It meows its way to Miss Carver before leaping into her lap.

"Oh, miss Midnight came to say hi."

Midnight glances to us then climbs to the head rest of the recliner and curls into a ball.

"Surprised she came out, usually she's a little weary of company."

I sip the coffee and starts to ask a question, but my buzzing phone diverts my attention.

I answer and Johnston doesn't give me a chance to say anything, "Just got a call about a vehicle fire east of us in a deserted patch of woods off Depot Road. Said the caller thought it looked like a Tahoe. Fire and EMS are on their way."

# 38

UPON DISCOVERING Agent Weatherby's charred Tahoe, we each dreaded what might lurk within the trunk. We were relieved to find it empty. K-9-unit officer, Barry Tyson, searched the surrounding woods with Rusty, but couldn't get a hit.

The dump site is roughly twelve miles from the McCrae's place. There's no note, hint, or anything. The MO and signature are different.

My mind is scattered and fogged. I need time to regroup. Chief Cunningham thought the same and demanded I go home and refocus.

I dropped Collins off at the station and did just that. Paul and Allen would stay with me while Officer Williams and Ferrell rotated on surveillance. Collins insisted he should keep the meeting with Pastor Sam Wicker intact. He left for Freewill Holiness as I pulled away from the station.

I glanced to the stereo when I reached my street, 5:49.

I pull into Paul's driveway and notice Allen's black Toyota pick-up parked behind Paul's gold Nisan van. I get out, stand by the garage door, and wait. A moment passes before the garage door comes to life and begins to lift. I step inside the garage and climb the small set of steps leading to the door. The door leads to his sunroom. As I push the door in, I feel a tug from the other side.  Paul.

"Hey girl . . . was just telling Allen I figured you were getting close. How in the world are ya?"

I smile and give him a big hug, pulling back, "Boy, it's been a rough day and I'm sure glad to see you."

Sandy rushes toward me, wagging her tail.

I squat on my calves and give her some attention.

"That bad, huh?" Paul asks.

"Yeah, there's a lot going on right now."

"Well, let me grab my things," we pass through the living room door, "Allen, are you about ready?"

He sits on the couch watching the local news station talk about the weather forecast.

He rises with a grunt, "Yeah . . . oh hey there Laurie."

"Hey Allen. Did he give you any trouble?" I question with a grin.

"Nah, not too much. He has been a little grumpy though," he smiles and cuts his eyes towards Paul as he disappears into the hallway.

"Hey! I heard that you ole fart."

Allen snickers as his shoulders begin to jolt up and down. He tosses a thumb towards the voice and says, "See what I mean?"

I wag my head and chuckle.

Paul and Allen gather their things and together we head down to my place.

I roll my window down and take my time easing along my driveway. I scan my yard and porch, looking for any sign of Morty. Nothing odd catches my eye. Of course, it helps that it's still day light. There always seems to be fewer glaring eyes in the light. It's in the darkness that they tend to multiply.

I can hear the cicadas begin to sing as their throaty voices travel with the breeze. They serve as a constant reminder of my coming demise.

I see Officer Williams seated in his car next to my cobbled stone pathway.

I shake off the fear trying to seep into my soul as I tell myself we have nothing to worry about. We have Williams and Ferrell rotating shifts, I have my Judge, Paul has his 12-gauge, and Allen has his .30-06. Plus, Collins will be here in a few hours.

We're safe.

I repeat the words to myself as if they're my new mantra, convincing myself of their truth.

Officer Williams steps out of his car as I park next to him. He rests his elbows atop the hood and interlocks his fingers.

Dressed in uniform and wearing a gentle smile below kind eyes, he dips his head, "Lieutenant. How we doing?"

"Hey Chris. I'm good. You?"

He bobs his head and glances about my home. "Good. I've been here for about three hours now and haven't seen anyone. I was hiding just off the road up there to see if anyone pulled in or anything. I never saw anyone, though. I'll be here for another two hours. Dean will be here by then. We have you covered Laurie. You're safe."

"I know that. Thank you, Chris. I'm going to go in and relax for a bit, if you need coffee or anything just let me know."

"Thank you, I'm good. I'm going to hide for a bit and see if anyone tries swinging by. Call me if you need me."

I sling the strap to my briefcase over my shoulder and shut the driver door, then open the back to let Sandy out.

"I will. Thank you again for doing this."

"Not a problem. It's what I'm here for."

Paul grunts something from the passenger seat as Allen helps him out, hooking his hands under his arm pits.

"I told Laurie we should have brought some donuts for ya," Paul says with a chuckle.

"Hey, I wouldn't object. Lemon filled is my favorite."

"Crispy cream or Dunkin?"

"Uh, I'd probably have to go with the double K on that one."

"Oh, alright then. I'll have to remember that."

Williams smiles and says, "Alright, you guys be safe."

"Thanks Chris. You do the same."

He dips below the roof of the patrol car and settles into the driver seat. He backs away, crunching over the pebble as the muffler pushes out gray smoke.

"Well, let's get inside. You guy's hungry?"

"Nah-nah, we ate before you came by," says Paul.

"You sure? I can fix a meal."

"No. We're good Laurie. Really. We had some oyster stew I'd fixed the other night," says Allen.

I brush some strands of hair from my face and help him guide Paul to the porch.

He's in good health for his age despite his trouble walking. Two hip replacements and a knee replacement certainly doesn't help.

We make it inside, and I go on to shower and heat up some leftover Chinese.

The day's light is slowly dimming as the sun sinks further into the unknown. I can feel the darkness crawl out from its hidden crevices as those ever watching eyes begin to multiply. As I sit in my recliner in the living room with Paul and Allen, I find myself glancing out the window to my left. If I listen closely enough I can hear the cicadas sing.

He's out there, and he's watching me.

During a commercial of *Mountain Men* (one of Paul's favorite shows) I stand and pull the curtain to the window.

Try looking in now you creep.

I force myself to be present with Paul and Allen as we enjoy some laughs at Paul's crazy stories. Once Collins gets here, I will peel away for a bit and spend some time looking over the new files.

I've already spent an hour on three separate calls from Chief Cunningham, Director Ramsey, and Agent Swanson. There's still nothing on Weatherby. I know in my gut it won't be good. We have not even made it to the third day yet and looks like he's already shown us who the next victim is.

Why Weatherby, though? She doesn't fit the victimology. Was it unplanned? Did she encounter him at the McCrae's? Startle him perhaps? Surprise him?

The questions linger in the back of my mind as I watch a rugged man dressed in heavy hunting clothes track a bleeding deer through snow covered mountains. Following the drops of blood, the white bearded man whispers how he has to be careful not to encroach upon a Grizzly or pack of wolves who may be guarding his kill. So, with each snow crunching step, the man's eyes dart about the forest as he watches and listens.

Wait a minute!

Is it all a trap? Is Morty luring us by taking one of our own? Leading us with a blood trail, only to ambush?

Is that why he took Weatherby?

Is it all a set up?

"You okay, Laurie?"

Why else would he want to take out a special agent?

"Laurie?"

"Huh? What? Sorry."

"Girl, you're going to have to relax a little. Don't let all of this stuff get to ya now," Paul says as he reaches from the end of the couch and pats my arm.

"I know. I just have a lot to process."

"Don't over think things. I learned a hard lesson about that when I was with Brunswick County. Being a detective is tough business as it is, so there's no need of making things harder on yourself. Only look at the facts. Never assume anything."

"I know. There's just so many pieces that could fit into all of this. It's hard to figure out which one's do which one's don't."

"When are they having the McCrae's funeral?" asks Allen.

"Sunday. They're supposed to have a memorial tomorrow night at Freewill Holiness."

"You're all going, right?" asks Paul.

"Yeah. We'll be there."

"You know how common it is for the killer to go to that type of stuff."

I bob my head, "I know. We'll set up a good surveillance."

"Good. That's good."

I rest my chin in the crevice of my left hand and glance to the window just to be sure there's no cracks in the blinds to be peeped through. The cicadas still taunt me with they're screeching. I can't help but wonder . . . what kind of monster may be lurking outside my window?

FreeWill
Holiness
Church

# 39

TUCKED DEEP WITHIN the wooded hills of Gray, rest a white planked church with a paint chipping steeple. A black ironed railing is attached next to bricked steps leading to red doubled doors with a black cross above them. The church could pass for one you'd expect to see on a rerun of *Little House on the Prairie.* The parking lot is covered with grassy patches of gravel as the church is surrounded by pine trees. A white Crown Victoria is parked next to a burgundy Honda Civic.

Behind the church is a cedar hewed swing set, with silver monkey bars and two green slides. Hand crafted picnic tables are scattered across the crab grass. Most of the tables are warped from the weathering. A doe and her fawn graze upon the grassy knoll about a hundred yards back.

The wind is growing as it begins to howl and tickle the tree branches, shaking them of their leaves and needles. The breeze arouses the cicadas to life as a slow rolling fog begins to settle in the church yard after having snaked its way between the pines.

If you were to open the glass storm door and unlatch the deadbolt to the back door, you'd find voices coming from deep within the sanctuary. And the aroma of freshly brewed coffee would be rather strong.

As you pass through a small kitchen, you see a door and as you near it the voices grow louder. You open this door and find that it leads into the sanctuary. Rows of cherry oak pews dressed in red velvet fill your vision. Two men are seated to the left side of the room. One man is dressed in black slacks with a white collared shirt, black tie, and a black sports coat. A gold badge is attached to his belt at the right hip. He has a note pad and is listening intently to the man next to him on the pew.

This other man is dressed in khaki pants with a navy and black flannel long sleeve. He has a bald head, an enticing smile, and kind blue eyes. He's a petite man, smaller than the one with the badge.

"It's been tough on Brett, you know. He was close to his sister and her family. Despite their ways, he still loved them."

"Despite their ways?"

"Well, you know, the way they treated Sarah and all the hard living and such."

"I see," Collins scribbles notes and takes a sip of coffee which was sitting on the floor next to his right foot.

"Mr. Wicker, do you think someone may have taken Sarah to get her away from that kind of lifestyle?"

The pastor of Freewill Holiness crunches his brows and blinks twice. He scratches the nape of his neck and says, "Huh, I never thought of that. Nah. No one comes to mind. I know Brett would never do such a thing. Take Sarah? Maybe, but kill his sister and brother-in-law? C'mon now, there's no chance. Brett doesn't have a mean bone in his body. You need to be looking at the dad."

"Jeremy?"

"No, Jeremy's dad. Richard. The grandpa. Brett said Amanda told him a handful of times that she was worried about him. She said he often threatened to take Sarah," Wicker pauses and takes a breath.

Collins crosses his arms and bites his pencil. "Go on."

Wicker tilts his head and angles his eyes to Collins. "Listen, Richard McCrae is a hermit and drunk. Pure and simple as that. He and Jeremy never did get along. A lot of the reason for the strife between him and Amanda. Brett said Amanda told him how Richard abused Jeremy as a kid. Although, Richard had changed a few of his ways, drinking was never one of them. He was always on Jeremy about his hard living, you know the drugs and thieving and what not. Brett told me one time that Amanda said she was worried what Richard might do."

"Why wouldn't Brett have told us all this when he had him in for questioning?"

Wicker shrugs his shoulders and takes a sip of coffee.

"What about the scriptures?"

"That I don't know. Because I know Richard doesn't have that kind of knowledge. And the cicadas don't exactly line up either."

Collins never mentioned anything about the cicadas. He stops in mid-stroke from taking notes and looks up. "Cicadas?"

Wicker notices Collins's tone and pulls his eyes from the red carpet. Wrinkled lines zigzag their way across his forehead, "Yeah. The cicadas."

"What about them?"

"You know, the cicadas that's been left at the scenes. The whole deal with that professor hanging himself at the museum. The cicadas."

"How did you know he was leaving cicadas at the scenes?"

Wicker scoffs and glances about the sanctuary, "Word travels fast in a small town my friend. Every word is heard. Believe me. Being the pastor of Freewill Holiness, I know. Gossip in a small town is as common as snow in Alaska."

Collins eyes him for a moment, deciding if he should let the matter go or press for more.

"Do you still practice snake handling?"

Wicker whips his head around, ready to defend. He looks Collins up and down and answers, "We do, and if that's why you're here I think you have better things to spend your time on."

"Why do you still do it?"

"Why, it's a showcase of our faith. It proves our belief and dependence on the Almighty."

"I'm just a little curious, you know. I mean I'm honestly surprised you continue such a thing after all the rumors and controversy."

Wicker lowers his voice and head, "That was a long time ago. Things have changed since then."

"Have they?"

He jerks his head up, "Of course."

"How so?"

"Well, yeah we believe in snake handling like Archie Whitaker did before all that began, but we also believe in something else. Something that strengthens our faith and proves to the unbelieving that the almighty is real."

"What's that?"

"The fire dance."

"Fire dance?"

Wicker nods his head, "Just like with Shadrach, Meshach, and Abednego. When acting in faith, we can touch the flame and not be burned. We can dance with fire and not even have the smell of smoke attach itself to us. It's the eighth wonder of the world my friend."

"Now you're just showing off. I thought lying was a sin, Pastor. One of the big ten," Collins turns up the white coffee cup with the words to a Psalm written in black cursive letters swirled along the outer diameter.

"It is," Wicker says with a face of stone.

"So, you're telling me that now you're not just snake handlers, but you're fire handlers too?" Collins asks with a restrained chuckle.

Wicker gives him a straight face as if he'd been sucked into another world, "That's right."

"Pastor Wicker, I appreciate your time and cooperation, but I think I'm going to hit the road before you start talking about casting out demons or summoning old saints, because I know that's probably next."

"Oh, we do that too."

"What? Casting out demons or summoning saints?" Collins asks with scrunched brows as he stands.

"I've performed more exorcisms in my time here than I'd like to admit. Must be in the water." Wicker says with a crooked grin as he stretches forth his bird-like claw to shake Collins hand.

Collins shakes it and once again, can't help but notice the delicate smoothness of the thing.

"It's been a pleasure Detective. You'll be here tomorrow night for the memorial?"

"Yeah, me and Lieutenant Daniels will be here. Begins at seven, right?"

"Seven it is. And if you'd like to witness our demonstrations of faith, we're having a revival Sunday night."

Collins gives it some thought as he passes Wicker the empty coffee cup. With squinted eyes and tight lips, "What time?"

"Seven."

"We'll think about it. Thanks again, we'll plan to see you at the memorial tomorrow. Take care."

"My pleasure. I pray much wisdom and guidance will be given you. I pray for your protection as well," Wicker says with a tight grin as he touches and squeezes Collins's left arm.

Collins dips his head and turns for the door. His heart thumps hard at a rapid pace.

"Oh detective . . ." Collins hears as he reaches for the door. He turns to face the man and sees him standing between the pews.

"Say hello to your boss for me. She's in my prayers as well."

Collins nods and walks out.

He quickens his steps, speed walking to the car, and wastes no time turning over the ignition. With a full note pad and a head swimming with questions, he lowers his foot further onto the gas pedal, creating as much distance as he can between him and Wicker.

# 40

**I HAVE SPOKEN WITH** Cunningham and Director Ramsey twice within the hour. We still do not have anything on Agent Weatherby. It has been ten and a half hours since her disappearance, and the clock rushes to its next tick.

I notice a pair of headlights beam down my foyer, pouring in through the window of my front door.

Paul jolts to the edge of the couch, dropping his feet from the ottoman, "Who's that?"

"Should be Collins." I say while crossing the living room and angling for the door. I peep through the glass and see another pair of lights floating behind the first vehicle. It is probably Dean checking to see who it is.

I unlatch the deadbolt and open my door to see Collins leaning into the open window of Dean's patrol car. He chuckles and slaps the roof of the car. Dean backs out and once again tucks himself away in the darkness.

"Was Dean checking to be sure it was you?"

Collins jerks his head as if my voice startled him, "Yeah. No word on Weatherby?"

"No."

Collins curses as he climbs the steps. His laptop bag is strapped across his left shoulder as it hangs by his left hip. His *.40 mm* Glock is holstered on his right.

I welcome him in and send the deadbolt home.

"Hungry?"

"No, thanks. I grabbed a wrap from Subway on the way over."

"Just make yourself at home."

Paul calls from the living room, "Who's my girl talking to in there? Better not be that hoodlum again."

Collins and I come around the corner.

Paul snickers behind his hand and hitches his shoulders as he darts his eyes away.

"Oh no. You're here?" Collins teases.

"Get on over here boy," Paul chuckles and slaps the couch next to him. "We got us a ballgame to watch. The Dodgers and Nationals are in a close one."

"Oh really? What's the score?"

I hear them talking as I put away a few dishes into the dishwasher.

"Nationals are up three to two. It's the bottom of the seventh, and the Dodgers just scored a run. Max Muncy hit a homer. The Nationals shouldn't taken out ole Strasburg. I think he had like ten strike outs or something. Isn't that right, Allen?"

"Yeah, that sounds about right. It was up there." Allen turns to Collins as he takes a seat, "So, how was the visit with the old snake handler?"

Collins breathes out a lip flapping sigh, "Interesting."

Paul wags his head, "Never cared much for stuff like that, you know? Always gave me the creeps. If God wants me dancing with snakes, then they better be an awful big prize waiting for me."

"Amen to that," says Collins.

I stand at the edge of the living room with a glass and bottle of Silver Oak in hand. "Anyone want a glass?"

They each decline my offer, so I go on to pour me a half glass and sit back into my recliner by the window. I take a sip and look to Collins, "So, how was he?"

He raises his brows and swallows. "I got some good information out of him, and I also got the creeps along with it. I couldn't stop thinking of how much he fits my profile."

I crane my head and narrow my gaze, "Really? How so?"

"Well, for starters, he drives a dark red, well cared for Honda Civic. He's well groomed, articulate, small but sneaky strong, charismatic, and he speaks in riddles. And get this . . . he knew about the cicadas."

I lower the glass of red wine from my lips, "What? How's that?"

Collins curls two of his fingers and says, "'Word travels fast in a small town my friend.' His exact words. And he kept talking about Richard McCrae."

"Yeah? What about him?"

"Talked about him being a drunk and how he and his son didn't get alone. Said he'd heard through Brett that Richard was threating to go to DSS and take Sarah away."

"How does he expect to do that when he's be on and off the streets for the past five years? He's out of his mind."

Collins, tightens his lips, raises his brows, and shakes his head.

"We've already looked into him. He was booked earlier that day for public intox. He was in a cell when Jeremy was murdered, so we know he could not have made it to West Virginia in time to dump Amanda's body. A man can't be in two places at once."

"Unless, he's a ghost," Paul says with a crooked grin.

I brush it off and take another sip of wine.

Collins bites his lip as his eyes gaze down at my rug which the coffee table sits upon. "I haven't thought of that one, Paul. Hmm. Anyway, I just played dumb and let the man talk."

"The profiler from the Bureau will be here tomorrow. Make sure you spend some time with her. Pick her brain, you know? She's set to give a briefing at three."

"Good. I was hoping she'd still be coming. I'll be anxious to talk to her."

"What's her name?" asks Paul.

"Shannon Carter."

"Oh yeah, I know Shannon. Well, I did at one time. Me and Ray worked with her in New Orleans a few times. That was back when she first got the job in Behavioral Science. She knows Douglas and Ressler and all of them. She was good. She helped track the Doll Maker and The Weaver."

"Really? I didn't know you worked with her. Maybe you two can catch up while she's in town."

"Yeah, I'd like that. I doubt she'd remember me though."

"Psh, what? Remember you? Are you kidding? Who wouldn't?"

"Right?" says Allen with a grin.

"I don't know. She's a sweet lady though, but boy don't press her buttons. She can be a pistol when need be. Kind of reminds me of you, Laurie."

"I guess I'll take that as a compliment then."

"Oh, it is. You're both fine ladies."

I spend another hour talking and cutting up with them. More than once, we bellied laughed until it hurt as we listened to Paul's crazy stories.

I look to my watch.

*9:32 p.m.*

I stand from the recliner, pass my baby grand piano, and take a hardcover from the bookshelf. A collection of short stories by Poe, Hawthorne, Dickens, and the like.

"Well . . . I'm going to leave you fellas alone for a bit. I need to decompress and sift over the case files. There's bottled water in the fridge and there's snacks and stuff in the pantry if you're hungry."

With that I retire to my bedroom.

Before I dive into the files from Dr. Langston and try to process all the recent events, I settle atop the covers of my bed, cross my legs and turn the page to an Ambrose Bierce story titled, *The Damned Thing*. I've heard of Bierce and may have read a few of his stories, but I've never read this one.

I engross myself in the story which is set some hundred years ago. It begins with a coroner investigating the mysterious death of a man named Hugh Morgan, who along with his hunting partner, William Harker encountered a wicked, unseen beast. It sent Morgan screaming in mortal agony as it ripped him to shreds like the stories of old British werewolf murders.

The tale then goes into the backstory leading up to Morgan's death. The hunting partner, William Harker explains how Morgan had been paranoid ever since he began having strange encounters with a presence he could not see, but only feel and hear. He knew the *Damned Thing* was always watching and plotting for his demise.

It wasn't until that day in the field when Morgan and Harker stumbled upon it, that the man's paranoia gained credibility. They thought they'd encroached upon a Grizzly.

The thing thrashed about in the bush and was sure to charge any moment. Harker blurted to his friend, "What in the devil is it?"

That's when he saw the sheer terror in the Morgan's eye. Fear washed down his face as he raised his rifle and aimed into the brush. He parted his lips and said in a dreaded tone, "It's that *damned thing*."

What was it? An omen? A demon? A beast?

Whatever it was, ended Hugh Morgan's life and sent him to a cold metal slab to be questioned by the coroner.

In a journal left behind by Morgan, with his last entry before his death he spoke how there must be a spectrum of color in which our eyes are not accustomed. He talked about how he'd seen flocks of birds shift and suddenly take to flight as if disturbed by some invisible force or presence. And how for centuries seamen had written how schools of wales and fish spook in an entire horde, darting away from an unseen entity. Morgan believed that the *Damned Thing* which had taken to tormenting him, must be from behind the veil. An entity. An omen. A wicked, abominable creature from somewhere beyond the realm of our known reality. An unknown thing from an unknown place.

Morgan believed that it is from this spectrum of color all supernatural and spiritual beings must reside. The last words in his journal were: "*And, God help me. The Damned Thing is of such a color!*"

The words of Archie Whitaker sting my mind as I remember him claiming to have seen visions of demons coming from the clouds and disappearing into the woods. It all sounds a little like this Ambrose Bierce story.

As intense and frightening as the story is, it is what I learned about the author that frightened me even more. After googling Ambrose Bierce on my phone, I found that twenty years after he penned *The Damned Thing* he mysteriously disappeared while visiting Mexico. What happened to him remains a mystery to this day, and a lot of people speculate he was taken by the unseen creature he'd written about decades prior to his disappearance.

My thoughts were reeling before with speculations about Archie's claims, but now I can't help to wonder if there may be more truth to them than I originally believed.

I sit my phone on my bed next to the book, and I rub my face with both palms. I take a deep, well needed breath.

I reach over to my nightstand and take up one of three manila envelopes from Dr. Langston. I pinch the metal hinges together and retrieve Hope Jamison's files.

With the new case files in hand and my note pad next to me, I spend the next two hours scanning each word and name with great diligence.

Everything Dr. Langston said is right here in the files. Her coming from Virginia, her troubled past, her claims of kidnapping, the diagnosis, the medication. Everything.

I hear Paul and the boys laughing in the living room.

I raise my vision and look to the back of my door as my mind is in another space. I shut my eyes and drag for sand.

If I don't figure this out, someone else is going to die. Another life will be taken, and another child will be abducted. How many will die before he's finished. When will he be satisfied? Why is he doing this? What's in it for him?

My heart stirs at the vibrating of my phone.

I sigh and lower my tired eyes to the screen.

*Restricted.*

"Hello?"

Static.

"Hello?"

Soft, raspy breathing.

My heart thumps as I can feel my carotid artery pulse and pick up speed. I swallow hard. "I'm listening."

"Tick-tock-tick-tock-tick-tock," deep and slow. It's mechanical as he gives the t's strong inflection, letting them roll gracefully off his tongue.

"What do you want?"

"You should know by now."

"Enlighten me."

"Why should I?"

"To relieve the burden. I know how much this must weigh on you. I know how difficult it must be to sleep, having so much pressing down on your conscience and heart. It's okay. You don't have to keep living like this. You can—"

"You cease your foolish speech, or I'll disconnect," he bites off with soul piercing venom to gain back his control and dominance.

"Why did you call me?" I ask as I head for my door to get Collins.

"Starts with S ends with M. You'll find two but not a third again."

"Don't do this. Don't take another innocent life."

"Innocent?" he hisses as if insulted.

I open the door and all of their eyes jerk to mine. I raise a finger to Collins and motion for him to get his phone.

"How could you think these people are innocent? How dare you say such a thing. These people are an abomination to the almighty. Can't you see that! I am doing the children a favor."

"What have these people done to deserve such wrath?"

"They've committed sins against God's most precious. I'm the one being sure the mill stone is placed about their neck. I'm the one tossing them into the sea. I'm the death angel. I am . . . the reaper." His words emit with a deep, raspy tone like an abandoned soul trapped in hell's eternal flame.

My skin crawls at his words.

Collins begins recording with his phone and holds it up to the receiving end of mine as I busy myself with jotting down notes.

"Well, what has Weatherby done?"

"Oh, the little agent? I did that for you, Laurie. I took care of the little pest. You'll never have to worry about that rat again."

"Where is she?"

"That shouldn't be of your concern. You should be worried about solving the riddle." He clears a phlegm and says, "It's simple really. Starts with S ends with M, you'll find two but not a third again," he says slowly as if speaking to a child. The voice altering device he's using crackles and hisses.

"Starts with S ends with M? Sarah McCrae?"

"Try again, darling."

"Listen, it's only a matter of time before this comes to an end. I don't want anyone else getting hurt. Just tell us where she and Weatherby are. You can come to the station. Do this peacefully, show us how strong and courageous you are by being a man and taking a responsibility for what you've done. Don't be a coward like all the others. Hiding like a little child—"

"Enough!"

I pull the phone from my ear and squint.

"I cannot be caught. You know why?"

I don't answer.

"Because I cannot be seen. I'm the death angel, remember?"

"When will it be enough?"

He chuckles, "I'm just getting started, darling. It's the year of my emergence. It will not be enough until all of New England is cleansed of its wickedness. I've only just begun. There will be more missing children in the next few days than you have had during your entire career. Meaning, more parents will die. Blood will be shed, sin will be atoned for, and the children will get a new start."

A soft whimper emits in the background.

"Who's that? Is that Sarah?"

"Ssshhh . . . don't worry detective, she's in good hands now."

The screeching from the flaky, ribbed belly of a cicada rips through the line followed by Morty taunting me with, "Tick-tock-tick-tock-tick-tock."

I curse and belt, "You coward. You're such a worthless coward. You're a weak little child, you hear me!"

Collins places his hand on my shoulder, trying to calm me but I can't be calmed.

The line goes dead.

I launch my hand back and sling the phone against the wall, sending it shattering in a thousand directions.

I melt to the floor as tears rush down my cheeks. I bury my face into my palms and sob. Collins lowers to his knees and pulls me into his safe arms. His warm embrace soaks up my hot tears as my cheek pushes deeper into his chest. I hear Paul's feet patter into the room.

"Oh baby," is all he can say.

"I can't do this anymore. I've failed them. People are going to die because of me. Because I didn't stop him," my voice trails off as a fresh wave of tears choke my voice and heart.

"I can't deal with all of this. It's too much," mucus clogs my words as my eyes sting with raw, unfiltered emotion.

"Ssshhh," Collins says as he rubs my back.

I pull back, rub my hands through my hair, and down to my face.

I force myself to my feet. Collins does the same.

Paul stands with teary eyes and opened arms, wearing a soft grin beneath that big white mustache.

I step in and bury my face into his chest.

"It's going to be alright now, ya hear? It's alright, don't go blaming yourself for all this mess. You can't do that. It'll take you to a place you don't want to go. Trust me, I know. You have to rest in the fact that you're giving it all you got and let God and fate decide the rest. This guy's going to mess up somewhere. Sooner or later they all do. You know that. Don't let him get to you. You're stronger and smarter than him, remember that."

I sniffle and pull back as I rise to my tip toes to kiss his cheek, "Thank you, Paul. I love you."

"Love you too, baby."

I spin around and find Collins knelt by the wall where my phone had just exploded.

"How are we going to track him now?"

"I'll have to call Director Ramsey. They can punch in my number and find what cell tower was pinged from the incoming call," I say as I hold out my hand, asking for his phone.

He hands it over, and I place the call to Ramsey.

Within fifteen minutes, they had a ping from a cell tower near the coast in Rye, New Hampshire.

"Starts with S ends with M," I say with one hand to my hip and the other to my forehead as I pace my living room floor.

"He said it's not Sarah. What else starts with S and ends with M?" Collins says as he sits with his elbows on his knees next to Paul and Allen on my couch. "Last time he gave us coordinates of the location, maybe S and M have something to do with the geography."

I stop and snap my fingers at Collins's words, "That's it. That's it! He wasn't talking about Sarah McCrae . . . he was talking about Salem. Starts with S ends with M. He's heading there now."

# 41

**THE RIDE DOWN WAS PLEASANT.** The *Grab-N-Go* convenient store in Salem will be locking the doors in just a few minutes. Gary Wade Duncan has made it just in time. He is two minutes earlier than his estimated arrival of *11:55 p.m.* The lights over the gas pumps are dim and blink sporadically as an array of moths and other organisms flutter about, seeking warmth.

Duncan's black Toyota Camry is the only car at the four little pumps. Shane Anderson is alone inside as he works the register. There is no other a soul in sight. Perfect.

Gary Wade Duncan has watched from a distance on numerous nights. He has even bought gas and snacks a time or two, all in effort to get a better feel for the layout and foot traffic. He knows where Shane lives, who he lives with, and how he treats his son, Connor.

Duncan's hands have taken to the tremors again as his heart pounds and beads of sweat trickle down his forehead. He steps out of the car and up to the pump, he inserts his card and begins pumping fuel. As he does so, he takes in his surroundings and looks hard for any would be witnesses. The coast is clear as he'd predicted. His pulse continues to surge as he watches the black digital numbers tick by. *20.84…23.39… 25.78…* he glances to his watch, *11:58.*

The sound of an engine along with tires crawling over pavement, pulls his eyes to the set of headlights turning off the roadway. The car eases into a handicap parking space at the front entrance of the store.

He curses beneath his breath, and guilt immediately washes over him for saying such a thing. He cut his eyes to the heavens and repents. How terrible of a thing to say.

The pump crawls on, *28.25…29.67…* he pulls his hand from his pocket and releases the nozzle from its little kickstand. With a few squeezes and clicks, he stops at *29.99.* Perfect.

He hangs the nozzle back and twists the gas cap with quick, fidgety fingers. The tremors continue to rage, so he shuts his eyes and steals a deep breath. The racing flood of unneeded thoughts slowly begin to ebb, and the twitch in his extremities come to a halt.

Good. That's it. Relax. You can do this. He tells himself. He takes one last deep breath and opens his eyes.

He watches as the door to the car parked in the handicap spot swings open. A teenage girl climbs from the driver seat of the beat-up Honda Civic and rushes inside.

Duncan checks his watch, *11:59.*

His top lip quivers as a wave of heat washes over him. His heart ticks faster with each pump of precious blood.

He opens his car door and lowers himself into the driver's seat. He watches through the passenger window as the girl crosses to the fridge and pulls out a bottle of water. He can tell by the packaging that it's raspberry flavor made by Crystal Light. It's the only bottled beverage he would ever touch and it's his favorite of all liquids. He even has one in the cup holder next to his thigh right now. He reaches for it, unscrews the cap, and takes a swig. What are the odds that this girl would choose his favorite beverage? It's more than just coincidence, isn't it? It's as if it is a sign from the heavens. Should he take her too?

As he wrestles with the thought, he takes out a peppermint candy from his shirt pocket and untwists the wrapper. He pops it into his mouth. He doesn't crunch it, but rather allows it to settle on his tongue where it makes out with his taste buds. As the peppermint begins to dissolve and change its shape, he leans over and pulls open the glove compartment. He retrieves a black rubber gripped hammer. He likes to call this his *Bone Cracker.* And many of bones it has cracked. He also picks up his dagger. Many of hearts it has stopped.

He tries hard to push away the thought about taking the girl as he watches her pay for the drink and rush back to her car. He must stay focused to do what he has come for. He swallows a gulp of peppermint flavored saliva and then follows it up with another drink of raspberry water. He draws in a long breath and lets its warmth roll from his nostrils. The girl turns over the ignition, the taillights wink red, and the muffler huffs a puff of smoke like a smoker with a cough. Duncan watches the girl pull from the parking lot and make her way to a red light where she sits for a moment before making a right turn and disappearing out of sight. Those red taillights vanish in the dark like a cicada slowly closing its eyes.

A thin smile stretches Duncan's lips as a slither of pride fills his heart. As hard as it was to do, he had just reigned in his own will and chosen to stick with the master's plan rather than act out of impulse. A scripture from the first chapter of James comes to life within his head, and he finds himself now repeating it with sharp concentration and attention to every detail. It was one of the scriptures his father would repeat to him every night before bed.

*Blessed is the one who perseveres under trial because, having stood the test, that person will receive the crown of life that the Lord has promised to those who love him. When tempted, no one should say, "God is tempting me." For God cannot be tempted by evil, nor does he tempt anyone; but each person is tempted when they are dragged away by their own evil desire and enticed. Then, after desire has conceived, it gives birth to sin; and sin, when it is full-grown, gives birth to death.*

Dragged away by their own evil desire . . . and sin, when it is full-grown, gives birth to death. Dragged away . . . sin . . . gives birth to death. Sin . . . to death.

Sin . . . death.

Shane Anderson comes to the doors with a set of keys. Gary Wade Duncan feels his heart knock hard against his ribs. He jolts to life and tosses the scripture to the far corners of his mind. He exits from his Camry, stuffs the hammer and dagger in the back of his pants, double checks that his pliers and dentures are his pocket, and enters a quick jog. He flashes a hand as he nears the door. Shane sees him, mumbles something, wags his head, and opens the door to let him.

"Just make it quick, alright?"

"Oh, don't worry my friend, this won't take long."

# 42

GARY WADE DUNCAN finishes his final touches and turns out the lights, leaving only a dim one on near the register. He scans the parking lot and when he is sure it's clear of eyes, he steps out and locks the door behind him. He darts his eyes about his surroundings as he crosses for his Toyota Camry. He angles around the front of it and opens the driver door. He sits down and latches the door shut. He breathes out a soothing sigh and glances at his watch, *12:06*. Nice.

A tight-lipped grin stretches across his smooth and well-kept face. Other than the few little freckles he left untouched with the new foundation, his skin is . . . well, perfect. Not a blemish in sight. It'd taken some time to apply the cream and cover up, but it was worth it. It always is.

He scratches the back of his head and the hair flows about his fingers. He shuts his eyes and pulls his fingers to his nose. He breathes deep and begins to quiver as he savors every last ounce of Amanda McCrae. Her scent is fading as it will soon be replaced with that from Mrs. Anderson.

They will never catch him. There's no chance. He has outsmarted them at every angle. Laurie should retire early before she causes herself more grief. He snickers as he marvels at his wit. He turns over the ignition and pulls away.

Mrs. Anderson would be in bed by now. At least she usually is by this time of night. He has completed his prerequisite of sixty-days of observation, which is the requirement he sets for himself before acting out any taking. He knows the Anderson's comings and goings, their likes and dislikes, habits and routines . . . everything.

With the Fulbright's offering to take Connor with them to Winter Island State Park, he was forced to deviate from the original plan. He must've ground a half inch off the enamel of his molars when he learned of the news. He's never liked surprises and this one was no exception. Not surprisingly, he created a new plan. Nothing can keep him from doing the will of God. Nothing. Having grown up in his father's friends church in the south, Gary Wade Duncan knows how important the will of God is.

He would come in through the back window as Mrs. Anderson slept. Sleep is such a mysterious thing when you pause to think about it. We spend a third of our lives dead to the world and completely vulnerable during the darkest hours. Therefore, you know with all the time you spend asleep, surely there has been times where you've been watched. Is that what causes you to wake in the middle of night? Is something or someone sitting next to your bed, watching? Or better yet, they may be lying beside you with an arm draped over your shoulder. There is no chance Gary Wade Duncan is the only watcher. Surely there is a plethora of unseen beings taking advantage of the opportunity to watch the living as they breathe the breath of life. Longing for that same breath to enter their lungs once again. Longing for life. Envious.

He would watch her chest rise and fall and when the time was right—it's always about the timing—he would pour out God's wrath. It would be quick and subtle. He'd shear her, extract the molar he needs to add to his dentures, bite her shoulder with the prior victim's teeth, and lastly but always the best part, stab her in the heart. If she's lucky, she would have already entered into shock. Some often do. It'd numb the pain slightly, but it wouldn't stop the fear from ravaging her heart and mind as she watches the reaper take her life.

He shakes his head and regains his thoughts. He goes back to the plan. After he finishes dealing with Mrs. Anderson's sin—*and sin, when it is full-grown, gives birth to death*—he would prop her up at the table so she could watch as he enjoyed a midnight snack. If he was lucky, there may be a plate of leftovers in their refrigerator. Perhaps, stew or soup. That seems to fit his mood at the moment.

After his meal, he would leave her in the living room as if she's watching television. He chuckled at the thought of leaving the remote in her cold, dead hand.

His body jiggles as he hits a pothole in the road while coming to a stoplight.

He will need to be at Winter Island rather early, so he can get there before the feds and pigs show up. The next shift at the Grab-N-Go would not be until eight, so if he was lucky it'd be about nine o'clock or so before they tried to contact the family. Once they fail at contacting the family, they will raid the Anderson home. They will discover the bald-headed misses propped up on the couch as Good Morning America discusses the latest news from the television set. It is at this point they will begin the search for Connor. After some time passes, they'll learn of him spending the weekend with the Fulbright family at Winter Island. They will raid the campground, turn it upside down searching for little Connor, and they will drag the Fulbright's in for interrogation. All while Gary Wade Duncan makes the trip back to Portland. And with God's favor he has nothing to worry about. All will be well, he need only trust.

He eases through the light, green hues reflect off the black, shiny hood of his Camry. He reaches for the knob to the stereo and turns up the volume. The station is programed to one of his favorite. Classical.

A few minutes in, Beethoven's fifth symphony begins to reverberate

throughout the cab as its trademark *duh. Da-duh, da-da, da-da-duh*, climbs its upwards projection of tune to penetrate his heart and soul. He basks in the genius of Beethoven's arrangement. Such beauty. His heart fills with delight as he savors every sound the string instruments speak forth.

He strokes his hand through the black curls fixed to his head and lets out a soothing sigh.

He can hardly wait to deliver Connor from such devils. It truly is a joy to snatch the children out of the pits of despair and offer them into the hands of those who will appreciate the gift God has bestowed upon us. How someone could be so cruel to an innocent soul, is beyond him. How a parent could do such things to their own flesh and blood is nothing less than an abomination. It is one in which is deserving of God's full and unforgiving wrath.

He knew the moment he met the Anderson's during the walk through of the home for rent, something wasn't right with Connor. The look in his eye told it all. And the more he watched over the next sixty days, God began to reveal it. He'd chosen Connor to be rescued. Shane and Donna will pay for their sins and Connor will be healed of his wounds, both physically and emotionally.

When the feds investigate who had access to the home, they will never find the realtor named Jim Ashe who showed them the home because Jim Ashe never existed. Jim Ashe is just one of fifteen personalities.

One of fifteen masks.

Just like Gary Wade Duncan.

# 43

DESPITE MY EFFORTS, neither Chief Cunningham nor Director Ramsey would budge on their decision to keep me grounded in Portland as the team headed to Salem. They said they wanted me and Collins to stay put in hopes of luring Morty into attempting to do something he shouldn't. We also appointed Williams and Ferrell to work together through the night to keep a tight surveillance of my home.

Detective White rode down with Agent Swanson and Chief Cunningham. The field office in Boston was alerted, along with state police, SWAT, and the Salem Police Department. Everyone knows to keep their eyes open. The officers in Essex and the surrounding counties have also been informed to be vigilant as they patrol the area.

It'd taken our team about an hour and a half to get there as they sped down I-95. I spoke via speaker phone with them most of the way.

I refreshed Cunningham and Swanson of what our UNSUB had said over the phone. They'd already heard Collins recording of it via email.

"And you're sure the girl's voice that you heard wasn't just a recording?" Swanson asks.

"No. It didn't sound like it. It sounded real."

"Why would he give you such a hint like that? Starts with S ends with M. For heaven's sake, everyone in New England would eventually think of Salem."

"Maybe he's giving up," Cunningham offers.

"No. I don't think so. I think he said it to prove to himself how good he is. To rub it in our faces. It's a control and dominance tactic. It's his way of showing he has all the control. That he's in power, not us. That's why he said it. It's what gives him the rush . . . the thrill. Outsmarting the good guys. Keeping and gaining more power. It's his drug."

"He's not going to do that. We're smarter than he is and deep down, he knows it," says Swanson.

"Just be careful. Please."

"We are Laurie, don't worry. We are," says Cunningham. "We'll stay in the area, and we'll be sure keep our eyes and ears open. We'll let you know as soon as we have anything. Try and get you some rest. Tomorrow is when we're going to need you."

I sigh as I gently brush my fingers over the keys of my piano. Not giving enough weight to strike a chord. I raise my head and look out the black window into the moonless night. Collins, Paul, and Allen are seated on the couch behind me.

"I'll try to. Be safe, you guys."

We end the call and I hand Collins's phone back to him.

"You need to get some sleep, Laurie. You look beat," says Collins.

"Geeze, thanks for the compliment."

"I mean it. You need some rest. They have everything under control. Tomorrow and the next few days are going to be crucial. Get your rest while you can."

"I know, Pat. But if you know anything about me, you know sleep is not in my vocabulary at the moment. It'll have to come by force, because I will not enter into it willingly. If I can't help them catch him in Salem, then the least I can do is go over everything here and try to give them some leads."

"Yeah, I know. Just be sure you're taking care of yourself. And try not to smash anymore phones," he says with a smile and pat to my shoulder.

I nod and yawn into hand.

"What are they doing down there, just patrolling the neighborhoods?" asks Paul.

"Yeah. They don't have much to go on at this point. They're working with DSS though to see how many kids in the area come from homes that would fit our victim profile."

"That's the thing though. A lot of kids and families fit the victim profile. There are a lot of messed up families out there," says Collins.

I nod and rub the back of my neck, "I know."

Allen aims the remote control and turns off the television.

"How is Dean doing?" I ask Collins. Dean Ferrell had called Collins on Allen's cell not long after I got on the phone with Cunningham and Swanson.

"He's good. Said he'll be out there until Chris takes over at five."

"Okay." I look at my watch, and it's already a quarter past one. "Guys, I'm going to go in here to look through the files and everything. Don't let me keep me you up. I know it's getting late."

"That's fine girl. You do what you need to do now. We'll be okay. Try to get some sleep too. You're gonna need it."

"I'll try."

† † † † † † † † † †

**THE AIR IS COOL AS IT BRUSHES** upon my flesh. Everything is black. The wretched odor of burnt trash hangs thick in the air. Leaves rustle and crackle with the breeze. The critters of the night are fully alive. Crickets, frogs, and . . . cicadas.

I can feel my body step down a sloping hill. The grass blades bend beneath my feet. Everything is still black.

I hear an array of splashes from what sounds like frogs diving into a pond for cover.

*The pond.*

My eyes flash wide.

I'm standing in our back yard, looking at the pond. The flood lights illuminate, glistening and refracting off the rippling water.

Something catches my eye at the banks edge. It's white and is floating like a log, but deep down I know it's not a log.

It's her.

My mother.

Her white dress floats at the surface. Her face is submerged, and her long blonde hair dances with the rhythm of the murky water.

My heart takes a lethal blow as all my air is knocked from my lungs.

The sound of sniffles rips through the air behind me.

I spin on my heels and at the top of the knoll, standing under our deck, I see my little sister. Amy.

Then everything turns black again, and this is when I awake. Gasping, sweating, heart racing, I jolt from my pillow and form an L.

The room is black except for my bedside lamp.

I glance to the alarm clock on my dresser.

In red digital numbers, it reads, 5:14.

I sigh and lower my head, pulling my hands to my face.

The floor creaks near my door.

Before I can raise my head to look, Sandy begins a curious growl.

I look and squint my eyes. A white flowing silhouette pierces the darkness by my door.

I blink and rub my face.

A soft hum enters my ears. My throat becomes dry and scratchy.

The figure floats towards me in a slow, sweeping motion as if it were moving through a liquid of high viscosity.

Gripping the bed sheets, I shuffle close to my headboard as my chest aches from the brutal knocking of my heart. Folders and files lie scattered across my bed. A few were laying on my lap, but they fell onto the floor when I moved. I must have dozed off while looking over the files.

The figure remains in the shadow between my door and bed, watching me. I can't see the face, but I know. I just know. It's my mother. She raises her hand and with a curl of her bony finger, she motions for me to come.

Gasping for breath, I slam my eyes.

Sandy lets out a sharp bark.

My whole-body jerks and begins to tremble. This is not the first time I've seen her like this. I've seen her before with her face all bloated and purple from having floated in our pond. Her lips plump, and her face drooped with death.

I make an effort to control my breaths as they rush out of my mouth. I dread seeing that ugly face. Please God, keep her in the dark.

"You're not real. You're not real."

The floor creaks again. This time closer to my bed.

I grit my teeth, and I feel a warm tear snake down my cheek.

"You have no control of me. Not anymore. Not anymo . . ."

The room goes quiet. The air is thick with her presence.

"NOT ANYMORE. NOT ANYMORE," I say while shaking my head with gritted teeth.

I swallow hard. I open my eyes.

She's gone, but my hearts leaps at the sight of a little girl standing next to my bed. Blonde hair and white dress. Harmless, loving smile and kind eyes. She's beautiful. An angel. She's my sister Amy.

I blink and she disappears.

While still trying to catch my breath, I turn and bury my face into the pillow next to me. Tears soak the silk material. I sob.

I pull up, place a hand to my forehead and glance about the room.

My head and heart swim with thick emotions.

Anger towards my mother, love and longing for my sister.

I will never forgive my mother for what she did. She was the cause for Amy's disappearance. She's the reason she was taken.

My jaw is tight as my teeth grind without my control. If it wasn't for my mother being the narcissistic, abusive, never satisfied shell of a woman, he wouldn't have chosen her. My sister would still be here.

I hate her for what she did to us. And I have every right for my hatred. How could a mother punish her children by locking them in the basement for days at a time?

No food. No water. No blankets. No nothing.

Just a cold, dark, stale basement.

All because we didn't meet her requirement of making straight A's on the report card for that quarter.

She deserved to drown in that pond.

My cheeks burn and my eyes sting with tears. I rub them and swing my feet over the bed to sit at the edge. I drop my face into palms, placing my elbows on my knees.

I stand and cross for the bathroom to get a glass of water.

My heart sink at the sight.

At the exact spot I saw my dead mother call for me, are drips of water upon my hardwood floor.

I kneel upon one knee and rake my hand over the wet spots.

I rub my fingers together, then dry them on my pajama pants.

She was here.

My mother was really here in her cold, rotting, and swollen flesh.

And so was Amy.

*Do not fear, the light will shine in the darkness.*

The words flow soothingly through my mind. My heart warms at the tender voice. It'd came from deep within my being. Whether my own voice or another's . . . I don't know. But I heard it speak the words. It was clear as day.

The words and voice seem familiar as if I've heard them before spoken from the same voice. A déjà vu moment one could say. A loving, warm presence enters the room and embraces me. I feel safe. I feel loved.

I don't know how to explain it, but I feel like I belong. Was it my sister's voice? God's?

It has to be my sister. Even though we were about a decade apart in age, we always had a special connection as if we were twins or something. We could finish each other's sentences like we knew the other's thoughts. Our connection was something special like the way twins have that supernatural feeling about one another. Amy and I had the same mystic ability.

Those words didn't come from the voice of God. Why would he speak to me? Why now after all these years?

I swallow hard. Thinking.

I get some toilet paper and mop up the water.

I go back to the sink and fill me a glass. I take a swig, and crawl into bed. Sandy jumps from the floor and curls next to me. I run my hand down her fur. She saw her too. What is all this about? Is Amy trying to tell me something?

I lay my head onto my pillow and think about the visions. The voice. The words.

I leave the light on, shut my eyes, and enter back into darkness.

# 44

**Saturday Morning**
**October 5th, 2019**
**Winter Island State Park, Salem MA**

HE'D BEEN WATCHING from the cover of a wood line adjacent to the campground for most of the morning. It was a little before eight o'clock when he began to see movement in the Fulbright's motorhome. It was half past the hour when the children stepped out. All four of them. Two young girls, an older boy about the same age as Connor, then lastly Connor himself.

He heard a women's voice come from inside, warning them not to wander off. It'll be interesting to see if they listen. Their obedience may very well be the difference that determines his plan's success. That was something he was always good about as a child. Obedience. Of course, it certainly helped that rather than being spanked, his father would stick him with a safety pin for punishment. He'd wear it clipped to the inside of his tee-shirts and any time Gary disobeyed, the pin would be unclipped and jabbed into his flesh until it couldn't go any deeper. He learned to deal with the pain by telling himself it was only a bee sting. He never considered his father to be mean, only strict. He learned to respect him a great deal over the years. However, he lost some of that respect once he got older and his father refused to listen to him speak about the voices within his head. His father always said it was demons trying to work their way in. He refused to get Gary help and just a few months after his sixteenth birthday, he forced him to live on the streets. The voices grew worse, and so did the tremors and twitches.

The screaming giggle of a child pulls him back to the present.

The motorhome is parked on the end next to a grassy spot and directly in front of the Salem harbor. The Fort Pickering

Lighthouse is a few hundred yard in the distance out on the rocks.

To Gary Wade Duncan's left, through the thick patch of trees, is the old gray blocked home that once housed the lighthouse watchers and their families.

The windows are long gone, having been broken by rowdy teens, and the doors hang open with broken hinges.

He watches as the children run about the grass, laughing, giggling, and enjoying life the way children should. Conner needs a family like this. He doesn't deserve all of the mess he has to deal with at home.

It wasn't long before one of the girls, who couldn't have been much older than five or six, wandered off to the old abandoned house less than thirty yards from the Fulbright's motorhome. The other three children were too busy playing to notice.

Gary Wade Duncan noticed.

As he sat, waiting for the perfect opportunity to strike, he hoped the kids would be brave enough to enter the abandoned home. It'd make his job so much easier. He could take Connor without them ever knowing.

His heart picks up speed as he watches the little girl stride closer to the house. She stops just outside the big wooden door to gaze upon it.

The other children finally notice her absence and rush to her side.

"Please go inside. Just go inside. It'll be so much easier," Duncan utters with soft breaths.

Squatted in the brush, he gently turns on his heels to face the children straight on.

They stand there for the longest time, obviously contemplating if they're brave enough to enter.

His heart soars when he sees the Fulbright boy push the door open. One by one, they enter. Lastly, after glancing over his shoulder and scanning the area, Connor steps in.

Gary Wade Duncan moves into position.

# 45

SHANE ANDERSON WAS discovered by his co-worker shortly after clocking in at eight. Anderson was left swinging upside down from the bathroom ceiling. He was stripped of his clothes, stabbed in the heart, and one pint of his blood was missing, but there was no puddle. A winged insect was carved into the right side of his chest, and he had a bite mark the back of his shoulder. Same signature and MO as the others.

Cunningham, Swanson, and White investigate the scene as officers swarm the Anderson's home less than twenty minutes away.

There was no sign of forced entry into the home. When the officers looked through a window and saw Mrs. Anderson sitting on the couch, they first thought she was asleep or high on narcotics. They had given the proper police knock, but she had not stirred. The officers force their way inside. Mrs. Anderson wears a wool beanie and sits with the remote control in her limp hand. Dried, flaky blood is streaked down her head and cheeks, her skin is a shade of purple and void of life.

After investigating and contacting family for the whereabouts of the child, they found a lead.

The Fulbright's. Winter Island State Park.

Field Agents, State Police, Cunningham, Swanson, and Detective White all rush to the campground near the Salem Harbor.

They did not contact the Fulbright's nor turn on their sirens. They will need to approach with stealth, surround the perimeter, and surprise him with force.

Their ETA is fifteen minutes.

† † † † † † † † † †

THE HOME IS DARK AND DUSTY, full of cobwebs, graffiti, and the odor of urine. Beer bottles and food wrappers lie scattered this way and that. A shirt or sock, a shoe or pillow tossed here and there.

"Hide-n-go-seek?" questions Jamie Fulbright.

Connor gulps, then gently nods.

Five-year-old Karissa clings tightly to her brother, eying the place with slow sweeps of her blue eyes. "I'm staying with you," she mumbles.

"That's fine. Me and Karissa will start counting first if you two want to go hide," says Jaime.

Kelly bolts away, and her feet pitter patter across the cold concrete floor.

Connor stands there for a moment as Jamie and Karissa turn their backs to him and begin counting. He hears Kelly climb a flight of stairs, so he follows. He turns and enters his stride. His eyes are pulled to the black fireplace full of shadows. Something about it was mysterious and sort of spooky. He rushes past it and angles up the stairs. Halfway up the steps, he stops and turns over his shoulder to steal a glance at Jamie and Karissa. And then to that creepy fireplace where he half imagined a monster crawling out of it. He jerks his head around and quickly conquers the stairs.

He hears Kelly's feet pound into a room before going silent.

"Four . . . five . . . six," coming from downstairs.

Connor cranes his neck about the hallway full of closed doors, then decides to return downstairs to the other rooms.

"Seven . . . eight . . . nine."

He scurries down the steps and disappears quietly into a back bedroom.

"Ten . . . eleven . . . twelve."

He finds a closet and tucks himself away in a dark corner. With his butt on the floor, knees to his chest, and arms wrapped around his shins, he waits within the shadow.

"Twenty. Ready or not here we come!"

Connor had left the closet door open which allowed it to welcome in a small glimmer of light. He can see a faint patch of steam with each breath. He shivers and tightens the grip around his legs. The window has been broken out, allowing a swift breeze to enter.

He hears footsteps climbing the stairs. They go for Kelly first.

Something rakes across the floor behind him.

He yanks his head around and peers into the dark. He can't see anything. He stretches out his hand, feeling aimlessly into the shadows.

The children laugh as they run among the rooms above him, but it's the weird noise that stirs loudly in his mind. He continues to stare hard into this shadow, deep within the darkened closet.

Squinting his eyes, and feeling in the dark, his hand lands on something. He jerks back and gasps. What was that? A shoulder?

He hears something shimmy across the floor towards him, but in a flash before he could scream, move or anything, a dark clothed figured had him in its grasp. A bony, black hand clinches tightly to his mouth. A strong smell that reminds him of a doctor's office fills his nostrils. Everything turns black, and his body turns limp.

† † † † † † † † † †

**SWAT TEAM, STATE POLICE,** and multiple field agents along with Cunningham, Swanson, and Detective White swarm the park by foot. Director Ramsey had landed in Boston a half-hour earlier and now enters the park with them.

They approach the Fulbright's motorhome on light feet. They motion for guests to remain silent and inside their campers or RV's. Ramsey climbs the small set of metal steps and gives a hard knock upon the door.

The motorhome squeaks as a pair of feet can be heard coming to answer. Guns drawn and ready for anything, the door swings open and every swat officer and agent tenses, ready to fire.

A large man stands with wide eyes, and a small petite lady stands in her robe behind him.

"Mr. and Mrs. Fulbright?"

They nod.

"We need you to step outside. Where are the children?" says Ramsey.

Climbing gingerly down the steps, "Uh-uh-uh-they-they-were just right-right here. What is this?"

"We need you both to sit here for a moment."

They sit at the picnic table as two swat officers enter the motorhome with AR-15's.

"You don't know where the children are?" Cunningham asks in a thin tone.

The man wags his head.

The wife sits trembling as tears flood her eyes. "What's going on? Where are the children," she asks with a shake to her voice.

"Director Ramsey?"

Everyone turns to the voice.

Detective White stands pointing to the abandoned gray blocked home.

Ramsey nods and motions the men into place.

Within moments they had the place surrounded.

Children's voices emit from inside, "Connor?"

"Connor, c'mon man, we're finished, you can come out now. You won," a boys voice echoes from the home.

Ramsey scrunches his brows. He takes a breath and signals his men inside.

The children get a start at the men's sudden presence. Their faces turn white and long as if having seen a ghost. Ramsey and Cunningham felt the same way when they realized they were too late.

Connor Anderson had been taken.

# Missing

# Child

## Connor Anderson

AGE: 8

SEX: MALE

HEIGHT: 3'10

WEIGHT: 67

HAIR: BROWN

EYES: BROWN

LAST SEEN: 10/5/2019 AT WINTER ISLAND STATE PARK, SALEM, MA

**IF YOU KNOW WHERE CONNOR IS OR HAVE ANY INFORMATION THAT MAY HELP INVESTIGATORS, PLEASE CALL 911!!**

# 46

I AWOKE TO Collins's voice from the living room a little after seven. Other than dreaming of being lost in the woods with a million cicadas screeching my name, my dreams were mostly a blank. I enter the living room and find Collins on the phone.

"Hang on a second, Chief. Here she is." He passes me his phone.

The call was from Cunningham. Just a checkup. Likely to be sure I hadn't slipped out of my window and began the trek to Salem. I can't say it didn't cross my mind. It was a little after nine when he called back to inform me of the Anderson murders, the raid on Winter Island State Park, and Connor Anderson's disappearance. I had heard most of it already through the scanner, so the news didn't come as a surprise, but rather a confirmation.

*Starts with S ends with M. You'll find two but not a third again.*
Precisely.
Same MO. Same signature.
Stabbed in the heart. Bite marks from dentures made from victim's teeth. Drained of blood. Scripture references. Drawings on the mirror. His name. My name. And next to Donna Anderson on the couch, was a jar containing a cicada.

The Fulbright's were taken in for questioning but were released a short time later. With their clean records and polished alibis, it was an obvious waste of time.

A massive manhunt ensued as officers checked every boater within the harbor, every camper, worker, maintenance man, you name it. Salem was essentially turned upside down and shaken with vigorous taps on the bottom, but like a shaker void of salt nothing came out.

How could he have gotten away so fast?

Must've had a vehicle nearby. Parked down a trail. Something. Or an accomplice drove by and picked him up. Or perhaps he simply drove in and out of the campground as if he were staying there, even waved on the way out.

Cunningham and Ramsey were both grouchy and could barely speak to me without blowing a gasket. White and Swanson weren't any better.

This quagmire is getting old fast. Not just for me but now for everyone. Of course, it doesn't help any that we still don't know where Weatherby is. That fact only adds fuel to everyone's flame.

I glance at my watch as I finish packing Paul and Allen some food to take back with them. Leftover turkey burgers, spaghetti, and some homemade ice cream which I had made last week.

*10:18.*

Collins and I are scheduled for an eleven o'clock meeting with Frances Whitaker at Morningside. Whether she will speak with us or not remains to be seen, but it will be worth a try. At least it'd allow me to give her Archie's gift. I'll also have to buy me a new phone on the way over.

The profiler from the bureau, Shannon Carter, will be giving a briefing at three. Agent Vasquez and Agent Turner will be flying in around that time as well.

We also have Sarah McCrae's vigil and her parent's memorial tonight at Freewill Holiness. That should be interesting.

† † † † † † † † † †

**"SHE DOESN'T LIKE** to be touched or looked in the eye. So, be careful. If you're lucky she'll be in a good mood. Otherwise, I wouldn't expect much for your time. Be patient with her though because she can easily be confused," a black-haired nurse tells us as she gently creaks open the door to Mrs. Whitaker's room.

I nod, "Thank you, ma'am," and step in. Collins is behind me.

The room is dark except for the light trickling in from the window.

Sitting in her wheelchair and peering out the window with the curtain drawn back, is an old, frail little lady. She has long white hair that is wrapped into a single braid which almost reaches the floor. She has a sun blotched hand to her cheek as her eyes gaze into the new day. Birds sing and rummage about in a cherry tree just outside the window. A hummingbird feeder stands in plain view.

I gently knock upon her door before pushing it on open, "Mrs. Whitaker?"

Nothing.

"Mrs. Whitaker?" I say easing closer.

She turns slowly. She has the bluest, most angelic eyes I've ever seen. It was only a glance, but I quickly divert my eyes away to respect her boundaries as told by the nurse. Her features are soft and kind. A lovely lady that must've been a true beauty in her day. Not that she isn't now of course.

She smiles. "Hello."

I place a hand to my chest, "I'm Lieutenant Daniels, and this is my partner, Detective Collins."

He raises his hand and smiles.

She shifts her eyes to him and nods with a kind smile then looks back to me. Her eyes pull at mine, but I fight the urge to look in her eyes, so I focus on the top of her forehead instead.

Holding the Origami Swan to my side, I step forward and hold it out. "This is a gift from your husband . . . Archie."

She gasps and pulls a trembling hand to her mouth. Tears well in her eyes. She takes it and holds it close to her chest as her mind appears to drift backwards to another place and time. Her lips quiver and tears trickle down her cheeks.

I glance about the room and find a box of tissues. I pass her a few and I am careful not to touch her in the exchange.

She sniffles and wags her head, "How did you get this? How did you get in?" Her brows arch.

I smile and lift my badge from my neck, "With a flash of this and a lot of conniving."

"How is he?"

"He's good. He looks well. Wanted me to give you that and tell you he said hey and he loved you."

She lowers her head and weeps into her hand.

Everything in me wants to reach out and touch her. You know, pat her shoulder, or squeeze her arm? Anything to show my sympathy.

She takes a drag of air through clogged nostrils. She dabs her eyes and face. "Will you tell him 'thank you' for me?"

"Of course."

"And tell him I said he better watch out for those loose women in there."

I chuckle, Collins chuckles, but Mrs. Whitaker keeps a stone face.

I reign in my composure, clear my throat, and say, "I'll tell him."

"Is he keeping a garden?"

My eyes had shifted to the cherry tree outside. Turning back to her, "Umm . . . yeah . . . yeah I believe so."

She turns and stretches for a small glass vase which houses two purple daisies. They are a little too far on the wilted side but may have one last chance of revival in them.

"Will you give him these? Tell him to plant them in his garden for me. I can hardly get them to grow here. Maybe he'll have better luck there."

A warmth courses through my body. I feel my own lip began to quiver. "Of course." I take the vase.

She turns and looks through the window, "He was only doing what he thought was best for that boy. You know that, right?"

I nod, "I know that."

"Archie was a good man. Still is. He never hurt a soul. Treated me like a queen and loved me when I'd forgotten what love was. After the death of our daughter . . . I didn't think I could live anymore, and I wouldn't have had it not been for Archie. Children were always special to us, especially after the miscarriage."

"I'm sorry to hear that. I didn't know."

She swallows and turns back to me, "Someone within that church is the cause for all this. I've been saying it for years. There was a bad breed that emerged from that church when all that happened. The Currie's were the ones I always suspected. I don't see the Wicker bunch doing anything, but them Currie's . . ." she shakes her head with tight lips and shakes a finger at me, "That's the one's you best look into, I've been saying it all along."

"The Currie's?"

"Gene and Barbara. And those youngins of theirs too. Something just wasn't right about them."

"Where are they now?" I question as I jot notes down in my pad.

She moves her head side to side and looks out the window at a flock of black birds. "Who's to say. They supposedly moved down south right after Hal took over. I never believed it though. I think they hung around. Changed their appearance, started going by different names, changed their cars, moved into another home. I think they're the ones involved in all this mess."

"What about Archie's theory?" Collins asks.

"What, the demons?"

He bobs his head.

"Yeah, there might be a little of that involved too. Have you heard the sounds yet?"

Collins and I look to one another with arched brows, then look back to her.

"You will. Trust me. Sooner or later you will."

"What sounds?"

"Like a metal chair raking across concrete. Only coming from the heavens. Or like an old door squeaking on metal hinges. It's the Angel's trumpets like it talks about in Revelation. When you hear that, you know one's near."

"One's near? What are you talking about?"

"Demons. When you hear the sounds from heaven, it's a warning. They're close. Believe me. Archie wasn't the only one that saw them."

I felt the hair on my arm stiffen. The Ambrose Bierce story of *The Damned Thing* flashes before my mind.

"They're invisible sometimes, you know? Other times they're not. Make's no difference. They're out there."

"So, you think the demons may be helping our killer?"

"I didn't say that . . . you did. All I know is there is more out there in this world than you might think. Just because you don't see them, doesn't mean they're not real. If you could just see beyond the veil," she pauses, shuts her eyes and allows a calming smile to stretch her lips, "But it's like I always say, 'If there's evil, then there must be good. Right?' I can assure you . . ." she takes the time to look us both in the eye, which makes me more uncomfortable than her it appears, "There is light and there is goodness. His name is Jesus. He's the only one the darkness bows to. As long as you have Him on your side, you don't have anything to worry about. The darkness will flee at the very thought of Him. He'll shine into the darkest of places, pushing away every shadow tucked away in a nook or cranny. No darkness can stand against such light. He's all that's good in this world. And you know what, you two can shine the same light."

I wrinkle my brow.

"You know why?"

A beat.

"Because we're all made in the image of God. Every one of us is designed with an internal candle and wick just waiting to be lit with the flame of our Creator."

I take a breath and look out the window at a Hummingbird feeding on some nectar.

"You want to catch this guy?"

I bring my eyes back to hers.

"Light your candles. The light will shine in the darkness and nothing can overcome such light."

"With all due respect Mrs. Whitaker, I gave up on religion many moons ago."

"Me too."

"Huh?"

"I said me too. I'm not telling you you need religion. I'm saying you need to spend some time with your Creator. Big difference."

I bob my head and rub a thumb over my palm.

"Is God good?" I ask the question before I even had time to think it. It just tumbled out with my breath. As much as I wanted to pull it back in, the question was out. *The* question I'd been asking my whole life. Is God good?

Mrs. Whitaker squints her eyes, tilts her head, takes a breath, and smiles. "I've asked that same question for many years—"

"You have?"

"Oh yes. I'm human just like you my dear," she pinches her arm and lifts an old dry, wrinkled patch of skin, "See here, I'm made of flesh and blood just like you. But you want to know my answer to your question?"

I nod.

She leans forward in her wheelchair, glances about the room, and says in a tone barely above a whisper, "You know the warm feeling you get inside when you hug someone you love? Someone you know loves you and always has your back. Maybe it's a parent, a child, a sibling, a spouse, a best friend. You know what I'm talking about?"

Paul and Amy are the two that pop into mind. They're the only family I've ever really had. And Amy's embrace is now just a painful memory.

"Yeah," my voice barely escapes from the dryness and knot catching in my throat.

"Is that good?"

I crane my head with arched brows and take my time before giving an answer. "Is that good? Yeah. Of course. How is it not?"

"What about the cry of a newborn baby? Is that good?"

"Absolutely."

"There's no darkness or evil in that, right?"

"Of course not."

"Because those two things I just mentioned are of the Light in which there is no darkness. That's God."

Good point.

I swallow and dip my head.

"You see God shows us His goodness every day, it's just sometimes hidden in the simple things."

"Well . . . what about the evil? What about the murders, the kidnappings? How do you explain that? Is that God's goodness?"

"Oh, c'mon. Don't be crazy. You're not saying God done those things are you?"

"Well he certainly didn't stop them, did he?"

"Honey, you know as good as I do there is evil in this world. Polarity does exist. If there is light than there will also be darkness. If there is goodness, there will also be evil. It's the way the world is. And it'll always be like this until we reach Heaven. The only place that will be perfect the way God intended earth to be before Adam and Eve were deceived by the serpent into eating that fruit. That was the moment evil entered the world."

A lull entered the conversation and to change the topic, Collins clears his throat and says, "Your husband said we should speak with Hal Resnick. Would you agree?"

"Hal's a fine man. A good man. You know he's kept a close eye on this mess. He knows a lot about the cases. He's really kept up with it through the years. If I were investigating, I'd be sure to talk to him."

"We'll be sure to do that."

A rattle began deep in her lungs, then crawled its way slowly up her throat. She doubled over, shoulders hitching, and coughing gut-wrenching sounds.

Her eyelids turned heavy as they hung half-way over her deep-set eyes. Her breathing quickened as she tried to catch her breath.

"Are you okay?" I ask as I lean close with my hands on my knees.

She nods with a hand to her mouth. "I'm fine. Who are you?"

I straighten and take a step back.

"Who are you? Who are you? Mandy. Mandy!"

"Sshh-sshh, it's okay. It's okay."

"Get out of here! Now!" she hisses.

It sends a chill down my spine to see such a scathing rebuke come from the seemingly kind and gentle lady we were just speaking with.

Feet plod down the hall across the tile floor.

"Mrs. Whitaker, it's okay-it's okay."

None of my word's sooth her. Her eyes are wild above a snarled nose and mouth.

I cannot believe how fast she changed.

The black-haired nurse reaches the room and rushes to her side.

"They're coming. They're coming!" Mrs. Whitaker begins to scream.

"Who? Who's coming?"

"The demons! They're all coming!"

"I think it's time for you to go. She's reached her limits," says the black-haired nurse named Mandy

I sigh and nod.

"Thank you for letting us speak with her. We'll come back another time."

"Please do," Mandy says as she busies herself with passing Mrs. Whitaker a container of pills and a cup of water.

"Thank you, Mrs. Whitaker. It was a pleasure to meet to you."

"Get on out of here. Go on," she says as she rakes her hand through the air at us.

I offer a gentle smile and step out. The last I saw of her, she was tossing her head back, downing her medication.

In the hallway now, "Boy, that was a quick change," says Collins.

"Yeah, it sure was." I say as I glare at the purple daises in my hand.

Archie will be happy.

# 47

"WHAT PLUS WHY equals who," says Agent Shannon Carter as she busies herself with aiming a clicker at the presentation screen. She is semi-retired, meaning she only works on cases such as this. The hair pullers for people such as I, but commonality for her. She has assisted in the capture of countless murderers and serial killers through the years, working on such cases from the Doll Collector, the Weaver, the Alaskan Hunter, Son of Sam, and the Green River Killer just to name a few.

I know her name and pedigree, but this will be the first time I've had the privileged of meeting her.

I sip on my coffee and jot notes in my pad as I sit in the stadium like classroom setting between Collins and Detective White. Agent Swanson and Sheriff Johnston sit on a row below us. Johnston is finishing up another one of his Zero candy bars. Agent Dan Turner and Agent Ricki Vasquez from the GTK case sit on the front row directly below Agent Carter. Chief Cunningham sits on a desk a few feet from Agent Carter, holding his glasses and biting one end as he cranes his head to the large screen. Director Ramsey stands to the side with crossed arms and one hand cradling his chin. The rest of the room is full of officers from surrounding departments in Portland and a few of the detectives working the Anderson case in Salem.

Agent Carter takes turns lecturing us about her philosophy and clicking to another slide filled with the gruesome photos taken from Morty's crime scenes over the years. The McNamara's, Anthony's, the Canton's, Shelton's, the McCrae's, and now . . . the Anderson's.

"If you want to know Picasso, you study his art. Same thing applies here. If we want to know who we're dealing with, we have to study his crimes. Why does he shear his victims? Was he sheared and humiliated by a bully or domineering parent when he was a boy? What is it about taking the victims teeth and making his own dentures to bite them with? Does he himself have bad teeth? Why does he like the cicada bug so much?"

Sheriff Johnston mumbles under his breath, "Because he's a frigging creep," and scratches at the scar on his cheek.

"Why is he leaving the scripture references? The drawings of skulls and angel wings? Why? Why? Why?" she says the last three words slow and with inflected importance.

She clicks to another slide. It is the bloodied bathroom mirror of the McCrae's.

"We are dealing with an individual who is extremely inadequate, possibly and most likely abused as a child, no sense of self value or importance, who has always been controlled, dominated, and humiliated by an older, manipulative relative. Until now."

She clicks to the bald head of Mrs. Anderson sitting upright on her couch with the remote controller in hand.

"Now at last . . . he is in complete control. Now, he is the dominator. The tables have turned. This isn't as much about the victims as it is about his own need to regain the power. This is his means of justice. He is carrying out the wrath of God for his own misfortune. This is a revengeful, angry, control hungry individual, who has whole heartedly justified his crimes in his mind. He won't stop until he's stopped. This kind of deranged individual will never be satisfied. He will always be hungry for more control. More power. More. More. More."

She pauses for a moment and scans the crowd.

I raise my hand.

"Yes?"

"Umm, what about the kidnappings? How do you see that fitting into all of this?" I ask before biting on the end of my pen.

She locks her hands behind her back and begins to pace. When she had crossed the entire platform, she stopped and removed her glasses. She cleanses them with a handkerchief from her black blazer and returns them to their spot at the tip of her nose. Her face is weathered from years of stress but has sharp features that give out a natural beauty. Silver sleek hair is brushed to one side and gracefully kisses her left shoulder.

"Perhaps, he is taking the children away from the abusive parents because he can sympathize with them. He knows what it's like to live in those types of environments. Hence, the reason for the orphanage that Hope Jamison came from. It's his way of feeling a sense of heroism."

"But this has been going on since the eighties. So, we can't be dealing with just one person. There has to be a cluster. A group. A cult."

She nods slowly and sighs.

"That was my next point. Our current suspect is likely not the only one involved. This could be a copycat of what happened in the eighties or this could still be the same organization. The same cult, group, or what have you. Regardless of how many may be involved, the one carrying out these murders, the one leaving behind the cicadas and writings, the one we know as Morty, he's the one I just mentioned. The one in need of control and dominance. Everyone else are just manipulated and brainwashed accomplices. Whoever began all of this is not the same person we're after today, but they are cut from the same cloth."

Ramsey clears his throat and looks over his shoulder to Agent Carter, "So, Mrs. Carter, what's your profile in this case?"

She begins with no hesitation, "Mid-forties to early fifties, white male, surprising strength and agility for his size, a split personality. A loner, self-loather, and impotent individual who hides his inabilities under the mask of a charismatic, confident, soothe talking genius, and who lives under a highly sophisticated image. Hence, the reason for the false appearance to Dr. Feltner as a Professor from UMass. Which explains his liking for classical music. Anything to contrast his lack of self-worth and feelings of inadequacies. Which was ingrained in him likely by a domineering parent if I were to place my bets. He is a highly intelligent individual with an IQ that would surpass any of ours by a wide margin. He will be drawn to dark colors due to the darkness residing within. He will likely drive a dark, low mileage car that will undergo regular maintenance and will not have a spot or blemish. That said I would be sure to check with the local mechanic shops to see if they have anyone on record that fits the profile. He will be well organized, likely to the point of OCD. Could have prior military or police experience, but nothing of stature. Would have likely AWOLed or failed the academy. A police and crime buff who will know the procedures of a crime scene inside and out."

A holy hush fills the room as she continues painting our serial killer. It is as if he is appearing next to her on stage, bone by bone, sinew by sinew, one piece at a time like a spirit becoming flesh.

"You will have likely already interviewed him. He will hang around any events which honor the victims. Be sure to stake out the victim's burial sites as well. He may feel some guilt for his actions and return to offer an apology. He would do this after midnight when it is darkest out. It is going to be someone you'd least expect. It'll shock you when you find him. You will have likely crossed paths with him and the others more than once before this is over. You may even come to consider him a friend or friendly nuisance. Someone who seems to be genuinely concerned about the case. Asking questions, prying and picking for answers. If you find yourself in discussions with someone like this, test them. Briefly and vaguely mention something about the case that is wrong and something that only the culprit would know. Then wait and see if he corrects you. If it's him, he'll correct you before he even realizes it. His pride and ego will demand it."

I feel a soft nudge on my arm. Collins.

He leans close and says in a quick whisper, "Maybe the guy at Ted's Diner is him, but I still think Wicker and that church is involved in all of this. I just feel it."

I whisper back, "Let's go tonight and tomorrow and see what we think after that."

He pulls back and nods.

I tap my pen to my notepad and point to the black figure I'd unconsciously scribbled while taking in the lecture. Just like the one Sarah McCrae had drew in her diary. Just like the one that reflected in my television the other night. A tall, black cloaked shadow with a top hat. The man in the black hood.

Morty. Gary Wade Duncan.

Him.

I watch as Collins's eyes expand. He shifts in his seat and shakes his head with a sigh.

". . . The person we're dealing with here, is the devil dressed as an angel. A wolf in sheep's clothing. Be careful who you trust and don't turn your back on anyone. I mean it. *Anyone.*"

After a few more questions, Agent Shannon Carter finished and stepped away from the podium. Agent Dan Turner and Agent Ricki Vasquez stood from their seats and approached her.

I lean into Collins, "We should go introduce ourselves."

He nods.

I rise and pat Sheriff Johnston's shoulder as I pass.

Closing the gap between the agents and ourselves, Mrs. Carter raises her attention to meet my eyes. She smiles.

Agent Turner and Agent Vasquez follow her gaze.

The room is full of chatter and shuffling feet. Like the end of a college lecture.

"Agent Carter, it's a privilege to finally meet you. I'm Lieutenant Laurie Daniels and this is my partner, Detective Patrick Collins."

"Pleasure to meet you. Hope this was worth your time."

"Are you kidding? My goodness, your insights were spot on."

"Yeah, and she didn't know about the guy from the diner until just now," said Agent Turner as he stretched forth his hand with a grin.

Collins and I shake his and Agent Vasquez's hands.

"Wow. That's amazing. I've heard so much about Behavioral Science and the Bureaus profiling tactics, but this is the first time I've seen it up close and personal. I must say though, it is not too far from Collins's profile. I think you were in the ballpark," I say turning to him.

He nods, "Yeah, they have their similarities." He looks to Agent Carter, "But yours is much more in depth. You definitely have the experience."

"Oh yes, unfortunately this isn't my first rodeo. I've been hunting serial killers my entire adult life it seems."

"So, you all were a part of the GTK case?" I ask.

They each nod.

Agent Vasquez goes first, "Yeah, that one was a doozy."

"At first glance, do you see any similarities?"

"What a copycat?" asks Turner.

"Maybe?"

He twists his head and rubs his chin before looking to Agent Carter, giving her space to go first.

"Yes and no."

I squint my eyes and crane my head.

"You see the GTK grew up in a similar environment as I discussed about this guy. The GTK was close to his mother and it was that bond that seemed to set him off. Everything he did, he did in an atonement for his mother's death. He believed that by killing all those people, it would somehow ease his mother's pain or grief in the afterlife. And other than a few victims here and there, he chose at random. There was not much planning involved. Whereas with your guy here, he's a master planner and control freak. He has to plan everything in advance or else he'd fall apart. The GTK flew by a whim. I mean for heaven's sake a stiff breeze could arouse him and get his juices flowing enough that he would be driven to kill the next person he passed along the street. He claims he was directed by an evil spirit he'd come to know as Kirkland. Which seems to be another personality buried deep within that was formed during his younger years in that cult he was a part of. He could shift and change on the drop of a hat. He couldn't control his impulses. Whereas, Morty here, controls every facet of his life. Control is what drives him. Control and dominance are his drug of choice."

"I see. Would there be any way I could speak with the GTK? You know, like a skype session or phone call?"

Carter looks to Turner and Vasquez.

Vasquez clears her throat, "We could try and arrange a phone call perhaps," she shakes her head and lowers her eyes, "But I really don't see them allowing it. Your best bet would be to show up unannounced with one of us. Between your badge and ours, we should be able to get you in. Jessie would be glad to speak to you and offer any insight he can, but the penitentiary would be the ones with the issue."

"Figures. Uh, Agent Carter would you mind taking a moment to discuss your profile with my partner here? I think it'd do him some good to compare the files," I say between glancing at her and Collins.

"Sure. Be glad to."

"Great. Thanks. Patrick, you want to show her to your office?"

"Yes, ma'am."

"Mrs. Carter, it was a pleasure meeting you. I'll speak with you again before you leave. I really enjoyed your presentation. You have been a tremendous help."

"It was my pleasure dear," she says as she squeezes my arm with a grin before following Collins.

After she'd taken a few paces, I spun around, "Oh, Mrs. Carter . . ."

"Yes?"

"You know a gentleman by the name of Paul Sealey?"

I could see the name swimming through her files, her eyes searching for the face to match the name. A big grin slowly stretches her face. She begins to chuckle.

"Paul Sealey. Oh boy, yeah, I know him. I helped him with some cases back in the seventies and eighties down in New Orleans. How is he doing?"

"He's good. He's actually my neighbor. He said he remembered you."

"Is that so? My word. You tell him I said hello. He's a good man. Always liked Mr. Sealey. He's a good one."

"I'll tell him."

As her and Collins walk off, I check my watch.

*5:16 p.m.*

The memorial at Freewill Holiness starts at seven.

As Agent Carter and Collins pass time going over the profiles, I spend my time getting to know Agent Turner and Agent Vasquez. I pick their brains about the GTK and other serial killers they have tracked down through the years. With their help and wealth of knowledge in the behavior of individuals such as the one we're after, I am confident they can help us catch our guy.

I just hope we can do so before he claims another victim.

# 48

"I STILL CAN'T BELIEVE how in depth this lady's profile is. I mean, it's literally like she knows the guy. I've never seen anything like it. I thought mine was detailed, but for heaven's sake she knows about his childhood, his favorite colors, wardrobe, you name it. It's amazing," Collins says while glancing out the window of my Suburban.

"I figured it'd do you some good to speak with her. She didn't get where she is in the Bureau for nothing you know." I flip my turn signal to take a right off I-95 as we head for the exit to Gray.

"I'm telling you right now, I really feel like it's someone here at this church. The moment I stepped into the place, I just picked up an eerie vibe."

"Well, let's not jump to any conclusions, but at the same token, don't turn your back on anyone either."

"The only thing that doesn't add up though is the size and stature. This Pastor Wicker guy is small and petite like. And he doesn't dress like the guy from Ted's Diner either. That's the part that's throwing me off. Unless, he dresses like that for a cover up. A disguise maybe. I don't know," he says while wagging his head and biting a thumb nail.

"Regardless, let's not assume anything. At least we're not alone anymore. With Agent Weatherby and the ongoing case in Salem, I believe we finally have everyone's attention. Turner and Vasquez said Quantico and Washington are like a hornet's nest right now. Every field office and police station across the Country knows what's happened. The airports, ports of entry, boarders, you name it, all know to be on the lookout for anyone matching the profile. So, maybe now we can finally begin to close the gap."

"I hope so."

"Me too, Patrick. Me too."

Coming into Gray off the exit, every light pole along the streets had a flyer stapled to the wood with a picture of Sarah McCrae, her description, a sentence asking for "your" help in finding her, and the word "MISSING" typed above it.

The town was already quiet to begin with, but now it just seems ghostly and dead.

Eerie.

An old Citgo gas station sits at the corner of a red light in town. The light inside is dim and the paint is chipping away along the blocked walls. It's old, rugged, and worn. A digital lit sign showing the gas prices, flickers as we pass.

The red light turns green, I let off the brake and proceed through.

"Woahhh!" Collins screams.

Tires screech across the asphalt, rushing closer at an alarming speed.

I catch glimpse of something green in the peripheral of my vision.

An old square bodied Ford Pickup lurches to a halt in the middle of the intersection, only inches from t-boning the passenger side and slamming into Collins.

A frail old man with pale skin, a bald head, and thick coke bottled glasses glares through the windshield at me. He snarls his teeth and flicks his hand at me, while growling a scalding rebuke. Even though he was the one that ran the red light. He shakes his head with clinched teeth and pounds the gas pedal. His tires bark as he speeds away.

Collins and I watch as the truck vanishes into the distant fog. The beady red taillights eye us as he disappears.

"IH8 PPL."

"Huh?"

"The license plate," says Collins.

"I hate people. Yeah, I 'd say that suits him."

"Yeah. You alright?"

"I'm okay. You?"

Collins nods and gathers his breath.

"I'm glad you saw him."

"That was a close one."

I rub my forehead and ease through the intersection.

Darkness descends more rapidly upon the town the deeper we go.

As we come out of a curve, my head lamps land on something large and black on the side of the road. I can't quite make it out.

"What is that?" Collins asks.

"I don't know. It's moving whatever it is."

As we near, it flaps its wings and takes flight.

A buzzard.

It was one of three that enjoy a deer carcass.

As I come closer, the other two hop around before taking to the air like their friend. Only these two decide to go right over my windshield. Their massive, black wings and ugly red heads almost skim the glass.

"That's one ugly creature isn't it?" asks Collins.

"Yeah. And as if their looks aren't creepy enough, they feast on the dead. Ever thought about that?"

"No, but I get your point. I think creepy would be an understatement," Collins says as he leans close to the side window to get a better look at the deer.

"Goodness. You see that?"

"What?"

"That thing was all cut up. Looked like it had claw marks down the side of it."

"Really?"

"Yeah. I mean big claw marks."

"Huh, maybe it was a bear or cougar."

Collins turns back and raises his brows, "Man, must've been wicked big whatever it was."

"Hmm. I don't know. There's no telling around here."

A few minutes pass.

"Is this where I turn?"

"Yeah. Take this right and the church will be about a mile down the road on your left."

"They're out in the sticks, aren't they?"

"You could say that."

I begin to see a light through the trees, and it illuminates a set of red doors with a large black cross hanging above them.

It is six-forty-one as I pull into the parking lot. About twenty cars or so are spread across the grass and gravel. Another dozen or so pull in as we climb out of my Suburban.

A church hymn plays softly from inside. It doesn't seem to be a recording either as it sounds more like a live band. Guitar, bass, drums, the whole nine.

The grass is slick from an evening mist as we stride across it. Crickets chirp and cicadas sing.

So far, the people look to be mostly of the blue-collar type. The men are dressed in jeans and flannels, maybe a vest here and there, but most wear ball caps and then remove them upon entering the church. The women are homely looking, with long hair and skirts as if it were a sin to take care of themselves. Who knows, maybe for them it is?

Then there are other people who do not appear to belong with the clique. These are the ones who are here simply to show their support of the missing girl. These people are from all walks of life. Young, old, rich, poor, you name it.

Collins and I reach the bricked steps leading to the red doors. A plump, middle-aged man who is dressed in a light blue button down and khakis, stands holding the door. He sports a fresh, clean shave that causes his double chin to press toward a third.

He greets us with a smile as his eyes lock onto our badges. Mine hangs from my neck and Collins's is clipped to his belt.

"So, you're the detectives?"

"That's right. Lieutenant Daniels, and this is my partner, Detective Collins. And you are?"

"Dale Conrad. Pleased to meet you. Appreciate you guys coming."

"Our pleasure. We just wanted to show our sympathy and support."

"Well thank you. Please, have a seat and if you need anything just let me know."

"Thank you, we'll do."

He motioned us in with a wave of his hand.

We follow behind an elderly couple and sit next to them at the end of a pew. Third row deep on the right side.

A table is placed below the preacher's pulpit in the center of the altar. Upon it, are pictures of the McCrae's, candles, and vases full of flowers.

The air in this sanctuary seems thin, like the walls are closing in. I've never been much of a claustrophobic, but I almost begin to feel as if I'm being smothered in here. My breathing has become too conscious in my mind, so I distract myself by examining the rest of the room. Trying desperately to tell myself it's bigger than it feels. The stage is about the size of my dining room and it would take only two steps from the altar to reach it. A round man, dressed in overalls with a thick gray beard, sits in a chair playing an acoustic six-string guitar. A tall and skinny man, with a face clean of hair but full of freckles, stands thumbing a bass guitar. In the back corner of the stage, caged behind a wall of plexiglass sits a young boy, not a day older than twelve, who keeps a soft beat on a set of drums. The trio is in mid chorus of Amazing Grace. Not that I know my hymns or anything, but I do know that one. I mean who doesn't, right?

On each side of the stage, there are two white doors which look like they could lead to a bedroom. Must be closets or something. Maybe where they count the tithes or break bread. Who knows? I turn to the right and begin to admire the beautiful stained glassed windows with their blend of yellow, red, and green hues.

The creak of a door pulls my attention. Brett Stephenson emits from the bedroom looking door to my right. He's dressed in khakis with a white polo shirt that is buttoned all the way to the top.

Another man follows close behind him. He wears a white button down with black slacks. Something about him reminds me of a little Tom Hanks. Maybe it is his hair or eyes. I don't know, but that was the first thing that popped into my mind when I saw him.

Collins leans close and whispers, "That's Pastor Wicker."
I nod.

Neither Wicker nor Brett pay us any mind. They are too focused on testing the microphone and fiddling with the cords.

The other two men and the drummer boy continue playing their hymn.

I look to my watch, 6:48.

I scratch behind my right ear and turn my head to take in the crowd behind us. I search and sift through the faces, while hoping he is here. He could be anyone of these people.

Anyone.

My eyes stop when they land on a couple seated at the back of the room. I've seen their faces before. Immediately, my mind goes to work trying to compute their features and decide where I've seen them before.

Then it dawns on me.

The diner. Ted's Diner. It is the couple I saw sitting behind us that day. The one's I felt were staring at us.

But what happened to them once the classical music started playing? When we began questioning people at the diner. They vanished, didn't they? Why?

Feeling my glare, the long-haired lady raises her vision and meets my eyes. I watch as she nudges her husband. He leans into her, then shifts his eyes towards me and Collins.

I smile and take a swallow before turning around to face forward. I wait a moment before scratching my left cheek and leaning to my right to whisper to Collins.

"The two from Ted's Diner?" he asks.

"Yeah. Don't look."

"Really? You sure it's them."

"I'm sur—I said don't look."

"Sorry."

"And yes, I do feel a vibe in this place."

"See, I told you so."

"He's here."

Collins face drains of blood and his eyes widen.

"I can feel him. He's close."

Collins pulls back. Face straight, eyes searching, scanning, thinking. He swallows hard.

I lean in once again, "Just stay calm and let's keep our cool. He'll come to us. He'll want to talk to me. Besides his taking to me, he's likely a police buff, remember? He'll be drawn to the badge."

Collins nods and scratches his sandpapered chin.

Not long afterwards the memorial begins. The music ceases as the three men leave the stage and sit along the front pew across from us.

Sam Wicker and Brett Stephenson step up to the podium with strained voices and misty eyes. They tell of their hope for Sarah's return, and the importance of everyone's prayers in the matter.

Wicker has a certain charisma about him that is quite inviting and drawing to say the least. Just the way he spins his words, the emphasis of his voice, the look in his eye, it all makes him seem genuinely concerned. But is he? I would like to hope he is. He even chokes up half through his speech, which forces Brett to take over.

He wasn't much better.

Brett tries to read from a script but keeps getting the words and sentences mixed up as if he has dyslexia.

If their actions were all for show to throw us off their backs, then they did a masterful job. As Brett struggled with his words, he ended by stepping off the platform to stand in front of the pictures of his sister and her family. He kisses his fingers and places them over the pictures, telling his sister goodbye and vowing to never give up on finding his niece, Sarah McCrae.

Once he finishes, Sam Wicker has his deacons pass out candles to the congregation. They dim the lights as our candle flames licked heavenward.

Wicker has us all stand as he leads us into a tear-filled prayer.

The sanctuary is split as half of us remain quiet, while the other half add to the prayer with their own words. A few even speak in tongues as they cry and wail to God.

My flesh crawls with cold bumps. Something just doesn't feel right. I keep opening my eyes throughout the prayer. In part to keep a watch on everyone, but also to be sure someone doesn't come dancing down the aisle with a snake. I keep a good watch at my feet too. I can't get the thought out of my head of a big Copperhead slithering up my leg.

After a few moments pass and as people sniffle and sob, their words end abruptly.

I raise my head to see Sam Wicker gripping the pulpit on each end as he sways side to side with his eyes clinched shut. His shirt is soaked in sweat and his cheeks are moist with tears.

An unsettling hush fills the air and so does an eerie presence.

Collins taps my elbow. "You feel that?"

"Yeah."

Something . . . or someone has entered the room.

It sweeps up and down the pews.  Watching us.

I glance over my shoulder to where the couple I'd seen at Ted's Diner were, but they're gone.

Fire ignites in my gut and rises through my chest before settling in my cheeks.

Who are these people? What are they up to?

I pat Collins's back and lean on my tip toes to say, "C'mon, let's go."

I step out of the pew and head for the door. Collins is right behind me.

People who are not of the clique, stand with their heads bowed and hands gripped upon the back of the pew.

Those of Freewill Holiness, sway to and fro as if in some sort of trance.

We make it to the door. I pull it open and step out.

Collins shut the door behind us.

I spin around to face him, "They're gone."

"Who's gone?"

"The two from Ted's."

The sound of a foot scraping over concrete fills the air and so does the smell of cigarette smoke. A deep, lung aching hack follows. "What's the matter?"

I turn and see Dale Conrad. The man who greeted us on the way in.

My eyes go to the cigarette he squashed out.

"I thought you may have been a deacon?"

His face wrinkles. "I am."

"I didn't know deacons smoked."

He chuckles, "Yeah, well ours here do. Something wrong?"

"I'm looking for a couple. They were sitting on the back pew against the left wall. The woman had long dark hair, she was maybe in her thirties or forties, and was wearing a long dark dress. The man had short hair, clean shaven, jeans and a flannel shirt. Know who I'm talking about?"

A shadow crosses his face as he stares at me for a moment without saying a word. Finally, he swallows a gulp and turns his eyes away. "I don't know who you're talking about. I've never seen anyone like that," he says with a meaty palm against a white column supporting the small overhang.

"You listen here, I didn't become Lieutenant with the homicide department overnight. Now, I know when something is up. It would be in your best interest to tell me what you know now, before I find out myself."

He glances at me out the corner of his eye, then sighs and scratches the back of his head.

"Alright, alright. But promise me you'll listen. It's important," he says with nervous eyes as he scans our surroundings. "And make sure that door is shut will ya?"

Collins checks it.

I look deep into Dale Conrad's brown eyes and say, "I'm all ears."

# 49

"SO. YOU KNOW about Archie Whitaker, right?"

"Yeah, what about him?"

"And the kid he hid in the basement?"

"Yeah."

He bites his lip and looks over his shoulder before leaning close and whispering, "The folks you're looking for are that kid's parents."

"What?"

He bobs his head and draws a deep breath.

My head swims with questions. Too many at once.

Collins clears his throat and asks, "How is that? That happened thirty years ago. They don't look old enough."

Dale looks me and Collins straight in the eyes, "That's because they're dead."

"You're joking, right? You got to be joking?" says Collins.

Dale wags his head with tight lips, "Every so often they'll show up looking for their boy. Us members never really see them, it's mostly the newcomers. But yeah, that was them."

"Ghosts?" I question.

"Call them what you like, I'm just telling you what I know."

I hug myself and squeeze away the shiver traveling up my spine. Looking out into the grass parking lot, I can hardly see the cars from the thick fog that'd begun to settle.

My mind goes back to the day at Ted's Diner as I think how fast the two of them disappeared. Much the way they did a moment ago in the sanctuary.

I rub my forehead and ask, "What happened to them?"

"No one knows for sure. After the boy was taken to an orphanage, they moved across Country and was never heard from again. Sister Whitaker found an article a few years afterwards of a murder suicide in New Mexico that she thought was them. Happened back in the eighties. Just a few years after the incident here."

I cross my arms and pinch my tear ducts. A dose of nausea tries to return with the sudden onset of a throbbing headache. I swallow hard and ask, "What were their names?"

"Uhh . . . Richard and . . . Rose Jenkins I believe. Yeah, sounds about right. The boy was a Junior. Everyone called him Richie."

The sound of an engine and the glare from a pair of head lights pull our attention.

Peering through the fog, I can make out a white van with a large number six on the side and equipment on the top.

Channel six news.

"Hang on a second, let me go see if this is Jessica or Tom," I say as I angle down the steps.

I retrieve the gray beanie from my coat pocket and pull it on. Striding through the grass and passing the parked cars, I reach the news van as the passenger clambers out.

She slams the door.

"Hey Jessica."

"Oh, hey Laurie. How are you? I figured you might be here."

"I'm good. Can you be sure we get a copy of the unedited tape once you're finished?"

"Uh, yeah sure. Whatever you need."

"Thank you. And if you don't mind, since we're here, I'd like for you interview me while you're at it. There are some things I'd like to say in case he's listening."

"Absolutely, we can do that. Are those people as strange as the rumors?"

I crane my head and look back over my shoulder to Collins and Dale Conrad still chatting by the red doors.

"You could say that."

"Listen Laurie . . ."

I turn back to face her. Her straight black hair rests over each shoulder as she is prepped and ready. I've known Jessica Willingham as long as I've been with the homicide division. We've worked well together over the years.

". . . I know how difficult these cases must be for you. And I know you're doing all you can. We know that. We do," she says with sincere eyes. "But take care of yourself okay. We need you Laurie, this county needs you. Don't you forget that."

"Thank you. That means a lot."

The driver, who also happens to be the camera man, is in the back of the van scrambling with equipment, making racket as the pieces ting against the metal.

"Give us a bit to film the intro and get a few shots of the place, then will come get you when we're ready for interviews. Okay?"

"Sounds good. Thanks again."

"You got it."

With that I march back across the grass.

The night is dark with a new moon. The blackness is thicker than tar and there is not a star in the sky. The fog slithers along the parking lot like a serpent.

With my hands tucked deep into my pockets and pulled tight to my body, I glance towards the woods at the back of the church. A soft creaking sound scratches my curiosity.

As I scan the darkness and fog, I notice a swing set maybe forty yards to my left and behind the church. Three swings sit next to one another, but one swings and creaks with the breeze.

Stop it Laurie. Stop it.

I say to myself and pull my eyes away.

But I have to look again, don't I?

All three swings are next to one another. Just the way they should be. I rub my eyes and continue to Collins and Dale.

"You're not afraid that the snakes will bite you?" I hear Collins ask as I come up the steps.

Dale leans close to him and whispers, "Well personally . . . yeah. I've been scared of snakes all my life, that's why I leave the snake handling for the others. Now, fire dancing is a different story. I can dance with some fire."

"Fire dancing?" Collins asks as he looks to me with a side grin.

"Oh yeah. Boy you get in the spirit and grab you a candle, there's not much like it."

"Ever been burned?" I ask.

He shakes his head. "You're coming tomorrow night, right?"

"Maybe?"

"Well, come on by and see for yourself then. It's something you'll never forget."

"I'm sure it is. Now, let's go back to the boy's parents, shall we?"

He looks out to the parking lot and shifts in place, "Yeah, what about them?"

"You ever seen them?"

He scratches his upper lip and lowers his eyes to my feet. He nods ever slightly.

"Has Wicker seen them?"

"Oh yeah. He's seen them." He says with a hint of a chuckle.

"What do you mean?"

"Well, let's just say they have a way of following you home sometimes. Especially the Wicker's."

"Really?"

"Yeah, Pastor Wicker and his wife have woken up before to the two of them standing by their bedside just looking at them."

"How long have you been coming here?" Collins asks as if to change the subject.

"Since I was a kid."

"Do you remember Archie Whitaker?"

Dale holds out his hand and rolls it side to side, "Kind of, sort of, not really. I mean I wasn't but four or five when all that happened. My brother was friends with Richie though."

"He was?" I ask.

"Yeah. He never could get over all that. He got into drugs once he got older. Ended up taking his life in high school."

I said, "I'm sorry to hear that," and meant it.

"That's okay. Hey listen, they're probably wondering where I'm at. Have you met Pastor Wicker yet?"

"I haven't, but Detective Collins has."

"Well come back inside, I'll introduce you."

# 50

**HE HEARD THE CREAK** of the door over the wailing and praying. Hopefully, it was her again. He had to admit, she was quite the sight for sore eyes. He enjoyed every second of watching her from a few pews behind. Her blonde hair had sat nicely over the back of her black coat.

Dressed in a flannel shirt with overalls, he blended right in. Wig and all. Even had enough hair left over to make himself a beard. After he added some gray, it looked quite realistic. The thick glasses and walking cane only added to his character. Gary Wade Duncan was a true chameleon. He could become whatever he needed to be at any giving moment. In this case he needed to look like he knew how to handle a deadly snake.

God would be proud of his wit and creativity.

A gut rattling and muscle quivering rush soared through him each time he looked to the pictures of the McCrae's below the podium.

Those two deserved every ounce of God's wrath and he enjoyed being the one to pour it out. It was quite rewarding to have their corpses join him as he enjoyed their dinner.

There she goes.

He watches as Laurie takes her seat three pews in front of him. Patrick Collins sits next to her.

Then a heavy-set man sits next to Collins. Looks like the guy from the front door.

The people begin to calm.

Sam Wicker raises his head and secures a firm grip on the pulpit as he wipes away the tears, "Thank you all for yielding to the spirit and allowing him to have his way tonight. One thing we can be sure of is this . . . no matter what happens, God has a reason for it all. He is in control of all this. We have to remain vigilant in prayer for this sweet girl. And let's remember to keep Brett in our prayers too," he says as he looks to him on the front left pew.

"Thank you all for coming and uh, let's keep the faith and keep believing for the miracle. Nothing is impossible with God. Nothing. Thank you all, God bless."

With that, the Pastor steps down from the podium and Gary Wade Duncan stands to his feet, steps into the aisle, and limps his way out the door.

**"IT'S NICE TO MEET** you Mr. Wicker," I say as I shake his hand. I'm struck by the coldness in his flesh. It's like shaking the cold, dead tail of a fish.

"Likewise. And please, you can call me Sam," he says with a gentle smile below kind blue eyes.

Chatter fills the sanctuary as people hang around telling of the latest gossip. After introducing us, Dale Conrad retreated to his post by the door.

"Thank you for coming and showing your support, means a lot to this town and especially to Brett."

"Well, you know I always take a case like this personal. I try imagine if it were my own family."

"That's a fine perspective. And you have quite the partner as well. One in whom I'm sure you're grateful for."

I look to Collins and grin, "Oh I am. He's a blessing that's for sure."

"I mentioned to him last night about our revival which will begin tomorrow night. You're both welcome to attend, we'd be glad to have you join us."

"You know Collins and I were talking about that on the way over. We may just take you up on that offer. It'd give us a chance to get to know you all a little better."

"Certainly, that'd be wonderful."

"Starts a seven, right?"

"Yes ma'am."

At his words a petite red headed lady with long curls comes up beside him and wraps her arm around his back.

"Cathy, this is Lieutenant Laurie Daniels and Detective Patrick Collins from Portland," he looks to us, "This is my wife, Cathy."

We each exchange hands and smiles.

"Our son, Steven, is around here somewhere. He's our bass player," Sam Wicker says as he eyes the sanctuary with an arm around his wife's waist.

"Oh, I love your hair. It's beautiful," Cathy says.

I smile and respond with, "Why thank you. So is yours. I had a friend once with hair just like that."

"Is that so?" her eyes shift to the table where the McCrae's pictures are set up, "Are you getting any closer with all of this?"

Her cut to the chase approach feels rather blunt. I eye her for a moment before answering, "Well, I'll just say this, we have plenty of puzzle pieces, but we need to locate the box to know what we're trying to build."

"I can only imagine," says Sam Wicker.

"You know this has really been tough on us here in Gray. Then to learn about the FBI agent and the murders in Salem . . . it really has everyone worried. I've been staying up until one or two in the morning talking on the phone with the women here. They're being sure to keep their doors and windows locked and some are even installing security cameras. I know of a few who won't even let their kids outside to play anymore. The schools are getting strict too, you know. A lot have even cut back on recess. That's how worried we all are."

"Well, you should be. I'd rather hear that than to learn you're not taking things seriously. It won't be long, and it'll all be over. Washington has really taken charge in making sure this guy is caught. We've got everything we need. The whole Country is keeping a close eye on it. It's just a matter of time."

I zeroed in on their mannerisms for any nervous twitches or quirks.

Cathy's eyes grew wider and locked onto mine.

Sam didn't flinch but instead responded with, "You know it's a real shame to have to live like this, worried about monsters lurking in the dark. Wasn't all of that supposed to go away when we got older?"

"Not in the real world. They just get bigger and meaner as you grow. You should spend some time in our shoes. You don't know the half of what really lives out there. It's a scary world."

"I can only imagine. But the scary part is, it's only going to get worse as time goes on."

I click my tongue against the back of my teeth and crane my head.

"Laurie?"

I spin around to see Jessica standing at the opposite end of the sanctuary near the front door.

"Are you ready?"

"Yeah, just a second," I tell her before turning back to the Wicker's, "Hey would you mind giving a quick interview about tonight? It's channel six news."

He balks for a moment, then looks to his wife for approval.

"Uh . . . yeah sure."

"It won't take long."

With that, we head to the door to meet Jessica. Her cameraman, Danny, waits outside with the equipment.

We did the interviews just in front of the double red doors and black cross. I went first, followed by Sam Wicker and a few others who'd attended the memorial.

We finished up, said our goodbyes and headed for the Suburban. I kept my questions to a minimum for the Wickers. The last thing I wanted was for them to get spooked and thank I'm on to them. I want them to feel they can open up to me and get comfortable with my presence. They need to trust me. And showing an interest in their church and beliefs would surely strengthen that trust.

Collins and I split at the hood of my Suburban.

As I raise my head with keys in hand, I see it.

I stop dead in my tracks.

"What? What is it?" Collins asks.

I don't say a word but ease closer to my windshield for a better look.

I pull the windshield wiper up and cover my hand with the sleeve of my coat to retrieve it.

A note.

Collins breathes deep and looks on over my shoulder at the piece of white folded paper.

I glance about our surroundings and wonder if he is watching us.

I carefully unfold it.

Three black bold words glare back at us . . . *I watched you.*

# 52

**I WILL DROP** it off with Blake and Natalie in the morning to see if it's the same handwriting," I say while bumping my turn signal to take a right to get back on I-95.

"So, you were right."

"What?"

"He *was* there," says Collins.

"Yeah. I knew I felt him. We need to talk to Wicker tomorrow night and see if has a list of all the members. You know, like a church directory. Names, numbers, addresses. I want everyone who goes there to be run through the system."

"That'd be good. What do you think about Wicker and his wife?"

I breathe out a sigh, "I don't know. Honestly, I can't say. I mean they're a bit weird and all, but you got to think . . . they believe God wants them to play with snakes and fire. So of course, they're going to seem weird."

"Yeah."

"I'm not saying I think they're innocent, but I'm not sold that they're guilty either. Not yet at least."

"What about this couple you keep seeing? What did he say their names were? Jenkins. Richard and Rose Jenkins?"

"Yeah. I'd rather not talk about that right now. Gives me the creeps."

"We'll have to ask Archie about them and see what he says."

I nod with my hands firm on the wheel as I peer through the fog creeping across the highway.

† † † † † † † † † †

**I GLANCED TO MY STEREO CLOCK** when we reached Paul's driveway. *9:23 p.m.*

He and Allen had hung out together for most of the day and had taken Sandy to the park for me. God knows that poor dog needs it, and I'm sure it does Paul and Allen some good to get out too.

I give a few knocks on his outside door leading to the screened in patio before creaking it open and stepping in. Collins follows behind me.

Footsteps pad from the living room to the door going to the patio.

"Is that my girl?" Paul's voice booms from the other end of the door.

"Yeah, it's me."

I'd called when we were just a few minutes away, so he was expecting me.

The door opens.

"Haha, there she is. How in the world you doing?" Paul says with a big grin and sparkle in his eye.

I laugh and give him hug. He eats it up.

"There's my man. How you doing boy?" Paul says as he pulls back and sticks out a firm hand to Collins.

"Mr. Sealey . . . it's good to see you," Collins says as he and Paul embrace with a manly hug consisting of a handshake, half hug and slap on the back. Their custom way of greeting.

We step into the living room. The TV is blaring as it broadcast the MLB playoffs. Even though Paul's Red Sox weren't in it this year, he still wouldn't miss the playoffs for anything.

I found Allen sitting in a recliner sipping on a can of Pepsi.

"Hey Allen. How are you doing?"

"Hey there Laurie. Doing well. How about yourself?"

"Doing good. Did he give you any trouble today?" I ask with a wry smile as I give a side glare to Paul who was shutting the door behind Collins.

"Hey, I heard that."

"I had to crack a knot on his head earlier. That man's getting ornery."

"Let me tell ya something . . . you try a crack a knot on me, you going to be drawing back a nub," Paul says as he passes into the hall leading to his bedroom.

"Oh, I don't doubt it. I remember you telling me of that rowdy Marine you whooped with a root." Allen says with a chuckle. "Did he ever tell you about that?"

"Oh yeah. He told me. I think the guy had it coming to him though."

"Yeah, well that's what wife-beaters get when they cross paths with me." Paul says from his bedroom.

Allen wags his head and whistles out a sigh as he rises to his feet, "Well, I guess I'll get going. Patricia and her husband should be getting close."

"Paul said they were staying for the weekend with you?"

"Mm hmm. Yeah, they're bringing the girls with them too. Haven't seen my grandbabies in a while. I sure miss em."

"Well that's good they're coming to see you. I appreciate you taking care of Paul and Sandy for me these past few days. Don't know what I'd do without you."

"Yeah, you've helped out a lot," added Collins.

"Oh, it's no big thing. I like hanging out with old Paul. He's my buddy. I tell him all the time he's the brother I never had."

"Oh, that's sweet," I say.

"Paul, I'm heading out, family should be getting close. I'll talk to ya in the morning, alright?" Allen hollers down the hall.

"Alright now, you be careful, have fun with your grandbabies," Paul's voice comes back.

"Alright, I'm heading out. Y'all be safe now and holler if you need me."

"We will. Thanks again, Allen."

"You bet." He says as he heads out the door.

"Paul what are you doing back there?" I ask as I enter the hallway.

"I'm coming, just had to grab a few things," he says stepping out of his bedroom and into the hall.

"I told Allen earlier, I feel like a kid again going for a sleep over. Got my knap sack full of clothes and goodies."

I snicker and shake my head, "Do you have your meds?"

"Yup. You got the Fox channel over there, right? For the ball game."

"Yeah. Don't worry you're not going to miss anything."

"Good. You know how much I like my ballgames."

"I know, well come on, let's get you to the house."

† † † † † † † † † †

**I SPENT SOME TIME WITH** Paul and Collins, watching the game, sharing stories, laughter and food. Something I needed more than I even realized. However, the longer I lingered in the moment, the more I felt the tug to my bedroom as it called me to spend the late hours of the night divulging once again into grotesque crime scene photos of the Morty case files.

I wiped down the kitchen, then told the men goodnight and headed for my room. That was two hours ago.

Here I am, sitting Indian style on my bed at one in the morning staring at the bloody photos sprawled across my comforter. Sandy lies next to me with her head across my lap. I stroke her neck with one hand and tilt a glass of wine with the other. The old bottle of Silver Oak is draining faster than I originally intended. Moments like these are the only time I care for the stuff. It's as if I can't really flip the switch to zero my focus until the red liquid touches my lips. A superstition, I guess. I don't know.

I sit the glass down on my nightstand and cup my face in both palms. Gosh, there's so much to decipher with all of this. How am I ever going to catch this guy when I have a mountain of information to work through. I feel like I'm attempting to dig a tunnel through it by only using a toothbrush. Really. That's what it feels like. I've never felt this overwhelmed with a case before. I mean for heaven's sake, Morty could be anyone.

That is what scares me the most.

Sensing my nerves, Sandy stirs and starts licking my arm.

"I know. Mama's getting crazy isn't she?" I say as I hold her face in my hands and kiss her forehead. Her ocean blue eyes comfort my soul.

"I'm sorry, girl. I'll give it up for the night."

I gather the photos and files and stuff them back into their rightful places before leaning across the bed to flick out the lamp.

It was a few hours later when I awoke to hoarse whispers and creaking sounds.

# 53

**MY CLOSET DOORS** are large glass mirrors that roll along a track. They make a squealing and creaking noise as they do so.

It was that noise coupled with the whispers that woke me.

The room is pitch black when I open my eyes. I am on my back with my head facing the hallway going to the bathroom. My alarm clock rest to my left on the nightstand showing its red digital numbers, 3:23.

I can make out the silhouette of Sandy as she lies still and quiet at the foot of my bed. I know she is awake because she keeps tilting her head at the sound of one of the closet doors rolling open. There is also the sound of whispers which are loud enough to hear but too low to make out the words.

I try to rise from the bed, but I can't!

I am paralyzed. The only thing I can do is think, breathe, and move my eyes. Everything else has shut down. My heart knocks against my chest as my hands begin to tremble on their own accord. My breathing quickens to short gasps. I try to scream. Tension builds in my chest. I want so desperately to scream but can't.

The closet door continues to roll along its track, squeaking ever so softly. It stops when it slides against the frame of the door which makes a light thud sound.

More whispers.

The room is so full of darkness that I can feel it. It is painful to angle my eyes in such a way to see Sandy at the foot of my bed. She is still quiet as she stares into the hallway.

The sound of long fingernails tapping against glass, pull my attention back to the hall. The pain in my eyes subside only a little.

What is that?

Wrapping around the glass door are five black bony fingers, tapping in a domino fashion upon the mirror.

My whole body now quakes as if attempting to shake out a fever. My teeth are clinched tight without my command, grinding upon each other, causing my jaw to ache.

Tears well in my eyes and blur my vision.

The bony hand is joined by another.

Whispers.

My heart skips a beat at the sight of a large, black figure climbing out of my closet. It is hunched at the waist with long arms that dangle passed its knees. Its head is full of black curly hair and its bones creak when it moves.

Sandy bolts off the bed and never says a word.

I want so badly to join her, but I can't. I try with everything I have just to flinch a muscle but can't. I am a stone.

My breath is now a pant, but I can now see it waft from my mouth. A chill has settled in the room. My tears now sting as they attempt to freeze in my eyes.

The creature continues to move closer with its whispers and creaking bones.

Closer.

*Creak.*

Closer.

Whispers.

*Creak.*

My heart is pounding.

Closer.

It now stands by my bedside, right in front of my face. Its black thighs only inches from my nose. It moves to the foot of my bed and squats down out of my sight. Its bones creak loudly when it does.

I slam my eyes shut and swallow hard. I hear the gulp. I feel the bed give and hear the springs recoil with the added weight. I open my eyes and angle them to my feet. My eyes ache again, and my vision blurs..

The thing is climbing in bed with me!

One arm slowly stretches forth and plants its bony hand next to my right leg. It does the same with its other hand next to my left leg before pulling itself closer to my face.

I straighten my eyes and shut them hard.

I feel it edging closer.

The bed gives with its weight and the thing continues to whisper. I can now understand what it's saying.

*"I see you Laurie, I see you. I see you Laurie, I see you."*

Its hands press down on both sides of my neck. Here it sits on my chest, hovering over me. Watching.

It takes a deep, raspy breath.

I feel its cold fingers on my cheek. It tilts my head straight as to get a better vision of myself.

I flash open my eyes. All I see is blackness. Just a black silhouette with a head full of curly hair.

*Please, just let this be over with. Please. I can't take it anymore.*

It leans close and presses down hard on my chest.

The familiar deep ache fills my chest as I hear and feel it crack under such weight. It feels like I am trapped in a vice grip that is slowly squeezing shut, inch by agonizing inch.

The life is being squeezed out of me.

I wince at the pain. My chest will collapse any moment. I won't make it through the night. This is it.

Then I feel the thing wrap its bony hands around my throat, squeezing. Its breath sounds like it is coming from a throat full of gravel.

I begin to choke and gasp.

My chest screams with agony as my breath and life comes to an end.

*I see you Laurie, I see you. I see you Laurie, I see you.*

It whispers over and over and over.

Thoughts rifle through my mind. Searching desperately for anything to hang onto. Anything to make it go away.

There is only one thing I can think that might have power.

The thought hits me like a ram's head to the gut and begins to transfer from my brain, but before it could even attempt to come out of my lips, the blackness dissipates. I feel the pressure of its fingers dissolve from my throat as its weight lifts from my chest. The thing vanishes from the room like a roach when a kitchen light flicks on.

I shoot from the bed, gasping, crying, holding my throat. I reach and fumble with the lamp, almost knocking it over. I find the switch and turn it on. It lights up the room and chases away the shadows.

I twist to the edge of the bed and continue to gasp. My heart beats so hard that every pulse hurts. My chest is on fire as it feels like I have a cracked sternum or collapsed lung.

My feet dangle over the bed, and my head collapses into the palm of my hands as all I can do is weep. My shoulders jolt as my entire body trembles.

I'd never felt such fear in my life.

Such darkness. Such evil.

Something moves from under the bed and brushes against my leg. I almost leap out of my flesh as my heart bangs hard like a ball bat to a metal trashcan.

It's Sandy scurrying out from beneath the bed. She leaps onto the bed and noses her way into my lap.

I pull my head from my hands and glance about the room. My eyes go to the hall and to the closet door. The door is shut as if it had never been open.

I fall backwards across the bed. I place the back of my left hand across my forehead and try to soothe Sandy with my right.

Then I say out loud what it was that made the darkness flee . . . *Jesus.*

I didn't even get to say it, I was still paralyzed when the thought crossed my mind. All I did was attempt to say it and whatever that thing was . . . vanished.

*The light will shine in the darkness. Do not fear.*

The moment that thought entered my mind the entire atmosphere of the room shifted. It was as if love itself had entered the room. I felt so much peace. There was no fear here. How could there be?

*Perfect love cast out all fear. There is no fear in love.*

Where were these thoughts coming from?

The pain from my throat and chest begin to vanish.

Was it all a dream? Had I imagined it all?

But it was so real. Even Sandy saw it.

So, this is why my chest has been hurting me. How many times has this thing done that?

I rise from the bed and angle down the hall towards the bathroom. I check the closet first though and slide it open, causing it to creak and squeal along the way. I brush my clothes away to be sure nothing is hiding behind them. The closet is empty of any black figure or intruder.

I stand back, close the door, and rub my face before heading for the bathroom.

I turn the light on and cross for the sink.

I splash water against my face. I take some deep breaths and look at my reflection. A faint hue of blue and purple marks are streaked across my throat in the shape of those bony fingers.

So, it was real.

God help me.

# 54

THE MARKS WERE still there the next morning. Lucky for me the temperature outside was cold enough for a scarf.

I wrestled with whether I should tell anyone. For the time being, I chose not to.

We took Paul home before heading to the station. Allen would be coming by shortly after we left. Chris and Dean were still taking turns patrolling the area.

The funeral for Jeremy and Amanda McCrae is at one o'clock. A Priest from a Catholic church there in Gray will be conducting it. The word on the street is that Pastor Wicker refuses to do so as he stands firmly by his conviction of only conducting funerals for members of his church. I assume Brett Stephenson understands.

It was just after nine o'clock when Collins and I reached the station. The mood was somber. There was still no lead on the whereabouts of Agent Weatherby. Nothing on the Anderson case in Salem, and of course, nothing new with the McCrae's.

Chief Cunningham was tucked away in his office with Agent Swanson. Swanson didn't sound too happy when I passed the closed door.

Collins and I reach my office a few rooms down. With a coffee in my left hand, I unlock the door with my right.

"Where did you say Detective White was?" Collins asks from behind me

"He was called out to Scarborough. A couple were robbed last night on the way home from their watering hole. The man was stabbed in the kidney. They're not sure he'll make it."

"Dang."

We step into my office and at the same moment, Cunningham's door burst open, smacking against the wall and causing the blinds to rattle against the door window.

Agent Swanson goes off on an expletive filled tangent that ends with, "You're wrong about this one, Leo. You'll see."

Swanson marches away without another word.

"Laurie . . . I need to see you," comes Cunningham's agitated voice.

Oh boy.

Collins wrinkles his brows at me.

I pat him on the shoulder as I pass. "Can you take the note down to Blake and Natalie for me?"

"Sure thing. I'll be in my office when I'm done."

"Thanks."

He follows me out the door.

I draw a deep breath and sigh it out before heading for Cunningham's office.

I round the doorway and find him seated on his desk with his back to me, chewing on one end of his glasses. His sleeves are rolled to his elbows. The room reeks of aftershave and sweat.

"Yes?"

He looks over his shoulder, then points to a chair.

I take a seat.

He stands from the desk, shuts the door, and crashes into the chair behind his dark brown desk.

He leans back and forms a tee pee with his fingers.

A moment passes. His eyes become distant as they glare to a picture of his family on the desk. A wife and two kids. Boy and girl.

"Laurie, the Bureau is breathing down my neck about Agent Weatherby. Swanson is losing his marbles and Ramsey is saying Quantico is wanting to take things over if we don't start pulling our weight," his eyes shift to mine as he leans forward, "Laurie . . . please tell me you're closing in. This can't keep going on like this. It needs to end, and it needs to end soon."

I swallow hard and nod, "I know. He's still following me. He was at the memorial last night and I feel for certain he'll be at the funeral today. Me and Collins were talking on the way over, if we want to catch him . . . I need to be the bait."

Cunningham pulls back and rests deeper into his chair as his eyes wander about the room.

"It's obvious he wants me. Let me be vulnerable one time and let's see what happens."

"You sure about this?"

"I'm willing to do whatever it takes. Collins said he'd go meet with Wicker at the church. I can stay late here one night, then make a pit stop on the way home, see if I'm being followed. Something along those lines."

"Let me think about it. We can work on the details, but you may be on to something."

"I think it's worth a try."

Cunningham bobs his head, then reaches for a cup of coffee on his desk.

He takes a sip and says, "You still think the church is involved?"

"I don't know. I can't really say one way or the other. It's a flipped coin to be honest. I need to learn more about them to be sure. I need them to become comfortable with me. Maybe then, they'll slip and say something they shouldn't. It'll be interesting to see what happens tonight."

"Well, be careful. Okay? I can have a few officers to patrol the area if you think you need it," he says before reaching for his jar of jelly beans.

"I think we'll be good tonight. Save it for the nights when I'm bait."

"Good deal. I appreciate your work Laurie. I know I don't tell you that often, but I do. I see what you're doing, and it doesn't go unnoticed. This case just has us all a little frazzled." He tosses a small hand full of the colored candies into his mouth.

"Thank you, Chief. I'm doing my best."

"I know you are. Give me some time to think things over. I'll let you know when I'm ready to do something."

"Sounds good. I'll be in my office until noon. Try not to bother unless you really need me. I'm going to dig deep into the case files for a bit. Make sure I'm not overlooking anything," I say as I stand from my seat.

"Thanks Laurie."

With that, I retire to my office for the next two and a half hours to  look over the files and to think about last night. I went through my coffee mug quicker than I intended to and took one bathroom break after the other as a result.

It's hard to gain my focus. Every time I zero in on the details of the case, I get a fresh vision of that thing hovering over me, pressing down on my chest and snuffing out my breaths.

I've studied sleep paralysis in the past, and I've seen its effects on people during my academic endeavors, but this seems more than just sleep paralysis. This was real and it was the most terrifying thing I've ever been through. Just the thought of last night's encounter sends a shiver down my spine.

I finally resort to saying Jesus each time I become burdened with the beast. I figured it was good enough to work last night, so I'd give it another try. And each time I did, my mind and soul filled with peace and light. Say what you want . . . that name is the only thing keeping me going at the moment. I wouldn't survive in that darkness long. It'd take me to the abyss. Thank God that at the mere mention of that name, light floods the scene, licking away every shadow or dark and unnerving feeling.

The name has power and for the moment, it's my only weapon against this present evil.

✝ ✝ ✝ ✝ ✝ ✝ ✝ ✝ ✝ ✝

**NOON ARRIVED SOONER THAN** I anticipated. Within no time we were on I-95 en route to the McCrae's funeral in Gray. An unmarked Chevy Tahoe driven by Agent Turner follows closely behind me, behind him and Agent Vasquez are two other unmarked cars.

Collins busies himself with the stereo. He stops when he lands on a classic rock station which has John Fogerty singing *Bad Moon Risin'*.

I love the song, but I sure hope the lyrics don't come true.

"So, Cunningham was willing to do it?"

"Yeah. He's desperate right now. I mean heck, we all are."

"Just don't let that desperation get you in trouble, Laurie."

I lean up to check the passenger mirror before getting off on the exit for Gray. "I know. I'll be safe, and there'll be plenty of back up."

"When are you thinking to do it?"

"Hopefully, tomorrow night or Monday."

He nods, then looks out the window.

It wasn't long after, we found ourselves pulling into the Oak View Cemetery where Jeremy and Amanda will be laid to rest. We weren't far behind the parade of cars of family and friends. We spread out and mingle in among them as they park. It's here we'd spend the next hour staking out the scene, while peering through binoculars.

If Morty is anything like your traditional serial killer, he'll likely show up. He'll want to see the family mourn. He'd bask in the knowledge that he was the one who chose the McCrae's last breath. It's a pride thing. Every killer's kryptonite.

Surely, he'll make an appearance.

# 55

"LOOKS LIKE BRETT'S taking it hard," I say while looking through the binoculars at the seated mourners. Brett has a fist balled to his mouth as his shoulders jar violently while an elderly lady attempts to soothe him. Dale Conrad, the deacon from last night, stands with a few others just outside the tent's reach. As we suspected, there is still no sign of Richard McCrae. It appears Sam Wicker was right when he said, "The man won't even show up to his own son's funeral." Tells me all I need to know about the family dynamics.

"You know, you never did tell me what happened? Remember when we were at Ted's the other day and the news was reporting the shooting of that crazed druggy? What happened?" Collins asks as I busy myself with looking through the binoculars. I take turns sifting the black clothed mourners, who are now tossing flowers upon the lowering coffins, and scanning the wood lines.

I lower the binoculars and take a breath. I allow my mind to travel back to that night.

"It was my third year working homicide. We were hot on the trail of this guy who was suspected of murdering and mutilating his girlfriend. We'd staked out the home for two nights without noticing even a breeze. But on the third night .. . he came back.

"Now, behind the home was a thick grove of pines that eventually led to a murky swamp. Chief Cunningham, who was still Sheriff at the time, saw the guy first. He came stumbling with an odd gait from the wood line. We confront him with our guns drawn. He flees and heads straight back the way he came. Through the thick pines. Myself, Cunningham, and about a dozen K9 officers and deputies, begin the pursuit.

There's a chopper overhead barking out directions through our radios. We fan out and make a big sweep through the woods. Two of our K-9's picked up a scent and sent us deeper into the woods. Cobwebs stick to our hair as branches slap us in the face. We can hear foot falls up ahead, so we know we're getting closer. Then there's this loud splash followed by an eerie silence. He'd reached the swamp. Now, keep in mind this happened about this time of year, so you'd be a fool to go swimming in that. You'd end up with hypothermia in a matter of minutes."

"Dang," Collins says as he adjusts in his seat.

"Yeah. So, we reach the edge of the pines, our lights hit the swamp, and right in the center of it is our man. He has his back to us with his hands to his hips like he's catching his breath. He's about waist deep I'd say. He's huffing and gasping for breath. We're all screaming as we shine our lights and train our guns to the center of his back."

I take a deep breath and rub my eyes. The memory strobes quick through my mind.

"He turns around to face us . . . he's smiling from ear to ear with the creepiest grin you could ever imagine. It reminded me of the Joker. Then he starts saying something in another language. He's spitting it out through clinched teeth as his voice strains with a hiss. You can see the tension and veins in his neck as he's almost growling at us. Whew . . . gives me chill bumps just talking about it."

"My goodness," Collins says as I glance out the window and place the back of my hand to my mouth.

"He sounded like a Priest speaking Latin or something. It was god awful. Then he looks down at his belly and slowly places a hand to his side before sliding it across. A bloody line appears. We couldn't see it, but he had a small razor blade in his hand. His gut starts oozing blood and he collapses into the water."

"For heaven's sake."

"But you know, the autopsy showed there wasn't an ounce of drugs or prescriptions in his system?"

"What?"

"Yeah, nothing. They ran test on his brain, and he was perfectly fine."

"Goodness, it's like he was friggin possessed or something."

"I know. It's creepy," I say as I reach for my mug of coffee between us.

"You don't think something like that is what's wrong with our guy, do you?"

I sip my coffee and give a slight chuckle, "Patrick, all of our guys are possessed in one way, shape, or form. Some just control their demons better than others."

"Well that's good to know."

"Consider it as my word of wisdom for the day."

A moment passes.

"You know Laurie, I've been thinking about something."

"Yeah?"

"I think we need to have a moment to decompress, you know? So, whatdayasay we grab a bite to eat tomorrow? Forget the case for the time being and just enjoy a meal together. As friends. I think it'd do us both some good."

I turn slowly and say, "Sounds like that could be called a date."

He blushes and begins to stutter.

"I'd love to. I think you're right. It would do us some good to disconnect for a bit."

He nods as a grin grows across his lips.

"Good. Tomorrow for lunch then?"

I shake my head and look out the window.

The warm touch of his hand on mine, gives my heart a start.

I turn back.

His eyes are moist.

"Thank you, Laurie. Tomorrow's her birthday, and it's always tough, you know?"

A knot forms in my throat.

"You're a good man, Patrick. Kelsey would be proud."

"Thank you."

I squeeze his hand and search the center console for a pack of Kleenexes.

As I dab my eyes, something catches my attention.

"You seeing this?" Collins asks.

"Yeah."

A black SUV had entered the cemetery from the road, traveling at a high rate of speed. Faster than it should along the narrow road that snakes its way up and down the hills between the gravestones.

Instead of slowing, it begins to pick up speed as it heads straight for the crowd of mourners.

Our radio crackles with a thousand voices. The sight of this SUV barreling for the mourners sends time into a crawl. I throw open my door and smash down upon the horn.

I hear Collins curse as the SUV jumps the curb and begins to sling grass and dirt into the air. The engine revs as it begins to plow through grave markers.

My heart pounds. I smash the horn one last time before bolting to the crowd as they begin to scatter from the coming carnage.

# 56

COLLINS AND I RACE toward the chaos. Agent Turner and Agent Vasquez are right behind us. People scream and scatter out from under the tent. The SUV plows into the coffins, knocking them open, and sending the McCrae's bodies flopping to the ground.

God have mercy.

The black SUV lurches to a halt atop one of the coffins. It's back tires are off the ground. The engine growls. Smoke and steam rise into the air. Pieces of black fender are tossed here and there. I unholster my Judge and pull back the hammer as Collins and I near the scene. I have five rounds of .45's and am ready to empty them any second.

Screams and cries of terror rip the air. It's like a war zone.

The back tires are still spinning and begging for traction as the car tilts back and forth atop the coffin. The tent is missing a leg which causes it to lean over the wreckage.

I come within a few yards of the SUV and yell for the driver to step out. Collins and the others quickly form a U around the back and sides of the vehicle.

The engine still revs, showing no sign of surrender. Either the driver's foot is still pressed against the gas or he has the accelerator set to cruise control.

I yell again, "Step out of the vehicle. Now. Hands in the air!"

I can see a head bob through the back glass. The driver is still alive and moving.

"Driver! Let me see—"

That's when I see a gun raise and aim to the subject's temple.

"Noooo!"

A single gunshot rips through the air as blood splatters against the driver window.

I curse through clinched teeth.

Agent Turner creeps along the passenger window with his gun drawn and peers inside.

I turn to Collins, "Patrick, get EMS. Now!"

The engine is still growling as the back tires continue to spin.

I ease around to the driver door with my Judge aimed and ready.

"I'm clear on this side. I'm going in," comes Agent Turner's voice.

I hear Collins end the call with dispatch before he joins me alongside the SUV.

I hear glass shatter at the passenger window.

Standing parallel now to the driver door, I see a bloody head slumped against the window. Blood and brain matter ooze down the glass.

The engine ceases.

Is this him?

Is it Morty?

Gary Wade Duncan?

I open the door.

The body slumps over and would have fallen out had it not been for the seat belt holding him in place.

My eyes scan his face, his features, but I don't recognize him.

Who is this?

He is dressed in jeans with a blue and white plaid shirt and a black sleeveless vest. Short gray hair with a salt and peppered beard. He looks to be in his fifties.

Is this him?

Turner and Vasquez lean in through the passenger door.

The SUV is empty besides hundreds of newspaper clippings, pictures, and the dead man.

"It's clear," I say pulling back and holstering my Judge.

I scan the cemetery.

The mourners are sobbing and shaking. Some had collapsed to the ground with their legs folded beneath them. We check under and around the SUV. The only person who was victim to the crash, was Jeremy McCrae. His body, which was caked in make-up, is wedged behind the front driver side tire. Amanda McCrae is sprawled out next to her casket about seven or eight feet to my left.

We back away from the wreckage and disperse through the crowd to check for any injuries. We do our best to provide first aid until paramedics arrive.

Brett Stephenson stands to my right and screams at the sky with his hands on his head.

Everything begins to blur at this point.

It wasn't until later that we were able to thoroughly investigate the scene and search the vehicle. What we found would only add more pieces to the already impossible puzzle.

It feels like I'm trying to solve a ten-thousand-piece puzzle in the dark.

But the light will shine the darkness, right?

God help us.

# 57

TURNS OUT WE were wrong. Richard McCrae did show up to his son's funeral. In a black Ford Escape filled with newspaper clippings of Morty's crimes, pictures of myself being interviewed or giving press conferences, and hundreds of copies of missing people flyers. Most were of the children that Morty had taken. Along with all of that was a six-page letter written on standard 8.5 by 11 printing paper, stapled together and stuffed in the glove compartment. Over and over, he stated, "The devil made me do it," and "Laurie's time is nearing." He ended with, "The devil's coming."

The last time I'd spoken with Sebago Police, Richard McCrae was set to be released this past Thursday. Though he was questioned heavily, swabbed for DNA, and inked for prints while incarcerated for public intoxication, nothing gave the interrogators reason to believe he was involved in the crime pertaining to the McCrae's. He had a clean alibi and no real motive to go along with the crime. I'd crossed Richard's name off my list not long after the investigation began.

Now I wish I hadn't.

† † † † † † † † † †

IT'S JUST AFTER FIVE, AND I FIND MYSELF tucked away in the conference room with Chief Cunningham, Director Ramsey, Collins, Agent Swanson, Agent Turner, Agent Vasquez, and Agent Shannon Carter. Sheriff Johnston and Detective White are still investigating the armed robbery in Scarborough.

Cunningham and Ramsey lead the briefing, using the white board and the projector screen. Ramsey directs the presentation with a clicker, alternating between slides of photos from the evidence at the scene. Pictures of the Ford Escape, the newspaper clippings, the bloody mess left of Richard McCrae along with a mugshot from his latest arrest.

"As I said in the press conference earlier. . . whether Richard McCrae is our guy or only a pawn," Ramsey raises his palms in the air, "I don't know. Going by the evidence, one could certainly argue that this was our guy. That is if he didn't have the alibi. How could Richard McCrae murder his daughter and son-in-law while he was in the process of being booked? Now, I'm not saying McCrae isn't involved, but I am saying he didn't kill Jeremy and Amanda, nor did he kidnap Sarah. It just isn't plausible."

He clicks to another slide as Chief Cunningham writes with a black marker on white board next to the screen. Cunningham clears his throat before turning and facing us. He stuffs his hand down the center of his pants to tighten the tail of his shirt. "With that being said, forensics were able to match the hand-writing. The letter in the glove compartment, the note left at Lieutenant Daniel's home and the note on her windshield last night . . . are all from the same hand. The note from the diner though, is not. However, forensics did say, it looked as if it could have been written with the opposite hand, due to its severe sloppiness and the similarity in the way the A's are formed. And we're working on collecting hand-writing samples of Mr. McCrae as we speak. We'll know if it's a match here shortly. So, this all means that either Gary Wade Duncan wrote the letter and planted it in the glove compartment then threatened McCrae to do what he did, or . . . McCrae's our man," says Chief Cunningham as he caps the marker and crosses his arms.

Ramsey clicks to another slide. This one shows the six-page letter. He reads in a slow tone, being sure to take in each and every word. "'Sin has been crouching at your door, Laurie. The Devil's been lurking and creeping behind you, waiting to strike, and ready to pounce. You let him in. You all did. Sin has to be dealt with. I am the vessel of God's wrath. I am the Angel of Death. I am the Reaper. And the time for Reaping has come. Your beautiful hair will be put to good use, that I can assure you. You may think this is my end, but my spirit will live on, haunting those left behind. I'm just getting started. The whole world will pay for their sins. It won't be long, and you'll hear the trumpet. The one that'll tear away the veil. Oh, that your eyes would see the hidden realm. Listen . . . can you hear it? The sky's groaning, longing for the day that the heavens will be opened, allowing the rest of us to come and reap the harvest. Dividing wheat from tare, good from evil. It won't be long my dear. It won't be long. The cicada's sing with joy as they await that day. It won't be long. It won't be long.' And he goes on from there with the same mumbo jumbo."

I raise my hand.

"Go ahead, Lieutenant," says Ramsey.

"McCrae is not our man. Gary Wade Duncan forced him to do this. He manipulated him just like he did Dr. Feltner. Morty is still out there."

Ramsey crosses his arms and places a hand along his jawline as he begins to pace. "You may be right, but we also have to consider the possibility that McCrae was somehow involved in all of this."

"I agree, but at the same token, I don't want us spending too much time on it either because I honestly believe it's a dead-end," I stand from my seat and approach the platform. "It's obvious I'm the one he wants—"

"But Laurie—" Cunningham interrupts.

"No, hang on a second, listen. If we want to put an end to all of this then I have to become vulnerable."

The air in the room turns thin as everyone becomes quiet. Every eye is on me.

"He knows now I'm too protected at home. He wouldn't risk taking me on my own turf. It'll have to be somewhere that I'm vulnerable. The street, the parking lot at Ted's Diner . . . the McCrae's."

Director Ramsey sighs and says, "Lieutenant Daniels, I admire your courage. I really do, but we can't risk losing anyone else."

"And we can't risk losing another innocent child either. Someone has to do something. It's me he wants and it's me he needs to get. It's the only way we're ever going to stop all of this. I have to do it. Please. Innocent lives are at stake here."

My mind goes to my sister Amy and all of the other children.

I have to do it for them.

Director Ramsey lowers and shakes his head. He turns his back, places his hands to his hips, and glares up at the projector screen.

Chief Cunningham steps forward, "Laurie, I know you're right, but for the life of me I don't want you doing this."

I swallow hard as I stare into his dark brown eyes.

"Trust me. That's all I'm asking for. Trust."

Director Ramsey turns and strides next to Chief Cunningham, "We can have agents and SWAT on standby in the vans. Put a wire on you to keep communications going. It's risky, but at this point it may be our best bet."

Cunningham nods, "Tomorrow night?" he asks looking to me and Director Ramsey.

I'm really going to do this. "Yeah . . . yeah, tomorrow night."

"I'll inform the field office in Boston and have an ample supply of men here by morning," says Ramsey.

"Good. I'll coordinate it with SWAT. Tomorrow night at the McCrae's?"

Ramsey and I both nod.

Cunningham sighs and cleanses the lens to his glasses, "Unless anyone has questions, we'll wrap up on that note."

The room is still.

"Okay then, we'll be in touch with the details. Everyone be ready for a stake out tomorrow night."

As people stand from squeaky chairs that fold back into position, Director Ramsey places a hand around my arm and leans close, "We'll hear everything. We'll have your back should anything go sour. You'll be safe, don't worry."

I whisper back, "Just get to me before he cuts my hair or pulls a tooth. I don't want him taking any souvenirs," and pat him on the arm before walking back to my seat next to Collins.

Collins face is drained of blood and his voice is tight, "You sure about this Laurie?"

"No, I'm not. But at this point what other choice do we have?" I say as I pack a few of my folders into a shoulder bag.

He nods and lowers his eyes to the carpet.

"Hey, I'll be okay. I can take care of myself. I'll have a wire. I'll be fine." I say all of that not just to reassure him, but myself as well.

He tightens his lips and tries hard to keep words from tumbling out.

"This has to end, Patrick. He can't keep killing and he can't continue to take innocent children. It ends here," I squeeze his elbow, "Trust me, I'll be okay."

I hope I'm right.

# 5.8

AS WE PULL into the dirt driveway of Freewill Holiness, Collins reads from their church sign, "'Old fashioned revivel. Seven o'clock. Guest evangelist: Ronnie Elms'. Huh, they don't even know how to spell *revival*. Doesn't surprise me."

"Yeah, me either. Listen, let's be sure to sit on the back pew so when they bring out the snakes, we can make a quick exit," I say with a grin.

Collins smiles, "Sounds good to me."

I park in the grass between a Toyota Camry, with more dings and rust than paint, and an old square bodied Chevy pick-up truck.

The moment I step out of the Suburban, I hear music with tambourines, hand claps, and shouting. An old time, foot stomping throwdown.

The only foot-stomping I'll be doing is squashing the head of a serpent trying to slither up my leg.

"Sounds like we might be late to the party," says Collins.

I look to the double red doors with the black cross above them and see a middle-aged couple enter. The door slams shut behind them.

"We'll see."

The commotion grows louder the closer we get. More handclapping, foot-stomping, tinging cymbals, guitar strumming, beating drums, and unharmonized singing. Collins reaches for the door and pauses.

"You sure about this?"

I nod.

He opens the door.

A wave of chaotic sound ambushes our ears. Inside, people are on their feet with hands either stretched to the heavens or fast at work to keep rhythm with the beating drum. Some people dance in place while others run circles along the perimeter of the room. We were almost trampled by two of the runners as we stepped into the sanctuary. They were long haired women with wild eyes and loosed tongues.

Up on stage, Sam Wicker paces to and fro with a microphone in hand. He shouts with a hoarse voice as he dabs the sweat beads on his forehead with a handkerchief.

"God said my people are to be separate, distinct, different. We can't be the same as everyone else, roaming about the world, doing what all the others are doing. We got to be separate, church. You hearing what I'm a saying? Separate. We ain't crazy! The one's out there doing what they want, living for the devil, they the crazy ones."

Collins and I settle quietly into the back corner of the room. Other than the couple I'd seen walk in just before us, our pew is empty.

Wicker waves his arm toward the front pew. I can't see for all the people standing in front of us. "C'mon up here Brother Elms. We need you to show these folks how it's done."

The parishioners cheer and holler as they clap and stomp.

Wicker stretches forth his hand and I watch as another bony, frail, and sun spotted hand takes hold. The music begins to calm.

It's a bald-headed man dressed in a white-collar shirt with a black tie. He struggles to conquer the two steps it takes to climb on stage. He supports himself with a wooden cane. His back has an arch near his neck, and it looks painful for him to raise his vision. He wears the thickest glasses I've seen since my grandpa in the seventies. He takes the microphone from Wicker and brings it to his shriveled lips.

"Ain't it good to be in the house of God tonight? Boy, let me tell ya, sure beats wandering the streets of this cold, mean world. Am I right?"

The crowd says "Amen," in sharp unison.

Wicker ducks behind the pulpit and opens a set of cabinet doors.

"The spirit of God is in the place. I said the spirit of God is in the place. Can you feel it? Whew-we. Boy, it's a getting strong up in here, let me tell ya," the old man then rattles off a dozen lines from another language. A handful of worshippers follow suit. I guess that's what they call "speaking in tongues."

Wicker straightens his spine. I lean to my left and look around a heavy-set lady in the pew in front of us. I squint my eyes to see what he has. I half expect it to be a snake or candle, but it's neither.

Instead, my eyes reveal a glass mason jar with a clear, watery liquid inside.

Wicker smiles from ear to ear as he swirls it around in the jar. He then shuts his eyes, mumbles a prayer, and holds the jar up high for all to see.

The old man lowers his head and sways it back and forth as he wears a tight grin, "We say we believe in God, and we say we believe in miracles. But do we really believe that? Well church, I don't know about you, but I know I do. And these signs shall follow them that believe; In my name shall they cast out devils; they shall speak with new tongues; They shall take up serpents; and if they drink any deadly thing, it shall not hurt them. The scripture said it and God as my witness I'm going to do it. Hand me that there strychnine brotha Wicker."

Strychnine? Dear God, he won't last ten seconds!

Wicker smiles and passes the jar of poison to the old man.

I rise from my seat.

The old man twists off the lid.

Horrified at what I'm seeing, before I can open my lips to protest, the man tilts up the jar and takes a long gulp. The music starts back up. Drums, guitar, tambourines, clapping, stomping, dancing, running, shouting, and speaking in tongues.

"These people are nuts. This isn't church, this is Russian roulette." Collins says as he grips the pew.

The old man does a half twirl while leaning on his cane, smiling, shouting, and speaking gibberish. Then he passes the jar back to Wicker, who takes it with glee and tosses back a slosh for himself. A bead of it trails down his chin. He wipes his mouth with the sleeve of his shirt and jumps off stage. He proceeds to make a quick lap around the room. My hand instinctively shoots to my hip next to my Judge.

The people were loud before, but now seeing their pastor leap from the stage and enter a running fit, it sends them all into a craze. The music gains speed and volume as does the worshipers.

Movement to the front right corner of the room gets my attention. It's from one of the closet doors. The one that I'd seen Wicker and Brett come from the night before. The door opens slowly to reveal a dark room. It's lit only by a small window which pushes in a white slanted hue of moonlight.

With my head now on a swivel, I jerk to my left at the loud wail of a woman.

The sight stalls my heart.

Snakes and fire.

Wicker holds what looks like two large Copperheads. He cradles them close to his chest, caressing them like babies. A long-haired woman holds a big round candle in one hand and waves her other over the flame. But not just over the flame . . . through the flame and in the flame.

As the lady turns around, I notice it's Wicker's wife, Cathy. As she dances and twirls in place with the candle, Sam Wicker enters the center aisle, marching and dancing his way to the pulpit with the snakes in hand.

My heart pounds as my mind screams for me to choose between my fight or flight instinct. My skin is cold. Or is the room cold? Either way, my body and flesh are chilled.

"I don't like this," I hear Collins say and as I turn to give a reply. That's when I see it.

Crouched in the open doorway in the front corner of the room, is a dark silhouette with short curly hair. The thing that tried choking me last night!

My heart bangs against my chest like a drum. My pulse quickens and shoots a splash of ice water down my spine.

I gasp at the sight of the thing hunched over, hiding in the darkness, glaring at me from it's black, eyeless face. It drops into a catcher's crouch and cranes its head like a dog.

That's when my instincts kick in.

I bolt out of the pew past Collins, yanking on his arm on the way out. We rush for the doors. Collins asks me questions as I drag him with me. The music and crazed worshippers rage louder behind us.

I reach the door and plow through it, down the brick steps and straight for my Suburban.

Collins stops and pulls away from me, "What the heck!? What is it?"

"It's that damned thing. I saw it. In there."

His eyes scrunch, "What are you talking about?"

I forgot he didn't know.

"Get in the car, I'll explain on the way."

I can't crank the Suburban fast enough.

When the engine fires up, I throw it in gear and speed away. Slinging gravel and grass as we leave those crazy nuts far behind. I honestly don't know which place is worse. Here or the asylum on Cushing Island.

# 59

"LAURIE. WHAT IN the world are you talking about? And Judas Priest will ya slowdown? You're scaring me." Collins says with wide eyes as he tightens his grip on the handle above the passenger window.

I train my eyes to the road and ease off the gas just a little. My breath escapes in quick gasps as blood thumps hard in my carotid artery. I rub at the soreness in my chest. My mind flashes back to the sight of that ungodly thing sitting on top of me and snuffing out my breath. I scratch at my throat and displace the scarf as I do so. I ponder whether I should show him the marks or not.

"You can tell me. I'll believe you."

I draw a deep breath and glance into the rearview mirror. I half expect to see the damned thing hunched over in the backseat and glaring back at me. I'm relieved to see the seat is empty and there's only fog and dust mixed in the scarlet hues of my taillights in the background.

"Okay but promise me not to tell anyone."

Collins looks at me with scrunched brows as his pale face shines through the darkness. "Of course. You have my word."

I turn on the interior lights and pull my scarf down just enough to show the bruised finger marks.

"Geez. What the hell? Who did this? Laurie, who the hell did this?"

I go on to tell him everything I knew about the creature that'd visited me the night before and how I'd just seen it again at the Wicker's. For the longest time, Collins silently processes the revelation.

I ease on the brakes as we near the red light leading to the ramp for I-95.

"Please, Patrick, you have to believe me."

Splashes of red light shines upon his face. He rubs his forehead and says, "I believe you, but what does this mean?"

His face turns a shade of green as the light turns.

I take the left and proceed down the ramp. "I don't know, but maybe Archie Whitaker isn't so crazy after all."

Or I'm just as crazy as he is.

Of course, I didn't say that out loud though.

† † † † † † † † † †

**WE REACHED MY DRIVEWAY** just after nine o'clock. We relieved Allen of his duties and picked up Paul and Sandy. Chris was on patrol and would be until midnight, then he would switch off with Dean.

I didn't tell Paul about what happened.

It was just after eleven when I retired to my room. Collins and Paul stayed up to finish watching a ballgame.

I was so exhausted both mentally and physically that within minutes of my head hitting the pillow, my world turned to black.

† † † † † † † † † †

**THAT IS UNTIL SOMETIME LATER WHEN I'M** woken to the feeling of being watched. My eyes were shut, but light brimmed before them as if someone had flicked on every switch my room had to offer. I squint and pull a hand to my face to shield my eyes. I peep beneath my hand and slowly glance about the room.

A radiant sparkle of light permeates the room as it seems to come from the foot of my bed. It's weird, because despite the odd vibe, I don't feel scared. My pulse is calm, and I don't feel threatened. Only curious.

I remove my hand for a better view.

The sight startles me, but again I'm not frightened.

A lady dressed in pure white from head to toe, stands at the end of my bed, looking at me with a tilted head and a one-sided smile. She's beautiful. Aged, but her complexion is pure and youthful. She gently turns and it looks like she is floating upon the air as her white gown flutters behind her in methodical waves.

Sandy sits to my left and stares up at the lady, while not saying a word.

I swallow long and hard. I blink more than once to clear any insanity that has overtaken me. No matter how hard I try to rationalize it all away, the lady still stands here and appears to wait for me by my door. She glances over her shoulder, gives a bashful smile, opens the door, and glides gracefully into the hallway leading to my living room.

Curiosity gets the best of me, and I swing my legs to the side of the bed, planting my bare feet to the cold hard wood floor.

A glowing light emits from the hall and pushes away the shadows. I round my bed and ease to the door frame. I lean against it and peer down the hall.

The lady in white continues into the living room with her back facing me as her auburn hair dangles along her dress which caresses the floor. She turns and angles for the front door. I can see her profile now and that one-side smile is still stretched across her lips.

Sandy eases alongside me as we head for the living room, following this strange, yet beautiful lady.

We come to the end of the hallway and enter the living room. It is lit only by a small lamp which sits atop a corner table between my recliner and the sofa where Collins is fast asleep. His face is turned into the couch, and his body is covered with two white blankets.

*Creak…*

I look to the front door and see it creaking open. White light seeps out and enters onto my front porch. A gush of cold air rushes in. I quicken my strides but am careful not to wake Collins. I reach the front door and step out. Sandy is right by my heels. I ease the door shut behind me. I turn to my left in just enough time to catch glimpse of the lady in white angling around the corner of my house. My pulse quickens as I see my breath escape into the cold with its ghostly steam. I fight hard to ward off the thoughts that this could be a trap, because something deep within me prods me onward. It feels like I'm being led. By what, though? Good? Evil?

I squeeze myself tight as I hear my teeth begin to chatter. My feet and hands are turning numb as my face begins to sting from the brisk air. The wind howls as it rustles the leaves along the wood line.

I look to Sandy standing up against my left shin. He is staring at the remaining trail of light radiating from the lady.

I draw in a deep breath, say a little prayer, feel the cold air enter my lungs, and angle off the porch for the lady. With Sandy right beside me, I begin to hear the lady whisper around the corner.

† † † † † † † † † †

**SEATED IN HIS PATROL CAR** and tucked away in a canopy of woods just off the road, Deputy Dean Ferrell had busied himself by alternating his eyes between his surroundings and Laurie's home just beyond the trees. His pulse quickens at the sight of a bright light piercing the darkness. It's like a lighthouse beacon shining out to the sea and cutting through the fog. Ferrell squints his eyes and realizes that the light is coming from Laurie's front door, because it's open.

He curses and shifts his patrol car into gear. He backs onto the road and crosses for Laurie's driveway. He can see the silhouette of something moving off the porch but can't make out who or what it is. Ferrell connects to dispatch and advises them to be on standby. He turns down Laurie's driveway and eases along in the darkness.

† † † † † † † † † †

**AS I CUT THE CORNER** of the house, my eyes find the lady standing directly in front of my cellar doors. She just stands there and glares at the double doors which lead beneath my house.

As I take a step forward, the lady raises her hand with a slow sweep and points a finger to the doors.

I stop.

She stands like this for at least two breaths before moving forward as if to enter the doors, but she vanishes like a vapor. Her light dims to darkness.

At that moment, fear enters my consciousness.

My heart drums as my lungs labor to take in the cold air.

What is she trying to show me?

I take my time reaching the cellar doors as more than once I glance over my shoulder and scan the woods to be sure no one was plotting an ambush.

It feels like a million beady eyes are glaring at my back. I hate this feeling.

The night is still and quiet, besides the breeze tickling the leaves above.

I reach the cellar doors and find the latch. The lock is gone. No reason for there not to be a lock. It's been months since I was last down there. Someone must have cut it. Unless they had my key.

The sound of gravel crunching in my driveway and the soft purr of a motor pulls my attention. I take a few steps back and look to the front of my house. It's Deputy Ferrell. I glance back to the cellar doors, then back to Ferrell.

"Sandy c'mon," I say as I angle to the front of the house.

As I near the driveway where Ferrell is seated in his car, the front door to my house opens up.

"What's going on?" Collins asks from a scratchy throat. Paul is peeping over him, rubbing his eyes.

Deputy Ferrell opens his door and steps out, "Everything all right?"

"Yeah and no," I answer.

Collins steps onto the porch and comes down the steps towards me. Paul is just behind him.

"Get some clothes on. Someone has done something with my cellar."

I watch as everyone's eyes grow wide.

They were thinking the same as me.

What the hell is in the cellar?

AFTER CHANGING INTO some more appropriate clothing to combat the weather, Collins, Paul, and I joined Deputy Ferrell by the cellar doors.

"Did you see anyone messing around out here?" I ask Ferrell.

"No, I just caught glimpse of the front door being open and that's when I saw you wander off the porch."

I didn't bother telling anyone about the lady. Now wasn't the time.

"Okay, well let's open it up and see what's going on." I say after a sigh.

Ferrell clicks on his Maglite and strides closer. He grips a handle. Collins joins him and takes hold of the other door handle. Together, they pull the doors open. A set of stairs, half hidden by the darkness, comes into view. Dust billows out like smoke clouds, swirling this way and that. The iron squeak of the rusty hatches pierces the air as the door's rests to the hinges limit. The stench of death greets us. It's not strong, but it's there. Ferrell calls for back up and unsnaps his gun before raising it to eye level. His Maglite clinched in the opposite hand, shining into the cellar. I'd already pulled back the hammer to my Judge. I hold it firm and angled to the ground in front of me. Collins draws his weapon too.

"Stay here with Paul," I say to Collins.

He nods.

"You be careful down there, honey," Paul says with a twist of worry in his face.

"Don't worry, we'll be fine. Just hang tight for a minute."

Paul scratches at his scalp through the wool beanie he'd borrowed from Collins and gives a reluctant nod.

I transition my eyes to Collins and keep them there for a moment.

He tightens his lips. I know he wants to protest me going down in the cellar. Having known me for as long as he has, he knows by now, it'd be a wasted breath.

I give a gentle smile and pull my eyes from his. I train them to the steps which lead into my dark basement.

Ferrell goes first, and I follow tight behind.

I feel my pulse soar as my heart knocks hard against my ribs. I feel a sudden heavy weight as if I'm being pulled down by the dread of what I might soon discover.

The wooden steps creak and groan as we descend.

Ferrell conquers the last step and plants a foot onto the dirt, creating a soft *thump*. He scans his light about the darkness. Nothing but my plastic bins, metal file cabinets, and an outdoor table and chair set fill our vision.

"If you're down here, come out not and show me your hands!" Ferrell says as he sweeps his light and pistol about the stale air and earth.

No answer.

There are plenty of concrete columns to hide behind, so we are careful not to be ambushed by someone on the other side.

The smell of death grows stronger, and my mouth begins to fill with bile.

Ferrell curses.

The area to our right is clear, so we make our way left beneath the living room and my bedroom.

"Come out now with your hands in the air!" I call.

Again, no answer.

We creep along, keeping our heads on a swivel.

A gust of wind rips by the vents and creates a high pitch howl that could've passed for a screech from the lady in white. Is she down here? Will she show herself to someone else? Is she hiding behind a column, watching us as we go.

My breath is now traveling from my mouth, partly from the cold air, and partly from dust that'd half clogged my nostrils. There also seems to be that weird heavy feeling in my core being which feels as if it is suffocating my heart and lungs. It continues to constrict tighter and tighter.

We pass beneath the kitchen and living room, and now make our way towards my bedroom.

I have my back to Ferrell to be sure no one flanks us. As I creep along behind him, he stops suddenly.

I bump into him and make a quick sidestep with my Judge trained at eye level. I plant my feet and form the proper stance.

My heart sinks to the pits of my bowels.

It's as if the world had come to a screeching halt. My mind fogs. My hearing wanes. I'm frozen in place.

Lying in front of us within Ferrell's halo of light, directly beneath my bedroom . . . is a black body bag. And it is full of someone or something.

"For Pete's sake, Laurie! What the hell is this!"

I don't answer. I can't. My jaw is locked.

Ferrell is stiff for a moment as his light begins to tremble upon the body bag. He cups the radio on his shoulder and calls into dispatch.

I step forward.

"Laurie, no. Wait!"

It's like a dream. My feet pull me to the body bag as if I'm floating like the lady in white.

Ferrell curses again.

Now within arm's reach of the bag, I squat atop my calves.

I feel Ferrell's hand on my shoulder.

I pull away.

With a trembling hand, I reach out and begin to tug at the metal zipper resting at the head of the bag. As I do so, I notice the deformity of the shape within it. There is a large lump where the chest should be. I swallow hard and continue to pull at the zipper. Under Ferrell's light, the bag begins to flay open like a cocoon. The lump moves just under my fingers as I hurry to zip past it. The screechy cry of cicadas rip through the air as a barrage of them crawl and scramble out.

My heart ceases and I jolt back, landing on my butt. I kick and squirm across the dirt. I saw what the lump was. It's a head. A bald one. It rests on the chest of a body. The eyes are glossed over with death. The mouth is stretched tight in mid-scream. It's the head of Agent Weatherby.

Ferrell curses and spins away, pulling his light with him and leaving the body in the dark.

I sit only feet away. Unable to move.

It wasn't just finding a body that'd filled me with such paralyzing fear and shock, it was the fact that it was the severed head of Agent Weatherby. And it was also the realization that she'd been staring up at me through the floorboards of my home, each and every time I laid my head on my pillow at night.

"What is it?" I hear Collins's voice.

Ferrell curses some more as he calls back to dispatch.

"Hey?" Collins again.

Him and Paul are beginning to chatter.

"Hang on, we're coming," Ferrell calls back.

The cicadas scream as they scurry about in the darkness.

As dispatch crackles over the radio, Ferrell jerks his light back to me and the body bag. He grips my arm and pulls me to my feet.

Together we rush for the steps.

I ascend the last one and crash to the earth. Knees weak, body numb and limp. I can hardly think.

Collins and Paul cross over and tend to me.

"What happened down there?" Collins turns and asks Ferrell.

"Oh, baby. Are you okay?" Paul asks as he rubs my shoulder.

Ferrell mumbles about the body bag and how he thought it may be Agent Weatherby.

Collins helps me to my feet.

Dispatch crackles again over the radio.

Sirens begin to sound in the distance.

I crash into Paul's arms. He holds me tight as I begin to sob.

Collins and Ferrell talk back and forth. The sirens edge closer.

Our discovery is going to make for a long night. And here once again is another puzzle piece to add to the mix.

The sound of those gravel throated cicadas sting my mind and remind me of Morty's words.

*Laurie will succumb to Morty! Laurie will succumb to Morty!*

How long before it's me in a body bag?

# 61

**WITH MY HOUSE ONCE** again becoming a crime scene, I now find myself wrapped in a blanket and seated on my couch. It's here where I'm questioned by Cunningham, Swanson, and Ramsey.

Paul sits next to me with an arm wrapped around my shoulders. Allen is in the kitchen and is being questioned by Officer Chris Williams.

My yard is marked with yellow crime tape as multiple news vans already line my driveway with reporters swarming in like flies to rotting meat. Collins, Detective White, Sheriff Johnston, Deputy Ferrell, Sherrie, and other CSI personnel along with Glenn Giles, are all in my cellar. They'd hauled in crime scene lights and have been fast at work for the past hour now.

"How did you not smell anything?" Agent Swanson asks.

I lift my shoulders with a deep breath and shake my head. "I never had a whiff of anything until we went down there. And even then, it wasn't too strong. The cold temperatures must've slowed down the decomposition."

Cunningham scratches his chin and crosses his arms in front of his chest, "He must've placed her down there on Thursday, soon after she went missing. It would have been about the only window of time where the place wasn't under surveillance. He had to do it right after Chris and Dean left the McCrae's. He was there watching them and waited for them to leave her by herself. He took her and rushed here to place the body before they showed up."

The room goes quiet.

"Meaning that that wasn't Agent Weatherby they passed on the way here. It was him," Ramsey says with a tightness to his voice. He curses and adds, "He used her hair as disguise."

I clinch my eyes and rub my forehead.

I feel the muscles in my face quiver as fresh tears seep from my eyes, "That poor girl."

✝ ✝ ✝ ✝ ✝ ✝ ✝ ✝ ✝ ✝

**THE FLASHING SOUND OF GLENN GILES'S** camera emits from the cellar. Crime scene lights are set upon tripods and push away the darkness trying to cover the body of Agent Weatherby.

The cellar swarms with hot, moving bodies as they comb and search every inch of the place while hoping desperately for fingerprints, boot tracks, or DNA.

Collins wears a mask and latex gloves and is squatted next to the body with Glenn Giles. As Glenn snaps pictures, Collins begins searching the rest of the bag. He uses a pen to comb at anything which looks like a promising lead. He holds a small flashlight with his left hand and searches with his right. He stops when he notices Weatherby's right hand is balled into a fist. That isn't natural. When death calls, the body relaxes which allows the fingers and hands to go limp. Weatherby didn't close her fist . . . her killer did. Why?

Collins leans close and rolls her hand over, so it'd be facing with her palm up. A folded white piece of paper is tucked within her grasp.

He nudges Giles.

"What?"

"Look at this?"

Collins gently pries her stiff fingers from the paper and pulls it free.

Another piece of printing paper with a message.

He unfolds and reads it aloud, "'I'm so glad you found me before I wasted away. I was afraid I would begin to stink before you realized I was down here. I tried to scream for you, more than once, but it's kind of hard to do when your vocal cords have been severed.'" Collins curses and looks away. He recovers. "'Though it was dark and lonely down here, I wasn't alone. I had the cicadas to keep me company. I'm sure you've found them by now. They're feisty little creatures. They love to snuggle, but be warned, some like to nibble. Though I was jealous of you, I always looked up to you, Laurie. I hope you remember that. Remember my soulless face, with my glassy eyes, staring up through the floorboards at you as you slept. Yes, I always did look up to you.'"

"Holy smokes," said Detective White who'd strode over to listen to the reading.

"Hey, I think I have something," comes a voice behind them. It sounds like Sherrie.

Collins, White, and Giles turn to the voice.

† † † † † † † † † †

**I WAS IN MID-SENTENCE WITH** Agent Swanson when my front door swung open. We turn and look over the couch to see Collins and Detective White coming down the foyer.

"CSI has DNA," says Collins.

"What? DNA? Where?" I ask.

"Sherrie found a black ski mask on the ground down there. She was able to extract a few hairs from it. They're taking it back to the lab now."

"It's a start," says Ramsey.

I nod, "At least we'll be able to test it with Richard McCrae. If there's no match there, then we can run it through the database and swab everyone within arm's reach if we have to."

"This could be the best lead we've had," says White.

"Let's hope so."

† † † † † † † † † †

**MUST'VE BEEN SOMETIME** after three o'clock when I laid down. I couldn't bear to sleep in my bedroom after the thought of Agent Weatherby being beneath me for the last two days, so I ended up in my recliner instead.

I was jolted awake sometime later by a nightmare of Agent Weatherby entering my home and wandering down the foyer looking for me. The last thing I saw before being jerked to my senses was her headless body gliding over my living room rug. Her shoulders were slumped, her hands dangled by her side, and she was dressed in a long black dress. She was whispering my name as she crept closer.

It was at this moment when I shot up from the recliner and gasped for breath. I sent my eyes darting about the room as I checked every shadow. Collins stirs on the couch next to me and is quick to reach out a hand to steady me.

"Geez, you're drenched with sweat. Are you okay?"

I feel his hand on my arm. My eyes are shut and moist with tears. I sniffle and swallow hard, wagging my head, "I saw her. She was right here."

Collins gives me a gentle squeeze, "I'm sorry."

"No, don't be."

"Just get you some rest."

I lean back and lay my arm over my forehead.

Collins pulls the blanket up, which I'd tossed to the floor, and covers me up.

What I did to deserve a partner like him, I'll never know.

"Thank you."

Within minutes I was out.

✝✝✝✝✝✝✝✝✝

**I STAYED THAT WAY UNTIL I WAS** awoken to a trio of knocks upon my front door. They weren't just any knocks either, they were police knocks. My heart drums and pounds with each pulse.

I rise and throw the covers aside.

Collins does the same on the couch.

I retrieve my phone lying on the coffee table . . . *9:17 a.m.*

*Bam! Bam! Bam!*

"I'm coming. I'm coming."

I angle for the door. Collins is behind me. I give a glance through the slim windows on either side and notice what looks like two men dressed in black. I figure it to be the Chief or someone from the station.

I open the door.

"Laurie. Detective Collins," Cunningham nods.

Director Ramsey stands next to him.

"May we come in?"

"Of course," I say with a wave of my arm.

They enter and I shut the door behind them.

Cunningham clears his throat, "Glenn is saying she's been dead since Thursday afternoon. Which is what we all expected. There is no sign of struggle or sexual assault. It appears he may have used some sort of wire to carry out the attack. Possibly cheese wire."

A beat.

"Sherrie received the results for the hair found in the mask," says Ramsey.

"And?"

"Nothing."

It felt like someone had sucked the oxygen from the room, leaving me deflated.

"We've swabbed everyone at the station. We need to get both of yours' and Mr. Sealey's."

I balk at his words, but I know it's necessary.

It's just that the thought of Collins or Paul being somehow involved in all of this, sends a chill racing down my spine. And then my gut became jittery at the thought of having to submit a DNA sample. What if they mess up in the lab? What if one of us were wrongly convicte—I stopped myself there.

I watch as Ramsey retrieves three plastic bags containing the swabs and pill bottle like containers.

"Sure, please come sit," I say as I show them to my living room.

"Well, at least we can begin the process of elimination. Now we have something to go on when we find a reasonable suspect."

They each nod.

"We need to check with the people at the church," Collins says.

"Definitely."

"Okay, you know how it works," says Ramsey as he'd slips on a pair of latex gloves and holds up a Q-Tip.

I nod and open wide. He swabs the inside of my jaw, then drops the swab into the container and bags it. He retrieves another bag and swab for Collins.

I rise to go wake Paul.

I reach the bedroom door and give a few knuckle raps, "Paul, are you up?"

No answer.

I knock again.

"Paul?"

I hear him grunt this time.

"Yeah. Yeah. Let me get some clothes on."

"Okay. Just checking. We need you in the living room once you're dressed, okay?"

"Okay, honey. I'll be right there."

I smile and head back to the others.

Ramsey is sealing the bag containing Collins's swab.

"When's the press conference?" I ask.

"Two," Cunningham waits a beat, then adds, "They're asking for you."

I give it some thought, and wag my head, "I'd rather not."

Cunningham dips his head, "Understood. Well, the crew is searching your cellar now. They'll probably be here for a while I'd imagine."

"I figured that much," I say as I pet Sandy by my feet.

The floorboards creak. We turn to see Paul coming down the hall.

"There he is," says Collins.

I smile and say, "Paul, this is Chief Cunningham and FBI Director Phil Ramsey. Guys, this is Paul Sealey."

They exchange handshakes.

"Paul, they found a mask in the cellar last night that had some hairs in it. There was no hit within the database, and they couldn't match it to any of our suspects so we're swabbing everyone we can to begin the elimination process. Would you mind if they took a DNA swab?" I ask.

His bushy white brows twitch, and I watch as he takes a gulp. For a second I thought he wasn't going to do it. Boy would that throw up some red flags.

Finally, he dips his head, "Course. If it makes everyone's job a little easier, I don't see why not."

"Good," says Cunningham.

Ramsey does the trick once more and bags it up. He and Chief Cunningham stand to their feet, shake our hands, and head for the door. We show them out.

"Are you going to be around for a bit?" I ask standing in my doorframe as they step onto my porch.

Cunningham says, "Yeah, we'll probably stick around for another hour or so."

"Okay. Well, I'm going to get dressed and see what's going on down there."

"Sounds good."

"Are we still on for tonight?"

Cunningham looks to Ramsey, and then back to me.

"That's up to you, Laurie. If you think you're up to it. We're ready if you are."

"I'm good to go."

They dip their heads and walk off my porch. I close the door.

I turn to see Collins and Paul looking at me with raised brows.

"I told them I'd do it. I need to go through with it. I think it's our best chance of catching him. If he's still out there that is. And honestly, my gut's telling me he is."

# 62

**Monday**
**October 7th, 2019**

COLLINS AND I WORKED with Detective White, Agent Swanson, Sherrie, and a few others of the CSI team until just after noon. The only mistake Morty made was leaving behind the mask. Even the note is free of prints. There is no boot tracks, secretions, or anything. At least we have the hair from the mask though.

Blake and Natalie are looking over the handwriting now to see if it matches with the other notes and letters.

My phone has been blowing up all morning. Jessica from Channel Six news has left a few messages, asking if I'd be up for an interview. I'm just not ready for that at the moment. Agent Vasquez and Agent Shannon Carter have both left me messages as well.

After we finished combing my cellar, Collins and I watched from my porch as the CSI vans and Detective White's black Crown Victoria crunched over the gravel as they backed out of my driveway.

I sigh out a deep breath and cross my arms. Yellow caution tape flaps in the breeze to the left us by the side of my house.

Collins places a gentle hand on my shoulder, "You doing okay?"

I nod slightly.

"You hungry?"

I turn and look to him.

"Want to grab a bite from Ted's?"

"Sure."

With that we head inside to get Paul and within minutes we were on our way to Ted's Diner.

But first I had to use the restroom.

† † † † † † † † † †

**ONCE AT THE DINER,** we took a seat in a booth and Collins and I ordered our "usual's" while Paul got a burger.

I prop my elbows on the table and form a tee pee with my fingers. I look out the window next to me as my mind busies itself with sifting wheat and rehearsing the plan for the night.

I turn to Paul seated next to me and say, "I know the Playoffs are on tonight and all, but please promise me you and Allen will stay alert for anything strange."

"Honey don't worry about us, we'll be fine. You do what you need to do, okay? Besides Chris or Dean will be in the area anyway. You focus on you. Ya hear?"

He pats my leg and gives a reassuring grin.

I bob my head and look to Collins, "Be careful tonight with Wicker. Don't let your guard down with him. Get what you need and get out."

He nods, "I'll be fine. Ferrell said he'd go with me."

"Good."

As I'd finish my word, I catch Stormy out the corner of my eye catering our food along. She reaches our table and begins passing out our lunch.

"Here ya go. Anything else I can get for you all?"

I glance about and answer, "No, I think we're good Stormy. Thank you, though."

"You're welcome, dear," she says with a smile and pat to my shoulder, "Enjoy."

As she walks away, I can feel the eyes of those in the diner on us. Must've been a dozen or so customers scattered about. A few regulars I knew, and few faces I've never seen. I subtlety keep my eyes on them all.

"My goodness what a burger," Collins laughs, "You going to eat all that?"

"Yeah and don't you go to thinking you gonna get any either. This one here's all mines," Paul says as he throws his hands around his plate, guarding it like a dog. "I see you eye balling it. Boy keep ya eyes on ya own," he says before emitting a low growl.

That sends us each laughing a good cleansing laugh.

"Paul, you're crazy," I say wagging my head.

"Yeah, well I reckon I've heard that a time or two," he says before stealing a big bite.

Feels good to have this moment. A chance to relax and spend time with those closest to me. I needed this. I don't know how much longer I can do what I do. Seeing the things I've had to see and facing the evils of this world can sure take a toll on you. I've been feeling that toll more than ever over this past week. If only the world wasn't so egotistical and fast paced, maybe it'd be a better place.

I marinate my thoughts in between bites of chicken salad. John Fogerty sings through the speakers above about how he wished it were true. That's such a great song. I don't think the man has ever written a bad one, at least not that I've heard.

"You know guys . . . today's always a rough day for me and I needed this," Collins says looking up from his plate to me and Paul.

Gosh. I'd forgot. It's Kelsey's birthday.

"I wish Kelsey could have met you two."

I reach across the table and squeeze his hand.

Paul clears his throat and says, "I'm sorry bud. I know how you feel. I lost my wife twenty-three-years ago. I wouldn't trade the years I had with her for the best things this world has to offer. She was special and she always will be. Just know this son . . . that love you feel in here," Paul stabs a finger at his own heart, "That's real. And that's her way of letting you know she's still with you."

Collins bobs his head and sniffles.

I give him one last squeeze then pull back.

I steal a deep breath and say, "Listen, I want you both to know how much you mean to me." I look them both in the eye, "And should anything happen tonight . . . I want you both to know that I love you dearly. I mean it. You're my family now."

Paul places his arm around me, pulls me close, and kisses the top of my head.

Collins adjusts in his seat and leans closer, "But nothing is going to happen tonight. Not like that at least. Right?"

I nod, "You're right, it's not."

I breathe deep and take a napkin offered to me by Paul. I dab the tears snaking down my cheek.

I pick up my fork and return to my salad as Bob Dylan begins to sing about how the times are changing.

God, please let this end tonight. I don't know how much longer I can go. This has to end.

† † † † † † † † † †

**"YOU SEE HERE HOW** the r is slanted and has that curl to it? Now look here at the note left on your porch with the jar. See?" Natalie says pointing a pen at the paper before us.

"Yeah, I see that. So, it's from the same hand? Same guy?" I ask.

"Unless we have someone who is meticulously copying the other, I'd say without a doubt it's from the same hand. And look when you place it under the microscope, you can really see it. He uses the same amount of pressure with each letter, the same arc at the end of each letter. Here, have a look for yourself."

I step forward and lean into the microscope. The rubber piece presses against my eye sockets as I peer through the lens.

"Oh yeah, I really see it now. Look," I say to Collins as I step back and give him a turn.

"I assume you've checked for any hidden code or message?"

Natalie nods. Her blonde ponytail dances as it dangles over one shoulder. She adjusts her black glasses and turns to look at Blake.

He finishes chewing on a bite from a deli sandwich which he holds in his hands. It smells and looks like turkey and cheese. He scratches the crown of his balding head with a free hand and says, "I've searched until my eyes began to bleed. There's nothing there. If there is, it's beyond my talent. It'd take someone from Davinci Code to crack that one, because I sure as heck don't see anything," he rubs a finger across his black mustache and takes another bite of sandwich.

Collins pulls back from the microscope, "He's arrogant, isn't he?"

Blake scoffs in mid chew.

Natalie raises a brow and nods sharply, "Yeah, I'd say so. Writing such large letters and using that much force, definitely shows his confidence and ego. Funny how our personalities can come out in our handwriting. I can tell a lot about a person just by the way they form their letters. This one thinks a lot of himself."

I nod.

Collins rub his chin with the back of his fingers. It sounds like sandpaper. I've never seen him go this long without being clean shaven.

Blake rises from his chair and crosses the room to toss his trash in a bin. "If the eyes are the windows to your soul, then your penmanship is the window to your spirit," he gives a half grin and tugs on his pants.

"What can you gather about this man's spirit," I question.

"Well for one thing, he's a control freak. Very orderly. With handwriting that precise, he's likely OCD. Everything has a place and everything's in its place. He's a routine type guy, a planner. Doesn't like surprises. Has to be in control of everything. Could be a germophobe, too."

I look to Collins.

He feels my eyes and gives me a glance.

Blake's words match his and Agent Canton's profile to a tee.

"Can you tell me where he lives?" Collins asks sarcastically.

"If I could, I would."

A beat.

Natalie adds, "And he's either well educated or well read. He's not trailer park trash by any means. He knows his grammar and punctuation. You're dealing with a smart man here. Maybe too smart for his own good."

"Well, thank you both for the work that you do. You're the best. If you think of anything else, and I mean anything, you let us know. Okay?"

Natalie bobs her head as Blake gives a smooth salute.

"I'll be around most of the day should you need me."

With that Collins and I leave the room and head down to forensics to see Sherrie.

I give a few knuckle raps on the lab door and step inside.

The room is dark as it is lit only by blue and white lights flashing from the different machines.

We cross to Sherrie, who is dressed in her white lab coat, where she sits on a tall stool staring at a computer screen and typing away. Her face is drooped a bit and I see bat her eyes as if nodding off to sleep.

"Hey Sherrie, anything new?"

"Oh, hey Laurie. Hey Patrick. Yeah, I was just about to call you as soon as I finished. We've got the results back. None of the swabs matched. So that at least clears everyone. But we also have a profile of the DNA."

I raise my eyebrows.

"Yeah. White male. Approximately forty-five to fifty-five. Red to brownish hair. Non-drug user and careful not to harm his hair with cheap products. He likely uses all-natural sources such as argan oil. Which says something about his personality I think."

My mind begins to wander at the details, trying desperately to match a face with the given characteristics.

"How old is the mask?" I ask.

"Oh, it's quite old. Not something he just picked up from Walmart if that's what you're asking."

"It'd be a wash to try and trace down the purchase, then?"

"Most likely."

"He's careful not to harm his hair. Has an arrogant personality, likely OCD." I begin to name off the list of his characteristics. "He's fascinated with bugs, particularly the cicada, and operates in his own delusional world . . ." A thought hits me like a fist and I blurt it out before I even realize it. "What about the Ottawa House? The-the-the patients at Cumberland Health. Former patients. What if he's from Cumberland Behavioral Health?"

Collins's eyes grow wide at my words.

"I have to get Langston on the phone. We have to get a list of his former patients."

Sherrie stands from her stool and winces at her back, but the excitement overrides her pain. "Laurie, you may be on to something here." After craning her back, she clutches her belly.

"If we find someone matching the description, they may have records that could contain his signature. I have to call Langston."

My thoughts rush as my heart pumps hard while I make a bolt for my office.

# 63

LANGSTON WAS UNAVAILABLE, but the lady who took my message understood the gravity of the situation. Especially after I threatened to get a warrant to search the place. Within minutes my email began blowing up with pdfs of the records of former patients going all the way back to 1975.

I forwarded it to both Collins and Detective White, and together we've sifted through the files for the past two hours.

"Why have we not thought about this before? I know he's in these files. He has to be." I say while sifting through the records.

Collins and Detective White are seated across my desk doing the same.

White leans back in the chair, takes a breath, and cracks his neck before pushing his glasses to the top of his head. "Yeah, there has to be a connection somehow to the asylum."

Collins reaches blindly for his cup of coffee on my desk as his eyes are fixed on the file before him. "Langston knows something. Hell, I think they all do over there. It's like they're hiding something."

A knuckle rap sounds on my door. I spin in my chair to find Chief Cunningham standing in my door frame. He looks tired and anxious. "We need to talk about tonight, Laurie. Can you come over to my office for a moment?"

"Yeah, sure." I look to Collins and White, "You guys got this for a minute?"

"Yeah, of course. Go ahead," says Collins.

I rise and follow Cunningham into the hallway.

I enter his office. He shuts the door behind me. Ramsey, Swanson, Turner, and Vasquez greet me.

I give them a smile and nod. "I'm hoping we can get a hit from those records. I have a really good feeling about that."

Chief Cunningham bobs his head as he sits at the edge of his desk with arms crossed. His tie is loose, and his shirt is opened a button around the collar.

"I hope to God you're right about this, Laurie," says Director Ramsey.

"So, as I said, we need to discuss the plans for tonight," Cunningham says.

I settle into a chair and rub my temples.

I hear someone clearing the Chief's desk, I look up to see him and Agent Swanson swiping things aside to make room for a map that Ramsey was busy unrolling.

I stand and angle closer. As does Turner and Vasquez.

It's a blueprint of the layout for the McCrae's property.

"We'll have vans stationed here . . . here . . . and here," Ramsey says while pointing with a stubby finger. "The SWAT team will be on foot here . . . and here. He'll never know we're there, until you need us."

I dip my head with a fist balled to my chin and my other hand tucked beneath an elbow. I take a breath, "What about a sniper?"

Ramsey nods and points along the tree line, "We'll have two. Here and . . . here."

"He'll know something is up with me being by myself, but hopefully the bait will be too tempting to ignore."

"Let's hope so," says Swanson.

We go on to spend the next hour plotting out the night. It was in the middle of our discussion about the wires I'd be wearing, that we all heard a set of feet pound down the hallway. The door swings open and rattles the closed blinds. We each jerk our attention.

Collins stands wide eyed with a stack of paperwork in hand. "I think we've got something."

# 64

I TAKE THE PAPER from Collins and give it a quick scan. The first page is all the personal information.

```
Name: Edward Lester Skinner
Age: 37 (as of 2000)
Height: 6'2
Weight: 197
Hair and eye color: Red and hazel
Hometown: Bangor, Maine
Condition: Multiple Personality
Disorder/Delusion of Grandeur/Bipolarism
Primary Care Doctor: William J. Langston
Treatment: Cognitive Behavioral
Therapy/Psychotherapy/Hypnosis
Medication:
Zoloft/risperiDONE/Sertraline
Booking date: 02/20/1990
Release date: 03/03/2000
```

"And look at the signature at the bottom," Collins says.

Chief Cunningham, Director Ramsey, and the others gather around me as we stand in the hall just outside Chief's office.

I bob my head at the similarities.

Then I flip the page to find a photo from 1990 of Edward Lester Skinner. He was twenty-seven years old at the time of booking. Though the picture isn't the best of quality, what stands out to me the most is his eyes. Just a dark void reflecting a barren emptiness. Wickedness. Evil. It's like staring into a black nothingness. I feel a cold chill slither up my spine as gooseflesh crawls down my arms.

Is this Morty?

"We've got to show Blake and Natalie. Did you find any relatives with this guy?"

Collins shakes his head as White speaks up, "Seems he's a real loner."

"Who admitted him?"

"Says he was found wandering the streets talking about the end times and how he was going to kill everyone before the world exploded. Bangor police received the call and an officer arrested him. After being looked at by a Psychiatrist, he was declared insane and a threat to himself and others. It's then, they decided to ship him off to Cushing Island where he'd go on to spend the next ten years of his life."

I shut my eyes and place my palm to my forehead.

"Collins get Langston on the phone for me. John, I need you to run the name, see if we have a rap sheet, car registration, address, the whole nine. I'll go show Blake and Nat. This is good," I say tapping the paper in my hand.

I turn to Chief Cunningham, "This could be the big break we've needed. If we can find him and get a DNA sample, we might just get a match with the hair left in the mask. It'd at least be enough for the D.A. to charge him with Weatherby's murder."

He bobs his head and retucks the tail of his shirt around his waist. "Let's pray to God this is our guy."

✝ ✝ ✝ ✝ ✝ ✝ ✝ ✝ ✝ ✝

**"LOOKS THE SAME TO ME,"** says Natalie as she peers through the microscope and compares Ed Skinner's signature to the handwriting left behind by Morty.

My pulse soars as my gut begins to quake.

"You're sure?"

"I'm positive," she pulls back and adds with a smile, "We've got ourselves a match."

"Thank God," I say looking to the ceiling and running my hands through my hair before resting them on the back of my neck.

"Thank you, Nat. Looks like I have some work to do."

I pat her shoulder and head for the door.

† † † † † † † † † †

**I RETURN TO MY OFFICE** where Collins had Dr. Langston waiting for me on line two. I pick up the phone and I'm greeted by the sound of heavy breathing.

"Dr. Langston?"

He clears a phlegm and answers with, "Yes, Lieutenant Daniels?"

"Yes. I'm calling you regarding a former patient of yours," I pause a moment, "Edward Lester Skinner."

A beat.

"Ed Skinner?"

"Yes. What can you tell me about him?"

Langston sighs as if concocting how he should frame his words.

"Dr. Langston?"

"Yes, I'm here. Mr. Skinner arrived here in an extremely vulnerable state. He suffered gravely from psychotic conditions of both MPD and Delusion of Grandeur, along with a bout of Bipolarism."

"MPD? Multiple Pers—"

"Personality Disorder. Yes. Mr. Skinner was an extremely intelligent and gifted human being, despite his condition. That being the reason for his admittance into our care. After many strenuous treatments that lasted for a total of six years, Mr. Skinner began to show signs of improvement. The number of personalities declined immensely from thirteen down to five. And at the time of his release, he was four years free of any MPD episodes. During his time here he engrossed himself with reading and learning. Everything from Science, Mathematics, Literature, Art, Biology, and Religion. Miss Daniels, when Ed Skinner left here, he was one of the wisest men I knew."

"Why didn't you tell me all this before?"

"Although Mr. Skinner was no saint, I cannot imagine him being in anyway connected to your crimes. He is a smart man, but he's not a killer if that's what you're thinking, Miss Daniels."

"And what makes you say that?"

He draws a deep breath which sends air rattling over the receiver, "Because I knew Ed Skinner for ten years. His heart would not be capable of such evil. I'm not denying the strangeness and eerie vibe he often emitted, that would be foolish. After his recovery, he did have a way of commanding a room. An uncanny ability to persuade and manipulate, but murder . . . not a chance."

"How many patients have stayed in his room since his release?"

"Oh goodness. Half a dozen. At least, perhaps more."

"I'll be sending a team of forensics within the next few hours. They'll comb the room for any DNA that may still be present. I know it's a long shot, but we may get lucky."

"I wish you well."

"Ever hear him talk of where he wanted to go once he got out?"

"Talked a lot about Bangor. Always said he wanted to go back home."

"Did he ever mention any family?"

"No. He claimed his parents died when he was fourteen. No siblings or close relatives. He lived on the streets until he arrived here."

"So, he liked it up in Bangor, uh?"

"That's correct."

"Well Doctor, thank you for your time. I expect you'll treat my guys with kindness and that'll you call should you think of anything you forgot to tell me?"

"You have my word."

"Thank you."

"Good day now."

I rest the phone back to its cradle and sigh out a deep breath.

Collins steps in, "We have a hit in Bangor. Field Agents and SWAT are en route to a house registered to an Ed Skinner."

† † † † † † † † † †

**I'M NOW IN MY OFFICE** listening to the police scanner and watching live video on my computer screen from a chopper cam as it hovers above a small two-story home in Bangor. The home of Ed Skinner.

The SWAT team scatters about the land like ants. Their guns are drawn and they're ready for action.

Voices crackle through the receiver.

I feel like I'm having a premonition of the plan for tonight.

Director Ramsey stands in the hallway with an earpiece in as he speaks with a field agent on scene.

We watch as a crew of men smash the front door in with a battering ram.

One by one they enter.

Voices. Voices. Voices.

A beat.

And room by room the word *clear* begins to emit.

Ramsey steps back into my office, "They've got nothing. Said the place is clean as a church suit. As if it could be sold today."

I lean forward in my seat, place my elbows on the table, and rest my interlocked fingers to my lips.

"And you're sure nothing came back from the DMV?"

Collins and White nod their heads.

"Must be using bad tags," I say out the corner of my mouth.

Cunningham curses.

"Tell them to—" I try to say, but the voice from the field agent crackles back to Ramsey.

He steps out again.

We watch him through the glass window as he stands in the hall with one hand to his hip and the other to his earpiece.

He wipes his face, then angles for the door.

"He says they found a hidden basement with chains and cages fit for a holding cell. The room's full of cicadas and newspaper articles of all the Morty murders."

"Ed Skinner's our man," Cunningham says, "But where is he?"

"If they don't find him, hopefully we will tonight. At least we know who he is and we're not going at this blind anymore," says Agent Swanson.

I hold out the papers containing his information we received from Dr. Langston. I stare at Skinner's photo, "So, you're the one who's terrorized New England all these years.

But surely you don't work alone," I look to Ramsey, "Tell them not to disturb anything. They need to back off and conduct a stake out. What if Skinner is down here? They need to give him enough time to come home, and then they'll need to conduct a thorough search of the place and collect all the evidence. I still think we should go forward with our plan for tonight, but if nothing happens then I will be up there first thing tomorrow morning."

# 65

**AFTER THE RAID** of Ed Skinner's home, we were all filled with a dose of confidence that we're on the right path. Ed Skinner's our man, but the lingering question that hangs in the room is . . . where is he?

Being careful not to cause too much of a disturbance, authorities pieced the place back together the best they could. They then set up a surveillance team consisting of a SWAT unit and a group of field agents. They'd give him 48-hours and if he was a no-show, then the home would become a full-fledged crime scene.

So, with all of that chaos, as the clock ticks onward, we are now forced to prepare for tonight's operation at the McCrae's. I just spent the last hour and a half in the conference room with Chief, Ramsey, Swanson, Turner, Vasquez, Carter, and a handful of SWAT officers and Intel guys.

The plan is set.

I'd arrive at the McCrae's by myself shortly after eight o'clock. SWAT, Intel, and our two Sniper's would already be in position. I'd have a bug under my shirt and wedge in my ear. I'd enter the home of the deceased just like I have countless times before, wander about, searching, listening, and looking for answers.

Collins and Deputy Ferrell would be meeting with Sam Wicker at Freewill Holiness around nine. This would serve a three-fold purpose. 1) To receive the church directory of past and current members, 2) To get the DNA swabs of Wicker and whoever else may be there, and 3) To ensure that if anything were to go down at the McCrae's that Wicker himself would have no chance of being directly involved. Just a way to help eliminate as many suspects as we can.

And Paul, Allen, and Sandy will be tucked away at Paul's place with Officer Williams keeping patrol of the area.

"Are you sure you're up for this?" Collins asks as we step out of the conference room and into the hallway.

"I'll be fine. Don't worry about me, just do what you need to do with Wicker. Get him talking and waste as much time as possible. Show some interest in his religion, that will get him going."

Collins takes hold of my arm and looks me deep in the eyes, "Laurie . . . please be careful."

I sigh then lean in and hug him. Our hug lingers a bit more than usual as neither of us wants to pull away. I pat his back then create space and hold him by his arms. I look into his dark blue eyes and say, "You've been the best partner and friend I could have ever asked for. I don't know what I'd do without you."

He tightens his lips and leans in to hug me once again, "Me either, Laurie. Me either."

A beat.

I pull back, "Well, listen . . . we're closer now than we've ever been. Sooner or later this is all going to end. His pride and boldness will get the best of him. We have to be ready for that moment. Tonight, might just be our chance."

"Let's hope so."

I glance at my watch, *4:53 p.m.*

"So, you're going to leave with Ferrell about eight-thirty, you said?"

"Yeah, we'll be at the McCrae's at the start, then we'll head over to Freewill Holiness. Wicker said they should be done by nine. I think the old man from last night will be there again."

"Brother Elms?"

"Yeah."

"Okay. Well, we have about an hour before things get busy. Let's use our time wisely and see what we can find on Skinner through the databases. Ramsey has already sent info into ViCAP and NCIC, but I want to do some searching ourselves. So, go to your office, search the databases and meet me in my office, say . . . by a quarter to six."

"Yes, ma'am. Sounds like a plan."

"Don't leave any stone unturned. And be sure to search social media as well," I say to his back as he paces down the hall. He raises a thumb into the air above his head.

With that, I head for my office. I enter and shut the door behind me. I settle into my chair and scoot close to the computer screen. I jimmy the mouse to awaken its senses and watch as blackness turns to color. A beautiful photo of Portland Headlight with a sunset in the background fills my vision. I type in my password and click away to our station's set of databases. With the files of Edward Lester Skinner lying in front of me on my desk, I go to work. I catch glimpse of his eyes staring at me as I work. I turn it over, take a deep breath, and return to typing.

† † † † † † † † † †

**IT TURNS OUT THAT OUR MAN ED SKINNER** is basically a ghost. Other than the house in Bangor being in his name and the records from Cushing Island . . . the man doesn't seem to exist. At least not under the name Ed Skinner. And the other name we have, Gary Wade Duncan, of course doesn't offer much either. I don't understand, if there's no criminal history under either of the names, why is he so careful not to leave his fingerprints? There are only two reasons that come to mind. 1) He's someone close to the investigation and he's worried he may be inked just to eliminate suspects. Just like we did with the DNA swabs, or 2) He has a criminal history and his prints are filed away. Without there being a criminal history, it leaves the first option as the most likely reason. But how is that? We know what he looks like now, we know his name and characteristics. Unless . . . he's disguised himself as someone else.

The thought stops my breath and sends a chill down my spine.

I feel Collins's hand on my forearm, "Are you okay?" He'd stepped in without me knowing it.

I swallow hard and look to him with my eyes wide. My mind is lost in deep thought. I scan his hairline carefully and search at his roots for any sign of red hair.

*Stop it, Laurie! For crying out loud, they've already did a DNA swab and test with the hair form the mask. Besides, how could I possibly think Collins could do such a thing. I have to get a grip on myself.*

The tick from the clock above me pounds into my head.

*Tick-Tick-Tick-Tick*

I clear my throat and lower my eyes, "Yeah. Yeah, just . . . thinking."

A pair of knuckles rap upon my open door and divert our attention.

"You ready?" asks Director Ramsey as two men from Intel stand in the hall behind him.

I sigh out a breath and rise from my chair.

"You've got this," Collins says with a firm jaw.

I nod and squeeze his arm.

✝✝✝✝✝✝✝✝✝✝

**AFTER GETTING BUGGED UP WITH INTEL** and going over the plan once more with Ramsey, Chief Cunningham, and Agent Swanson, I told everyone bye and wished them luck. They returned the gesture. I headed for my Suburban and left the station by myself just after seven-thirty. The SWAT team and Intel vans were already in position at the McCrae's as they await my arrival. The blacked out Suburban toting Cunningham, Ramsey, and Swanson would leave the station just a few minutes after me.

Collins and Deputy Ferrell were already on scene as well and tucked away somewhere within the woods just off the road in Ferrell's cruiser.

I rode in silence most of the way. No radio. No phone calls. Just silence.

My mind rambled with thoughts as I rehearsed the plan.

I got off I-95 for the exit to Gray.

I stole a glance in my mirror and found numerous sets of headlights shining back at me. After a few cars turned off, I found what looked like a Suburban tailing about ten car lengths behind me.

I wipe a greasy palm on my pants leg and take a deep breath.

My heart hammers at the knowledge of my closeness to the McCrae's.

"God, if you're really up there, please keep us all safe tonight. God help us catch this piece of scum. Please."

As I ease onto a side street that'd take me through the back country. The road seems to narrow as it is eaten away by the abundance of vegetation. My lights beam off pine trees and bushes as I angle around the curves.

Other than the roar of my tires licking at the asphalt, my thumping heartbeat is all the sound I can decipher.

I grip the wheel with firm hands and the hard leather presses against my palms.

My body feels numb. There's a tingling sensation in my gut.

I breathe deep again.

The McCrae's mailbox comes into view.

"God help me."

My black Motorola radio crackles with a hiss as Ramsey says, "We're a few minutes behind you. We'll cut our lights once we near the location. Everyone's in position. Our guys can be right beside you at your word. Snipers are set and waiting. Turn your bug on. From here on out, we'll be in your ear."

I reach beneath my shirt and find the device. I press a button, and then press a button on my earpiece.

I ease into the McCrae's darkened gravel driveway as pebbles crunch and ping off the bottom of my Suburban.

"Can you hear me?" I ask.

"Roger. Stay calm and do what you do best. You've done this a thousand times. You're just here to get information."

Ramsey's words pour into my ear as the McCrae's dark home filters into view. First, it's only a black silhouette, an empty shell of a home where life once was.

The smell of death still lingers. That's a hard odor to rid.

I sit motionless in my cab for a moment as I take turns staring at the home and scanning my surroundings.

Watching. Listening.

Is he here?

"We see you. When you're ready."

"Okay, give me a second."

I roll down my window and listen to the wind tickle the trees as crickets sing from the shadows, and of course there's a plague of cicadas which screech into the night.

The house in front of me has an eerie feeling that it is now more of a tomb than a home. Residences of violent homicides often carry that vibe. It's like the energy has been changed.

I double check the cylinder on my Judge. Five rounds of .45's.

I rub my forehead and face.

"Okay. Let's do this."

# 66

AS THE SOUNDS OF NIGHT sting my senses, I cross for the front door which is still the color of blood. Grass and leaves crunch beneath my steps. My breath steams out into small clouds and rises to the moon above. Once at the door, I hear a cricket do his magic somewhere in a crevice, and I use my key to slice the seal in the corner of the door frame. I insert the said key and unlock the deadbolt.

With my Maglite in hand, I unsnap the holster containing my Judge. I grip the doorknob and give it a twist. The door pops open with a creak and I shine my light inside. Death's stench greets me. Maybe my senses are heightened, but the odor seems stronger than in previous days.

With my right hand resting on my gun and my left sweeping the light about, I ease down the foyer and shine my light down the hallway to my right. I pause here to listen.

Nothing.

I turn straight and make my way into the kitchen. I check behind the island and any other place someone could hide.

Satisfied, I turn to the living room and sweep it with my light.

I go on to check every shadow the place has to offer, and I'm satisfied that I'm the only one present in the home. At least for now.

"Clear," I whisper.

"Okay. Good. Snipers have you in sight. Try to stay near the windows if you can, so if anyone tries to approach you from behind our guys will have a clear shot."

"Only if necessary. Otherwise I want him alive. I want someone that can talk. Dead people aren't very good communicators."

"10-4."

With that I slip on some latex gloves and begin to conduct a thorough sweep of the place once again. Other than a few portraits hanging in the hallway, there aren't many family photos. Which speaks of two things: 1) The McCrae's lack of finances, and 2) Their lack of family unity.

The discord among Jeremy and Amanda was likely her reason for not having such photos. The ones she did have were mostly of Sarah. And in those, Sarah barely even gave a smile. More like an empty, hopeless, stare.

As I pace along the floors, the wind begins to pick up strength and thrusts itself against the house. A sudden gust shifts the home along its foundation, which causes it to creak and groan.

"Anything?" I question in just a little more than a whisper. "No. Nothing."

I raise my wrist and press a button on my watch to lighten the screen, *8:22 p.m.*. I hear it tick three or four times before I lower it away.

Collins and Deputy Ferrell will be heading to meet Wicker in just a few moments.

I glance about the home and glare into the shadows.

*C'mon you piece of scum, show yourself. Let's get this over with.*

† † † † † † † † † †

**COLLINS RIDES SHOTGUN IN FERRELL'S** patrol car as the two ease back onto the asphalt. Ferrell waits until he rounds the curve to cut his lights on. The McCrae's home is now out of sight and tucked behind the grove of pines behind them.

"So, it's true? They really handle snakes and all of that?"

Collins nods and raises his Styrofoam coffee cup to his lips.

"Yeah. It's pretty wicked."

"Dang, dude."

A beat.

"So, are you and uh . . ." Ferrell says with raised brows, ". . . the boss getting along all right?"

Collins turns and scrunches his brows, "Man, c'mon. It's not even like that. Yeah, me and Laurie are close friends, okay? But it's just that, nothing more."

"I'm just saying man. A beautiful woman like Laurie and a good-looking dude like yourself, I figured maybe you two were seeing each other," Ferrell says with a sharp grin.

"Well yeah, we see each other every day but not like that. We have a strong bond which working these kind of cases can give, but like I said, we're just friends. Besides, I still haven't got over dealing with losing Kelsey."

"Look, I'm sorry man. I didn't mean to—"

"No, it's fine. Don't worry about it," Collins says after taking another sip of coffee.

The two go back and forth with small talk as they make the ten-minute drive over to Freewill Holiness. The conversation changes gears once the church sign comes into view.

Collins clears his throat and says, "Remember, we're only here to eliminate suspects. Let's keep the mood light. Make them think we're their friends. The last thing we want is for them to feel that we're on to them and give them a reason to clam up. We have to keep things fluid and keep them talking. And stay alert."

Ferrell rolls past the dim lit sign and onto the gravel path leading to the grass parking lot.

Only two cars remain. A burgundy Honda Civic and a black Ford Explorer. Ferrell comes to a stop a few car lengths next to the Ford.

A flickering bulb, which hangs in the ceiling of the overhang where the red double doors wait with the black cross above them, draws in a horde of moths and other night bugs as they dance around the light.

Ferrell cuts his lights off and the two sit for a moment. The muffler huffs out gray smoke into the brisk air.

Darkness crouches behind the church as the silhouette of a cedar hewed swing set rest within it. One of the swings sways with the breeze. The towering pines, which surround the land, stretches forth their branches over the church. Their affect looks like the shadows of monsters playing on a child's wall during a lightning storm.

Collins looks over to Ferrell, "Are you ready?"

A beat.

"Yeah. Yeah, I'm ready."

They exit the car and cross for the steps. They're careful to scan their surroundings along the way to be sure no monster can leap from the shadows and pounce on their jugulars.

They conquer the brick steps and now stand at the door beneath the light where the night bugs dance. Their little wings flutter and flap, while at times tinging against the glass of the bulb.

Collins breathes deep, then exhales. His breath escapes in small vapors. He gives a few knocks and waits. With his head down, he glances to Ferrell as the two listen for movement.

Footsteps begin to thud near.

Collins watches as Ferrell takes a gulp.

The hardware and inner mechanism of the door starts to rattle.

The door swings open ever slightly and creaks on rusty hinges along the way.

Wicker comes into view as he holds the door open. Not Sam, but his son, Steven. He greets them with a smile and welcomes them in.

He eases the door shut behind them.

† † † † † † † † † †

**"ANYTHING?" CHIEF CUNNINGHAM** asks Agent Swanson as he scans the woods with the FLIR binoculars. They're parked in their Suburban just down the road from the McCrae's. The house is barely visible through the trees.

Sheriff Johnston and a deputy are parked behind them.

Ramsey unbuttons his jacket and adjusts the knob controlling the heat.

"No. Nothing."

Ramsey scratches his cheek and says, "Just be patient. I have a good feeling about this. He'll show eventually. It's too tempting for him not to."

"Sshh. Listen. I thought she said something," says Cunningham. "Everything okay, Laurie?" Ramsey asks after pressing a button on the small black device he holds in his hand.

"Yeah, I'm good. I'm just mumbling as I make my way through the home. If I need you, you'll know."

"10-4."

Swanson continues to scan the darkness for any signs of life. Any white blip mixed with red and purple. Any outcropping of a man. But only darkness returns his vision.

✝ ✝ ✝ ✝ ✝ ✝ ✝ ✝ ✝ ✝

**"MY DAD SAID YOU WERE COMING.** I'm Steven. I saw you the other night, but we didn't get a chance to meet." Wicker says as he turns back to them from shutting the door.

Collins was busy looking the place over when Steven Wicker said the words. He returns his eyes to the pastor's son and says, "You play bass, right?"

"Yeah, sure do."

"How long have you played?"

"Oh, goodness. Most of my life I guess. I must've started when I was about eight or so."

"I see. So, is your dad around? I saw his Honda but didn't recognize the Explorer. Is that yours?"

"Yeah, he's in the back." Steven says turning and looking to the closet door where Laurie said she saw the creature. "And yeah, the Explorer's mine. You need the church directory, right?"

"Yup."

"I can get it for you," Steven says as he passes them and heads in between the pews towards the altar.

They watch as Steven reaches down to lift something from the seat of a front row pew. A thick white binder. The church directory.

"Do you have any siblings?" Collins asks.

"No. Just me," Wicker says with a smile as he passes Collins the binder.

"So, this is it, uh?"

"That's it."

"How far does this go back?"

"Oh, I think to about 71 or 72. Something like that."

"I see. Well can you get your dad for me? There's one more thing I need from the two of you while we're here," Collins says as he lowers his eyes and reaches into his inner coat pocket for the swab kit.

Three quick gunshots stop his heart. Fire spreads across his thigh. He flinches and snatches his hand from his pocket to go for his *9mm* on his hip. In his left peripheral, he catches glimpse of Deputy Ferrell stumbling backward into a pew as he grasps at his chest. He then falls to the floor like an abandoned puppet. A dark silhouette streaks by the back wall of the church. Steven Wicker still stands beside him. Collins brings his gun up to train it on the dark figure and fires off one round before hearing Steven draw near. Collins jerks to his right but is met with a sharp sting along his neck. He feels a rush of liquid pour in beneath his skin. Like a hornet stinger full of venom, only this was a needle from a man's hand. He throws an elbow in Stevens direction. Connects. Fires off a round. His shot hits the pulpit. Wood splinters off. Steven kicks his knee, giving it a sickening twist. Collins winces and squeezes the trigger twice more. Sending stray bullets into the ceiling. Collins stumbles to his left. Steven punches him in the kidney and wraps his arms around him.

Collins curses as he turns and throws another elbow into the man while trying desperately to aim the gun to his gut. Steven knees him in the groin as the two struggle for the gun. Collins's breath is sucked from his lungs as his world begins to spin.

His vision fades in and out with blackness. Time slows to a lull.
Sound ebbs. His body becomes numb. His eyelids feel like cinder blocks and they begin to close without his approval.

"Ssshh. Easy now, Detective. That's it, go to sleep. I promise this won't hurt too much."

# 67

**I SPENT THE LAST** half hour combing through the home before finally making my way down the hall to Sarah's room. I now stand at the door as I prepare myself to enter.

*It's okay. You can do this.*

"I miss you so much, Amy. Please, help me stay strong. Help me find this guy." I say as I wipe away a tear snaking down my cheek. Amy's face fills my mind along with flashes of police lights and barking search dogs. I shut my eyes and shrug off the memories.

I twist the knob and enter.

I raise my light and shine it about the room. It's the same as before with all of the Disney characters, fairy's, and splashes of purple and pink.

I cross to her window.

"Can they see me?" I whisper.

A beat.

"Yes, they have you in sight." Ramsey says in my ear.

I step back from the glass and rest on the side of her bed. Faint light from the moon filters in and creates a geometric shape across the floor and edge of her bed. Dust particles float in the center of it like fruit gnats.

I rub my fingers above my brows then shift down to drag for sand across my eye lids.

"Where are you, Sarah?"

Ramsey's voice crackles in my ear, "What was that?"

"Sorry, I'm talking to myself." I sigh and rub the nape of my neck.

My heart hammers at the sudden sound of scratching coming from the closet doors to my right. It sounds like little claws. It could be a rat.

I stand carefully and the bed springs creak as I do.

The scratching stops.

I ease my way across the room and stand still before the closet doors.

After a moment of stillness, the scratching continues.

I checked this closet earlier when I cleared the house and didn't find anything. The scratching gets louder as it rakes across my mind. It sounds like little claws tearing away at cardboard.

For heaven's sake, if it's a cicada—

I fling the doors open and shine my light.

The sound stops.

"Is everything okay?"

I wait a moment to give a Ramsey an answer.

"Laurie?"

"I'm fine."

There it is again. The scratching comes from my left this time. I shift some shirts and send the close hangers raking along the metal shelving.

My light lands on a box. A cardboard shoebox.

The scratching emits again. Louder.

My heart knocks hard. A bead of sweat trickles in my eye. I blink away its sting.

"Laurie, talk to me. What's going on?"

"Not now." I say with raspy whisper.

I rest my fingers on the lip of the box and shine the light with my right.

I open it.

The screeching of a cicada greets me.

I jolt back and crash to the floor with a thud.

Ramsey curses.

"I'm okay-I'm okay. I promise. It's a box with a cicada. I don't need back up. Not yet."

I transition to my knees and crawl back into the closet. I find the cicada crawling up one of Sarah's shirts. I turn back to the box, which is full of leaves and a wet sponge to keep the cicada alive. There is a note folded neatly with a red ribbon tied across it.

Ramsey is in my ear again, but I block him out and steady my light on the note.

**Hello Darling**

I open it. It's typed with Courier font again and this is what it says:

*Hope you like my gift. He's a real sweetheart once he gets to know you. He loves to cuddle. I found that he particularly likes it under the covers. You can have the box too but be sure to keep the sponge moist. Oh, and change out the leaves once every few days. He likes bark and grass too, so don't be afraid to change it up.*

*Anyhow, that is beside the point. How have you been? Still no sign of Sarah or Connor I see. Don't worry, they're doing just fine. They're better off this way. You really should spend more time catching the bad guys. I'm only doing you a favor. I'm separating the wheat from the tares. The good from the bad. It's a marvelous thing I do, if only you had eyes to see.*

*Until next time my dearest Laurie.*

*Yours truly,*

*Morty.*

*GWD.*

*The Reaper.*

I hear Ramsey spitting out curses as he threatens to send in the SWAT team.

"No. I'm fine," I pause a moment to settle my thoughts. "It's another note. From Morty. I'm fine, don't send anyone in yet."

My pocket buzzes.

I retrieve my phone.

*Restricted.*

# 68

IT'S ONLY STATIC at first, but I know it's him. I hold the phone to my ear without saying a word. I can hear him breathing on the other end.

"So, you've discovered my gift I suppose. You're in Sarah's room, aren't you?" his voice is deep and contorted as its altered by a machine.

I stand, exit the closet, and cross slowly to the window. I press my back against the wall next to it and peer around for a quick glance.

"Where's your partner? Rather odd for you to be alone. Would you care for a dance, Miss Daniels?"

I scrunch my brows and pull the phone from my ear as I glare at his words.

I breathe deep and say, "Listen, I read your letter. I think I understand now."

"Hmm, now we're getting somewhere. I knew you'd see."

"Talk to me, Laurie. You have to tell me what's going on in there." Ramsey says.

I ignore him and say, "You're right. It is a marvelous thing that you do and I'm sorry it's taken me this long to see that. They all deserved what you did to them, but the question I have to ask is . . . what are you doing with the children?"

A long breath and static return my words.

"I'm giving them a better life. A life in which their parents could never offer. The chance to become more than just beggars for the rest of their lives. I'm giving them the chance to be something."

"And how is that?"

"You'll see soon enough, my dear. You'll see. You're awakening has only begun. Soon you'll see more clearly. Trust me, Laurie."

I shut my eyes and clinch my jaw to keep my tongue from lashing out. It takes all I have not to tell him what I really think. I can't do that though. I have to keep him calm. I have a job to do.

"I do trust you and I want to know more. I want to see as you see."

He chuckles slightly. More breaths. More static.

"That takes years of practice my dear. You've only just begun," he coughs and adds, "Listen, don't let them waste time trying to find me. I'll be long blended with the shadows before they ever even begin the search. It'd be futile and vain. It would be best to find your partner. Be a shame if something were to happen to him."

"What have you done?!"

"Tick-tock-tick-tock-tick-tock."

My eyes blur and my gut turns to fire. The heat rises to my throat and chokes my words as the smoke clouds my mind.

"Wher—"

The line goes dead.

I stomp my foot to the floor and curse.

Ramsey is in my ear again.

"Did you get any of that?"

"Yes, we got it! What the hell are you thinking?"

"Not now, we have to speak with Collins and Deputy Ferrell. Have any of you talked to them since they left."

"Yeah, Pat texted Cunningham when they arrived at the church. But I don't think anyone has heard from them since."

"Okay. I'll try calling him. If we don't get any answers, here's how I want it to go down. I want me and Sheriff Johnston to go to the doors. You guys tag along, but don't show yourselves. If nothing has happened at the church, the last thing we need is for them to see a bunch of FBI Agents and SWAT vehicles. I don't want to give them a reason to think we're on to them. Let me and Johnston go, and you guys hang back in case we need you. Can you do that for me?"

I was already dialing Collins as I waited for Ramsey's reply.

"Yeah."

"Okay. I'm dialing Patrick now. Have someone try and ring Ferrell too. Tell Johnston to be ready, I'll pick him up here in just a second. Have some guys stay here to search the area with the FLIR. Maybe get a chopper in the air too. Morty has to be close."

"10-4."

"Patrick's not picking up," I say after the fourth ring. "It just went to voicemail."

I leave a quick message and send him an urgent text. I pocket my phone and rush out the room. I have the shoebox and note tucked under my arm. I left the cicada to wander about Sarah's closet.

I make it out the front door and slam it shut behind me. I have no time to seal it up.

I reach my Suburban and do a quick 180 out of the driveway. Tires sling gravel as I race to where Johnston and the others await. I reach him, he jumps in, and together we speed for Freewill Holiness.

# 69

**THE DIM LIT SIGN** of Freewill Holiness comes into view as I round the last curve. I flip my turn signal up and angle down the gravel slope. I cut my lights and ease next to Ferrell's patrol car. A few spots down is a burgundy Honda Civic and a black Ford Explorer. Other than the light hanging above the double red doors, everything is dark.

Ramsey crackles in my ear to tell me they'd parked down the road and that the SWAT team is circling the church as he spoke. Cunningham and Swanson coordinate with them as they make their way through the thick grove of pines which surrounds us.

"C'mon," I say to Sheriff Johnston as I reach for the handle and pull the door open.

He clears his throat and rubs his cheek where the hook shaped scar is at.

I place my feet to the ground. I dart my eyes about as we approach the steps of the church. Crickets sing within the shadows. The wind howls as it rips at my face with sharp attacks like venomous fangs from an adder. I feel a million eyes on me at once as the feeling of being watched is overwhelming. I check over my shoulder twice as we angle for the front doors of the church.

Is he here? Watching me this very moment? Tucked away within the trees, watching me with his beady, wicked eyes?

I take a deep breath and climb the steps. Mine and Johnston's boots clack along the way.

The flutter of moth wings sounds above as they swirl around the light.

My mouth is dry and full of a strong iron taste like blood. I run my tongue along the back of my teeth to rid the stale flavor.

I hover my right hand over my Judge after unsnapping my holster. I lean my ear against one of the red doors. The woody texture presses against my flesh.

Nothing.

I look to Johnston and nod.

I give three quick knocks. Police knocks. And wait.

With my eyes at my feet and ear angled to the door, there's only silence.

I raise my vision to Johnston and nod once more.

I rest my left hand to the golden thumb latch. The grooves of the cold metal kiss my flesh. I press some weight into it. The latch clacks, and with a soft push, the door opens. I ease the door all the way open and peer inside.

Sheriff Johnston is behind me with a hand over the pistol on his hip.

Together we make our way in. We're careful of our steps.

Empty pews fill my sight before my eyes are immediately drawn to the closet door on the right. The room where I saw the black creature last night. The door is closed this time, thank goodness.

As we continue down the center of the pews, something comes into view which stalls my heart. It's droplets of blood which begin in the aisle before crossing between a set of pews towards the side wall. The blood drops end at a door. There's also a red stain near the front of the altar.

Instinctively, my hand grips my Judge and retrieves it from the holster. I hear Johnston draw his weapon as well.

Listening and watching, we step lightly while making our way to the first row of pews.

"I have blood stains. Send back up but with stealth. Don't let them barge in on us. This could be a hostage situation," I whisper to Ramsey.

Ramsey replies, "10-4."

I first thought I was hearing things. That my mind was playing tricks on me. But then I heard it again.

Chanting.

Sounds as if it is coming from below us.

I turn and look to Johnston. His eyes are at his feet with his head tilted. Listening.

I turn to the side door where the blood trail ends. I stretch my left hand under my right arm and rub my fingers together to get Johnston's attention.

He keeps his head down, but his eyes raise to meet mine.

I toss my head to the door and ease closer while staying along the wall to keep the floor from creaking.

I pull back the hammer on my Judge.

Johnston follows me.

The chanting continues below us.

After sliding along the wall, we make it to the door. I reach out my left hand and rest it upon the knob. I listen for a moment . . . then carefully pull it open.

With my gun trained at eye level, I scan the room.

A kitchen. Nothing but an empty, messy kitchen, and a blood trail leading to another door.

The aroma of some sort of potluck dinner fills the air. Beans, corn, ham, casseroles, deserts, and the like. The leftovers are stuck to the dirty dishes resting in the sink. Two long tables, which are joined to one another, wear a white sheet with food stains. A few fold away chairs sit on the floor and are scooted back from the table.

I look to the left and follow the blood trail to this other door. It looks like it could lead to a basement.

There's more chanting beneath our feet. Voices string together with a flowing cadence.

My nerves pull taut like guitar strings. My heart thumps like a bass amp. Icy fingers tickle my spine, but my feet carry me onward to this door.

With Johnston just behind me, I stop when I reach the door, and listen.

The chanting continues.

Ramsey is in my ear again, "They're in."

"Copy," I whisper back.

I take a deep breath and push the door open just enough to see in. The chanting grows louder. A dark set of stairs descend into a dusty cellar.

I push past the fear leering down upon me and enter through the door. I plant my right foot upon the first riser and begin the descent into darkness.

# 70

**THE DOOR HAD SWUNG** freely on its hinges and it now hangs in the air over the steps. The walls are dark colored cedar planks and are splashed with an amber hue of a dancing flame.

I move to the left side of the stairs and press my back against the wall. I ease down the steps with my weight distributed to this one side to keep the wood from creaking. With my Judge gripped tight within my wet palms, I make my way down, one step at a time. My ears fill with the chanting voices. I bend low to get a better view.

I see someone cloaked in black with their back facing me. Morty? They stand swaying side to side before a table. They chant something in an unknown language. Sounds like Latin maybe. Upon this table is a red cloth and a row of candles. The person is standing in front of something on the table . . . or someone. Their wide frame is made even wider by the cloak they're wearing, and it blocks most of the view. My heart knocks at the sight of the lower half of a body. Black boots hang off the table on the left side. It's either Collin's or Ferrell. I can't tell. And towering above this person in black is a statue. It is a man's body but with a ram's head and a finger pointing skyward with the palm facing out.

The chanting stops.

So does my heart. He must've heard us.

I steady my aim to the back of the person I believe to be Morty.

"Great and mighty master . . ."

The booming voice echoes and travels along the walls of the cellar.

As he continues to talk, I use his words as cover and ease down three more steps. I'm now only two from the floor.

"I ask that you please find this offering acceptable and may this man's life give you strength."

Seeing the silver glimmer of a blade was like taking a ram's head to the gut. I watch as this person raises the blade to chest level. I can picture it clearly in my mind. He's going to slice their throat and watch them bleed. Whether it's Collins or Ferrell, I still can't tell. But this can't be Morty, it doesn't fit his MO or signature.

Time slows. I feel like I'm moving beneath water.

I reassure my aim and rest my finger tight upon the trigger. The cold metal licks my skin. I attempt to shout, but before I can even get a word out, the breath is knocked out of me. Someone dressed in another black cloak had attacked me from the right side. They emitted out of the shadows like a wild beast. My gun discharges and sends a deafening blast ringing through the chambers. Fire spreads up my right side, beginning at my oblique and ending at my armpit. Carried about with the tackle, I land with a thud to the cold, stale earth.

*BAM!*

Sheriff Johnston fires a round and yells for the person to drop the knife.

The person that'd attacked me is now on top of me and pinning me to the ground. They growl and snarl over me. Another flash of mortal pain tears at my right side again. I feel deep pressure, then a sudden release like water gushing from a bottle. I hear a blade pull from my flesh. They've stabbed me once and now they're about to stab me again!

Still dazed by the ambush, I watch as the black cloaked figure yanks the blade high above its head. The hand squeezing the blade is about to come down, hard and fast.

With my left forearm shielding and ready to block any blow, I struggle to aim my Judge.

Johnston's feet pound down the last few steps. I hear the other person drop the knife.

God, please help me or Johnston get a shot off in time.

My vision blurs. All I can see is the shadow of a man as he sits atop me. My breath is being snuffed out as his weight is crushing my chest. Flashes of my nightmarish encounter with the creature from my closet, fills my mind. With his hand held high and clinching a sharp, bloody blade, he pulls it down toward my heart. He screams as loud as he can. My ears ring with all the chaotic noise.

I swing my Judge and struggle to pull the trigger. A million thoughts scream through my mind.

*BOOM!*

# 71

VOICES. VOICES. There are so many voices. My head swims with turbulence and feels that at any moment it may lift off my shoulders like a balloon releasing its air. My body is numb. I could be free falling through the sky for I know. I just feel so empty, void, and weightless.

I gasp and suck in a room full of air. My eyes flash wide. Wooden floor joist from the dark basement fill my vision. I'm lying on my back and something heavy lies on top of me.

"Get on the ground now!" I hear Johnston yell as he races towards me.

A thousand footsteps pound across the floor above me. SWAT is coming. Their voices begin to call out, and a half dozen feet land on the steps. More follow as they begin to pour in. Their lights bounce off the walls and sweep the room. They call out orders and Johnston rushes to my side. He takes the body and pushes it off of me. It flops to the ground and its lifeless glare stares into my eyes.

I recognize the face as belonging to Brett Stephenson.

I swallow hard and try to speak. "Coll-Coll-Collins. De-Dean-Dean," I begin to mumble.

Voices. So many voices. The air is full of sound, but it's chaotic like static on a television.

My eyes take on a sudden heaviness. I fight with all I have to keep them open, but no matter how hard I try, they begin to close. My mind swims again. Blackness clouds my sight. The voices fade.

† † † † † † † † † † †

**SHERIFF JOHNSTON PRESSES HIS** thumb to her carotid artery.

He curses.

"I've got a pulse, but it's weakening. We have to get her out," he says as he cups his radio against his shoulder and calls into dispatch.

Johnston places one arm under Laurie's shoulder blades and the other beneath her legs. He rises and turns for the stairs.

He looks over his shoulder to the table where the body still lies. There are too many men in the way to see who it is.

"Who is that?"

"It's Detective Collins sir," a gruff voice replies.

Johnston curses and spins back for the stairs. Laurie's limp hand swings in the air as he pushes himself up the flight of steps.

Footsteps pound through the kitchen and edge to the door.

"Watch out-watch out! I'm coming through. Make way," Johnston calls out.

Two Field Agents press their backs to the wall.

Johnston steps through the door and crosses the kitchen. He's met at the door going into the sanctuary by Ramsey, Chief Cunningham, and Swanson.

"Get outthaway-getoutthaway!"

They jump back. Eyes wide.

Johnston rushes towards the main entrance and collapses next to the door. The other three are right behind him.

"EMS is five to eight minutes away. At least. We have to stop the bleeding," says Agent Swanson as he lowers to his knees and begins to shed his jacket. He shoves the wad at Laurie's side. She gasps and jerks at the touch. Her back arches. Her eyes flash open, but the pupils are missing as only the white appear.

"Roll her to the side," says Cunningham as he now kneels beside them.

Ramsey is pacing behind them with a phone to his ear.

"Where's Collins and Deputy Ferrell?" Ramsey asks.

"I didn't see Ferrell, but Collins is downstairs."

"How bad?"

Johnston curses, "I don't know. Just tell them to hurry and get here!"

The front door swings open as three more SWAT guys and two officers enter. They glare at the mess before them and thud towards the commotion coming from the kitchen and basement.

Cunningham checks Laurie's radial pulse and holds it for a moment.

"What do you have?" asks Swanson as he presses his jacket to her side.

"It's there, but faint. God have mercy."

They watch as her color turns a shade of pale white. Her lips become blue and purple.

Ramsey holds the phone to his shoulder and says, "They're about a mile away. Just keep pressure on it, they're almost here."

With that, he rushes away for the kitchen door.

Johnston slaps Laurie's cheek with the back of his fingers, "Stay with me now, c'mon. Laurie! Hey!"

A distant siren begins to pierce the air.

# 72

**Tuesday**
**October 8th, 2019**
**Portland Police Department**
**12:07 a.m.**

DIRECTOR RAMSEY stands with crossed arms in front of the one-way glass. In the interrogation room on the other side, sits a young man with his face lying on the table. His hands are cuffed and chained to a metal ring in the center. Director Ramsey turns to Agent Swanson and says, "He may be all we have, so we have to get something out of him. See what you can do."

Agent Swanson crosses for the door, dressed in black slacks and white shirt with a black tie, while carrying a stack of files in hand.

Ramsey spins to Agent Vasquez and Agent Turner standing behind him, "Any word on Daniels or Collins?"

"Chief Cunningham said she's still in surgery and is in critical condition. So far, they've had to remove her Gallbladder, a portion of her Liver, and I believe he said she's received a blood transfusion as well. Said she flat lined twice on the way to the hospital and once again during surgery. The doctor told them that the guy barely missed her kidney and had he hit that, she wouldn't have made it to the ER. She's going to be lucky if she pulls through," Agent Vasquez says as she lowers and wags her head.

Turner adds, "Yeah, and Collins is in surgery too. He was shot in the thigh and had a bad reaction to whatever these people injected him with. Doctors said it appears to have stopped his heart because the brain scans show he lost oxygen for a dangerous amount of time. Cunningham said he'll be lucky to live, and if he does, he'll never be the same."

Ramsey cradles his chin with a hand and shakes his head. "Have mercy." Is all he can say as he turns to watch Agent Swanson enter the interrogation room after the door gives off a loud buzz.

Swanson drops the files in front of the man's head. They land with a thud, and the man jerks as if he had been sleeping. He straightens and rubs his eyes. He leans back in the chair and stares at Swanson with a firm jaw.

"Steven Wicker?"

The man nods slightly.

"I'm Special Agent Frank Swanson. FBI. May I ask how old you are?"

"23."

Swanson nods and begins removing his tie. He places it on the table, then grabs at his back and winces. "Man, you better enjoy being young because once age hits you . . ." Swanson gives a smooth whistle and cranes his head, " . . . boy you'll wake up with more aches and pains than you ever thought possible."

Swanson lowers himself to the floor. With his back flat, he pulls one knee to his chest and holds it for a good stretch.

Steven Wicker leans up in his seat and peers over the table. He tilts his head and scrunches his brows.

Swanson winces and huffs out painful sighs as he tugs at his leg. With each pull, his back pops and cracks.

Steven Wicker's face twists at the sounds.

"Ever had back problems?"

Wicker doesn't answer.

"Don't worry. You will eventually," Swanson says as he switches legs.

"No, I already do. I have a stress fracture in my lower back. Happened in my junior year of high school. First game of the year, I jumped for a high pass and was tackled from behind."

"Oh, so you were a football player, huh?"

Wicker nods.

"Me too. I was a linebacker for my high school. You said you jumped for a high pass, were you a receiver or tight end?"

"Tight end."

Swanson bobs his head and grimaces as he tugs at his knee. His back pops again.

Ramsey watches with a half grin as Swanson continues to develop dialogue between Steven Wicker and himself.

"He's good," says Agent Turner.

Ramsey nods.

Swanson rises from the floor with a grunt and takes a seat at the table. He rubs the corner of his eye, then feels for a pack of cigarettes in his shirt pocket.

"You smoke?"

Wicker nods.

Swanson reaches across the table and unlocks the handcuffs. He pulls out the pack of cigarettes, takes one for himself, and holds the pack out for Wicker.

With the two of them sharing a smoke, Swanson leans back and crosses his leg. He places a small ashtray in the center of the table.

"Alright, let's get down to business. If you help me, I can help you. You get to determine how bad this is for you, okay? The choice is yours. If you're honest with me, man to man, you might have the chance at parole one day. If you clam up and try to be mister wise guy, then this could get real ugly for ya, real fast. You understand?"

Wicker takes a drag on the cigarette and exhales through his nostrils.

"So, the thing I want to know is . . . why?"

Steven Wicker drills Swanson with his icy eyes and takes two long breaths before answering, "It's what Satan wanted."

"What's that supposed to mean?"

"It means things are not always as they seem," he says before taking another long drag on the cigarette.

Swanson shuts his eyes and scratches an itch on his forehead.

"So, the church thing was just a cover up?"

"Let's put it this way, everyone has their basement of secrets, ours just happened to be at church."

A beat.

"How long have you been doing this?"

"For a little while?"

"How many are they?"

"What, bodies?"

Swanson nods.

Wicker flicks some ash and says, "Six. They're out back beneath the swing set. You can count them yourself to be sure."

Another beat.

Swanson stares into his eyes as if searching for a soul.

"Who's all involved?"

Wicker tightens his lips and smirks. He takes another drag.

"You're doing good, so don't shut down on me now."

Wicker rolls his eyes and puffs smoke into the air, "Just me and Brett."

"No one else?"

Wicker curls his bottom lip and wags his head.

"Why did you kill your parents?"

"They would've gotten in our way, and sooner or later they would've figured things out."

"So, your mom and dad weren't involved?"

He shakes his head.

"What about the McCrae's?"

Wicker scoffs, pulls his face back, and angles his brows, "If you think we're involved with all of that and the kidnappings . . . you're wasting your time here, pal."

"Don't play games with me. I know you did it."

Wicker shakes his head and flicks more ash, "Wasting your time."

Swanson takes a short drag and coughs out the smoke as he leans on the arm of his chair. "Alright, you said they were six bodies beneath the playground. Who are they? Give me some names."

Wicker sighs, "I don't remember their names, okay? I never learned them."

"So what were you doing with them? Was this some type of cult ritual or something?"

"You could say that. Brett got me into it. He studied Eastern religion and astrology a lot. A little African voodoo was mixed in too."

"Basically, what you're saying is that you were into sacrificing and such?"

"A little, yes.

"But, you're saying the McCrae's, the Anderson's in Salem, and all the others through the years . . . you guys had no part of?"

"That's what I said wasn't it?"

"Watch it."

Wicker tosses his hands up and tilts his head to the side with a smirk.

"Why would you try to kill Detective Collins? And why did you kill Deputy Ferrell?"

"Same reason we killed my parents and stuffed them in the closet. They were in the way."

"And what do you get out of doing this? What's in it for you?"

Wicker grinds the cigarette into the ashtray and places his elbows on the table. He leans in to Swanson. His head angles a few degrees to the side, his brows turn down, and the corners of his lips rise on each end. He speaks in a low, steady tone, "Everything."

Swanson doesn't move, but only stares back into Wickers dark eyes, searching for that soul. He'd go to search for it for another two hours.

After the long pause, Swanson puts his cigarette out and stands.

"Hands together."

Swanson tightens the handcuffs back and takes the ashtray and files. He turns for the door.

Ramsey lets out a deep breath as Swanson returns to the room behind the glass. He slaps him on the shoulder, "Good job."

He shook as if he suddenly been overtaken by a cold gush of air, "Man, the vibe that dude gives off . . . whew. That's evil incarnate right there my friend."

"You done good, though," says Agent Vasquez.

"Turner is speaking with an excavation crew now. Looks like ourselves and Glenn Giles may be in for a long night," says Ramsey.

Swanson rubs the nape of his neck, "We have to rush the DNA swab. If these two aren't connected to the hair found in the mask at Laurie's . . . well I'm afraid we may have had more than one serial killer lurking the streets of New England."

"You think he's telling the truth about all of this?" asks Vasquez.

Ramsey sighs, "We'll know here shortly once they've dug up the playground and Quantico has the chance to run the DNA samples. We have a mountain of evidence to sort through, so surely something will become of it."

"Let's hope so," says Vasquez.

Swanson places his hands to his hips and stares at Steven Wicker. "For heaven's sake, we've got to get to the bottom of all this."

# 73

SEATED IN A WAITING room down the hall from the emergency surgery unit at Maine Medical Center, Paul adjusts in his seat next Sheriff Johnston. Chief Cunningham had stepped out to make another phone call.

A tv high in the corner plays a muted rerun of *Everybody Loves Raymond*. Two middle-aged ladies and a man likely in his thirties fill the remainder of the room. One of the women has a terrible cough that sounds as if it may start a worldwide epidemic. The other woman is curled into a ball as she rests her eyes with the hood from her sweater covering her head. The man has his face buried in his phone and ear plugs dangle along his neck.

Nurses and doctors pace the halls. Their voices and clacking shoes echo along the walls. The sound of equipment and machines rolling on squeaky wheels, the thud of doors barging open, and the smell of disinfectant, all add to the storm of emotions raging in Paul's soul.

Paul blinks and rubs his eyelids to fight away the invading sleep which inches its way to victory. He leans up in the chair and takes both palms to do a loop around his face, head, and neck. He shakes his head and mutters, "She's gotta pull through this. She has to."

Johnston rests a hand on Paul's back and gives him some pats, "She's a strong lady, Paul. She will be fine."

He only says that to smooth Paul's worry, and it doesn't do much to help. "And gosh darn, she'd be lost without Collins," Paul says as he interlocks his fingers and cracks his thumb knuckles. "That boy's gotta make it. Judas priest, what a mess."

Johnston curses under his breath and says, "These sick people are going to pay for what they've done. They don't deserve to take another breath if you ask me. They need the death penalty."

The sleeping lady in the hoodie stirs in her seat at Johnston's words. She yawns, gives the two of them a good look, repositions, and falls back to sleep.

"I just can't believe they did this. And that deputy of yours. He seemed like a good man no more than I got to know him," Paul says as he straightens and leans back in the chair.

Johnston says, "Yeah, he was."

A door clanks open and a pair of feet pad down the hall. They enter the waiting room. Paul and Johnston spin around in their chairs to catch sight of Doctor Pollard angling towards them. He stands before them, dressed in white scrubs and a green cap with his mask pulled below his chin. He sports a salt and peppered goatee.

They watch as he takes a breath. "Gentlemen . . . she is out of surgery and is now in recovery. We were able to stop the internal bleeding. She is in stable condition—"

"Oh, thank heavens," says Paul.

"We will have to keep a close watch on her and keep her sedated for a few days to be sure her body is responding properly to our treatments. As I stated earlier, she's a lucky girl. The blade just missed her kidney. It was also only inches from her hepatic artery and portal vein near the liver. Had he hit either one of those . . . we wouldn't have been able to save her. And had it not been for the swift action taken on scene to slow the bleeding, she wouldn't have even made it here. You guys gave us the chance to save her, and without you she wouldn't be here."

Paul tosses a thumb to Sheriff Johnston. "He was one of them on scene that helped her."

"Well, you done a good job Sheriff. Well done."

Johnston nods and said, "Thank you, doctor. But you're the smart one. I appreciate what you've done. Now, what about Detective Collins? Any word on his condition?"

Doctor Pollard nods and says, "Yes, he is in post op now. We have him on a ventilator to help regulate his breathing. We were able to flush the digitalis from his system."

"Digi what?" Paul asks.

"Digitalis. It's a form of heart medication which taken by the wrong dosage can lead to some harmful side effects. Mr. Collins had a severe reaction to the dosage and entered digitalis toxicity. We expect him to recover, but what that recovery will look like is uncertain. Remember, as I stated before, his heart appears to have stopped before regaining its pulse; however, a very weak one. Which resulted in his brain being deprived of oxygen for a dangerous amount of time, and that can quite possibly have lasting effects upon him."

Johnston sighs out a breath. "How would they have gotten a hold this stuff. The digi . . . talley's?"

"You'll want to see if anyone within the family had heart conditions. It is a common drug prescribed to help those fighting congestive heart failure. It's ironic actually, that the same drug which can treat the heart condition can also stop the heart completely when administrated in high doses."

"Okay. I see. Well thank you again, Doctor."

"My pleasure. If you want to go home and get your rest, it'd probably be in your best interest. I know you want to be here for them, but they currently do not need any visitors at the moment. It's important they have their rest."

"Of course. Sure. Whatever is best. Thank you, sir," Paul says as he stands with a grunt and stretches forth his hand. The doctor removes his glove and shakes Paul and Johnston's hands. He nods with kind eyes and returns to where he came.

"You sure you'll be okay with Allen and Officer Williams?" asks Sheriff Johnston.

"Oh yeah, I'll be fine. Don't you worry about me."

Johnston clears his throat and says, "Okay, well let's get going so we can get you home. The Chief and I have some work to do. The church is buzzing right now."

"Yeah, let's go. I know you boys are chewing at the bit to figure this thing out. I appreciate you staying up here with me."

"No problem, Paul."

They leave the waiting room and make their way down the elevators where they find Cunningham outside at the main entrance. They fill him in on the news and head to their car.

They drop Paul off at his home with Allen and Sandy. Officer Chris Williams patrols the area.

Chief Cunningham and Sheriff Johnston then head for Freewill Holiness to see if the Wicker kid is telling the truth about the bodies beneath the playground.

† † † † † † † † † †

**SURROUNDED BY THE GROVE OF PINES** and tucked away in the foothills of Gray, Freewill Holiness stands out like a lonely star in a sea of empty blackness. Above the pines, a wispy fog lingers and snakes its way about as it's carried with the chill breeze. Yellow tape outlines the perimeter of the church, and on the back side, a crowd is gathering. Bystanders do their share of rubbernecking as news reporters do their jobs of informing those at home. Two helicopters circle overhead.

An owl hoots in the distance, but its voice is muffled by the purring engine of a CAT backhoe fast at work. The claw tears away and unearths where the suspected bodies have been laid to rest. According to the Wicker's twenty-three-year old son at least. The swing set has been moved aside, and the swings sway by themselves. Spotlights and flashlights are in abundance as officers, detectives, FBI, and CSI men and women in Tyvek suits scatter about the land. They watch and wait for the backhoe to strike something dead.

Detective White turns to Sherrie, who is dressed in her white suit that is tighter than usual because of her growing belly, and says while leaning close so his voice can rise above all the noise, "When are your friends from Bangor getting here?"

"They said by daybreak. Lord knows we're going to need them if all of this is true."

White nods and trains his eyes to Glenn Giles who stands next to the widening hole, watching for any sign of bodies and relaying directions to the operator running the backhoe.

The machine swings the bucket aside and empties a pile of dirt, then returns for another scoop. The bucket sinks and make an odd sound.

Glenn Giles shoves a fist into the air and leans close to the hole. The backhoe stops and lifts the bucket away. Giles waves his hand. Three men with shovels draw near.

White and Sherrie angle closer for a better view.

Giles lowers himself into the hole. As White and Sherrie approach, the sight that'd pulled Giles's attention, comes into view. A black and lumpy trash bag.

Giles cranes his head from the hole and looks to White and Sherrie. With tight lips, he takes a deep breath.

White turns around at the sound of a car rolling close.

Cunningham and Johnston.

They ease around the church and rest twenty or thirty yards from the excavation site.

The two exit the Sheriff's Tahoe and stride to White and Sherrie.

White approaches them.

"What do we have?" asks Cunningham.

"We've just started, but I think we may have our first body. Come take a look."

By now, the three men with shovels were carefully digging around the black trash bag which is beginning to show the outline of a body.

Cunningham curses and rubs the back of his neck. He turns and ganders at the crowd behind the yellow tape. Three separate news vans are lined along the road with reporters pouring out breaking news and updates as fast as they can manage. He looks up and spots two news choppers. He looks down to Detective White and says, "This is going to be a long night."

The crew would go on to pull five more bodies from beneath where the swing set had once rested. Some were just bones with stringy hair, while others still wore their flesh.

Death lingered in the air. A stench. A heaviness. Lives had been taken. Family's destroyed.

And somewhere behind the shadows, those cursed cicadas joyfully sang their nightly song.

# 74

**THE DAYS FOLLOWING** the discovery at Freewill Holiness, news stations across the Nation were flooded with the story of a snake handling church where human remains were discovered beneath their swing set. If it bleeds, it leads as they say. As new information rolled in, more information rolled out for the public eye and ear. The little church in Gray had gained national notoriety overnight. Steven Wicker along with the help of Brett Stephenson, murdered six people before taking the lives of Sam and Cathy Wicker, Deputy Ferrell, and attempting to murder Detective Collins and Lieutenant Daniels. The six bodies discovered beneath the swing set ranged in age from twenty-seven to fifty-eight, and none were connected to the Morty case files. All of the six individuals were determined to have been homeless prior to their murders. The bodies of Sam and Cathy Wicker were discovered in the prayer closet behind the stage and pulpit. Each had a single gunshot wound to the head and ligature marks around their hands and feet. Deputy Ferrell was discovered next to them and had died from two gunshot wounds to the chest. It was also discovered that the digitalis medication used upon Detective Collins was stollen from an elder lady within the church which Steven Wicker had done some handy work for.

Along with the grizzly details of course came the coverage of Morty and the emerging awareness of Ed Skinner. And after hosting a barrage of news conferences and interviews, the Portland Police Department and FBI were left exhausted while attempting to piece together the quagmire pile of evidence with the absence of two of the region's best detectives.

Now the third day after her stabbing, the doctors plan to wake Laurie Daniels. Paul, Chief Cunningham, and Sheriff Johnston stand by her bedside as Doctor Pollard and a staff of nurses enter the room.

"Okay, todays the day. Let's begin."

† † † † † † † † † †

**STANDING IN A SEA OF BLACK, MY VISON FAILS ME.**
A heaviness weighs upon my chest. Darkness seeps through my
flesh and suffocates my heart. I know I'm running, because I
can feel my arms and legs pumping as my feet grab for traction.
But it feels like I'm beneath an ocean of dread. My movements
are slowed as if the air has been turned to molasses. My heart
pounds in my chest, my carotid artery thumps hard along my
neck. I can hear a raspy breath emitting behind me along with
the sound of thudding feet. I feel my way through the darkness
and grope blindly at the inky blackness. I hear whispers. Sharp
and quick. They come in deep octaves. They are full of rage and
jealousy. My breath is now escaping in quick gasps. My lungs
beg for air. I feel like I have just drunk a gallon of gas and
swallowed a flaming match. My head swims with questions
that I somehow know will never be answered. I try to scream,
but my lungs are void of air. My voice comes out as only a
useless, pitiful whimper. Where am I? Who's chasing me?
Who's whispering?

I turn and look over my shoulder.

Blackness. Only blackne—

My heart knocks at the sight.

Two bulging red eyes jar up and down in fast pursuit of my
soul. They're gaining ground faster than I can possibly move.

I hear a deep, demonic like laughter that chills every fabric
of my being. It sends a charge of static electricity over my arms
and causes the hairs to stiffen as tiny bumps fester across my
flesh.

I yank my head around and charge further into the
darkness.

The laughter and heavy footsteps rush closer. The whispers
grow louder as if their owner's lips are only inches from my
ears.

With my last stride, my stomach drops twenty floors. I've
run off a cliff!

I'm now falling helplessly through space. Through this dark
void that is eager to eat me. To have me. I can feel its desire for
me.

With my sight being useless anyways, I slam my eyes and clinch them tight. I lock my jaw hard enough to crack my teeth. My blood feels like it's taken a transfusion of concrete. My heart struggles to pump the dense liquid through my veins. Gravity pulls at me with its death grip. Its cold fingers wrap around my heart and squeeze like a hungry snake with fresh prey. I continue to fall faster and faster, into this bottomless pit. Wind rips at my face and hair.

I force open my mouth and belt out a scream from the very being of who I am.

Though no intelligible words are muttered, I know in my heart that I'm screaming for God. For him to save me from this darkness. To rescue me.

At that instant, a powerful and booming explosion blasts at my eardrums. A radiant flash of light stings my eyes. A warm gust of air thrust against me. I'm no longer falling. I now stand on secure ground. I have my wits about me again. I crack open my eyes, one at a time. The darkness that had once encamped me is now replaced by a beautiful white light. The glow of this light outlines majestic mountains and waterfalls, ginormous trees, sapphire skies with transparent clouds, and free flowing rivers of emerald water. The evil whispers have now been replaced by the sweet chirps of sparrows rummaging about the trees and flying carelessly with the refreshing breeze. My soul's been renewed. I feel at peace. As foreign as this place seems, somehow I know I'm home.

My face twists into a euphoric grin, and I stretch out my foot to take a step. I'm stopped by a voice. *Not yet my dear child. Not yet.*

The voice is soothing, calm, joyful, yet bursting with a controlled authority.

I pull my foot back and turn to look behind me. A beaming light full of golden and bronze hues fill my vision. I shield my eyes with my forearm. I want to ask a question, but the voice is already answering.

*This is the place I have prepared for you. But this is only a fraction of it all. There's plenty more my child, plenty more.*

The voice chuckles.

*I am the Light in whom there is no darkness. I am the Light of the world. Darkness is its own kingdom with its own ruler. Here there is only*

*Light. Be one with me as I am in you. Be what you already are, my child. Be the Light, and the darkness will flee.*

My heart floods with emotion. I feel I should cry, but the tears won't form. How can one cry in such a place as this? I breathe deep and inhale the refreshing air scented with lavender and jasmine.

*That's it, bask in my presence. You'll need your strength my child. For there is more for you to do. Abide in me and go in my strength. I am with you always, even to the ends of the earth. Be the Light my child, be the Light.*

My eyes become heavy as blackness slowly refills my vision. Sound begins to travel in distant waves like when you're awakening from a deep sleep. Voices surround me. Lights flash and pop. I can feel myself swimming back to reality. The surface of my conscious draws near.

# 75

**5 months later
Monday March 2nd, 2020
Portland, Maine
3:43 p.m.**

HOURS HAVE TURNED to days, days to weeks, and weeks to months. The seasons have changed. The holidays have passed. The winter's snow has melted and relieved the trees of their heavy burden as it has splashed the earth and turned everything to a slippery slosh. The days will continue to grow longer as the sun becomes more social and giving of its presence.

Though time has passed, my memory of what took place at Freewill Holiness has not. My heart still aches the same today as it did the moment I awoke and learned of the tragedy that happened that night. Nothing could have prepared me for learning of Deputy Ferrell's death and Collins's close encounter of it. I feel as if I've been capsized by a rogue wave of frustration and guilt while left to fight for survival amidst an ever-maddening sea of despair. The only relief I have from that god-forsaken nightmare is the fact that Morty . . . or Gary Wade Duncan or Edward Lester Skinner . . . whatever the heck his name is, has been silent since I last spoke to him at the McCrae's. However, we're only in the fourth month of his "emergence", and that fact has me holding my breath because I know it's not a matter of *if* he strikes again, but *when.*

✝ ✝ ✝ ✝ ✝ ✝ ✝ ✝ ✝ ✝

**TOURISTS MILL ABOUT, GOING THIS WAY AND THAT.** They wear light jackets and take turns snapping pictures, laughing, and peering through quarter paid telescopes at Cushing Island or the light on Ram Island Ledge. With sapphire skies and an emerald ocean, the view is nothing short of picturesque. The sun tickles the water with its warm fingers and glistens off the sea, but the wind howls past as if the

Atlantic is in a constant scream. Raging gusts rip on to shore, tearing away at anything and anyone in its path. Waves crash against the rocks as gulls squawk and hop along shoreline, pecking at small fish and critters trapped in the tide pools. And it is here along this rocky shore that the envy of all lighthouses resides . . . Portland Headlight.

After my release from the hospital, I was placed on an undisclosed leave of absence and I spent the first two weeks tucked away within my darkened home. Only going out to pay Collins a visit at the hospital. At Paul's prodding, my best coping mechanism became taking a scroll at least twice a week by Portland Headlight. The sights and sounds remind me of my vision of paradise. Sometimes if I listen close enough, I can hear the voice calling my name.

I had to do something, because the grief and guilt added with the constant nightmares had become too much. I felt so empty and hollow. I'd become void of myself. My mind stayed fogged, trapping me in a thick cloud of hopelessness. I'm just now able see a faint silver lining. If it wasn't for Paul, I don't know that I ever would have crawled out of bed. I would have most likely died there. I still have a ways to go, but with each day I'm finding that I'm healing little by little.

And so is Collins.

It's been five months since his injuries, and he is still recovering. Though he has made tremendous progress, the injuries he sustained that night have unfortunately left him maimed for life. He now suffers a stutter in his speech as certain words are difficult for him to form. Especially anything beginning with an L, I, or S. The left side of his face has a droop to it like you see in stroke survivors, and he also has a limp now. His vision will often blur and fade with no warning. And he is just now able to care for himself again. The doctor expects him to spend another few weeks in the rehabilitation center before being allowed to return home. I told him he was welcome to stay with me until he gets back on his feet, but he insisted on staying with his brother in Dover, New Hampshire. It's only about an hour away from here, so Paul and I will be paying plenty of visits.

I still find it hard to believe that it all really happened. I knew something was off about the church, but my God, who would have ever suspected there being bodies buried beneath the swing set?

The nightmares still visit, but not near as much as before. During the first month after the incident, every night I would find myself either trapped in that darkened space being chased by the red-eyed creature or being led to my cellar where I'd find the headless body of Agent Kim Weatherby. A few times the dream of the man in black, the snakes seeping beneath my door, the spinning the chair, and the young girl who looks like my sister, would visit me as well. Whichever nightmare it was, I'd awake in the middle of the night often between the hours of two and four, gasping for breath and darting my eyes about the room. Satisfied I was alone, I'd crash to my pillow and drift back to sleep.

The creature from my closet has visited me more than once too. I believe I've woken about three or four times now to it sitting on my chest, smothering me. The last was about two weeks ago. My chest is still sore from that night.

Now, as I rest my arms on a metal rail overlooking the Atlantic with Cushing Island glaring back at me across the sea, I begin to mumble, "I should have never let them go to the church alone. I should've known better. Sometimes I think the department is better off without me." I turn and look to Paul with a hand to my mouth. My vision is blurring with tears, but the wind dries them as soon as they attempt to streak down my cheek.

Paul places an arm around my shoulder and says, "Sweetie, now I know this is hard on ya, but girl you can't keep blaming ya self. Fate and death work alone, they don't ride anyone's coat tails. All this would've happened rather you'd had your say or not. You gotta believe that."

I draw a deep breath and turn my eyes back to the Atlantic. Portland Headlight stands tall just feet behind us. I watch as boats streak past, leaving a trail of white caps. A ferry angles for Cushing Island. I lower my head and sniffle.

"You've got to move on. You can't give up on the case now. You've had time to gather yourself, now's the time to get back in the game. You need to speak to Cunningham. They need you over there, sweetie. These children need you, and Amy would want you to get back into things."

I shut my eyes and lean into Paul's breast. I can no longer keep the dam of emotion in place. My body jerks as the flood of pain and guilt release.

"Sh . . . shhh . . . sh. It's alright now, girl. Let it out. We're going to get through this. They need you back on the case. You were closer than you ever been. You can't give it up now. Don't just throw yourself right back into it though. Work slow. Start on the outside and work your way in. It'll come to ya. Justice may sleep, but it never dies. Sooner or later, he's gonna slip, and you've got to be ready to catch him when he does. You can do this, girl. I know you can. You're no quitter."

I swallow hard and pull back, "Thank you, Paul. I needed that today. I love you so much."

"I love you too, girl."

My eyes linger back to Cushing Island.

"The place is calling ya, huh?"

I nod, "I still have Mrs. Whitaker's flowers which I need to give to Archie. Besides, a visit back after what all I've learned would likely do some good."

I feel Paul's eyes.

I turn and see him smiling with glistening pupils. "I knew you weren't no quitter."

"I'll take it easy, but you're right, I need to do this."

"And what about trying to talk with the guy in North Carolina?"

"The GTK?"

"Yeah."

I dip my head.

"Good. I think you could learn a lot from a guy like that. And if he's willing to help the way they claim he is, you need to take full advantage of it while he's offering it."

"And I need to see this Hal Resnick fellow that Archie had mentioned." I turn my head to the left and scan the trail along the cliff, searching for an empty bench to sit on. The trail is congested with a river of moving bodies. I locate one of the benches, but it's already taken by an older couple. I shift my sight to the right and search for the other bench. After peering through passing legs and swinging arms, I find it, but it's taken as well. By a young boy. His head is facing his lap where he looks to be twiddling his thumbs in between glances to the ocean. His feet swing freely from the bench.

I push off the rail and straighten my spine. I raise my glasses to my forehead and squint for a better view.

"What is it?" Paul asks.

"There's a boy over there by himself. Can't be much older than nine or ten. I don't see anyone with him. Surely he's not here alone."

"Really?"

"Yeah, look. Can you see him?" I say as I point in the boy's direction.

Paul angles his head a bit and leers that way, "Honey, I can't see that far. All I can see is a bunch of blurry people walking the trail."

After watching the boy in between glances for another five minutes or so and not seeing anyone with him, I nudge Paul and say, "C'mon, let's go see who his parents are."

Together we angle beside Portland Headlight and cross for the trail lining the rock face shoreline. We join the flow of traffic and continue along with the river of people. We pass the older couple on the first bench. We smile and nod at one another. The boy is now about a hundred feet ahead. As we near him, I dart my eyes in search of any relatives or friends. He still seems to be alone.

We reach him.

"Hi there. Nice out today isn't it? Mind if we join you?"

He raises his head and locks eyes with mine. His right eye wears a faint shade of yellow. His eyes stop me and for the longest time we just stare at one another, neither of us being able to say a word.

Paul clears his throat and that pulls me from my trance.

I glance around us and say, "Where are your parents?"

The boy still doesn't speak, instead, he lowers his head and looks to the empty spot on the bench next to him.

Paul and I accept the gesture and take the seat.

"Are you here alone?"

He shakes his head.

"Well, what's your name?"

He doesn't answer.

"I'm Laurie. I'm a police detective here in Portland. This is my good friend, Mr. Paul."

"How you doing, kiddo?"

The boy raises his head, looks to me, to Paul, and back to me.

"My name's Seth."

"Oh, it's nice to meet you Seth. What's your last name?"

"Roe."

"Where do you live?"

He turns and lifts a finger, pointing over our left shoulder, "Rocky Hill Road, just over the hill."

My mind travels back to the numerous crimes I've investigated along that road. Not the greatest of areas.

"You walk here?"

"No, I rode my bike."

"Do your parents know you're here?"

He shrugs his shoulders.

"Well listen, you don't need to be out here all by yourself. There are some bad people in the world right now. What's your parent's number?"

"No, you can't call them. They can't know I talked to a police officer."

"And why is that?"

"Cause, they just can't."

"Does it have something to do with your eye?"

He turns away and crosses his arms.

"Honey, I can help you, but you have to be honest with me."

"I know who you are," he mumbles.

I lean closer, "What did you say?"

"I've watched you for a while now. You're the one from tv. The detective they've talked so much about," he says facing me. "I hoped you'd see me," his eyes fall back to his lap, "No one else does."

I straighten and look over to Paul. I bite my bottom lip and turn back to Seth. I gently place my hand on his shoulder and begin a sentence, but his reaction cuts me short. He flinches and shifts to the end of the bench.

I pull back my hand and take a deep breath.

"I'm sorry, Seth. I just want to help you. Did one of your parents do this to your eye?"

A long pause. Finally, he nods.

"Okay. Who? Mom or dad?"

"Both."

I draw back and mumble some special words to them. None which a boy his age should hear.

"Tell me what happened, Seth. I need to know the full story in order to help you."

He interlocks his fingers and begins to rock to and fro. Now, he won't look at me.

"I have to know Seth. You can tell me."

He shuts his eyes but continues to rock. His lips part and he begins with, "Daddy was drunk one night and Mama was searching for her pills—"

"What pills?"

"Her sleeping pills. She calls them something that starts with an M."

"Melatonin?"

"Yeah, that's it."

"Okay. Then what happened?"

"Well, Mama accused Daddy of taking her pills and they started fighting. He started throwing stuff. Plates, cups, whatever he could get his hands on. I come running into the kitchen to see what's going on and that's when I get hit across the eye with the saltshaker."

Paul says, "My goodness, son."

"Oh honey, I'm so sorry."

"Mama comes running over to check on me. Daddy stands over us and says, 'He'll be alright. He needs to toughen up anyhow and quit being a little pansy.' After placing a towel on my face to stop the bleeding, Mama whooped me for being nosey."

"What?"

"Yeah, she said I shouldn't have been so nosey and that it was my fault I got hit with the saltshaker."

"Honey, that was not your fault. You didn't do anything to deserve that. When did this happen?"

"A few weeks ago."

"Has anything happened since?"

"No."

"I tell you what. Let us take you home. You can put your bike in the back of my car. I'll stop a few blocks down from your house and when the coast is clear, I'll let you out. But I'll need to drive by to see the place and get the tag numbers from your parent's cars. Does that sound like a plan?"

Seth nods.

"Okay, let's get you home."

Together we rise from the bench and make our way to my Suburban in the parking lot. I open the back hatch and help Seth place his bike inside.

We settle into our seats and I turn over the ignition. My mind sorts through a million ideas of how to protect Seth from becoming Morty's next victim. I have my contacts in DSS, so I will have to see what I can do. Though I know that the recent incident will likely not be enough to do anything, because even Seth claims the saltshaker was just an accident and a "whooping" isn't much grounds for abuse. Unfortunately, we'd have to have more than that to do anything.

My eyes daze through the windshield as we follow the snaky path leading out. We climb a small hill and I begin to hear Seth in the back seat. I blink my eyes and shake away my daze. I look to the rear-view mirror.

". . . I just knew that if I could somehow meet you, then maybe you could help me."

I try to swallow the lump forming in my throat, but it lingers still.

"Sometimes I wonder if I'd be better off like the others," he says looking out the window as he rests his chin along his arm as it lies upon the window seal.

"Seth, have your parents ever hurt you on purpose? You know, other than whooping's?"

He gives it some thought.

I pray he says something that'll give me some leverage.

"No."

I sigh.

"I guess not."

"Are you sure about that?"

He nods, "You can turn down this street here, so we come in from the back way."

I follow his instruction and turn to Paul, "Will you grab the pen and note pad in there?" I say pointing to my glove compartment, "Jot down my name and number for him, will ya?"

"Right up there by the big yellow house is fine. It's empty and the people who live around it are never at home."

"Seth, where do you go to school?"

"Dora Small."

It's less than ten minutes from his house.

I ease to a stop in front of a two-story yellow home that looks like it could collapse at any moment. Weeds and vines have overtaken it. A small tree leans against the right side, likely uprooted during the Nor-Easter we had a few months ago.

I help Seth with his bike and lower my hatch.

"Here, take this. If you ever need help and don't know what to do, you call me. I know some people who may be able to help you. I will do my best. But promise me . . ."

I bend down and place my hands to my knees, so I can look him straight in the eye, ". . . no matter what, you will not talk to any man that you don't know. Okay? No matter what, especially if you're alone. I don't care how cool or nice of things he says he has don't listen to him and whatever you do, don't go with him. It's important."

He nods.

"Promise me."

"I promise."

I straighten and sigh out a breath. I extend my hand. He removes a hand from his handlebars and meets mine.

"I'm going to get you some help, okay?"

"Thank you," he says as he pulls his feet to the pedals and pushes off the asphalt. I watch as he angles down the street.

As I make my way back to the seat of my Suburban, I pause and stand in the doorway. With one hand on the door and the other on my car, I do a careful scan of my surroundings. Nothing unusual. Just a quiet, semi-vacant neighborhood.

I settle into my seat and shift the gear stick to drive. I proceed to follow Seth and keep a good distance behind.

"The kid's downright pitiful, isn't he?" Paul says with a wag of his head as we watch the boy meander his way down the street ahead of us.

"I just pray to God we can do something for him."

Seth slows at a stop sign, then takes a scroll to the right. For the moment he disappears behind the house sitting on the corner, but as we near the stop sign ourselves, he comes back into view about a dozen blocks down the street.

I sit at the crossway for a moment, watching as Seth turns left into a driveway. He glances back to us.

I make the right down Rocky Hill Road.

I take inventory of the houses we pass along the way. It's a mixed bag. Some are run down and greasy looking, while others are decent enough.

We reach Seth's place.

A red 90's model Ford Taurus sits in the driveway. The bumper is cracked and hanging free in the wind on one side. The license plate is stuck in the back windshield. A big rust spot covers the top of the trunk.

The yard is littered with scattered trash: Beer bottles, candy wrappers, fast-food cups, and burger boxes.

Junk lines the pathway to the front door. The storm door is open and hanging only by a screw it seems. A shutter hangs crooked and shingles are missing on the roof. The brick home is overrun by vines.

"Whew wee. Somebody don't know what it means to do a little up keeping. My goodness," Paul says.

The place could easily pass for a home which Morty would choose. The thought grips my throat with an iron fist. A heaviness fills my chest. My hand begins to tremble as it rests upon the leather wheel covering which is now greased with sweat. My head swims, leaving me feeling like I'd taken one too many sips from my bottle of Silver Oak.

I breathe deep as we continue by the place. I turn my eyes back to the road and shake the wave of dread that has washed over me.

I have to help this kid. I've got to do something before Morty does. God help me.

# 76

**I SPENT OVER** an hour on the phone with Linda from DSS as I informed her of Seth Roe's situation. Other than sending a social worker out to make them clean up and watch where they throw the saltshakers, there's not much more they can do. I kind of figured that much. Looks like I'll have to handle things myself.

I called Doctor Langston's office and managed to speak with a nurse. They'll be expecting me tomorrow around one o'clock. It'll give me a chance to get Archie Whitaker's flowers to him which I've somehow managed to keep alive these past few months. It'll also do me some good to speak with Langston again. Especially now that we know about Ed Skinner.

I also spoke with Chief Cunningham and Director Ramsey over the phone. They both agreed on the benefits that a visit to Mr. Jessie Randolph, AKA "The GTK" would bring. They're working on forming a team to fly down with me now as we speak. So, it looks like I'll be catching a red eye down to salty Carolina within the next few days. Randolph is currently on death row in the Robeson County State Penitentiary of North Carolina. I'm holding out hope that he'll be cooperative with me and offer some insight into the mind of a serial killer.

And I've got to get around to meeting this Hal Resnick guy too. Maybe I can arrange that once I get back from the South.

Anyhow, I need to get some dinner going. It's already going on eight o'clock. I offered dinner to Paul, but he said he had some leftover Lasagna he was going to eat when he got back to his place.

I cross to my kitchen sink and rinse out my wine glass. Paul's house is through the woods. His porch light peeks out beyond the limbs just visible by the small window above my sink. I take a washcloth and clean the inside of a cup, then rest it on a dish towel to dry.

I go on to fix some Lobster bisque and enjoy another glass of Silver Oak before retiring for the night. All while hoping and praying I can avoid the nightmares that often stalk me in my sleep.

† † † † † † † † † †

**I SURVIVED THE NIGHT** without being chased by the red-eyed creature, confronted by a headless Weatherby, or sat upon by the demon in my closet. It was a goodnight.

I spent the majority of my morning sifting through the case files I'd tucked away in my metal safe high upon a shelf in the back of my closest.

With the revelation of Morty being a former patient at Cumberland Behavioral, the similarities between the death of Maria Santorum and my mother are obviously more than just coincidence. I now know and fully believe that Morty murdered or at least assisted in the suicides of both women. I know for certain that he's somehow involved in the disappearance of my sister Amy. Her disappearance would have been just six years before Morty was committed to Cumberland Behavioral. Which means he would have been around his early twenties when it happened.

I sigh and rub my hands over my face. The files and crime scene photos lie scattered across my couch and ottoman. I look to my watch, 11:27. I better get going.

I gather the files, stuff them back into their folders, and return them to the safe in my closet.

I grab my coat lying on the bed and change out the .410 shells in my Judge to the .45's.

I check Sandy's food and water then lay out some pee pads in the hall in case she has to go before I get back. I shouldn't be gone too long. I give Sandy some love and cross for the door. She follows me out. I give her one last rub on the head, shut the door, slide the deadbolt home, and angle for my Suburban.

The passenger ferry St. Croix awaits me in Long Wharf.

† † † † † † † † † †

**"HOW ARE YOU FEELING TODAY?"** I ask Collins as I pull into the crowded parking lot of the Wharf.

I hear him adjust in his bed as he says, "I'm-I'm doing okay. I'm still a little sore from the therapy yesterday, but it's getting better. What are you up to today?"

"That's good. I'm actually retracing our steps to Cumberland Behavioral. I just pulled into the wharf's parking lot. Langston is expecting me around one."

"Oh really? Are you going by yourself?"

"Yeah. I'm not staying long though. I'm going to speak with Langston and say hello to Archie. I have those flowers that his wife gave us awhile back. I thought I'd surprise him with them. I should have already done this."

"That's nice of you. I'm su-sure-sure that'll make Archie's day. I wish I-I-I could be with you. I-I hate for you to be by yourself. You be careful out there, La-Laur-Laurie."

"I will. Don't worry about me. I'll be fine. So, the doctors are letting you go home in a few weeks I hear."

He scoffs out a chuckle, "Yeah and I can't wait to bust out of here. I thought about doing what Tim Robbins did in his cell on Shawshank. You know, dig a hole through the block wall and cover it up with a poster or something."

"Yeah, I guess I should have brought you some stone chess pieces, huh?"

"It would have been nice."

We laugh for a moment as the space between us grows silent.

"You still believe he's out there, don't you?"

I take a second to answer. "Yeah. I do."

He takes a deep breath.

"I met a kid yesterday at Portland Headlight."

"Oh yeah?"

"He's only eleven, and he was there by himself."

"What?"

"He told me some things about his parents that has me worried. They fit the victimology profile perfectly. I've already spoken with Linda at DSS, but there isn't much they can do. I'm going to keep an eye on the kid and pray to God Morty doesn't take notice."

"Did his parents know he was there by himself?"

"No, I don't think so."

"And L-Lin-Linda can't do much about it?"

"No, there's not enough evidence to go on. You know how the system works sometimes."

He sighs. "La-Laurie, promise me you'll be careful out there."

"I will. I promise. You just worry about getting better, okay?"

I find an empty spot and shift to park. I reach into the passenger seat and grab my briefcase. I take my thermos of decaf from the center console.

"I-I am. You know if you need help with the files, I can look things over here."

"I know, and I appreciate that Patrick. But you need your rest. There'll be plenty of time for you to sift through files later. Listen, I need to go. My ferry departs in ten minutes. I'll call you tonight, okay?"

"Okay. S-s-sounds good. Be careful."

"I will. Talk to you later, bye."

"Bye."

I hang up and look out across the parking lot towards the marina. My mind goes back to when Collins and I were here back in October. Only days before that life changing night at Freewill Holiness. My heartbeat catches in my throat and releases a flood of emotion. One of the reasons I haven't been back to Cushing Island is for this exact reason. I knew I'd be faced with memories from the day we came here.

I suck in a gasp of chill air as warm tears roll gently down my cheeks. I dab at them with a tissue and wipe at a small amount of mascara I was determined enough to apply before I left the house. My chest weighs heavy as if it has a cinder block lodged in it. I swallow hard and try to settle the weight. It dissipates slowly, but half of it decides to remain.

"Patrick . . . I'm sorry. I'm so sorry. I'd do anything if I could somehow trade places with you. I feel terrible about what happened to you and Deputy Ferrell that night. It should've been me."

I close my eyes and lower my head. My lips begin to tremble as I feel the tears welling again. I smack the wheel enough times to sting my palm. I pull my hand to my face and pinch the bridge of my nose while leaning my head against the window. A wave of nausea settles over me as my entire body begins to quiver. My gut twists into knots and from somewhere deep within the inner chambers of my soul, a wave begins to grow. It rises through my chest before crashing at my face and leaking through my eyes and nostrils. It's too strong to restrain. My shoulders jar violently as I begin to weep without sound, before groaning so hard it hurts.

*Girl you can't keep blaming ya self. Fate and death work alone, they don't ride anyone's coat tails. All this would've happened rather you'd had your say or not. You gotta believe that.*

I hear Paul's words amidst my sobs.

Then I hear these words, *Be what you already are, my child. Be the Light, and the darkness will flee.*

At those words, my mind travels back to my vision of Paradise.

*Be the Light, my child. Be the Light.*

I pull in a deep breath and open my eyes. My vision is blurred, and my eyes feel stingy. I sniffle and look up into my rearview mirror to wipe away the mess residing on my face.

My chest is free of the cinder block, and I can breathe again.

I take a few calming breaths and glance at the time on my stereo, *12:24.* The ferry boards at twelve-thirty.

I swallow hard and reach in the back seat for the flowers. I hold them in my lap and admire their life and beauty. I open my door. I stand in the door frame and glance about my surroundings.

Unlike last time I was here, the sky is blue and there is hardly a cloud in sight. The sun glistens off the ocean as it laps into the marina. People lean along the boardwalk railing, looking out to the water as others busy themselves by working to fill their stomachs by the food trucks. Gulls are in abundance, squawking with horsed laughter and calls for a mate. Chatter from the crowd mixes with the gulls. The wind wrinkles an American flag angled off one of the food rucks. Fishing boats rumble along, passing in and out of the port with nets or lobster cages stacked high on the stern. The aroma of fresh lobster rolls and bisque fill the air. There's also the odor of raw fish wafting by.

A loud clack gives me a start. I look towards the far end of the boardwalk and see a man in yellow overalls stacking wooden pallets beside a small white building.

I throw my briefcase strap across my shoulder and lock up. I take a sip of my coffee and cross for the boardwalk railing. The vase containing Archie's flowers are in my free hand, cradled tight against my ribs.

I reach the board walk and watch the water lap against the concrete wall below. To my left sits the St. Croix. The bell for boarding should ring any moment.

I keep a watchful eye for the pale old captain that guided us last time, but so far, I've yet to see him.

I take a sip of coffee and relish the savory flavor as I peer out into the open Atlantic where numerous sailboats and ferry's join the fishing boats. My eyes are drawn heavenward at the distant horizon and it's here they rest as my mind sifts through a pile of information and memories.

Moments pass and I'm pushed out of my daze by the quick tolling of a bell.

People angle for the ferry ramp. The St. Croix's boarding and it's time to head to Cushing Island.

# 

MINGLING IN AMONG the crowd, Morty thuds across the metal boarding ramp onto the St. Croix. His boots plod along the steel only feet behind Laurie. He watches as she passes the ticket master and angles for the bow. Her blonde hair is played with by the wind as it gracefully dances upon the shoulders of her black peacoat. Such a beautiful creature. A quiver rummages throughout his body at the sight. His eyes twitch behind his black aviator glasses. His molar teeth chatter as he pulls in a breath. He still needs her tooth to complete the set.

A Cannon camera dangles about his neck as he oohs and ahhs as if seeing Portland for the first time. Yes, today he will be a tourist. A tourist with a thick French accent. His beanie and scarf keep his new hair at bay. He decided black would look nice on him today.

Keeping his eye on her, he angles for the stern and leans over the railing to begin looking over his pictures. Mostly of Laurie as she made her way from the Suburban to the wharf. His face twist into a tight grin.

The ferry's engine grows and huffs out a puff of gray smoke. The captain shifts into gear and together they leave the marina.

He knows the time to kill will come. There is no question. It must be done. He cannot allow anything to keep him from the mission. Killing is all about timing and Laurie's timing is drawing near. He can hear the cicadas sing of her coming demise.

It won't be much longer.

# 7.8

"WHY IT'S NICE to see you again, Lieutenant Daniels," says Dr. Langston as he stands from the chair behind his desk. The nurse that'd showed me to his office, smiles and walks away.

"Likewise," I say while scanning the room and taking my time to enter.

"Oh, you've brought me a gift I see."

"Uh, it's not for you. Archie's wife sent it with me," I say with a slight grin.

"Oh, that's kind of her. How is she?"

"She's well."

"Please, have a seat."

"I'm good, I'll stand for a moment."

I cross for one of his many bookshelves and pass over the many titles. Mostly of Psychiatry, Psychology, Human Behavior, and the like.

"I'm so very sorry for the tribulation that has befallen you over the past months. You have my sincerest sympathy."

I turn and give a kind smile as I pull out a hardcover with the title, *Broken Minds: The Outcast of Society*, "Thank you, Doctor."

He rounds his desk and comes near.

"I apologize for not having seen it. I should have suspected Edward Skinner all along," he rubs his forehead. "For the life of me, I cannot find the reason that I didn't. Perhaps, it was due to his charm, but I still should've had my suspicion. I'm deeply sorry for my negligence."

"No need to apologize. It is what it is, Doctor. I'm sure Edward Skinner can be a gentleman when the time calls for it. Likely enough to fool even myself," I say as I thumb through a dozen or so pages of the text.

Langston shifts to my side, places his right hand upon the bookshelf, and removes his glasses. "I never would have imagined that Mr. Skinner could have been capable of such atrocities. Not if my life depended upon it."

Boy, his British accent sure is thick today.

"Of all the different species which exist on earth, man is by far the most dangerous. You'll know if a bear desires to kill you, but man . . . man can look you in the eye with tears streaming down his cheeks, just before raising a gun to send you into eternity. I'm afraid we are capable of anything, Doctor Langston. No one is immune. Evil doesn't discriminate."

Langston raises his eyes to mine and bobs his head.

"Now, I know you've been swamped by the feds, and I know you've spilled your guts about Skinner . . . but *I* need to hear it for myself. What was he like? Who was Ed Skinner?" I say while placing the book back into its place.

Langston watches the book slide between two others. His eyes enter into a daze, and he draws a deep breath. "You'll need to sit. Please," he says with an extended palm.

I sit in the chair across from his desk, and I place the vase of flowers atop the cherry oak.

Langston settles into his seat.

A half hour into our conversation, Langston says, "Skinner, at least the version of Skinner which I came to know, was an extremely intelligent man. He considered himself a philosopher, and I never chided him for it either because . . . well, he was. He was a philosopher and intellectual man who when confronted with something he didn't understand, would spend countless hours in exhaustive study until his understanding was enlightened. It's just the way he was. He had an alluring presence, you know? Very likeable and easy to get along with. Yet, there was a sense of superficial charm about him. Like it was a mask he wore to hide the real Skinner within. Because no matter how charming and kind he was, there was just something about those eyes that told another story. I should have known," Langston says as his eyes wander behind me.

"But every time I brought him in to discuss his progress or concerns which I may of had . . . he would answer every question so fluently and eloquently that if I didn't know any better, I would have mistaken him for a professor from some high esteemed university."

"You had mentioned before that he was diagnosed with severe MPD and Delusion of Grandeur. How many personalities were you able to find?"

Langston draws a breath and lets it out through puffed cheeks. He leans back in his chair and interlocks his fingers in his lap. "Through various tests and consultations, I was able to discover a total of thirteen. But in all honesty, I always believed there could be more. Now that I know what I do, I believe it may be these other personalities who are responsible for the crimes."

"Which would explain his reason for keeping them hidden by the mask of kindness."

"Correct. If Ed Skinner truly is the murderer, then he was hidden within his crowd of personalities. Prior to his recovery, I remember stating to Dr. Brown, that I believed he may have fifteen or more personalities, but it was only those thirteen which he chose to reveal during our studies."

"So, you're saying that Ed Skinner is not really our man, but rather a home in which our killer happens to reside?"

Langston nods.

I continue, "Morty could be any one of those hidden personalities tucked away within the mind of a genius slash savant."

"Yes."

"Which would account for the reason you never suspected Ed Skinner of being the killer because psychologically speaking, he isn't. The killer is a dark personality dwelling within his mind who manifests when his twisted desires need quenching. It is one of these personalities, tucked away in the dark chambers of his mind, who is to blame. That's Morty. The Angel of Death. That's Gary Wade Duncan."

Langston nods again, this time while holding his interlocked fingers to his chin.

"Doctor, now I know the file states that Mr. Skinner was involuntarily committed by Bangor Police, but were they ever able to determine who his family members were? Did he ever mention his parents or siblings, friends, relatives, that sort of thing?" I question after scribbling notes into my pad.

"The only answer I ever received from him was that his father passed when he was a young teenager and that his mother moved south. He claimed he had a few siblings, but they moved off and started their own families. He said he hadn't spoken with them since. When I asked about their names, he'd always say he'd rather not have them involved. No matter how hard I pressed, he never gave up their names."

"Did he say what he was going to do once he got out?"

"Yes, he had plans to attend UMASS and earn a degree in Entomology. He told me once that he had taken a liken to it a few years prior to his release. It surprised me. I thought he may want to explore philosophy or religion. That seemed to be most interesting to him for a majority of the time he was here. Though he did have quite a diverse spread of study. He really enjoyed learning anything new, regardless of the subject at hand. As I said, he was quite the intellectual."

"I see."

"I must say, Lieutenant Daniels, I'm pleased to see you are back on the case. I was worried about your well-being."

I raise my eyes from the note pad, "Well, thank you Doctor. I'm doing just fine, though. Now you had mentioned something earlier about his anger and ego when he first arrived. Could you expand on that for me? I don't recall getting the full details. I believe we were sidetracked by what the officer had to say. The one who found him, that is."

"Oh yes-yes. I guess we did lose track, didn't we? Well . . . from the moment he was committed, I knew Mr. Skinner was in an extremely vulnerable state. His mind was quite fragile, and I believe that had it not been for his intellect, I likely would not have been able to bring him back. After a few months of testing, consultation, and experimenting with various meds, I was able to have him sedate enough to the point where he could conversate with a sense of normality. However, there were times when he would still lash out in violent tantrums, thrashing about the halls, injuring our patients and nurses. More than once our orderlies had to restrain him and place him into solitary confinement.

"One such incident happened with Mr. Willis Frank. The two of them were playing chess. They'd played numerous matches and if I recall correctly, Mr. Skinner had won all but two of the dozen or so matches."

"That's a long time to play chess."

"Well, when they get something on their mind, you'd be amazed at how consumed they become with it. Anyhow, Mr. Frank began accusing Skinner of cheating. Of course, that didn't sit well with him. That was one thing I learned through the years. You never question Edward Skinner's morality or integrity without paying the price. That was the button you avoided at all cost."

"What happened?" I ask leaning to the edge of my seat.

"Well, he almost killed Willis Frank. He beat him with a chair leg before finally attempting to choke him with it as he sat upon his chest. If our male nurses hadn't of gotten in there when they did, there's no question in my mind that Mr. Frank would have lost his life that night. But the man I saw who beat Mr. Frank, was not Edward Skinner. It was one of the personalities I was never able to meet. For the life of me I tried to draw that character out during our consultations, but he was tucked so far away, that it was beyond my ability to do so.

"The following day, I paid Skinner a visit in his confinements. He immediately dropped to his knees and pleaded for forgiveness of his sins. While sobbing to the point of convulsion, he stated over and over that he didn't mean to do it. That it was the devil who made him do it."

"Did he ever do anything like that again?"

Langston shakes his head and removes his glasses to give them a rub with his white lab coat.

"After he was removed from confinement, he stayed holed up in his room like an abused puppy. He never once turned his lamp light on, and we almost had to force him to eat. All he spoke of was how sorry he was. As soon as Mr. Frank recovered from his injuries, Ed Skinner followed him around relentlessly begging for forgiveness. To the point that it'd become harassment. I had to bring Skinner in and sit him down right there where you're sitting . . ."

My gut turns in knots and my skin begins to crawl at the thought as I glance about the armrest of the chair. The armrest upon which Morty once sat.

"... and reassure him of his forgiveness. I thought I may need to bring a priest in to read scripture and anoint him or something. But after a few days, he finally let it go and returned to his normal self."

A beat.

I raise my eyes from the chair, "So as I said, Edward Skinner is not the killer, he's only playing host. One of the other personalities who likes to hide within the shadows—likely this Gary Wade Duncan guy—is the killer. That's Morty."

Langston nods, "And there lies your problem. I can answer questions all day about Edward Skinner, but I hardly knew Gary Wade Duncan. The only time I ever saw him was the moment he tried to kill Willis Frank. I never had the chance to properly meet him."

I dip my head, close up my notepad, and rise from my seat, "I understand. Well, thank you Doctor for your time. You've given me enough for now. I have plenty to think about."

I send forth an open palm. It is greeted by the large, smooth hand of Langston's.

"I guess I should take Archie's flowers to him. Is he in his room?" I ask lifting the vase from Langston's desk.

"I believe he is outside tending to his garden."

"Even better."

✝ ✝ ✝ ✝ ✝ ✝ ✝ ✝ ✝ ✝

**AS I MAKE MY WAY DOWN** the halls, zig zagging with every cut and corner, I pass through the sparkling lobby that seems so out of place and exit out a back door where the gardens await. I step onto a cobble stone pad which serves as a promenade that parallels a courtyard full of luscious displays of colorful flowers and greenery. In the center is a large oak tree that scales the walls in height. It reminds me of the tree of life. Patients in their white gowns are scattered about and crouched low like catchers while tolling at their masterpieces. Plucking weeds and picking at less than perfect petals like a monkey picking flees off another's back. Other's hover their gardens, sprinkling water on them from pales with tiny holes.

I stand here for a moment to take it all in. After a moment of watching everyone, I begin to search for two people in particular: Archie Whitaker and Hope Jamison.

Birds sing above as they take turns fluttering from tree branches to the wall's ledge. A cricket chirps to add to the bird's song and the low chatter among the patients. Most of them were talking to themselves as only a few were in conversation with others.

I scan their faces, looking for—ah, there's Willis Frank and Cynthia Harden. Both are working on separate gardens but next to each other.

I'm surprised to not see Dorothy Bledsoe with the two of them.

Willis tosses a shovel full of soil to the side, then rises and cranes his back with a grimace. He sees me and stares for just a moment before a large grin stretches his face. He nudges Cynthia and points to me. I toss a hand and offer a gentle smile. Together the two of them drop what they're doing and stride over.

"Miss-miss-miss Dan-Daniels. How-how are you-you?" Willis says stretching forth his hand.

"Hi Willis, I'm great. How about you? Hey Cynthia."

"I'm-I'm goooood."

"Hey there beautiful. Where's that handsome detective of yours? Mr. Gregory peck?" Cynthia asks.

"He uh . . . um . . . couldn't make it today. He's working on something else right now."

Cynthia's eyes sparkle, "Oh, must be top secret?"

I nod, "You could say that."

"What-what brings you-you—"

*Eeeerrrrr-aaaahhhhhh-creeeeaaaakkkkkk!*

What the heck is that! I cringe and squint my eyes as I look heavenward. Willis covers his ears and clenches his jaw while shutting his eyes. Cynthia gazes up with an open mouth.

A hush fills the courtyard as every patient goes silent while craning their necks towards the mysterious sound.

It's what Frances Whitaker told me and Collins about. Like the mix between a metal chair being dragged across concrete and a trumpet that's been ran over by a semi-truck.

                          

Is this what Morty talked about in the letters? Is this one of the trumpets from Revelation which he talked so much about in the past?

I watch as every patient's gaze locks on the heavens. Some shield their eyes with a hand and stand without moving a muscle, while others smile and laugh as they bound on their toes, waving their arms to the sky.

Willis removes his hands from his ears and with hesitation, glances up. Cynthia stands in a trance and wears a big grin.

The birds slowly return to their song and the cricket to his chirping. Then one by one, the patients lower their heads and fix their attention back to their gardens.

My heart gets a start when a hand gently squeezes the back of my elbow. I bolt around and find a dark skin lady with beautiful features. Nurse Omora.

"I'm sorry, I didn't mean to startle you."

I draw a deep breath and smile, "It's okay. Goodness."

"My apologies. You heard the sound though, right?"

A beat.

"I did."

"Yeah-yeah-yeah that-that was a goooood one. Man that-that hurt-hurt-hurt my ears."

"No, Willis, that was beautiful. You should've heard it fully. Magnificent. Just gorgeous," Cynthia says before shivering in place with a euphoric rush.

I turn to Omora with my eyes begging for answers.

She bobs her head, "Uh, Willis, Cynthia, do you mind giving us a moment?"

They nod and head back to their gardens.

Omora interlocks her fingers behind her back and begins to pace along the cobble walkway. I follow beside her on the right.

"A phenomenon that scientists and astronomers have yet to explain. Some say it's atmospheric pressures, shifting of our satellites, a passing meteor, a breaking of the sound barrier . . . a sign of the end times."

Our feet click and clack along the stone.

I look past Omora to the gardens and patients to my right, "That's the first time I've heard it."

She turns her head to meet my eyes, "I can't begin to tell you the number of times I've heard it."

"Wow. And how long have you been here?"

"Seventeen years."

"Have you mostly heard it here?"

She bites the inside of her left cheek and gives it some thought, "I'd say the vast majority, yes."

"When did you first hear it?"

"Uh . . . sometime during my first month here, I believe."

"Do you know how long it's been happening here?"

"I'm not sure, but I know Dr. Langston has spoken of it before. I want to say he first heard it a few years after they moved here and began the renovation of the Ottawa House. So, sometime during the eighties, I guess. Because, if I'm not mistaken, I believe Dr. Langston has been here since the mid-eighties."

"I see."

So, Ed Skinner would have heard it while he was here.

"No one knows what it is. There are tons of videos on the internet from all over the world. My family in India has even heard it."

"Really?"

"Yeah, look on YouTube when you have the chance. It's rather interesting. Is that a gift for someone?"

"Huh?" I ask as my mind is busy sifting wheat.

"The flowers. Are they a gift?"

"Oh this? Yes. It's for Archie Whitaker. It's from his wife, Frances."

"Oh, how sweet. He'll be delighted."

"Can you show me to him?"

"Of course, right this way," Omora says as she makes a quick cut to the right, leading us down a cobble walkway in between the gardens. Patients mingle among us as we enter their domain. Some gawk and sneer as we pass, others just stare with a blank face. They're eyes are void of life and their mouths drooped in a drug induced drawl.

Coming to the back corner of the gardens, Polish tulips, rose bushes, and yellow daises begin to multiply. I see an elderly man's back hunched at the spine as he sits with his knees pressed into the earth. His hands are fast at work.

We stop some ten feet away.

"Mr. Whitaker?"

"Huh?"

"Mr. Whitaker, you have a visitor."

I hide the flowers behind my back.

He stops his work and cranes his head around with a stiff neck.  His face is drenched with sweat and smeared with dirt. His eyes bound from Omora to me. A smile grows across his face. He wipes his brow with a forearm, then pushes himself to his feet. His knee pops loudly, he grimaces but manages to stand.

"Lieutenant Daniels . . . my my my. It's good to see you, dear. I would offer a hand, but I'm not the cleanest joker in the bunch at the moment," he says with a smile.

"That's perfectly fine Mr. Whitaker. It's good to see you as well. I have something for you," I say as I reveal the vase of flowers.

His eyes sparkle. "You give her my Swan?"

"I sure did, and she wanted me to give you this in return."

I watch as he steps forward with quivering lips and tears welling in his eyes.

Omora pats my upper arm and says, "I'll leave you two alone for a moment. Let me know if you need me."

"Thank you."

Archie stretches with a trembling hand, and I pass him the vase. You'd thought it was full of diamonds.

He takes it with both hands and marvels at it, then clutches it tight to his chest and sways back and forth as if he were hugging his wife. With his eyes closed and tears beginning to stream down his cheeks, I watch as his shoulders jar up and down.

"Thank you. Thank you. Thank you," is all he can say through his breaking voice.

I swallow hard and wipe a tear snaking my cheek, "You're welcome, Archie."

He lets out a deep puff of air and opens his eyes, "How is she?"

"She's good. She said to tell you 'thank you' for the Swan and that you better watch out for loose women in here."

A smile cracks his lips and he wipes his eyes with the heel of his hand. He sniffles and his eyes goes back to the vase. "Oh man. It's like really having her here with me."

He turns and eases himself to the ground at an empty spot in his garden. Perfect for two daisies.

He sits the vase next to him and reaches for a miniature spade shovel. He begins to dig. "I can't tell you how thankful I am. You have no idea how much this means to me."

I smile and move beside him. "I think I do, Archie, because you can't hide the kind of love you two share. You can't hide that kind of light."

He cranes his head at me and smiles then returns to planting the daisies.

If only somehow the two of them could see each other. It's a shame they've been separated this long.

"Miss Daniels?"

I clear my throat, "Yes?"

"I'm sorry about what happened. How are you doing?" he says as he wipes his brow and straightens his spine with his knees still tucked under him.

"You know about everything?"

He nods, "I keep up with the local paper. One of the gifts I've received for my good behavior. That and my Victrola."

"I'm not going to lie . . . it's been hell. Between dealing with my physical pain then dealing with the grief and guilt of what happened to Collins and Deputy Ferrell, along with Agent Weatherby. I've seen some dark days over the past few months."

He tightens his lips and lowers his gaze to his hands resting on his thighs, "I'm sorry, Laurie."

"So, you know the truth about Freewill Holiness?"

He nods with a shameful look in his eye.

"Do you believe Sam and Cathy had anything to do with it?"

"No. I don't think they did. Sam and I disagreed on a lot of things, but I don't think he could have done something like that. Sam and them meant well, they just got a little too caught up in their religion. It's a downright shame that his boy did that to them. I blame Brett for most of it. He must've really brainwashed that kid."

I angle a brow and dip my head.

"But girl, don't let those two heathens or that church's weird ways ruin God for ya. Don't go a thinking that every church is hiding secrets like that. I hate you had to experience all of that. There are a lot of good churches out there. Far more good than they are bad. The question you have to ask yourself is this . . . what is the center of their focus? Religion or Jesus? That's how you tell, right there. Jesus didn't suffer the crucifixion just so you could follow a bunch of manmade rules. No, He willingly gave Himself up to suffer the worst death of His time, so that we may be reconciled with God. Jesus restored our standing with the Almighty. Religion and rules won't save you. If they could, then Jesus died in vain. You got to trust that his blood and death paved the way for you to get to heaven. There isn't anything you can do to earn it. It's called Grace. Am I making any sense to ya?"

I swallow and nod, "More than you know."

"Good. Good. I didn't mean to go into all that. I just don't want all of that putting a bad taste in your mouth. Those two weren't serving God. They were straight up serving the devil. I'm sure you know that by now."

"I do. Something I'll never forget."

"I'll say this then I'll hush. You have a light about you, honey. The world may not see it, but I do. You may not feel it or know it, but God is using you in a big way. Trust Him. And know this girl, God is so much bigger than religion. Jesus didn't die for us to have to follow a million different rules, he died so we could have a genuine relationship with Him. He loves you more than any earthly mother or father ever could. He wants the very best for you. Just the mention of your name brings a smile to His face. He loves you. Always has and always will. Remember that for me, will ya?"

"I sure will, Archie. I will."

He takes a deep breath and asks, "So, have you met Hal yet?"

"No, but I'm going to soon. Hopefully by the end of this week. I've been off the case since I was hospitalized. So, I'm just now getting back in the groove. I have a flight to catch tomorrow. I'll be out of town likely until sometime Friday. Hoping I can meet him then."

"I see. Where are you heading?"

"North Carolina. You ever heard about the GTK?"

"Of course, who hasn't."

"And the San Bernardino Phantom?"

He nods.

"I'm going to meet with him in prison. I'll interview him and see if he can give me any insight into what it's like to be a serial killer with religious motives."

"Goodness. I hear he's helping people though. I read in the paper a while back about him doing prison ministry. It said he's a preacher now."

"That's the word on the street. I guess I'll find out."

A distant rumble of thunder drums through the sky.

"Guess I better finish up. I heard they're calling for an evening thunderstorm. That's what the weatherman said on the tv in the cafeteria this morning."

"Okay, Archie. I'll let you get back to what you were doing. It was good seeing you. I'll try to come back in a few weeks and see how your daisies are doing."

"Sounds good, Detective. Thank you again. You be careful now. You're in my prayers."

"Thank you, Archie. You take care, okay?"

"Yes ma'am, you too."

With that I turn and head back through the gardens the way Omora and I had come.

I find Omora and ask about Hope Jamison, but she tells me she's been in bed all day with a terrible migraine. Which is something she's apparently been struggling with lately.

So, having fulfilled my purpose of the visit, I thank Omora and call for a taxi to pick me up at the gate. Maybe it'll be the old man this time, Don Graves. He was a nice fellow.

I notice I have two messages. One from Cunningham and one from Ramsey. Should be about the details of our visit to meet the GTK.

The thought of meeting such a man creates a chill which starts at my calves before trailing up my body and ending in the back of my neck to send the hairs standing on end.

The GTK.

*The* GTK.

Should be an interesting visit.

# 79

AFTER SETTING EVERYTHING in order and packing my bags, by two o'clock the following day, I found myself boarding a Citation flight with Detective White, Agent Dan Turner, and Agent Ricki Vasquez. We flew into Fayetteville, North Carolina where a federal issued black Tahoe awaited us. From there we headed to the Hampton Inn downtown and checked in just after 10 p.m.

I tried to get some sleep on the flight down, but the best I managed was no more than a half hour or so nap. My mind was just too busy sifting through everything. From the case files, the enigma lurking within the gates of Cumberland Behavioral, visiting the GTK, worrying about Seth Roe and that whole situation, and then of course worrying of Paul's safety despite Williams keeping watch. Not to mention the ever-accusing voice of guilt and grief. Collins should've been the one sitting next to me on the flight, not White. Deputy Dean Ferrell should be rotating patrol with Chris Williams, and Agent Kim Weatherby should be tagging alone with Agent Swanson back at Quantico.

So, after entering my room on the bottom floor of the hotel, I quickly changed clothes and crawled beneath the cold, soft hotel covers. I didn't even bother turning the lights or tv on.

I thought I should've been out like a light, but for the life of me, I can't fall asleep.

A million questions run through my head, followed by a severe vibe of uneasiness. I feel naked and vulnerable, like my every move is suddenly being watched. Like I'm not alone in the room anymore. I take a deep breath and crack one eye lid open just enough to peak between my eyelashes. I scan the room, check the bathroom door, and the door leading to the hall. I feel so . . . unsafe for lack of a better word. Like I've stumbled into a lion's den and at any moment will be feasted upon. I wiggle my toes and fingers, just to be sure I'm not having another sleep paralysis episode. Which I shouldn't be because I don't remember falling asleep.

I take a deep breath, toss the covers back, and swing my legs to the floor. I reach and twist the switch for the bed lamp on the nightstand. The darkness hides as the light licks away the shadows. I push off the bed and angle for the door. I double check that the lock is engaged. Then it dawns on me . . . I never went in the bathroom.

Someone could be in there.

Morty.

Oh c'mon, how is that even possible? How could he have made it in the room before me? I have to get some sleep, but before I retreat under the covers, just to ease my nerves, I'll check the bathroom and behind the shower curtain. And so I do. Empty. Just like they should be.

I step out of the bathroom, turn out the light and close the door behind me.

Before I get back in bed, I drop to my knees and reluctantly check beneath it. No monsters. No Morty.

I sigh and crawl back into bed. I turn out the light. Darkness returns.

My eyes land on the bathroom door as its darkened silhouette glares back at me. I keep waiting for a pair of bony black fingers to wrap around it, before the creature in my closet crawls out with creaky bones and rest atop my chest like it has done before.

I say a prayer and reassure myself, then gently close my eyes.

Blackness turns to red as the last thing I see is the back of my eyelids.

† † † † † † † † † †

**THE MORNING ARRIVED QUICK.** We checked out just before 7 a.m. and made a round by the McDonald's drive-thru for some coffee and breakfast. Of course, all I got was a parfait, anything else would have likely sent me into cardiac arrest by the time we entered onto the interstate. We then made the forty-five-minute drive to Robeson County Prison just off I-74 in Lumberton.

A light mist had begun to fall on the drive over as the sun remained tucked behind the clouds. Green trees dusted with pollen line the highway and state road leading to the prison. I noticed after we landed yesterday how my nostrils became slightly clogged and my eyes irritated. I've sneezed more since we made it here than I have in the past month. The falling mist should do this place some good.

I wipe my nose with a tissue as Agent Turner turns into the driveway. We ride beside a block building before coming to a guard shack. A muscular guard with an M-16 greets us. With a flash of Agent Turner and Agent Vasquez's badges and a quick explanation, we make it through the gate. The correction officers are expecting us between eight and nine. It's eight-o-six now.

We follow along with the guard's directions and ease our way to a parking lot in the back.

"He still doesn't know it's us that he's seeing, right?" Detective White asks, sitting beside me in the back.

"No, he knows he has visitors today, but I told them not to tell him who."

White nods at my words.

"I think that's a good idea. Less chance of him changing his mind," says Vasquez from the front passenger seat.

"I think that's where he said we'll go in at," says Turner with one hand on the wheel and the other pointing to a door.

He finds a spot, which isn't hard to do. Only about a dozen or so cars are parked here. He shifts the gear stick and kills the engine.

I grab my note pad and shoulder bag containing the case files. Together we exit the Tahoe and stride across the asphalt.

"You ready to do this?" White asks.

I turn and look up at him, "Of course."

As instructed, Agent Turner presses the button next to the door. After a moment of waiting, a loud buzz rings out and the door swings inward to reveal a small white room with a glass enclosed office where a lady sits in a chair. She motions with a finger towards us. We step inside and angle to her. Her voice comes with a static hiss and a flat, careless tone as she speaks through the glass using a speaker box, "How can I help you?"

Agent Turner clears his throat and retrieves his badge. The lady squints her eyes, removes her glasses and rest them atop her head. She leans forward.

"Agent Dan Turner . . . Behavioral Analysis Unit. The Bureau has sent myself, Agent Vasquez, Homicide Lieutenant Laurie Daniels, and Detective John White here. . ." Turner says with a toss of his hand to each of us, ". . . to interview one of your inmates. Jessie Randolph. Director Phil Ramsey has spoken with your supervisor and the correction officers. They're expecting us between eight and nine today. Randolph has been informed of a visitation as well."

The lady searches each of our eyes, "One moment," then rises with a grunt and makes her way to a door behind her.

About five minutes pass before she returns with an older gentleman. He has white hair and a thick white mustache to accentuate a deep scar running across his cheeks and nose. He makes his way out of the enclosed office and steps from a side door. He eyes us and nods, his face is void of an expression, "So you're the Feds, huh?" he places his hands to his hips.

Turner slowly raises his badge.

The man sucks on his teeth and rolls his tongue across the back of his lips, "Well, glad you survived the trip down. Arlen Rogers," he says with an extended hand.

"Agent Dan Turner."

We each introduce ourselves and shake hands.

"Follow me," Arlen says before leading us to the door he came from.

After passing numerous offices and cutting this way and that through sharp hallways, we enter a long corridor void of any doors except the double doors waiting for us at the end. A few of the overhead lights flicker. The clacking of our shoes echoes off the walls.

"Where will we be meeting him? His cell or?" I ask.

"I'd suggest you meet him at his cell if you want to make the most of your time. He'll be more open with you that way. He can be shy at times, so it's best to make him as comfortable as possible. The crime reporters and doctors usually start there, then as they get to know each other, they'll move round. But I'd definitely start at his cell. I'll get you some comfy chairs to sit in."

"What like Agent Starling did with Doctor Lecter in *Silence of the Lambs*?" Agent Vasquez asks with a chuckle.

"Something like that," Arlen says with a grin and wink. "But in all seriousness, I don't think you have anything to worry about. Randolph's more of an Ed Kemper type than the cannibal Hannibal. You'll see."

As we near the doors, voices begin to grow from the other side. Arlen stops by a silver pad on the wall. He raises the badge hanging from his neck. A loud beep emits, and the doors swing open, pushing inward.

Another long corridor, only this one has doors on each side with small slits like a mailman would use.

Cells.

Laughter. Chatter. Cursing. Arguing.

Arlen is forced to raise his voice to be heard over the noise, "These are mostly your rapist and murderers. Most are here for life sentences. They have two hours a day outside their cell. They can choose to either spend it in the cafeteria or in the yard."

We nod and continue to follow behind.

The inmates peek through letter like slits in their cells and scream or whistle to get our attention. Me and Agent Vasquez are called more names than I care to mention.

Arlen rebukes them as his voice thunders throughout the hall. That settles most of them, but a few still murmur and cat call.

"I apologize ladies."

I dip my head.

We continue down this long corridor before finally coming to a pair of elevators tucked away in a cubby to the right. Much like you'd find within a hospital.

"Let me guess, he's kept underground?" I ask.

Arlen cranes his head and tightens his lips. "I guess we figure since they're on death row, they might as well get used to being underground. It won't be much longer and underground will be their permanent residence."

I swallow and look to my comrades.

White scratches his bald head. Turner draws a deep breath, and Vasquez is busy scanning the ceiling tiles while chewing on the inside of her lip.

I adjust my shoulder bag containing the files and ask, "Any word yet on his sentencing?"

"He has another trial set for the summer. With his case and all, I'd imagine it'll be awhile before they can settle on anything. It could be another twenty years before he's finally executed. There's just too many people split with it. You know how it can be."

"But he's not like the others, right? At least not anymore?"

"No comment."

"So, you have your doubts about his changed behavior?"

"I'll just say that I'm waiting to see how long it last before he gets tired of pretending."

The elevator dings, and the doors spread open slower than I'd expect. They creak and whine. The interior looks like it may have been salvaged from a pile of rubble during World War Two. A dim light above stammers with a tick sound. The air is stale when we enter.

Arlen presses a button wearing a large D. It buzzes. The doors roll shut. The descent begins with a bump.

"Whew," says White from the corner as he grips the railing.

"How far down?" Turner asks.

"Three floors."

The light winks out then stutters back to life.

The mechanisms pulling us underground, whine, hiss, and clank. A soft beep counts the floors.

We come to a stop with a quick jolt. A buzzer pierces the air. The doors start. They peel away, revealing a dilapidated dungeon of a room where the walls are made of beige cobble stone and the floors a slick solid piece of gray tile with black specks tossed here and there. A dismal taste lingers in the air. It's a bitter mix between disinfectant and mildew.

"Right this way, please" Arlen says while stepping from the elevator.

We round the corner and pass through a door which he unlocks with his badge.

The door leads us to another long hallway with cobble stone walls and gray tile floor. Except this one resembles a tunnel as the ceiling is rounded. We walk along in the center, and the air sings of our every step. To our left there is a middle-aged lady with glasses who sits behind a computer at an information desk. Behind her stands an officer with a shotgun cradled at his waist. To the right is more of the dimly lit tunnel. A few of the lights are missing their bulbs and the others flicker like stars.

Arlen leads us to the lady at the desk. Her neck is bent as she cradles a phone between her shoulder and chin, with her fingers typing away. Arlen tosses a hand in the air and smiles. She nods back, but eyes us carefully.

"Follow me," Arlen says as we continue down the long tunnel like corridor. At the end is a large door with five separate locks. A middle-aged officer sits in a chair beside the door and is armed with a pump action shotgun across his waist. He has one leg crossed over the other and is busy reading a John Grisham paperback. He notices us and stands as we near. Large letters rest above the door: **DR.**

"How we doing, Freddy?" Arlen asks.

Freddy dips his head and retrieves a ring of keys, "Not too bad, yourself?"

"Doing well, doing well. These fine folks have an appointment with Jessie."

"Is that so? He said something about having visitors when I made my morning rounds," Freddy says looking over his shoulder at us while jiggling the locks. The mechanisms disengage and metal latches slide away with clanks and clatters. The door pops open with a slight hiss of grungy air.

Freddy straightens and steps aside, holding the door for us, "Welcome to death row, folks."

My carotid artery thumps hard along my neck as I feel my pulse soar past a hundred beats per minute. The blood drains from my fingers to aid my hammering heart. I blink away the sting from a bead of sweat that'd found its way to my eye.

Arlen clears a phlegm and raises his hand, "Last cell on the right. Should you need me, there's a buzzer on the wall down there."

We enter carefully. One by one. I went first.

"Oh, and be sure not to get to close to the bars, because some like to bite," he says with a half chuckle. "Good luck."

# .80.

THE TUNNEL IS LONG and lined with more cobble stone walls like a dungeon in a haunted castle. The overhead lights are circular lamps like you'd find at a bar above a pool table. Their strength is not near enough to light up the darkness. The foul odor of urine, sweat, and musty earth strikes my senses. The door latches shut behind us as the deadbolt slides home and echoes among the dismal chambers. We're now locked in with society's most vile and wicked creatures. The air has a chill to it like you'd imagine a dark tomb may have.

At the end of the tunnel, my eyes find four chairs waiting for us in front of a cell.

To my surprise, the place is rather quiet. Except for the soft water drip puddling somewhere in the shadows. I feel my blood rush through my ears.

No voices. No clanking among the cell bars.

Eerie. Quiet.

I look to the others out the corner of my eye. Neither say a word as their eyes search the place with darting sweeps.

Someone sneezes from a few cells down to break the silence.

This isn't a tomb of the dead or dungeon of monsters. People actually live here.

"C'mon," I say while taking a step forward.

The others follow behind me. Our shoes thud and clack off the tile. The first row of cells on either side contain only a small cot and sink. Void of any soul.

Then one by one, the souls emerge as we continue along.

There is a man to the left of us, who has a thick gray beard and beady black eyes. He lies in small bed with the covers pulled to his neck. His head never moves but his eyes watch us like a haunted painting as we pass.

I shift my eyes to the right and see a man lying in bed on his back with an arm tucked behind his head, reading a paperback.

The next cell down, a man paces from one wall to the next like a caged Tiger as he mumbles to himself with his fists knotted by his sides.

The cell across from him houses a giant of a man who leans into the bars with his hands coiled around the metal. His eyelids are stretched tight and he sucks his lips in to reveal big yellow teeth. His extends his tongue and licks at the air.

The next few cells are empty.

We're about two thirds to the end where our seats await us.

I glance at a cell to my left and see a man standing by a urinal in his cell. He has his back to us, and I see two bold, black letters upon his white jumpsuit: **DR**. He whistles an out of tune version of *Jingle Bells* above the sound of peeing.

His neighboring cell houses a lump beneath the covers. Still sleeping.

The cell across to the right there is a man covered in more tattoos than flesh who sits Indian style in the floor with his eyes closed. He appears to be lost in meditation.

A loud cat call cracks the air. I turn to my left to see a man grabbing at his crouch and wearing a toothy grin. His eyes are bugged out like one of those little pug dogs. He watches us as we pass. I hear him mumbling and pressing against the metal bars behind us.

The next few cells are empty as we come to the cell of Jessie Randolph. AKA the GTK.

The light above flickers then winks out. Behind the bars, the cell is dark and only a silhouette of a human sitting on the side of a cot can be seen.

We sit down in the fold away chairs. Mine squeaks as the legs rake across the cobble stone. Agent Turner's does the same.

It's quiet now. So quiet I can hear the other three's breath.

My mouth feels as if someone has just crammed a cotton ball into it. I swallow hard and toy with my watch, moving it about my wrist.

I open my mouth to begin a sentence, but am cut short by a smooth, calming voice from the darkened cell, "Hello."

I clear my throat, retrieve my note pad and files, and reply with, "Hello, I'm Homicide Lieutenant Laurie Daniels. I'm here with Detective John White, Agent Ricki Vasquez, and Agent Dan Turner. We are needing your help in solving a series of crimes that have taken place along the New England Coast, particularly near the Portland area."

"The Maine Killer? Morty?" the voice asks as the dark silhouette stands from the bed. The worn-out springs creak as they're relieved of his weight. He comes closer to the cell bars. The light winks on above us.

I'm slow to answer as I watch this dark form emerge from the shadows and enter into the light. He's dressed in a white jumpsuit and wears black glasses like John Lennon liked to wear. Jessie Randolph steps to the bars and coils one hand around the metal. He tucks the other arm behind his back. He glares slightly above us as if we were standing.

"Yes, that's correct. Can you help us?"

He bites his bottom lip and lowers his head to the corner of the cell, then rubs the back of his neck.

A beat.

"I've heard about you, Daniels."

"Is that so?"

He nods his head and releases the bar. He crosses to the other end of the cell. His right arm swings by his side and I can see that it is missing from the forearm down.

"You were almost killed."

"Yes, yes I was."

"I'm sorry. And I'm sorry for the loss of your deputy. I mean that."

"Thank you."

"You know it was a false religion that inspired me to kill?"

"Yes, I know."

"A cult. Just like your church in Maine. A cult's environment is a prime breeding ground for evil. Evil increases with compound interest as the late C.S. Lewis was once quoted. And with cults, I like to believe it pays a hefty dividend as well."

I lower my eyes and begin to scribble in my notes.

"However, I do not believe the killer you seek comes from such a cult."

I look up and glance at the others on both sides of me.

Turner adjusts in his seat. White crosses his arms, and Agent Vasquez jiggles her foot as her leg is crossed over the other, lady like.

"And why is that?"

"He's too smart. He knows too much information. He's a scholar. A philosopher if you will. Cults only focus on their religion. They shield you from the outside world. They hate wisdom because wisdom equals power.  Your killer is too versed in multiple subjects to come from a cult. He's his own man. He's not connected to the church. You simply found a snake in the process of turning over rocks. I may be wrong, but I don't believe the church and Morty are connected. The church was only a pawn in his game."

"And what leads you to say this?"

He stops and places his back to the cell wall, then slides down slowly. He scratches the back of his head and replies, "I have my sources. My brother James and his family visit me twice a month. They were the first to inform me of the killings. And of course, my preacher friend David Hoffman always brings updates from the paper to read to me. Once I learned of the re-emergence of this killer you call Morty, I knew it wouldn't be long before you or the Feds showed up. I was sure to do my homework, so that when you did visit, it'd at least be worth your time."

"Well, thank you. As you and I both know, time is of the essence with a case such as this."

"That it is," he says after sighing out a breath. "Your friends are rather quiet, surely you haven't tricked me into believing you're accompanied by agents only to have Freddy, Arlen, and Melanie aid you in such a ploy."

Agent Turner clears his throat, but White speaks first. His deep authoritative voice booms among the chambers, "I can assure you that we haven't come this far just to flatter you with trickery. We're here because we need your help."

"I see. And you are?"

"Detective John White."

"And how long have you been on the force, Mr. White?"

"Eight years with Homicide and Robbery, three as a patrol officer prior to that."

"Very well. What about the agents, do they speak?"

"We're more of observers," says Vasquez.

"From the Behavioral Analysis Unit, am I right?"

"Yes," says Turner.

"Profilers?"

"Yes," they say together.

"Tell me, how close was the profile?"

Turner looks to Ricki then looks back to Jessie Randolph seated in the floor with his back to the wall, face turned upward.

"Close enough."

"No-no-no, now we all know *close enough* isn't *good enough*. Am I right?"

No answer.

"You were wrong. You were close, but you were wrong. From what I've gathered from the news, Ed Skinner wears many masks. You're not just profiling one man, but multiple. He has graduated from the pity parties of believing his conundrum to be a setback. He's now using his weakness as a strength. The Ed Skinner you may see plastered on the screens and in the newspapers is not the man you're looking for. Skinner could be any among you and you'd never know. Because remember you're not looking for Ed Skinner, you're looking for Morty."

I raise my vision from the notepad and ask, "Why does he do it?"

A beat.

I watch as Jessie Randolph pulls in several breaths while framing his words. He slides up the wall with a grunt, then angles back to the bars in front of us.

"Because he has to. A killer kills because he has to. Because the wickedness within is consuming him from the inside out. With Morty, it's become an all-consuming, never satisfied hunger for more. A gnawing, eating, craving. And not only that, but he believes he's doing God a service. He's acting as the reaper and is cleansing the earth from its wickedness. It's his passion. This kind will not stop on his own. He will continue to kill until he encounters the Light. That kind of darkness can only be driven out by the Light. Trust me, I know."

"What about the kids? Why take the kids?"

"There's only two answers I can give. One, he's killing and believing he's sending them to heaven to escape the pain and suffering of this world. Or two, and I pray to dear God I'm right, he's forging their names and changing their appearances enough so he can send them to organizations he's working for, in effort to give the kids a better life."

A beat.

"If you were in our shoes, what would you do?"

"I'd pray."

"Good answer."

He sighs, "At this point, I believe it may be your only answer. You will all be in my prayers and I'll have my family and friends pray for you as well. And I suggest you give it a try it yourself, because you're going to need all the help you can get. Trust me, there's a lot more going on than meets the eye."

The light stammers again.

"How did you do it?"

"The murders?"

"Yes."

"Why, that was many moons ago," he sighs through puffed cheeks. He scratches at his chin, "You see *I* never killed anyone. The evil within me did. I never killed anyone because I wanted to. I killed because I had to. There's a difference. And there's a switch that is flipped prior to the killings. You no longer view the person as human but more so as a means to an end. A *thing* to be used. I was working for a power greater than myself and I became a laborer of darkness. But thank God I was delivered. I was rescued by the Light of the World and I'll never be the same. Both physically and spiritually," he says thudding his nub against the bars.

"My sin cost me my sight, an ear, and half my arm. Which were the very things I took from so many. But thank God it didn't cost me my soul. Thank God I saw the Light. Evil is real my friends, but so is the goodness and grace of God. Without it, I'd be dead and rotting in a place many miles south and far worse than this."

"Would you kill again if you could?" asks Agent Vasquez.

A long pause.

"Not if my life depended upon it. I've done enough killing for one's lifetime. My passion now is in giving life, not taking it. He has changed me from the inside out, I'm a new man. My desires and passions have changed. Like I said, I'll never be the same."

"Do you fear what awaits you in the afterlife?" asks Agent Turner.

Randolph shakes his head, "I can face God on judgement day with a clean conscious, you know why? Because my faith is not based on my works, but on the grace and blood of Jesus Christ. His blood has cleansed me and made me new. My sin has been eradicated and forgiven. There's nothing to condemn, because now when God sees me, He see His son Jesus in me. That's the good news my friends. If God can forgive me and give me a new life, then well, there isn't anything too dirty for grace. Nothing."

"Okay enough with the mumbo jumbo, let's get back to why we're here," says Vasquez.

"My apologies, ma'am. Yes, going back to the case."

I clear my throat and proceed with, "Mr. Randolph, I know that you suffered a traumatic childhood and that that had a tremendous impact on your life and crimes. Do you believe Morty may have experienced a similar upbringing?"

"Perhaps that's why he has such a thing for killing parents who are unworthy. Maybe it's his way of taking revenge on his own parents. As if each parent he kills, he's fantasizing what he wished someone would have done to his parents. He's taking the kids because that's what he wanted someone to do to him."

"Hmm, that's a good point," I say while taking more notes.

"My gut says he's a lone wolf type of guy. I really do not feel he's part of a cult. If he is working with others, it's a pretty small group in my opinion. Maybe just a few helping hands if any at all. He's so good at deception and disguise, he could do all of this on his own. Just doesn't feel like cult work to me. Don't bank the house on it, but I know a cult inside and out and this doesn't feel like one."

After going back and forth like this for the next hour or so, the clank of the chamber doors gives us all a start. I turn to see Freddy holding the door for Arlen. Here he comes thudding down the long corridor.

I look to my watch and see its just after eleven.

The cells stir as voices begin to rise.

"Feeding time," says Randolph.

Arlen reaches us and wears a tight grin, "Well now, did we discover anything worth exploring?"

"We certainly did. Thank you both for allowing us to visit. This has been truly insightful and encouraging," I say as I stand from my seat.

"Good. I'm glad. Well, I hate to run you off, but lunch will be served in a few moments, so I wanted to get you out before the exodus to the cafeteria begins."

"No worries. We understand. Again, thank you for the opportunity," I turn to Jessie's cell, "Mr. Randolph, I can't tell you how much I appreciate your time and honesty. You've given us some excellent information that I'm confident will aid in our investigation. It's been a pleasure."

"You are very welcome, dear. I'm always glad to help in any way I can. You all be safe heading back North now, okay."

"We certainly will."

"And remember . . . pray. It's more powerful than you think."

"I sure will. Thank you again."

And with that, we make our way out as we pass through the various halls and tunnels. We reach the aged elevator and ride it back to the surface of earth. Out of the darkness and into the light.

# .81

ON THE FLIGHT back aboard the FBI Cessna Citation, I mulled over the words exchanged with Jessie Randolph and could hardly wait to get back to my office. I thought a lot about Seth Roe and his situation, so I made myself a mental note to reach back out to Linda with DSS to see if anything new had emerged. I thought about Paul and Sandy. And of course, I couldn't help but think of Collins and how much he would have enjoyed this trip. I also noted to myself the need to talk to Hal Resnick, and I figured I should pay the Carver's a visit while I'm at it, just to see how they're holding up.

It must've been a few hours into the flight, when my brain finally had enough and decided to leave me high and dry. Then my thoughts became dreams and my worries nightmares.

One such nightmare sent me jolting awake and gasping for breath as I had to be comforted by White and Vasquez. Turner was too busy snoring.

I dreamed I was on board the plane but was awoken to the screech of a million cicadas. When I opened my eyes, the cabin of the plane was filled with the crawling and screaming insects. I looked down the aisle to the door leading to the cockpit. The door flung open and broke off the hinges. A gust of air filled the cabin, followed by a thick swarm of cicadas. As they fly and screech about, a man emits from the cockpit and strides for me. He's covered head to toe in cicadas. I know it's him. My stomach takes a quick dip as I feel the plane descend into a nosedive. Louder the cicadas sing. Morty edges closer. His hands stretch for me. Two bright red beams of light flash where the eyes should be. His mouth drops open and elongates to create a deep, black void. A grotesque shriek emerges and a horde of cicadas flood out, bolting straight for me. Faster the plane sinks through the sky, and louder the cicadas sing. Within seconds I'm covered in them. Their tiny, hairy feet crawl and scurry across my flesh. I force open my mouth and begin to scream. Instantly they flood my mouth and rush to the back of my throat. I feel them enter my lungs. My screams are turned to cicada screeches. That's when I'm woken by the jostling of my shoulder. Agent Vasquez.

My pulse must be soaring over one hundred and fifty beats. I'm drenched with sweat, but my flesh feels cold and clammy like. My head spins like a carousel and throbs as if a tiny demon were behind my eyes picking away with a hammer and chisel.

Vasquez squeezes my arm, "Breathe Laurie. C'mon now, take it easy. It's just a dream. Just a dream. You're safe. We're here Laurie, we're here."

"Here take you a sip of this," Detective White says as he passes me a cold can of Ginger Ale. I take one sip and hand it back.

I blow out a series of short breaths and try desperately to gain control of my pounding heart. I swallow hard and close my eyes. I feel my bottom lip begin to tremble as my eyes start to sting. My chest weighs heavy like a bowling ball. My short breaths turn into a soft cry. I clench my jaw and try to control it.

"Ssshhh, sshhh, it's okay. Laurie, it's okay," Vasquez says as she wraps her arms around me and squeezes hard.

Tears leak down my cheeks as fear pounds at my heart like a battering ram, trying with all its strength to burst in and suffocate me.

The plane does a quick jolt as if we'd just rode over a speed bump. My heart starts and I flash my eyes open.

Vasquez pulls back and holds me at arm's length with her hands just above my elbows, looking me in the eye, "Listen, we're going to catch this guy. This will all be over soon."

White pats my shoulder and settles into the seat next to me, "Look, if you think you need more time before you come back to the case, Laurie, I—"

"No. No, I've had my time. I'm ready," I say nodding my head before reaching for the Ginger Ale between me and Detective White. Vasquez stands and crosses to her seat across the aisle from us. I take a sip and pull in a deep breath.

"I saw him."

"Who?" she asks.

"Morty."

"Did you see his face?" White asks.

I shake my head.

"But you saw him?"

"Yeah. His face was covered in cicadas. The whole plane was crawling with them. He was standing right there. We were crashing."

Silence.

I thought I heard White gulp.

"Dear god," says Vasquez as she processes my words.

"Maybe we should listen to Randolph," says White as he stares vacantly ahead while tightening his grip on the arm rest.

"What's that?"

"Pray."

† † † † † † † † † †

**WE MADE A SAFE** landing at Portland Jetport soon after seven o'clock that evening. I survived the flight without any more nightmares. Of course, the fact that I stayed awake the rest of the way might've had something to do with it.

I returned to the station with the three of them and climbed into my Suburban. I made it to my side of town a little after eight o'clock. I made a pit stop to see Paul and pick up Sandy. I spend about an hour with Paul before heading home.

With Sandy by my side and my Judge on my hip, I insert my house key and send the dead bolt away. I push the door open with my left hand as my right rests atop my Judge. Sandy bolts inside and disappears around the corner of the foyer, heading for her bed in the living room.

I take a step inside and close the door behind me. I engage the deadbolt and pocket the keys. I go on to make a quick sweep of the house. The closets, under the beds, behind the shower curtain, et cetra. Everything is clear. It's just me and Sandy.

I go on to warm some leftover lobster bisque and try to have a relaxful evening by crashing on the couch and flipping channels until I land on an airing of *Where the Heart is*. A movie I've seen a thousand times, but never fail to watch again when I come across it. I needed something light and heartfelt.

Anything to relieve me of my world for a bit. An escape if you will.

So, I enjoyed my bowl of lobster bisque with a glass of Silver Oak and laughed and cried with Natalie Portman, Ashley Judd, and Sally Field. It was a good night. One that bid me well before the coming dawn. A busy day awaited and so by ten o'clock—after checking under the bed and within the closet—I was beneath my covers and praying for God to keep the nightmares at bay.

† † † † † † † † †

**I SPENT MOST OF MY** Thursday at the station, tucked away in my office with a closed door. I spoke to Linda who said DSS made a visit to the Roe's place yesterday and did what I expected them to by shaking a scolding finger and tell them clean up. Nothing more could be done with the current situation, but at least the school knew to keep an eye out for any signs of abuse. Like the week of school which he missed when the mother claimed he had the flu. Just so happens that that was about the same time as the saltshaker incident.

After some digging, I was able to find Hal Resnick's number and give him a call. He'll be expecting me tomorrow afternoon between two and three. He's younger than I thought. The file says seventy-nine, but he sounds like he crawled straight from the book of genesis. His voice reminded me of a raspy James Earl Jones.

The rest of my day was spent combing over every file our records had to offer. I started at the beginning and worked my way through to the Anderson murders in Salem last fall. And just for good measure, I looked through Ed Skinner's file from Cumberland along with the other two hundred or so files Langston turned over to us. I went through four cups coffee in those three hours it took to sift the files. After needing some time, I turned to my computer and headed over to YouTube. There I searched *strange sounds coming from sky* along with the meaning of dreams and nightmares. To my surprise, just as Omora had said, there were hundreds if not thousands of videos about the sounds I've heard. All without an explanation. I thought about Morty's notes, his letters about the trumpet, and his references to Revelation. I thought about Archie Whitaker saying he saw demons emit from the clouds, and I thought about all the rumors through the years of the locals claiming to have seen similar things. Then I thought of *The Damned Thing* by Ambrose Bierce and his belief about the creature of "such a color," and how he eventually disappeared in real life.

Is Morty of such a color?

Is he the grim reaper? The death angel? The devil?

Who is he?

Is Ed Skinner, Morty? Or is Ed Skinner just the hands and feet of Morty and Morty's really a spirit? The death angel.

Gosh, I've got to stop all this wild speculating, it's going to put me in there with Archie.

Anyhow, I make it home just after eight p.m., and immediately take Sandy out for a walk around my house. Give her a chance to get a breath of fresh air and relieve herself, while also allowing me to check my lock on the cellar doors. Secure. Last thing I want is to have another decapitated body rotting away beneath my bedroom floor.

With my hands tucked deep within my coat pockets, I draw a deep breath through clinched teeth and tuck my neck between my shoulders before letting it out. Wasn't quite cold enough for my breath to steam but couldn't have been far from it. The calendar might say March, but it sure feels light early February to me. A gentle breeze rustles the leaves above us as I stand waiting for Sandy to finish sniffing and doing her business.

The sky is clear without a cloud in sight. The night is dark with no moon, but only speckles of stars tossed here and there like salt. An owl calls in the distance and joins the chirps of a crickets.

"Sandy c'mon, hurry up."

She sniffs one last time and gets a start. She bounds to her left and finds a spot to her liking.

I turn and peer through the trees at Paul's place. The lamp from his living room is visible through the window.

Sandy finishes and jolts past me to head for the front porch.

"Don't worry about me, I don't mind being left alone in the cold," I say with a chuckle as I cross and follow behind her.

I make it inside and lock the door behind me.

I go on to fix a bowl of homemade salmon stew and enjoy a glass of Silver Oak before retiring for the night. But not without one last glance beneath the bed and behind the closet door and shower curtain. Just for good measure.

I crawl beneath the covers and pray to God to keep the nightmares at bay and to somehow help me catch the grim reaper.

God have mercy.

# .82



**Friday afternoon**
**March 6th, 2020**

I ARRIVED AT the station around six this morning. I've spent the past five hours sifting through case files, coroner reports, pathology findings, crime scene photos, and scribbling on my white board with colored markers. In between all of that I was sipping my coffee and whispering pleas for help. About eleven-thirty the soft knuckle raps of Sheriff Johnston pulled me from my work. He asked if I wanted to grab some lunch at the new Japanese restaurant in town. I gave it some thought and felt my stomach plead like a toddler tugging on a parent's arm. The toddler won, and so I soon found myself riding into town with Sheriff Johnston.

Amidst our conversations over the meal, I told Johnston of my meeting with Hal Resnick today, and Johnston offered to tag along. I told him I would be fine on my own, but he was more than welcome to accompany me. So, after lunch we began the twenty-minute drive north to Yarmouth.

Traveling along I-295 we listened to classic rock tunes from the 70's and 80's. Everything from Boston, The Steve Miller Band, Bob Seger The Beatles, Creedence Clearwater Revival, and whatever else fit into the time of the drive.

While paying attention to google maps on my phone, I relayed the directions to Johnston and told him to make a left at the stop sign onto Oak Street. Which wears its name with pride as a dozen or more oaks line the road on both side. Their branches spread over us like bony fingers. The road is dark from their coverage. There're only three houses along the street, and that's counting Hal Resnick's on our right. Johnston pulls into the sloped driveway. The concrete is cracked and looks like tributary streams on a map as weeds fight their way through the crevices. Resnick's place is a small single-story home with crimson brick and a slanted roof. A sagging overhang is supported by two white columns.

As we pull in, John Fogerty begins the second verse of *Long as I can see the Light*. Johnston shifts to park. I look to the clock on the stereo, *1:53*. I draw a deep breath and relish the moment. The refreshing, soothing tone, rhythm, and melody wash over me like a well needed douse of cold water after long day in the dessert. Neither me nor Johnston say a word until Mr. Fogerty finishes. I know good music when I hear it, and I think Johnston does too.

The jockey comes on for a moment before the station turns over to an array of ads. I look to Johnston, "Are you ready?"

He takes one last sip of coke and nods.

We climb out and shut the doors. The thuds send a group of red backed black birds scurrying from a nearby oak. They call out their displeasure along the way. A yellow striped cat leaps from a wicker rocking chair and scampers off the porch. He runs along, low to the ground, and makes quick glances over his shoulder before disappearing around the side of the house. A black cat trots across the yard from the left. It greets us with yows and gentle eyes. He follows us onto the porch where he does figure eights between my legs. I press the doorbell and lower to pet the friendly cat. I scratch his head, then rub beneath his chin. He soaks it all in and strikes up his motor. His eyes turn googly as if he were at a massage parlor. I chuckle at his sweetness and rise to the sound of heavy feet thudding through the house.

"I'ma coming. Who are ya?"

I clear my throat, "Lieutenant Daniels . . . Portland Homicide. I spoke with you yesterday."

The feet reach the other end of the door, and I hear the lock unlatch. The front door opens to reveal a heavy-set man with a white scruffy beard and disheveled hair. He has small beady eyes that rest too close to the bridge of his nose. His thick glasses ride below his eyes as he tilts his head low to look over them. Dressed in a light blue button down with black suspenders connected to khaki pants, he pushes the glass storm door open with a shove of his forearm.

"Come on in where it's warm," he says as he holds the door for us.

We step past him with kind nods. Once inside, it was like falling into a cat litter box. The acrid odor of urine and ammonia hits my nasal cavity like a whack from a hammer. Whew.

The living room is dim and lit only by the slim light passing through ruffled blinds. It looks more like an office than a living room. The walls are dark green with white trim. Bookshelves line the wall, with neatly stacked hard backs, before coming together to form a v-shape where his television sits in the cubby of an entertainment center. Newspaper is tossed everywhere, and the hardwood floor crawls with cats. At least a dozen or more. Of all sizes and colors. Most greets us with loud yows, but a few retreat either behind the couch or entertainment center.

Resnick shuts the door behind us and slides the deadbolt home.

"Well, you'll have to excuse the mess. I used not be like this, but after two knee replacements and three back surgeries, I don't feel much in the mood for picking up after myself if you know what I mean. Here let me get you a place to sit. You're not allergic to cats now are ya?"

His voice has that yankee twang to it, but with the woodsy accent, not the one from the city. Just an old northern backwoods type of thing.

"Oh no-no. They're fine. I'm quite the animal lover myself and if it wasn't for my Huskey hating them, I'd have a few myself," I say as Hal shews a few cats from the couch with a wave of folded newspaper.

"I hear ya. Please, y'all have a seat," he says aiming his paper. "Hal Resnick by the way. Pleased to meet you folks."

Johnston and I shake the man's chubby hand before sitting.

Resnick crashes in a beige recliner on the right of us. He leans to his left with a grunt and twists on a lamp.

"Now, that's a little better isn't it?"

"Yeah, sure is."

"Can I get you anything? Coffee or . . ."

"I think we're good. Thank you though."

"You don't sound like you're originally from around here? You've got a little southern in you, don't ya?"

"Yes sir, I grew up in North Carolina before moving here to attend the University."

"U of Maine?"

"Yes sir."

"I see. So, you said old Archie told ya about me?"

"He did, and he spoke rather kindly of you."

"He did, did he?" he says scratching at his wrist where a silver watch looks to cut his circulation.

"Archie said you knew the Wicker's fairly well."

Hal scoffs and shakes his head, "I knew something wasn't right about them folks. I just had a feeling, ya know. Now I never would've imagined their boy was a devil worshiper and what not. I mean heck, I just figured maybe they toy with the money or something. Sorry scum rascal."

Hal adjust his glasses and coughs into the crevice of an elbow.

A chubby gray and white cat leaps into his lap and curls into a ball. Hal strokes its neck with an open palm.

"I hope they get him good when he goes to trial. What was the other one's name again? Brad Stowe?"

"Brett Stephenson."

"Yeah-yeah, Brett Stephenson," he says bobbing his head as he begins to rock in the chair. It squeaks with every move.

"What about what happened with Archie Whitaker? Do you believe he really saw the things he did? He claimed you saw them too."

Hal lowers his eyes to the cat and gives it a few strokes before answering quietly, "I did."

"Is that so? Anyone else?"

He nods, "About four or five not counting me and Archie. They were older. They're all gone now."

"So, you believe Archie only kidnapped the boy to protect him from the . . . 'demons?'"

"Of course," Hal says with a quick snap of his head, "Archie's a good man. He was only trying to protect that boy.

He'd seen too many go missing over the years and knew if he didn't do something that boy would've been next to go."

I swallow and scratch the back of my neck. The image of Seth Roe flashes before my mind.

*What if I were to—gosh, stop it! No, Laurie. No!*

I bat my eyes at the floor and hold them shut for a hard squeeze. I open them and roll my tongue about my inner cheek.

"Do you believe the demons are responsible for the kidnappings today?" my tone is less than convincing. I can't believe I'd even ask the question. I hear Johnston adjust in his seat next to me.

Hal tightens his lips and sways his head, then tosses up an open hand as the other strokes the cat. "I don't know, ma'am. All I know is what I saw. I know demons are real, not just because I've read stories about them in the bible, but I've seen them with my own eyes and I've felt them before too. I can't tell you how many times I've been woken in the midd—"

Before he can even finish his words, I feel myself shifting to the edge of the couch, leaning in.

"Middle of the night to the feeling of being watched. Like something dark and wicked was standing right beside my bed, glaring at me like a cheetah licking his chops at a wounded fawn. I've even been woken to the sound of my floor popping like somebody stepping across my bedroom. I sit up in bed and glance about the room, flick on a light. Nothing. But boy, you want to talk about an odor. Whew wee, do them jokers stink or what? Smells like somebody been boiling eggs or something. I don't know why they bother me so much, because all it does is cause me to start praying and the moment I do . . . the feeling disappears, and it isn't long before the odor does too.

"Now I'm not trying to convince you to believe like me. You both grown adults, so you believe what you want to. I'm just telling you what I know based off my experiences," he says glancing to both me and Johnston with a tilted glare. His glasses have fallen to the tip of his nose once again. "Ya know about the Mi'kMaq Indians right?"

We nod.

"Okay, now they have a bunch of different beliefs. Some I believe myself and some I'm too sure of, but for the most part I think there's some truth to what they're about. They have a number of creatures they believe in. One being the Culloo."

"What's that?" Johnston asks.

"Well, ya see it's an evil angel that looks like a giant bird but sort of resembles a man just a bit. They say it's got wings like an eagle and thick hairy legs like a man. It supposedly has these sharp talons it uses to snatch up the children as it sweeps down from the heavens and carries them off, never to be seen again. I have a buddy who attends the Mi'kMaq's annual Pow-Wows and who likes to think he's good friends with a bunch of them over there. He's done a lot of remodeling work for the tribal elders and what not. He says that they are all worried that the Culloo may be responsible for all these missing children."

"Really?" I ask as Johnston scoots to the edge of his seat.

"Yes ma'am. Now your guess is as good as mine, but I know I saw something that day. I'm not saying it was a Culloo, but their description is mighty close to the thing Archie, myself, and the others saw. But there's one other thing that has them all worked up to."

"Yeah? What's that?" I ask.

"It's this other thing they like to call the Chenoo."

I scrunch my brows and give him an odd look.

"Ever heard of a Wendigo?"

I purse my lips and tilt my head side to side while turning my hand over, back and forth, "Yeah. Kind of. Maybe, I don't know."

"Well the Chenoo is pretty much the same thing, 'cept it doesn't fly. It's an evil spirit that roams the woods searching for something to eat. It mostly eats deer and other large animals, but the legend is that it'll eat people and children too. And when it does, it's spirit will turn them into the same thing. Now I know you're going to think I'm crazy here, but just hear me out. When all that was going on with Archie back then, just before he got taken away, Archie, myself, and a few of the other men who liked to hunt, kept finding deer lying in the woods half eaten and torn to shreds with these large claw marks the size of a man's hand."

His words sent my mind back to the night when me and Collins were on our way to Freewill Holiness. When we saw that deer on the side of the road with all those claw marks.

"Now we reported it to the DNR, but they just kept saying it was a big cat or bear. But every time all this junk gets stirred up with this Morty fella, seems like the hunters start finding deer out in the woods torn to shreds by those large claw marks. And some folks from the Mi'kMaq tribe have already found at least a dozen or so they say. Again, I'm not trying to convince you of anything or twist your arm in to believing me. I'm just telling you what I know."

"So, you think all this could have something to do with evil spirits?"

"I don't think it. I know it."

"But how is that? I mean who's writing the notes and letters? Who have we been talking to? A spirit?" Johnston asks.

"No. No, you're dealing with a man. Ed Skinner. Flesh and bone. But what I'm saying is, you don't do the things he's done without there being an underlying evil offering a helping hand. There's more to all of this than meets the eye."

"I've heard that before."

"It's true. Look, all I'm saying is, I think the Indians might be on to something. I know the end times are getting close and the book of Revelation has some creatures and things in it that'll downright scare ya socks off. The bible talks about weird demons and creatures which are quite similar to what the Indians talk about. Maybe because the end is nearing, these sorts of things have been sort let loose if you will. Like the veil separating the spiritual world from the physical is thinning. Which is allowing us to get a glimpse at what lies beyond the veil."

"Maybe that's what the noises are about," I mumble absently to the floor.

"Pardon?" asks Resnick.

"The noises. The chair being drug across concrete. The screechy trumpet from the sky. Have you heard it?"

Hal half chuckles as he turns his eyes from mine and looks to his cat. He rubs its head and its purrs become louder. "Oh yeah. Can't nobody explain it either, can they? Even the smartest men on earth are dumb founded by nature's mystery.

Kind of like the Seneca guns in New York and down the coast along the Carolina's. Ever heard of them?"

I nod.

"What is it?" asks Johnston.

Resnick coughs and says, "Seneca guns. Them loud booms near the coast down South that nobody can explain."

"Oh yeah-yeah, I think I know what you're talking about."

The sound of a roaring engine from a big semi-truck zooms past us. I turn and look through the window behind the couch.

"Goodness, he was getting it wasn't he?"

"Oh yeah, them truckers fly up and down this road. They like to use it as a short-cut back to 295. One reason why I keep most my cats in the house. Only got two that stay outside. They're more the rambunctious type. Rat chasers, ya know. I got them both neutered, so they want go roaming as much. Less chance of them crossing the road."

Something moves and shifts behind the entertainment center.

"Oh, that's Skylar back there. He's a big scaredy cat. He'll stay back there till ya gone. He's not much of a one for company."

We hang around for another half hour before I felt I had what I came for.

"Well, Mr. Resnick—"

"Please, just call me Hal. Now that we're pals," he says with a chuckle.

"*Hal.* Thank you for seeing us. It was a pleasure to meet you."

"Oh now, the pleasure is all mine. I hope I was able to enlighten you a little bit."

"You certainly have." I stretch forth my hand and hold out my card. "If you think of anything else you should tell me, please give me a call."

"I sure will. I know I've sure been praying for all you folks. I know this is a mean world out there and you're going to need all of the help you can get. If you ever feel like talking again, just swing on by. My doors always open."

"I appreciate that, Hal. I guess we need to be going, I have some things I need to take care of back at the station. Remember, you call if you think of anything else or if you ever need anything. Okay?"

"We'll do. You fine folks are going to get this devil. I can feel it. It won't be long."

With that we make our way out. Johnston trudges us back to 295 en route for the station.

So, now I'm not only facing a deranged serial killer with multiple personalities who stalks me like a cat, but who also may be working with spirits from Revelation or Indian folklore.

Perfect.

God help me. No, wonder Archie Whitaker took that boy.

# 83

AFTER SPENDING THE rest of the evening in my office, I'd done enough digging for one day and decided to clock out just after eight o'clock. Detective White is busy working on a few other cases but is also working with some newly hired detectives in combing through evidence of the Morty case files. We're all trying hard not to let the files go cold. The Bureau, despite the billions of other murders and violent crimes they're sorting through, is still working desperately to help me and the department track down Ed Skinner and the missing children. I've spent the last few days speaking over the phone with Director Ramsey and Agent Swanson as they decipher the information I keep sending them to plug into the ViCap and NCIC databases.

I step out of my office and lock it with my set of keys, I breathe out a sigh and adjust my shoulder bag. The station is empty except for Sheriff Johnston, Chief Cunningham, the ladies working the front desk, and Sherrie and her team of forensic scientists working late in lab.

I give a knuckle rap on Johnston's window as I pass. He tosses up a hand as he sits reclined in his chair with a phone cradled against his neck.

Before I even parallel Cunningham's office, I hear him going off on a tangent with some choice expletives. I near the window and see his shadow pacing to and fro. His door is slightly cracked. I don't bother gaining his attention.

I tell the two girls at the desk to have a good night before exiting the station. A grumble of thunder emits from the dark sky as rain begins to fall, drumming the asphalt with a steady beat. I make a quick dash across the parking lot, while covering my head with my jacket the best I can.

I crash into the driver seat with a sigh and crank up some heat.

My radio plays something soft from Al Green, and I begin the trek home.

†††††††††††

**BEING SO LATE AND MY BODY NOT FEELING LIKE** cooking up a meal, I stopped at the drive-thru Subway in town to grab a tuna wrap.

I called and checked on Paul. He was busy flipping channels between a March Madness basketball game and a Red Sox exhibition game. I told him I had some leftover salmon stew and lobster bisque I'd bring him tomorrow evening. I made plans on the way home from the station to drive up to Gray tomorrow and spend a few hours around the McCrae's place to refresh my memory a bit. While I'm at it, I'll give the Carver's a quick visit.

The rain had eased and turned into a floating mist once I reached my house. I made it inside, sat my things down, grabbed a rain jacket with a hood, and took Sandy out for a walk. I gave my cellar lock a quick check and was relieved to see it hadn't been tampered with.

Waiting on Sandy, I stand with crossed arms looking to the heavens, half expecting to see a winged creature or hear the chair drag across a concrete cloud. I thought about Archie Whitaker, and I thought about Seth Roe. I never thought I'd say this, but maybe kidnapping the kid wasn't such a bad thing after all.

A rustle in the woods to my left gives my heart a start. I spin and glare into the thicket. I listen hard for a moment.

Sandy pauses and stares too.

Everything is eerily quiet.

†††††††††††

**CROUCHED LOW UPON HIS HEELS AND HUGGING A** thick pine while dressed in all black with a large hood, Gary Wade Duncan eyes Laurie from the shadows and savors every second. Such a beautiful creature the creator has bestowed upon us. A shame what he had to do. But if he didn't, she'd stop him. Something he'd vowed could never happen. He can't let the creator down. He has to do it. There is no other choice. It must be done.

His eyes blink on their own and his body trembles with a euphoric rush at such a sight. His breath quickens as his heart pounds against his ribs. The muscles in his face twitch as he cranes his head side to side. His hands have the tremors again and he rolls the imaginary pill between his right thumb and index. The medication would help, but he doesn't like the way it makes him think. The meds would only fog his mind, and right now it is important his mind stays clear. He can't become distracted. He must focus and do what he's called to do.

He breathes deep and sighs as he watches her turn and head back inside. The door closes behind her.

Gary Wade Duncan lowers his head and retrieves a mason jar from his deep coat pocket. Within the jar crawls a cicada. He smiles as the creature's little hair covered feet walk upon the glass to make subtle *ting* and *tick* sounds. Duncan closes his eyes and prays for strength to do what must be done.

Soon it'll all be over.

Soon the cicadas will sing.

Soon Laurie will succumb to Morty.

# .84

HEAVY. HEAVY. Sitting on my chest. A mucus filled hiss. Something wet dripping onto my face. My body trembles as if I've been left out in the cold, but a warm putrid blast of air caresses my face. My windpipes cinch as they're clutched in an iron fist. I flash open my eyes. Darkness. I feel so small. Like I'm free falling through an eternal black void. I can't breathe. I can't move! My throat tightens, and I feel cold bony fingers wrap arou—

*I see you!* A thin, raspy voice whispers into my ear.

"Jesus!"

The moment the word emits my mouth, the dark figure with curly hair let's out a shriek and leaps from the bed. It lands on the floor with a loud thump before vanishing into a smoky black vapor. I jolt from the bed to form an L while grabbing my neck with both hands and sucking in gasps of cold air. My eyes dart about the room. I hear Sandy growling, but it sounds muffled like she's under the bed. My neck is sore and stiff. It's painful to move and swallow. The familiar ache in my chest has returned.

"Jesus Christ," I say as I reach for the lamp. I twist the knob. Light sweeps away the darkness.

It was the thing from my closet again. The thing from Freewill Holiness. It'd ventured out and climbed onto my chest to try and strangle me.

I swing my feet off the bed. Sandy crawls out and begins to sniff about the room. She edges down the hall and stops at my closet door where she begins to bark.

I glance at my clock. The red numbers show 3:33. I push off the bed, palm my Judge from the nightstand, pull back the hammer, and angle to the closet door. I flick on the hall light along the way.

I stand in front of the closet door where Sandy sniffs at the bottom. I tighten my right hand around the rubber grip of the Judge and sling the door open with a quick shove of my left. It rolls along its track to the right.

With my feet planted firm and my gun now squeezed within both sweaty hands, I make quick sweeps and brush back my hangers full of shirts and blouses.

Nothing.

Sandy continues to bark.

I sigh out a breath, relax the hammer on the Judge, and lower to ease Sandy. With some loving reassurance, she subsides and crosses back for the bed where she waits as I head for the bathroom to relieve myself and examine my neck.

I stand and flush then angle for the mirror.

Once again, there is bruising which is turning my skin a pale shade of blue and purple.

"Jesus," I say at the marks. Then I look to the ceiling and say it again. This time more so as in asking for help.

† † † † † † † † † †

**I AWOKE THE NEXT MORNING** to the piercing buzz of my alarm clock. Seven-thirty. I snoozed it once and crawled out of bed with the next go around. I make my way to the bathroom and flip on the light before standing in front of the mirror to examine my neck again. I wince at the touch. It proudly wears blue and purple streaks. I breathe deep and rest both my palms on the sink counter while looking at the mess of a woman staring back at me through the mirror. My blonde hair is disheveled with bed head and dark bags tug at my eyes. A red mark from the indentions of my rings, which I'd slept too hard on, is streaked across my cheek. Boy do you look rough.

I wipe my eyes with both palms before leaning back into the mirror. I look myself dead in the eye, "You can't let this devil win. You can't let him beat you. You're stronger than him, Laurie. You have to be the Light. Be what you already are. You can do this. Stay strong. Jesus help me."

I feel my lips begin to quiver as tears sting my eyes. I wipe a tear with the sleeve of my shirt and take a deep breath. A gentle voice echoes in my spirit.

*I am with you. I will never leave you nor forsake you. Even in the darkness I am here. Trust me.*

I clinch my eyes and nod. Another tear slips out. I suck in a gasp of air and swallow hard, wincing as it goes down. I open my eyes and run my fingers through my hair. I take up my toothbrush and give my mouth a good cleansing.

I go on to take a shower and enjoy a quick breakfast before gathering my things and heading out the door. Not without giving Sandy some loving of course. I climb into the driver seat of my Suburban and head to Rocky Hill Road to make a pass by Seth Roe's home before beginning my day.

The underlying thought that I can't get out of my head is: What would've happened to that kid if Archie had not of taking him?

† † † † † † † † † †

**I COME TO THE STOP SIGN** at the crossroads, and I take a right onto Rocky Hill Road. I slow down as the Roe's home crawls closer on my left. The road hisses as it's still damp from the prior evening's rain. The home and yard are quiet. Their red 90's model Ford Taurus sits in the driveway with the bumper cracked and hanging free in the wind. I figure they're still in bed, so I pull off the side of the road across the street a little ways down from their home. I eye the place and wonder what goes on behind that front door. I wonder if Morty knows about it yet. Is it really such an evil thing that Morty does? Killing the parents, yeah of course, I'd never condone such a thing. But taking the kids out of places like this? Well, it'd be easy to rationalize. Yet, the question that stings my heart the most is .. . how many others are out there just like this? I might not be able to help everyone, but if I can somehow help this one then maybe I'd be doing my part. The urge to act is growing stronger and truth be told, it's starting to scare me. If DSS will not do nothing, who will?

I readjust my grip on the greasy wheel. I close my eyes and rub my neck with a grimace.

The sound of tires rolling over asphalt gives my heart a start. I glance to the rearview mirror and see a white pick-up truck edging closer behind me. I slide low into my seat and lean my elbow onto the center console where I cradle my chin into my palm until the truck passes. Once out of sight, I raise back up and glare once again to the house.

*There's other ways Laurie.*

I nod to myself as I bite my bottom lip, drop the gear shift to drive and head to I-95 for Gray.

† † † † † † † † † †

**I PULL INTO THE McCRAE'S** driveway just after nine o'clock. I sit for a moment and finish my coffee. Looking about the place, one would never imagine the things that happened here. Yeah, perhaps it's a bit *junky*, there's no denying that. But there's thousands of junky homes across Maine, New England, and the rest of the United States. Why here? What's so special about the McCrae's? Out of all the homes he could have chosen, why did Morty come *here*? Where did he cross paths with them? How did he know the McCrae's were like this? He had to see them out somewhere or already know them. Then followed them home or maybe was even invited over for dinner, who knows? Perhaps he installed their cable or fixed a leak beneath the sink. Having exhausted our resources, we know it's not the mailman, UPS, or FedEx man. And we know it's not one of Sarah's teachers. So, who is it? If Morty is a man such as Ed Skinner, then how did he come to know the McCrae's? Or at the very least, know of them? For that matter, the same question can be asked about the Anderson's in Salem. How did he know about them? Is this a ring of people? How many Morty's are there?

A gentle breeze brushes by and tickles the leaves of the surrounding trees. Riding along one swaying branch, is a chubby Brown Thresher with its head tucked tight to its chest behind its wings. The ban of sunlight pierces through the clouds as the light pushes away the tree's shadow, sending the light crawling towards me before enveloping my car and snaking past me.

I finish my coffee, say a quick prayer, then step out of the Suburban and stand in the gap between my open door. I scan my surroundings. The two-story home with white siding, black shingles and shutters, the front door the color of blood, with two small white columns supporting a dilapidated overhang standing before me. The grass is still high with scattered Miller Lite cans, blonde headed barbie dolls, and the trampoline with the safety net around it that sits to the right side against the woods. To the left and directly behind the home, is the brown corn field. The old building and pick-up truck press against it.

I look in the distance to my left and see the Carver's place about a hundred yards or so off the road, resting in the center of the corn fields. My gaze lingers on the aged farmhouse with crooked shutters and aging cedar planks. Even at this distance I can see the repairs it could use. Poor lady. As if it's not enough to have a paraplegic son to care for, she's been left to live in a place like that. A shame her husband left her in that kind of shape.

A cawing crow pulls my eyes back to the McCrae's. I watch as he struts along the roof's peak. He watches me with twitchy eyes as he cranes his head back and forth.

Rather than begin by entering the home, I start by spending the first half hour casing out the land. Searching for ease of access and places to hide. Thinking like a killer. But no matter how hard I try, I just can't wrap my mind around the fact that he did this by sneaking in. I honestly believe he was let in. Hence, the reason for no sign of forced entry. I think he knew the McCrae's personally. Their murder was personal. Meticulous, but personal. Just like all the others. I think they knew their killer. I think they are all somehow connected. But how?

As those words eat at my psyche, I decide I've done enough searching outside and begin to stride across the yard for the blood colored front door. I slice the seal and unlock the door. It pops open and the faint odor of death greets me. Not near as bad as before, but it still lingers.

The home is dark, except for a trickle of sunlight slipping in through a half cracked blind in the living room. The blood droplets on the kitchen island are still here. Of course, now the blood has lost its contrast though and has browned from the breakdown of the red blood cells and their hemoglobin which have released iron atoms that are normally protected from the highly chemically reactive oxygen molecules. A little something I've learned from Sherrie over the years.

I pace the floors of the home with a Maglite in my left and my right hand hovering the Judge on my hip. After a thorough sweep, I'm satisfied that I'm all alone. I allow myself to enter into my zone and begin talking to the empty tomb of a home. Asking questions that only the dead would know. Stopping in each room and visualizing what must've took place. I allow myself to become a fly on the fly on the wall so to speak and watch as the crime unfolds. I start by standing in the foyer facing the front door. I imagine hearing the doorbell ring. I hear feet thud from the hallway. Amanda McCrae passes me and goes for the door. She opens it. A dark figure stands at the entrance, and his face is covered within a black hood. He looks like the Grim Reaper. Amanda knows this person and welcomes him in. I watch as she turns and heads for the kitchen, the figure trails behind her. They both pass me. I get a whiff of peppermint when the person I imagine to be Morty goes by. I follow them both into the kitchen. The two carry out small talk. Amanda then turns her back and that's when the figure retrieves a hammer. I watch as he pulls back to hit her with it. He swings and connects. A sickening thud rings out. Amanda collapses. He straddles her body and looms over her. I hear feet patter down the hallway. Sarah McCrae. I watch as Morty ducks behind the kitchen island. Sarah's enters from the hall and begins calling for her mother. I almost bring myself to exit the vision. I force myself to watch as Morty leaps from behind the island and takes hold of Sarah McCrae, wrapping a hand around her mouth. I flinch and make a jolt forwards. Morty snatches his head and looks me in my soul. I gasp and flash open my eyes. I find myself gripping the island with white knuckles. It feels like a jack in the box had just burst open in my chest. I dart my eyes about the kitchen. I'm all alone.

Maybe Morty is more than just a man. Maybe this really is the Grim Reaper. If so, how can I stop such a being?

I walk into the living room and turn to look back into the kitchen. I run my fingers through my hair and keep my hand on the back of my neck once I'm finished. I steady my pulse by pulling in long, slow breaths. I swallow hard with a grimace and readjust my scarf to be sure the marks stay covered.

I cross for the McCrae's couch and take a seat. I rest my elbows to my knees and cradle my face into my palms.

"God help me. Show me who this is, so we can stop it. If there's a better way of doing things, then show me how to find this guy."

I pull my head up and glance at my watch, *11:23*, then turn for the big window looking out to the corn field where I can see the Carver's home in the distance. I've spent enough time here to stir my memory, I think it's time to pay the Carver's a quick visit before heading back south to Portland.

# .85

**AS I CRAWL** along the Carver's long dirt drive, with dust trailing behind and pebbles pinging off the under carriage of my Suburban, I can't help but notice a strange buzz sensation dispersing across my body. Like standing too close to the television set or some other source of static electricity. It began in my guy then rose to my chest before crawling out of my mouth and spreading across my flesh. A warm tingling feeling. Odd.

I place my left hand to my stomach and hold it there until I shift to park next to the Carver's 1980's Ford pick-up. The rusty brown Oldsmobile still rests on cinder blocks in the front yard. The passenger window is shattered while the seats inside are ripped and showing their yellow cotton. I swallow hard and steady my breath. The static feeling slowly dissipates. I've never done that before. Is it a side effect of something the black figure did to me last night? Is it my heart reacting to all the stress? Anxiety maybe?

I rub my face and step out. I angle to the wooden steps leading to the wide ranch style porch with rocking chairs scattered here and there. The shutters still hang crooked and the paint on the cedar shakes has chipped more than before

I expected to be greeted by the chocolate Labrador with gray whiskers as last time, but he never showed himself. Maybe death has taken him. He looked like he was more than halfway on the journey home the last time I saw him.

I pull open the screened storm door, which creaks with a loud whine as it swings along its rusted hinges, and I give a few knuckle raps upon it.

I wait a moment. Nothing.

Again, I knock.

Something stirs deep within the home, and I hear Miss Carver croak out after clearing a phlegm, "Coming. Hold on a second."

I release the screen door. With the shocks worn out, it lands back in place with a smack.

Heavy feet thud through the home, edging closer.

The curtain in the small peep window of the door shifts back to reveal her large eye and hairy eyebrow. She stares at me for a moment and then disappears. I hear the mechanism of the deadbolt disengage. The door swings open. Miss Carver stands with a big grin as she's dressed in the same dirty dress as last time.

"Well, hey there, how you doing?" she says chewing on something that looks like the remnants of a ham sandwich maybe.

I chuckle, "Doing well. Just thought I'd drop by and see how you were holding up. Be okay if I come in for a moment?"

"Sure-sure, come on in darling."

I step in and she shuts the door behind me. I see their black cat, Midnight, scurry into the hall and out of sight. I figured Phillip would be parked in front of the tv, but he's not. His chair is there, but it's empty. I scrunch my brows and raise a finger, "Where's Phillip?"

"Oh, he's still in the bed. Not much of a morning person. Usually don't wake till about noon."

"Really?"

"Yeah, c'mon grab ya a seat there," she says waving a hand to the couch. "Can I get you anything?"

"Oh, no-no I'm fine thank you. I won't stay long."

"Well hang on just a moment, I'll go see if Phillip is up to having company. I'm sure he'd be happy to see you," she says crossing for his wheelchair in front of the tv.

"Oh, no that's okay. You don't have to wake him just for me."

"Well, it's about time for him to get up anyway. If I don't wake him, he'll have trouble sleeping tonight."

"Okay, well do whatever you need to do. Do you need any help?"

"No-no, I got it. Between tugging on him all these years and packing on the pounds after I passed menopause, I reckon I done turned into a hefty ole gal," she says with a crooked grin as she wheels the chair from the living room, disappearing into the hall. The chair's wheels squeak like an old gurney in a cold morgue.

"Oh, don't say that."

"It's true. And I'm not ashamed to say it either. I'll be right back, hun."

"Okay, let me know if you need me."

No answer

I scoot back a bit into the couch and begin to eye all the knick-knacks scattered about the shelves. Everything from glass figurines of the local lighthouses such as Portland Headlight and Nubble Light to name a few, Red Sox memorabilia, a signed baseball, among other things. On the mantle below where the tv hangs in the corner, are electric candles and other decoratives such as a little Jesus carrying a crucifix. And beside that a sculpted set of Libra scales. I hear some movement deep within the home, so I turn my attention from the tv and land on the coffee table in front of me. Newspaper lies crinkled and turned to the obituary section. A half a cup of cold looking coffee sits next to it.

As I turn to glance at the end table between myself and the recliner where Miss Carver usually sits, I catch glimpse of something black streaking from the hall and into the living room. Adding to the sight in my peripheral is an ear piercing, screechy wail that I know all too well.

A cicada.

I jerk around to see Midnight in desperate chase of a fleeing cicada. Midnight scampers through the living room with its eyes wild and body crouched low as it grasps with its black paws at the creature fluttering and screaming about the home.

My heart pounds. My senses shove to over drive as I begin darting my eyes. I jolt to my feet and flash my hand over top my Judge, ready to draw at the drop of a hat. My eyes blink fast as I feel them widen. I feel the blood drain from my face and hands to rush to my heart and brain. My leg muscles tighten as my feet quickly spread into an athletic position, preparing me to run. My flight or fight instinct is in full effect.

A loud clatter emits from behind the tv, and the cicada sings as Midnight closes in.

I feel my grip on the Judge clench down like a tourniquet. My eyes sweep every inch of the place, anticipating an ambush. I glance to the door. My heart knocks. My breath becomes labored as if the oxygen in the room has suddenly been sucked out by a vacuum.

The thudding of slow approaching footsteps from the hall, stalls my heart.

He's here!

# .86

THE FOOTSTEPS FROM the hall add to the sounds of the cicada and Midnight behind the tv. Standing now with my Judge gripped tight and trained at eye level to the wall, I follow the sound coming down the hall.

"Stop right there. Not another step!" I belt out.

They stop.

A deep masculine voice pierces the air, "Now darling, you haven't even giving me the chance to properly introduce myself. Where are your manners?"

The hair on my arms and neck straighten.

I hurry and retrieve my phone to connect with Cunningham. It beeps and dings along the way, but there's no service.

"I'm afraid that won't be possible my dear. Not with the cell jammer turned on," comes Miss Carver's voice, "And don't bother thinking of your CB in the Suburban. He cut the wires while you were in the McCrae's house."

My heart sinks as my head swims in confusion. I shoot my eyes up to the opening in the hallway and am doused with a glass of cold water that travels from the back of my calves to the nape of neck before penetrating and gripping my heart with icy fingers, squeezing like a vice.

Standing before me is Miss Carver and her large self-next to a tall, lanky, *standing* Phillip Carver. He wears a wide grin as he looks down at his hands held close to his chest. A cicada crawls in and out of his fingers like a roly poly held by a toddler.

I feel my entire body begin to quiver as my bones freeze into place. With my Judge trained to the two of them, I feel my heart seize.

Slowly he raises his eyes to meet mine. Their black void swallows me alive. I've never seen such wickedness in one's eyes before. My heart skips a beat as that icy glare tries desperately to suffocate my pulse.

The cicada behind the tv has quieted as now the only sound coming from it is the crunching of wings and legs as Midnight chomps down to enjoy a tasty snack.

"Hello Laurie. Nice to officially meet after all these years. I feel like I've known you forever. I guess I have though after watching you for so long."

I suck in air with quick pulls through my nostrils. My words catch in my throat as I'm unable to emit anything.

With a quick toss of his hands as if releasing a wounded bird, he lets the cicada go. It flutters through the air, like an overloaded helicopter, and sinks quickly to the floor.

"Say hello to little Sandy."

I scrunch my brows at him, and keep my aim trained to the two of them while watching the cicada in my peripheral.

"Hands on your head. Hands on your head, now!"

He smiles and wags his head slowly. Miss Carver glares at me with a tilted head.

"You'll have to kill us both. If you think we're going to just let you cuff us and drag us in to show the Chief . . . you're gravely mistaken darling. But if you kill us, you'll have no one to fill you in on the details. You'll be left in the dark once again—"

*Hellllllppppppp! Pleeaaasseee! Hellllllppppppp!*

The distant screams come from below. It sounds like a child.

"Don't worry, he's fine. Just a little afraid of the dark that's all. It'll grow on him after a while. Always does."

"Besides we've already got a family waiting on him," adds Miss Carver.

"Wh-who-who is that?"

"I think you know," replies Phillip.

"Connor Anderson?"

He tightens his lips and shakes his head, "C'mon Laurie. Think darling. Think."

*Helllllppppp!*

My blood turns cold and my heart weighs heavy in my chest as if it'd just received a transfusion of concrete.

"Seth Roe?"

"Ding-ding-ding. We have a winner folks! Well done, Miss Daniels. Well done."

There was a murder scene behind that door on Rocky Hill Road this morning, and I didn't even know it. I sat across the street staring at a house which likely holds two corpses.

"Are the parents dead?"

He smiles big and looks to Miss Carver, then back to me and bobs his head, "Oh yeah. You could say that."

As my mind already swims with a million ideas and possible scenarios, the revelation of them having Seth Roe only adds to the chaos. Think Laurie, think. If I kill them both now, I will severely hamper our chances of finding the other children and solving the cases. I can't kill them. I need them alive. But how am I going to do that with no cell service or call for back up?

*Hellllpppp!*

"Hang on Seth, I'm going to get you out!"

"So, the way I see it, you have three choices my dear Laurie. You can shoot us dead here as we stand. Remind you we're not armed—"

"And how do I know that?"

He breathes out a sigh and looks to Miss Carver, then lifts his shirt to his navel and spins in a circle. Nothing.

"Go on, show her, so she'll believe us," he says with tight lips as if I'd just insulted him.

Miss Carver does the same as Phillip.

"As I was saying. Now that you see we're not armed, if you kill us right now, you'll be killing two unarmed human beings. Something you'll have to live with for the rest of your life. I don't think your morals would allow that. Number two, you can try to walk us out at gun point and maybe even attempt to cuff us once we're at your Suburban. But I promise you, that won't happen without a fight. Two against one. Not only that, we vastly outweigh your little frame. Without that gun, you wouldn't stand a chance and you know it."

He pauses to let his words settle.

"And three, you could walk out that door, drive away to the nearest cell reception, which would have to be at least two miles away to get outside the jammer's radius, and make the call for back up. By then we'll have vanished like ghosts and Seth Roe will soon become the next little face you see plastered across every light pole in town and broadcast on every television station across America. He'll become Nancy Grace's next product and the entire Nation will know, 'That is the boy they failed to save.'"

A beat.

"What will it be my friend?"

I stand silent with my aim locked to his chest.

"Well, if you're not going to choose—"

Before finishing his words, he makes a bolt down the hall. I fire a round but miss. Four shots left in the cylinder, six more tucked in my inner jacket pocket.

His heavy footsteps pound through the home, shaking the old floor and walls.

"Don't move or I'll kill you right here and now, you understand me!?" I say to Miss Carver with enough venom to drop her dead where she stands.

She stands frozen in the opening of the hallway.

"Turn around, hands behind your back. Now!"

She does so.

I pull out my cuffs and snap them into place.

"Take me to them," I say with my Judge jammed in the small of her lumpy back. She winces as the metal digs into her.

Together we make our way down the darkened hall.

Other than our feet creaking the floorboards, all is quiet. I keep my head on a swivel. My eyes dart every which way, including over my shoulder to prevent an ambush from behind.

Other than the door at the end of the hallway, there is only one door and it is open to reveal a small bathroom on the left. I check it before continuing towards the door at the end.

Memories of the night at Freewill Holiness flood my mind. I know I'm making a mistake. I know that with each step, I'm inching closer to my tomb. With my senses heightened, I'm aware of the ticking from the second hand on my watch. I can hear Morty's voice in my head. *Tick-tock-tick-tock-tick-tock.*

Jesus help me.

The door grows closer. We stop outside it. I give Miss Carver a good yank on the cuffs and say, "You do anything stupid and you're getting a forty-five round caliber bullet that'll go into your back like a quarter and come out through your stomach like a cash register. You'll be dead before you hit the floor. Understood?"

She nods.

I reach around her and twist the knob of the door. I open it only a few inches, then step back and say, "Pull it open with your foot."

She hooks her toes around the corner and tugs it open. A dark stairwell greets me. A chain to a bulb dangles above the first step. I snatch it down. The chain makes a *tink* sound and the light stutters to life. The stairs descend about a dozen risers into darkness. A stale odor of mildew and earth wafts through the air. I hear a cricket behind a horde of muffled cicadas, sing joyfully from the shadows.

"You turn the lights on, or else Miss Carver gets her foot blown off. It's your choice."

A beat passes as we stand at the top of the stairwell.

I hear a switch flip and three sets of florescent tube lights come to life.

"No need for violence my darling. Not yet," his raspy voice bites the cold, stale air.

"Go. Slowly," I say poking Miss Carver with my Judge.

Together we descend. Step by step. I turn and check the back of each step as we go down. Each has a board, so there's no open gap. No chance of a hand reaching through and grasping my ankles.

The ticking of my watch is overtaken by the sound of classical music and singing cicadas. I use Miss Carver's size to my advantage and keep myself tucked behind her broad shoulders, I only peer up just enough for my eyes to see what lies before me. The further we go down, the more the full range of the basement comes into view. I stop on the second to last riser and check my immediate right and left to be sure no one charges out of the darkness like last time. I don't think I'd survive another attack like the one Brett Stephenson offered me.

Three glass windows line the top of each wall. Faint light trickles in between the silhouettes of bushes. Directly ahead in the center of the basement are three rectangular glass aquariums with mesh screen lids. Lights hang in the corner of each. Leaves, sticks, and sponges are scattered across the bottom where cicadas sing and crawl about. It's a hatchery, and it's similar to what Dr. Feltner had in his basement at the museum. Beyond the cages and on the far back wall, my heart gets a start at what I first thought were a dozen or more people glaring at me through the shadows. I strain my eyes and see that it's not people, but mannequin heads. Some wear wigs which I assume are made from his victims, while other wear human like masks with white holes for eyes. This is his changing station.

Next to the mannequin heads, sits a large box like container that almost scrapes the ceiling and must be at least ten foot wide. A black sheet covers it as if it belonged to a nifty magician. Faint muffled cries emit from it. Seth.

My instinct is to rush forward and snatch him from the cell, but I know that'd be a mistake. Morty would surely emerge from the darkness and snatch me up.

In the back left corner, there is an old vinyl record player with the lid propped open by a wooden stick. It plays a soft instrumental arrangement like the one left in the tool shed with Amanda McCrae.

The left wall is lined with bookshelves packed to their capacity with mostly hardbacks and textbooks, a few being paperbacks. If I strain hard enough, I can make out some of the titles among the bookshelves. Most which belong to either Psychology, Criminology, Religion, History, Mathematics, Biology, or Entomology. One shelf below the textbooks is lined with John Douglas and Mark Olshaker paperbacks regarding Douglas's career as an FBI Agent tracking down and interviewing America's most prolific serial killers. Morty has definitely done his homework. It looks like Dr. Langston was telling the truth about Ed Skinner's love for reading and self-education. This is Ed Skinner's dungeon. This is where his different personalities reside.

I shift my focus to the right wall and scan its distance. The wall is covered in cork board. A large map of the Northeast is pinned in the center with red and yellow pins supporting blue string that ties to each creating lines, just like real investigators often do. Newspaper clippings, photos, articles, anything pertaining to the Morty cases over the last two decades, cover the surface of the cork boards. Joining it all are photos of myself. Most are taken through the open blinds of my home. I'm either sitting in my recliner reading a paperback, watching tv, playing my piano, or outside in my yard with Sandy. Then there were some of me boarding the ferry for Cushing Island. Ones where Collins was with me and ones where he wasn't.

How long has he been stalking me?

The rattle of chains pulls my eyes to the back wall where the box shape is covered by the black sheet. Seth muffles another cry. A lock's mechanism fills the space. A door creaks open. It's a cage. Still seated carefully in the shadows, I can just make out the silhouette of a figure. He steps out, then shuts the door and locks it back. The black sheet falls back into place, almost touching the earth floor.

The figure stands in the shadows, so that all I can see is his waist down. The chest and face hide within the shadow.

"So, what do you think. Laurie?"

I don't answer. I tighten my grip on the Judge and push it deeper into Miss Carver's back. I feel her pull away as the barrel digs into her flesh.

"Let Seth go or I'll kill her right now."

"Oh, Laurie. C'mon now. We all know you won't do that. You're not a murderer. You do that, then what makes you think you're any better than me?"

A beat.

"Oh, I have something I think you'll enjoy," he says flashing out of the darkness and striding for one end of the bookshelf next to the record player.

"Stop. Stop!"

"Easy-easy. Geez. You're trigger happy aren't you?"

He reaches the bookshelf and retrieves an album cover that was resting atop a row of books. He holds the album cover before his eyes, marveling at it as if he'd just discovered an ancient relic. He shifts his gaze to mine and holds the album out for me to see.

"Tartini. My favorite collection. It includes his greatest work, the Devil's Trill Sonata. You know he claimed to have been visited by the devil in a dream? He told the dream to a friend of his and said he dreamed that the devil appeared to him and had asked to be Tartini's teacher. At the end of the music lesson, Tartini handed the devil his violin to test his skill. The devil played with elegant virtue and delivered a magnificent performance. So beautifully executed with such superior taste and precision was the Devil's performance that the composer felt his breath taken away. Have you heard that tale, my dear?"

I hear my heart thump in my throat as all I can do is stare.

"It has the quote in his own words right here on the back. Listen to this . . . 'One night, in the year 1713 I dreamed I had made a pact with the devil for my soul. Everything went as I wished: my new servant anticipated my every desire. Among other things, I gave him my violin to see if he could play. How great was my astonishment on hearing a sonata so wonderful and so beautiful, played with such great art and intelligence, as I had never even conceived in my boldest flights of fantasy. I felt enraptured, transported, enchanted: my breath failed me, and I awoke. I immediately grasped my violin in order to retain, in part at least, the impression of my dream. In vain! The music which I at this time composed is indeed the best that I ever wrote, and I still call it the 'Devil's Trill', but the difference between it and that which so moved me is so great that I would have destroyed my instrument and have said farewell to music forever if it had been possible for me to live without the enjoyment it affords me.' Isn't that amazing!" he says with glee as he removes the vinyl album from its cover and gently places the black disc onto the spindle.

Static fills the air, then comes the thump of the needle resting into place, followed by the soft, tranquil playing of a violin.

He closes his eyes and breathes in a deep shot of ecstasy with a tight grin.

I'm left quivering near the steps with my Judge crammed into Miss Carver's lumpy back. I rummage the thoughts passing through my brain and try desperately to plan my next move.

He turns towards me and takes three steps.

"You come an inch closer and you're both dead!"

He stops and sighs out a deep breath.

Tartini's *Devil's Trill* now plays over the muffled cries of Seth Roe and the singing cicadas.

"If I were to be honest, I'd have to say I am rather surprised it has taken you this long to get this close to me. I just couldn't resist the urge to unveil the secret any longer. I yielded to my flesh, but it'll be okay. I'll still get what I want in the end. Do you know why I led you to Devil's Den Hallow, Laurie?"

"Enlighten me."

"Oooh, such attitude. I love it. If you followed the crimes of the GTK, which I'm sure you must have, you would have likely connected the dots. You see, the GTK is more than just an inspiration, we're both products of the same origin. Myself, the lady you call Miss Carver there, and my father all use to attend the cult which the GTK's dad created. Though we never knew each other very well as we would only attend once or twice a month, we knew enough about them to know—"

"That was in South Carolina. So, you're originally from the south like me?"

"I grew up only minutes from where you lived. I watched you every summer as you and your family floated over to Bald Head Island. You've always been a gift to my eyes, Laurie. That's why I insisted we follow you here."

He reaches softly to his neck and begins picking with his thumbs. He gains traction and I'm left in awe as he carefully removes the fake skin containing the mask of Phillip Carver. He sheds the skin like a cicada sheds its shell. He tosses the face of who I'd known to be Phillip Carver, to the ground where it crumbles in a pile of silicone.

Standing before me now is Ed Skinner. The man from Cumberland Behavioral Health Center.

But the question I'm left with is . . . is this Ed Skinner or the psychopath Gary Wade Duncan?

He paws at his face, which wears a thin red beard.

"Remember me?"

"Get on the ground. Now!"

"Or what!" he barks, "You going to shoot me? Is that you're plan?" he says thrusting his chest forward. His brows angle as his face twist into a snarl.

I feel Miss Carver tighten, "It's over Ed. This is it. There's no way out of this."

He yanks his head to her, "Shut up, yes there is!", and sears her with those icy, beady eyes.

So, this is Gary Wade Duncan. This is the man we've called Morty for all of these years.

He smacks a palm to his forehead and begins pacing in a tight line. He huffs out thin patches of air through clinched teeth in between low mumbles.

"Where's the cell jammer?" I ask.

He ignores me and continues pacing.

Miss Carver stammers, but manages to get out, "Bedroom. My-my bedroom. In my nightstand drawe—"

A flash of searing, hot pain strikes my face as the back of Miss Carver's skull smashes into me. I hear something in my nose and cheek pop, cracking like a pistachio shell. The blow sends me reeling backwards and crashing to the earth with a thump hard enough to sting my tailbone. Tears fill my eyes and distort my vision. My breath is now only available with gasps through my mouth. My head smacked the ground when I landed, sending a throbbing headache throughout my brain. My world begins to spin as nausea tears at my gut, ripping away at my consciousness and tossing me into a sea of disorientation.

The sound of thrashing footfalls adds to the shrill of Tartini's high E on the violin as it blasts through the vintage record player. I try to pick myself up but am immediately slammed back into the earth as Morty pounces onto my chest, stabbing bony knees into my sternum and ribs. Cold fingers quickly seize my wrists. They're jerked above my head before being stretched tight and squeezed with one large, calloused hand. I feel and hear him dig into his pants pocket as I struggle and squirm. I rotate my hips and knee him hard in the buttocks as I try desperately to reach the soft spot that'd be sure to send him curling to the floor. No matter how hard I struggle, my best efforts are in vain. He has me. There's no way out of this.

He was right. Laurie will succumb to Morty.

# 87

THE CICADAS SCREECH and sing along with Tartini's Devil's Trill. Somewhere in the corner of that black metal cage, Seth Roe whimpers through a gag, squirming, and rattling the chains that bind him. All the while his only hope of freedom lies on her back with a psychopathic serial killer sitting atop her chest.

I feel his weight crushing my breath as my mind reels into flashbacks of that ghastly creature sitting upon me in the midnight hours. It was a premonition of my coming death.

I struggle to buck him off of me, but every attempt comes in vain. He smiles big to show his grungy, yellow colored teeth, and it's now that I realize he's wearing dentures. The dentures which are made from the teeth of his victims.

"There some things I will need from you, Laurie. I think you know quite well what they are." Morty pulls his hand from his pocket. I try to crane my head up enough to see, but only get a glimpse.

A sledgehammer of dread and fear barrels into my chest at the sight.

A box cutter.

For heaven's sake he's going to scalp me and add my hair to his collection.

No one knows I'm here.

I'll vanish just like Weatherby and who knows, maybe end up beheaded beneath the home of someone from the station. Probably Sheriff Johnston or Chief Cunningham or Paul—Jesus Christ! No!

A burst of energy courses through my veins at the thoughts. I jolt and jerk, scream, kick, but nothing works.

"Ahh, Laurie," he says with a sigh while holding the knife in his right and clinching my wrists above my ahead with his left, "Isn't it beautiful? Hear them sing, Laurie. Hear the cicadas sing! Laurie will succumb to Morty. Laurie will succumb to Morty! Isn't it beautiful?"

"No. Stop it. Nooooo!" I scream while grinding my molars.

I watch as he places the box cutter onto my belly and reaches back into his pocket. He pulls out what looks like pliers and says, "This will be for the tooth extraction of course. I apologize for not having any novocaine. Your adrenaline will have to suffice."

He leans close and stops only inches from my face. His warm breath is sickening. It smells like a mix between potted meat and peppermint.

"Sh shhhh my child. Which do you prefer first? The scalping or the extraction? Or would you rather me slice your throat first?"

The salty, iron mix of mucus and blood trickles from my nose into my mouth. I blink to clear my vision.

A deep-rooted fear rips into my soul like a wild animal with fresh prey. An inky blackness covers me like a blanket. Oxygen is scarce.

Morty's beady black eyes pierce my soul as he sits atop my chest, hovering over me like the wicked creature from my closet.

I feel my soul begin to evaporate. Is this what dying feels like?

"You'll likely bleed out before I finish my last cut. I believe that may be the best choice. I hate to have you mess things up as you squirm while I cut into your scalp or pull your tooth. It'd be a true tragedy for you to ruin your hair by squirming like a wild hog and cover it all in blood. Your hair is much too beautiful for that."

"Please. Please. Don't do this," I try to say with dignity and courage, but it comes out weak and timid.

He sighs and pulls his face from mine. He clutches the pliers and marvels at them as he opens and closes them.

"But you know I do. It's not like I didn't tell you this would happen. I even gave you the cicada to remind you of your coming demise. Nature's way of remembrance. Christ did the same with Simon Peter, did he not? Do you recall the story of

Peter's betrayal and how Christ reminded him of it with the call of the rooster?" he wipes his nose with the back of his right hand, still clinching the pliers, "You knew this would happen. Why you didn't think you'd live forever, now did you? You can't play with hot coals and not expect to be burned, Laurie."

He takes the blade off my belly and clinches it within his teeth.

His face tightens, forcing the veins in his neck to bulge and his eyes twitch like someone would who has a tick from Tourette's syndrome. He pulls in a room full of air through his flaring nostrils.

I feel the pressure release from my wrists, but it's immediately fixed to my throat. His grip cinches harder and begins to choke my breath. I pound my hands into his forearms, but I'd be better off hitting a brick wall. I kick and squirm. My oxygen leaks out at an alarming rate. I feel my air way begin to close. I hear my breath emit in short, pathetic gasps and whimpers. This is it.

He sits the pliers to the ground and takes the box cutter from his mouth. My eyes bulge at the sight of it clutched tight within his hand. He slides the button to fully extend the blade. I try to swallow just a fraction of air but can't. A throbbing pain rips at my entire larynx. I hear things pop that shouldn't pop. More gross noises emit from my throat as he squeezes even harder.

Perhaps I'll black out before he slides the blade across my flesh, sparing me the agony and horror of hearing the blood spill and gurgle out of the open wound.

My eye lids take on a surprising heaviness. I'm not going to be able to keep them open much longer. Some of the last things I see before they permanently shut, are the grinning face of the devil named Morty and the glowing tube light mounted to the ceiling. I hear him laugh beneath his breath. I hear Tartini's Devil's Trill on the turntable, and I hear the cicadas sing their chorus.

*Be the Light. The Light will shine in the darkness.* I remember with sharp clarity despite my sudden weariness. The name forms in my head, but I have no air to say it.

Jesus.

I feel my lips move like fat cold worms. They're likely blue and purple from the lack of blood supply. My hands and feet feel like ice cubes as my body desperately tries to send blood to my brain and heart. The body's last-ditch effort to survive. My eye lids sink close.

Blackness.

Followed by a sudden influx of memories. Dreamlike, but memories, nonetheless. Both distant and near. From my earliest childhood days to the past year of my life. Dimethyltryptamine or DMT. The body's attempt of keeping my brain alive.

I feel something sharp and cold dig into my neck. I feel no pain, only pressure.

Just get it over with. Send me to the lig—

A sickening crack pierces the air, followed by a grunt. I feel a sudden shift atop my body, the pressure disappears. The fingers around my throat release and the cold blade pulls back. My memories fade, being replaced by blackness, then red from the back of my eye lids.

It's like I'm at the bottom of a swimming pool, pulling, pulling, grasping hard for the surface. A dim light begins to replace the darkness of my eye lids. I feel my airway return to its form. I flash open my eyes and suck in a deep gasp as I surface from the deep. Only seconds from death.

Miss Carver stands at my feet with her head twisted to the right. Her hands are still cuffed behind her back. She must've kicked him.

I follow her eyes and see Morty curled into a ball but squirming while grasping at his jaw and temple. He's growling with building anger. Any moment he's going to rise and kill us all.

I jerk my head to the right where I think my Judge must've been slung during my fall. I dart my eyes across the dirt for it. Sweeping my eyes side to side, hoping, praying to find my only hope of survival. And yes, I have no choice but to kill him now. It's either kill or be killed. Me or him.

I hear him shift in the dirt behind me. Short gasps of air burst out through what sounds like clinched teeth.  I know he's pushing to his feet and at any moment will pounce on me again.

I blink hard to suppress the tears leaking out. More blood and mucus trickle into my mouth, this time from the back of my throat. The thick glob almost gags me, but I manage to spit it out just as my eyes find the black L-shaped object within a patch of shadow about ten feet from me. My heart leaps at the sight.

I hear Miss Carver whimper an apology as Morty growls a scathing rebuke towards her.

I scamper across the earth for my Judge.

The sound of feet shuffles behind me.

I stretch into the shadow, grasping my hand into the darkness, hoping to find the handle of my revolver.

My fingers scrape the black rubber grip.

I hear and feel Morty closing the gap.

I'm dead if I don't kill him now.

I stretch one last time. My forearm muscles tighten with the reach. I palm my judge, slam back the hammer and do a quick roll. Pull the gun up to eye level and clinch it tight between both hands.

Just as I spin, I catch sight of Morty rushing towards me with the box cutter ready to slice and dice.

Time slows to a crawl.

It feels like I'm moving beneath water.

Dreamlike.

Sound ebbs away.

Whether subconsciously or not, I can't say but I swear I hear the tick of my watch as my finger pull against the cold metallic trigger.

*Boom!*

A flash of fire erupts between us.

The shot echoes among the walls with a deafening blast.

Carried by his momentum, Morty crashes face first into the dirt beside me. Unmoving and as good as dead.

I hear Seth scream with a shrill cry from his cage. Miss Carver stands with her hands behind her back, eyes wide in shock.

I scamper to my feet and snatch the box cutter away that'd tumbled a foot from Morty's hand in the fall. I close the blade and pocket it, then step back to create distance. All while keeping my gun trained to his back.

I reach for my throat and pull back bloody fingers. Not enough to kill me, but it was a good start.

I look to Miss Carver, "On the ground, now. Get on the ground!"

She doesn't hesitate.

I spit away more blood and mucus which tries to slither down my throat. I wipe my nose with the sleeve of my shirt, doing so gingerly. It was already beginning to numb, but has a throbbing sting to it. I slow my breath for a moment, switching from short gasps to long, deep pulls.

Having my wits about me and giving myself ample time to take it all in, I draw in one last deep breath through my mouth. The stale, cold air hits my lungs with a slight burn.

With my Judge trained to his back, I edge closer.

A pool of blood builds near his head. His face is twisted away from me, arms lying lifeless by his sides. Closer now, I see a jagged hole in the back of his head. His hair is stained with blood.

Standing over him now, I lower onto my claves and with my un gunned hand, roll him over. His limp body flops as he twists to his back now. His right arm thumps to the earth, sending a small patch of dust particles into the dim light.

With his mouth stretched wide, I can see that most of his top teeth have been shattered by the bullet.

Morty is dead.

I stand to my feet and glance to Miss Carver lying in the dirt.

"Stay right there," I say full of regained authority.

My ears still have a ring to them from the gunshot and my head still reels from the backwards head butt to the face and the crash to the dirt. But nonetheless, with my Judge gripped tight between my sweaty palms, packed with three more .45 rounds, I ease my way to the cage covered in a black sheet containing Seth Roe.

The turntable still plays Tartini, but the cicadas are now eerily quiet as if their listening to my every move.

I reach the door that I'd just seen Morty exit and lock behind him. I lift the black sheet enough to glance inside. It's dark, but I hear Seth in the far-left corner.

"Seth, honey, it's okay. It's me Laurie. It's okay honey, I'm going to get you out."

He cries through a gag. A chain rattles in the darkness.

I look at the door and see a gold Master lock clamped shut through a chain. A metal latch is locked above that. It'll take not one, but two keys to get him out. Morty should have them both.

I turn around and see Miss Carver still on her belly. Then look and see Morty still lifelessly in the dirt where I'd left him.

"Hang on a second, Seth. I have to get the keys."

He whimpers a response.

I cross the basement and squat beside Morty. No need to check a pulse, the hole in his face is enough to answer the question. I take a breath and cram my hand into his pockets. His left pocket is empty, except for a peppermint candies and a few pieces of loose change. It's his right pocket where I find a small set of keys. I pull them out and cross back to the cage. They jingle along the way.

The third key I try, unlocks the gold Master lock. The chain falls to the floor with a loud clank, and the six key unlocks the latch. I slide the dead bolt away and step in. I angle to the dark corner where Seth's dark silhouette awaits. I holster my Judge and retrieve my phone for light.

Seth glares back at me through the light. His eyes are red and wide with fear. His body trembles with raw nerves which are stretched thin. His cheeks are wet with tears. His dirty blond hair is sweaty and disheveled. A piece of duct tape holds a wad of cloth in his mouth. His hands and feet are chained together.

"Sshh sshh, it's okay baby, I'm here now. Sshh you're okay, you're okay. You're with me now. Everything's going to be okay," I reassure him as I fumble through the different keys. Finally, I find the right ones. The chains fall way as I unlatch their locks. I pull him to his feet and gently remove the tape and gag as I draw him near to my left side while we make our way out of the cage.

He cries into my side as we stumble through the darkness and into the dim light. I pull my Judge from my hip and train it to Miss Carver's back.

"Up. Now."

She hesitates this time at my command.

"I said up!"

She sighs and rolls to her side, then sits up with her feet cradled beneath her.

I step over and give her a tug.

Once on her feet, I step back and train my gun to her and pull Seth tight to my side.

I wave the gun to the stairs, "Take me to the cell jammer. Now"

Together we make our exodus from the basement.

I shield Seth's face from Morty as we pass. I give a quick reassuring look to his lifeless body. There'd be no rising with that body. He's deader than dead and it doesn't take doctor to know that.

We climb the steps and re-enter the hallway. I shut the door behind us, then continue to follow closely behind Miss Carver as we march for her bedroom.

Once there, I can't help but notice the filth. Looks like something that'd belong to a caveman. Clothes and old food plates lie scattered everywhere I look. The dust is thicker than a dusting of snow and is caked upon every inch of the room.

She stops at the side of her unmade bed, "It's in there, top drawer beneath the folder."

"Step away and go stand over there," I say with a wave of my gun to the opposite side of the bed.

I bend at the waist and tug the drawer open. It comes out uneven. With one swipe, I find a small black box the shape of a nine-volt battery but three times the size and with antennas and buttons. A small green light flashes from it. I pick it up and find the off button.

I sit it on the nightstand and retrieve my phone. I watch as my service switches from a circle with a line through it to four bars.

With my Judge trained to Miss Carver, I place a call to Chief Cunningham and cradle the phone to my ear.

"Let's go. Outside to my Suburban. Now."

My call begins to ring as we make our way out of the god-forsaken house.

It's on the fourth ring as we exit the front door and step onto the porch.

"Come on Chief. Of all times, you have to pick up now," I mumble to myself. The storm door slams shut behind me and we descend the steps. Pebbles crunch beneath our feet, Cunningham answers on the fifth ring.

"Hey Lauri—"

"I'm at the Carver's, the McCrae's neighbors. Morty's dead. I've got Miss Carver at gunpoint. I have Seth Roe with me. He's fine. You're going to need to send someone to his house on Rocky Hill Road. My nose is broken, and I've got a cut on my throat, but other than that I think I'm okay. Get here as soon as you can."

The line goes silent.

"Did you hea—"

"Yeah-yeah, I heard you. Judas priest. We're on our way. You're sure he's dead?"

"Yes . . . I'm sure. Thank God."

# 88

**5 months later**
**August 8th, 2020**
**Portland, Maine**

AFTER MY ENCOUNTER with Morty—who indeed turned out to be Ed Skinner disguised as a twenty-three-old mentally disabled and paraplegic man named Phillip Carver—with the cooperation of Miss Carver we were able to recover seven large file cabinets containing enough information to keep us working daylight to dark for the next four weeks. That's even with the help we received from Quantico.

There were three orphanages in total, one in Eastern Germany, one in West London, and one in South Africa. These three orphanages are responsible for working together with Annette Carver in taking the children, of which she claims were from foster parents here in the states. With a changed of names, haircuts, and enough threatening and brainwashing, along with funding from the orphanages, she'd then ship them off across the pond via a red eye. They'd be welcomed into the orphanage and later purchased by a wealthy family oblivious of the child's true background.

Just three weeks ago, we were able to locate Connor Anderson and Sarah McCrae. We found Sarah living happily with a big firm lawyer and real estate agent in London. Connor lives with a wealthy family in South Africa who owns and operates a large car manufacturing plant in Johannesburg.

After me and a few of my friends from Quantico flew out to each of the homes for a quick visit, I left whole heartedly believing that the children were better off with their new families. I've facetimed them both since our visit in order to keep in check. Though thousand of miles apart and an ocean away from their original homes, both Sarah and Connor could not appear to be any happier. I rest with peace at night, knowing they're growing up in homes where they are loved and provided for beyond their wildest dreams. They now have a chance of becoming something one day, other than a redundant version of their good for nothing biological parents.

Although we were able to link Edward Lester Skinner to at least twenty-one murders dating from 2002 to 2020—not considering he likely aided in the suicide of Maria Santorum who leapt from the cliffs of Cushing Island in 2002—the other nine that took place from 1986 to 1997 are attributed to his father, Earl Howard Skinner. We also learned that Annette Carver was actually Earl's sister, meaning she was Ed's aunt, rather than his mother. Her husband had died in a car wreck when she was young and is said to have never changed her married name.

After living a life of horrible abuse at the hands of their parents, Earl and Annette decided to take matters into their own hands and help children who may be suffering similar circumstances. From 1980 to 1998, the two lived together and claimed to be common law husband and wife. Earl would do the dirty work of murdering the parents, while Annette would take the children in and nurture them, coercing them into never telling anyone and promising to give them a better life. Promises which they very well kept.

A few years before Ed's release from the asylum, his father's health began to deteriorate and in 1998, Earl Howard Skinner died of pneumonia and septicemia after complications with his recent diagnosis of lung cancer.

At Ed's release from Cushing Island, after infusing himself with wisdom from his years of reading and learning while booked in the mental asylum, he teamed with his aunt and soon picked up where his father left off in 1997. Ed committed his first murder and kidnapping in 2002, which was the year I became Homicide Detective. He went on to kill six people that year and would kidnap a total of five kids. Thirteen years later, he would kill another eight people and kidnap a total of four kids. The seventeenth year after his first murder, he killed a total of seven people, including Agent Weatherby, and kidnapped Sarah, Connor, and Seth.

Through enough digging, along with the confession of Annette Carver and what Morty said that day in his basement,

I have reason to believe that Earl Skinner was the one who killed my mother in 1984, not herself.

And we were able to connect them to the For the Greater Good cult from which the GTK originated. By searching through enough court records and files, we found that Earl and his sister Annette lived in Oak Island, North Carolina. Only twelves miles from my hometown of Southport. They lived there from the late seventies to the early eighties and would travel to Georgetown once or twice a month to involve themselves in the rituals of For the Greater Good. Ed is believed to have joined them.

According to records and Annette Carver, we were able to determine that Earl Howard Skinner and his son Ed operated the ferry from Southport to Bald Head Island during those years. This would have been around the time my family and I vacationed there, using that same ferry. They would have both watched us board and exit the ferry numerous times during those years. So, this is likely when Ed's obsession with me began. And my family were their first victims. Likely with constant prodding from Ed, the trio followed me to Maine where they'd eventually continue what they begun in North Carolina.

As for the rest of the missing children . . . we're still searching.

The total number, according to the files and Annette Carver's words, seems to be around twenty-four. If you include my sister Amy.

Speaking of which, after having chased down numerous leads and threads, I've successfully found. Yes, you read that right. I found her. She lives in San Diego with her heart doctor husband and two precious children. She herself is a practicing attorney specializing in criminal law. A tough cookie you might say. I've spoken with her on the phone at least a dozen times over the last two weeks and must've facetimed her and the family at least half that many.

It took her some time to comprehend the revelation. Her memory of early childhood is vastly fogged as she was taken from us when she was only six years old. But with enough memory jarring from myself along with some DNA tests, she's a believer, and she is indeed my sister.

I tried reaching out to Jared in Colorado in hopes of having a sibling reunion, but he's yet to return my calls. Nothing new there. It's been eight years since I last spoke to him.

Nonetheless, here I am sitting in a window seat 35,000 miles above the Grand Canyon, and only hours from hugging my sister who I've been missing for the last thirty-six years.

And someone very special to my heart is sitting next to me. Patrick Collins. Though it hasn't been easy, he has made a strong recovery and other than walking with a slight limp and dealing with an occasional stutter, he's doing quite well for himself.

And yes, Seth Roe's parents were both murdered by Morty. Same MO and signature, only different victims. That said, I'm currently weeding through mountains of paperwork in efforts to gain custody of Seth Roe. I'm working with the state in securing full parental rights. Seth is at home now with Paul, probably watching a baseball game and eating hotdogs as Sandy begs for a crumb.

Though I had trouble seeing it before, I see it now.

The Light does shines in the darkness.

# Epilogue

**2024**

AFTER SOLVING THE Morty case, I decided that it was time for me to retire from homicide. I've seen enough through my years of homicide investigation, and I honestly don't know that I could handle another case involving a serial killer. It takes a lot out of you. My first check-up after the case was solved, showed I had not one but two ulcers along the lining of my stomach. The pain in my chest has subsided thank God, and I've yet to be visited in the night again by the creature in my closet. I've also been told I have a symptoms of PTSD. I think you probably know the reasons why.

As I had last mentioned, I was in the process of attaining parental rights for Seth Roe. After working with the state through countless hours of phone calls and interviews, the rights were granted. Seth Roe is officially my adopted son, and he now lives with me, Patrick, and Paul in San Diego.

We made the move from Portland three years ago and bought a house together just ten minutes from my sister Amy and her family. But I knew I couldn't just move out here and pick up some ordinary job. I had to use my skill and experience to help make the world a better place. So, together with my sister, we've created a foundation called *Amy's Hope.* Through it we are able to help families of missing children by offering them hope and encouragement while also providing private investigation services in the search of their missing children.

Since our founding in 2022, we've successfully located over two dozen missing children. Of course, not without the help of my friends at Quantico. We've also been able to locate eight so far of the missing that were taken by Earl and Ed Skinner. Only one of the eight lives in the US, the others are scattered throughout the world.

As for my friends in Portland, before I headed West I was able to work out an agreement with the State and Cumberland Behavioral which allows Archie Whitaker to pay weekly visits to his wife Frances at Morningside. A guard accompanies him from Cushing Island to Long Wharf, where he is then picked up by a good friend of his named . . . Hal Resnick.

It allows me to sleep a little better at night knowing that Archie and Frances will spend the rest of their days cherishing their sacred love by likely exchanging origami swans and daises among other things. I hear Archie's garden is one of the most splendid in the whole institution. And with his wife's help and guidance, why shouldn't it be, right?

At Portland Police Department, with my retiring, Detective White was promoted to the ranks of Homicide Lieutenant and has taken over my responsibilities. And of course, Sheriff Johnston is still chasing bad guys and keeping things in order. The two will call me every so often. Sometimes just to check in and other times to ask for advice on a case they're currently working.

I hated to leave Portland behind, but I couldn't be any happier here in San Diego. Finding my sister was one thing, but then to get to live just minutes from her and her family is a true blessing. And we even started going to church with them too. Me, Patrick, Paul, and Seth. But this one is a real church, nothing like the one that almost killed me in Gray. These people are genuine. The real deal. Where Jesus is the focus, not religion. It's a big difference.

With Paul's age sending his body into a decline, he's been forced to take on a walker if he wants to get out and about. Not that that would keep him from going on our evening walks by the harbor at Shoreline Park though.

As a matter of fact, that's where we are right now. The sunsets are beautiful here. Sometimes it's the whole gang, other times, its just me and him, and of course Sandy.

As the sun dips further into the sea, sending out a cascade of colors sparkling atop the water while the gulls sing their applause, I turn to my left where Paul is standing with his hands along the railing and his eyes gazing at the sunset. I know those words were right.

The Light shines in the darkness.

† † † † † † † † † †

**SEATED IN MY OFFICE** downtown with a phone cradled to my ear and on the line with a family from Washington state regarding their seven-year-old son who's been missing for four days now, I hear a set of knuckle raps upon the window of my door. I spin in my chair and see it's my sister Amy. Everyone thinks we're twins as we have the same blonde hair and hazel eyes. She has her phone in one hand and a stack of files in the other.

I scrunch my brows. She mouths, "It's important."

Collins walks up behind her with more files in hand. I recognize the look on his face at once and know that whatever it is that they have will likely be earning most of my time over the coming days and weeks.

"Excuse me just a moment. I'm sorry, I have a call I need to take. I'm going to need to put you on hold just for a second, okay?"

The mother sniffles and mumbles, "Okay," on the other end.

I place the call on hold and ask Amy and Collins, "What is it?"

She swallows deep and begins with, "I think it's a human trafficking case. I have the files here," she says with a glance to her left hand. "Her name is Lyndsay Cole. She was eleven when she was abducted. That was in 2019. The family is on the line now. They're coming from South Carolina. They're just off I-10 in Palm Springs, heading this way."

"What?"

Collins clears his throat after taking out his toothpick and says, "Yeah. They've been searching ever since and now have enough information to prove it may be human trafficking. They have s-som-some good leads but need our help to take it a st-st-step further."

I nod absently. Human trafficking. Are we ready for this? My mind wanders to the darkness lurking in the shadows of our world as it snatches our children away right before our eyes.

*Be what you already are. Be the Light, Laurie.*

The light will shine in the darkness, right?

"Yeah-yeah, okay. Let me speak to them."

Amy passes me the phone.

"Hello, this is Laurie Daniels."

The following pictures are from my time visiting the
Portland, M.E. area back in the summer of 2017.

## PORTLAND HEADLIGHT AND A LOBSTA' ROLL

## CELLAR DOORS AT PORTLAND HEADLIGHT WHICH GAVE ME THE IDEA FOR LAURIE DANIELS CELLAR SCENE.

## NUBBLE LIGHT IN YORK, M.E.

THE ABANDONED HOME OF FORMER LIGHTHOUSE OPERATORS AT WINTER ISLAND STATE PARK WHERE CONNOR ANDERSON WAS ABDUCTED.

Thank you for reading *The Reaping!* I hope you enjoyed it as much as I did writing it! If so, I would be grateful if you'd be kind enough to leave a review on Amazon as reviews truly are the life blood of any Author's career.

## About the Author

I am a former college baseball player turned writer who thoroughly enjoys the outdoors, whether it be fishing, kayaking, hiking, and exploring new places, or watching a game of America's greatest pastime. I'm an old soul at heart, so I love old music (especially classic rock from CCR, Bob Seger, Bruce Springsteen, or vintage rock and roll from Chuck Berry, Muddy Water's, Elvis, etc) old movies and antique items. I own a Victrola Turntable in case you're not getting the picture yet. I'm an avid reader and writer of Mystery, Horror, and Suspense. I enjoy reading Stephen King, Ted Dekker, Frank Peretti, Thomas Harris, Steven James, C.J. Box, and James Lee Burke to name a few. I also enjoy a fun/inspiring Southern Story as well such as Where the Crawdads Sing. I was a top ten finalist in Inkshares 2018 Mystery/Thriller contest. I am a member of the Horror Writers Association. I hold an MBA from Coastal Carolina University and am currently practicing real estate in Myrtle Beach. You can find me on Instagram, Facebook, and YouTube to stay up to date with my latest work.

You can find me on Instagram, Facebook, and YouTube to stay up to date with my latest work.

**Instagram**: randall_lane31
**Facebook**: Randall Lane Fiction
**YouTube**: Randall Lane Fiction
**Amazon**: Randall Lane Fiction

# Other Books Available

If you enjoyed *The Reaping* then you'll likely enjoy my latest novel *Devil's Den* as well. Available on Amazon! The book trailer is posted to my YouTube channel.

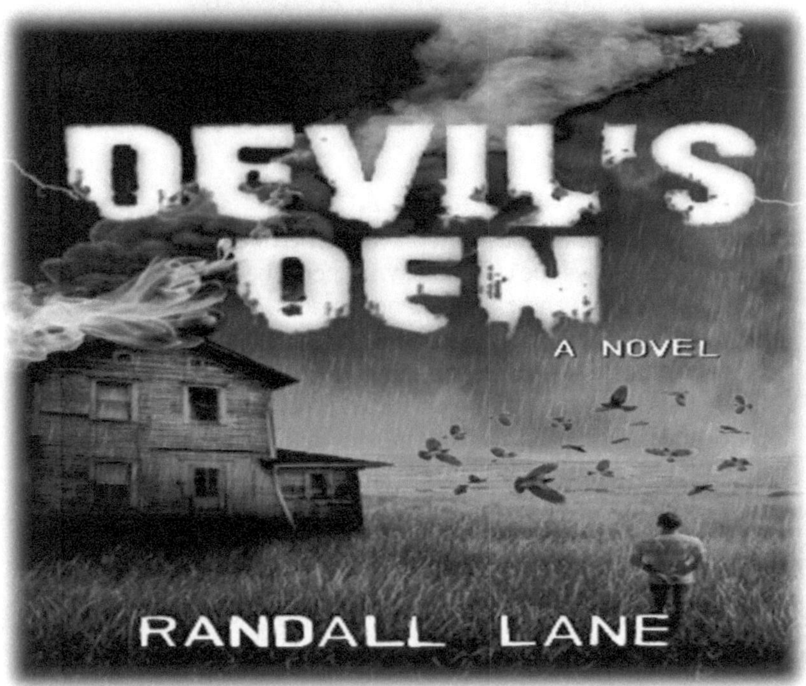


*Synopsis.* The year is 1989 and as Detectives search for a local serial killer, James and Rebecca Randolph can't help but wonder if it may be Ethan, the new co-worker of James. After causing a horrendous accident at the Georgetown International Paper Mill, Ethan vanishes before further questioning. Locals are quick to term him the GTK or Georgetown Killer. 25 years later, after relocating to Holden Beach, James and Rebecca find themselves once again in the cross hairs of the GTK. As they consult the spiritual guidance of Native American Friends, they soon learn there is a lot more going on than meets the eye. Embarking on a Journey from Darkness to Light, passing through the Devil's Den along the way, they gain a whole new perspective of the saying, "Good vs Evil."

I also have my novel *Omah*, available on Amazon too! To watch the book trailer, head over to my YouTube channel. (Randall Lane Fiction.)

*Synopsis:* After a string of mysterious disappearances and encounters in Northern California, Game Wardens are less than surprised when six-year-old Tyler Jacob's vanishes by the South Fork Eel River while fishing with his family. As the family is riddled with guilt and on the verge of losing hope, Native Americans from the local Yurok Tribe step in to help spread light on the recent events. While pushing through the vast wilderness and majestic Redwood Forest in search of his son, Randy Jacob's soon learns that what he once thought was just a Legend may actually be a living and breathing creature after all. As hours stretch into days and the clock rushes forward, can Tyler be found before it's too late.

Be sure to check out my collection of short stories titled, *Night Terrors!*

INCLUDES EVERYTHING FROM GHOSTS, ALIENS, BIGFOOT, WEREWOLVES, SKINWALKERS, STRANGE DISAPPEARANCES, AND MANY OTHER CREEPY MYSTERIES.

# Inside Look at Chapter 1

# of Randall's next Novel

# OLD
# GHOSTS
# OF THE
# VALLEY

**A NOVEL**

**RANDALL LANE**

# 1

# Chapel Valley, NC

# October 2023

# 3:33 p.m.

Carol Gore is a fifty-nine-year-old divorced mother of two, who lives alone up in the backcountry of the Blue Ridge Mountains. She has lived in the same house since the early nineties. She and her husband, Steve, moved to the area after he'd picked up a mining job in the town of Chapel Valley. It was also around this time that Carol learned of the Abbott cult. A co-worker from Piggly Wiggly wouldn't shut up about the sweet little Abbott family and its parishioners, so Carol finally relented and accompanied her to an event at the compound. That was all it took for Carol to become hooked.

As Carol thinks back to the moment she first stepped foot on the Abbott compound, she subconsciously rinses off a few glass plates from previous days meals. Skylar, her white Himalayan cat, is busy weaving in and out between her feet. The tickle brings her back just in time to hear the strange noise. Carol thought she'd heard something earlier but only brushed it off as a play upon her ears. Must be the house settling or something, she'd said to herself. Isn't that what we always say? Or at least what we always hope for, right? What if we're wrong though? What if we're not alone during all the times we think we are? What if someone or something . . . lurks within the shadows and watches without our knowing?

As Carol asks herself these questions, she hears it again. The sound is unmistakable this time. The creaking of a floorboard beneath a sturdy, unwelcomed foot. All day she had fought the eerie feeling of being watched. It seems a presence had been hovering just over her shoulder. She's being too paranoid, she'd thought. Things are different now. To think she's still being watched . . . well it'll just end up driving her crazy. She can't allow herself to go on thinking this way. They would end up throwing her away to the place where people drift along in white gowns, while being force fed medicine and whipped into submission. She'll never go back there. She'd made a promise to herself, and she's determined within her heart to keep it.

No amount of self-encouragement can eat away the growing feeling she has of being watched. It is stronger now than ever before. The home is quiet other than the running of the faucet, and the black and white film playing in the living room. Carol stands frozen with her back to the rest of the kitchen. She looks down to find Skylar staring behind her. Together they listen.

Creeeaaak!

Skylar hisses and enters in a low crouch, his ears flare backward, his hair stands straight. Carol feels someone in the room. She turns just enough, so she can scan the room with her peripheral. She goes over the China cabinet full of Grandma's dishes and scans over the kitchen table. Her heart leaps at the big shadow of a man standing in the kitchen's door frame. She gasps and drops a dish. The crash of the shattering glass fills the room. She fights the urge to look directly at the man, knowing that the chance of her survival will quickly diminish should she see his face.

Skylar emits a low growl and backs up to be between Carol and the sink cabinet.

"What do you want?" Carol asks with her words sticking to her throat.

A moment passes.

"You."

Creeeeaaaaak!

The dark man takes a step.

"Stop. Don't come any closer."

He stops.

She grips the sinks hard enough to hurt her fingers.

"Look at me."

She shakes her head.

"Carol."

Her heart sinks at the knowledge of this mystery man knowing her name.

"Carol. You have to look at me. It's very important."

She clamps her eyes shut and shakes her head again.

She hears him breathe deep. He holds it, then sighs.

"I don't want to do this Carol, but I'm afraid I have to. You're leaving me no—"

Carol snatches Skylar up and bolts through the side door of the kitchen for her bedroom. Heavy thuds pound towards her. She slams the door shut and engages the lock. She rushes to move a chest of drawers against the door.

The dark man slams against the door as soon as Carol slides the furniture into place. The door rattles hard on its hinges. She stumbles backwards with one hand to her mouth, and the other reaching blindly for the bed.

Her heart will surely explode any moment as adrenaline courses through her veins in an icy rush. Her legs meet the edge of the bed, and she bruises a heel against the metal railing below. She winces and bends to tend to the pain.

The door rattles hard once more. Skylar growls again before going into a frantic search for cover. Another hard thud pounds against the door.

As Carol rubs her heel, she begins to hear a faint but hoarse whisper coming from under the bed. The scratchy voice stalls her racing heart and sends her body freezing in place. Movement comes from beneath the bed. It sounds like something crawling across the hardwood floor. Carol jerks herself up and looks toward the window. A sudden thought hits her. What an idiot. Last week she'd nailed the windows shut after fearing someone was secretly entering in the night. In her efforts to keep someone out, she ends up trapping herself in. She must break it. She races over to a nightstand and begins to search for something to break the glass.

The whisper under the bed becomes more audible now. Between the thuds against the door, she can make out the words. It's saying, "Come near my dear."

Carol yanks open a drawer to her nightstand and pulls out a hammer she's used for hanging pictures. She tucks her face into the crevice of her elbow and takes a swing. The window shatters. She rakes away the shards along the seal and rushes over to the nightstand. As she begins to swipe away the clutter, lamp and all, the thing beneath the bed growls loudly. Carol catches a glimpse in her peripheral of a long, bony hand reaching out from beneath the bed, aiming for Carol's ankle. She screams and jumps backwards. The thing continues to growl. Its pale fingers fall limp to the hardwood. Its nails make a loud tapping sound.

Carol hurries and places the nightstand beneath the broken window. The door thuds again as she climbs upon the nightstand.

She wiggles through the window and falls to the ground. Her hip barks in protest. She grunts and manages to get to her feet. She hears her bedroom door burst open. She doesn't turn back to look but makes a break for the grove of pines.

Running and stumbling her way into the tree line, she pushes away the swipes of bony branches. Her tender feet scream with every poke and jab from the sticks and pine needles. Her lungs burn like they've been doused with gasoline and lit to a flame. Her breath steams into the frigid air. Running between the pines, she retrieves her cell. Moments later she finds the contact she's looking for and places the call.

Panting and glancing over her shoulder, she waits for her son to answer.

# Coming in 2024!

## Tales from Uncle Joe

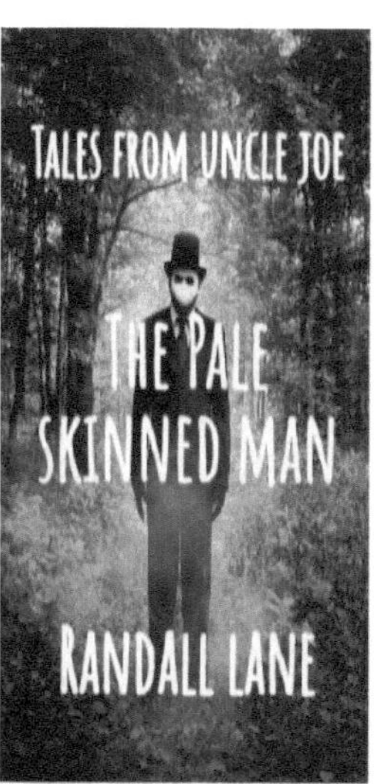

TALES FROM UNCLE JOE
MUTILATIONS
RANDALL LANE


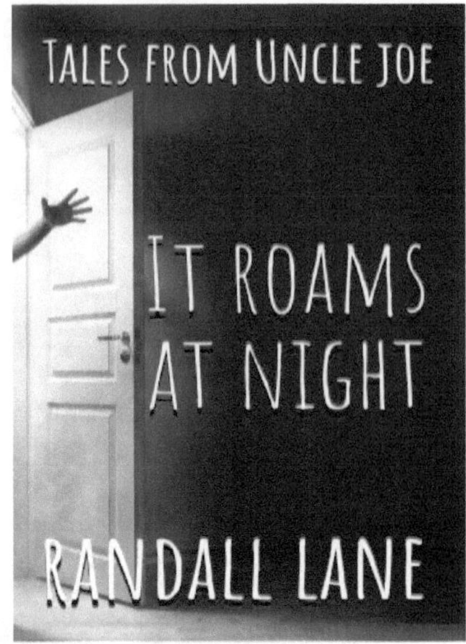

TALES FROM UNCLE JOE
IT ROAMS AT NIGHT
RANDALL LANE

TALES FROM UNCLE JOE
AN INSIDE JOB
RANDALL LANE

Thank you once again for joining me on this journey through story. From one reader to another, may we all continue to find ourselves as we escape into the written word.

Till next time!

All the best,

*Randall Lane*